BRUMBACK LIBRARY
3 3045 00164 8423
T5-CVM-053

Byte Me

Other Five Star Titles
by Pauline Baird Jones:

The Last Enemy
The Spy Who Kissed Me

Byte Me

Lonesome Law Man #2

Pauline Baird Jones

Five Star
Unity, Maine

Lonesome Law Man Series, Book 2

This novel is a work of fiction. Names, characters, places, and incidents are either the product of the author's imagination, or, if real, used fictitiously.

Five Star First Edition Romance Series.
Published in 2000 in conjunction with Pauline Baird Jones.

Cover Art "A Mile High in Denver" by Lulu Vargas.

Set in 11 pt. Plantin by Christina S. Huff.

Printed in the United States on permanent paper.

Library of Congress Cataloging-in-Publication Data

Jones, Pauline Baird.
Byte me / by Pauline Baird Jones.
p. cm—(Five Star first edition romance series)
(Lonesome law man ; bk. 2)
ISBN 0-7862-2857-1 (hc : alk. paper)
1. Computer crimes—Fiction. I. Title. II. Series.
PS3560.O52415 B9 2000
813′.54—dc21 00-046235

Byte Me

Prologue

Overhead, tiny pinpoints of light gave depth to the moonless night sky, while thirty stories down, miniature streetlights made a path for the occasional car to follow. The silence was so deep, Phoebe Mentel heard her own breath whispering in and out of her lungs. She leaned on the parapet and studied the tower across from her and her companion, taking the moment to find her focus and quiet her mind.

"You ready?" he asked. She turned as he dropped his bundle of equipment at her feet and knelt to extract the rocket launcher. He was dressed to steal in deepest black. Only his eyes gleamed out of the dark, eyes far too blue to be true.

Lucky for her, she didn't need true. She needed *there*.

"I was born ready." She spoke softly, but her voice, lightly laced with her mother's Southern charm, sounded loud in her ears. Also dressed to blend with the night, she'd covered her chin-length hair with a black stocking cap and smeared her face with blacking until only her brown eyes were visible.

His smile came fast and white, cutting into his dark silhouette like a lost Cheshire cat before fading back into the night. He readied the launcher, then used the parapet to steady his arms as he sighted in on the shadowy outline of the tower opposite.

A pop. A hiss. A double strand of rope snaked across the gap between the two buildings in a gleaming, silver arc. A muffled *clunk* found its way back to their ears.

He tugged on the rope until the grappling hook resisted. He tested it for give. There was none. He leaned back, using his full weight to tug again. It still held. He secured their end with brisk, practiced economy, then bent to check his climbing harness. When he'd shouldered his pack and was securely anchored to the rope, he looked at her.

Phoebe adjusted her earpiece. "You receiving?"

He nodded. "You?"

"Soft and clear."

"Catch you on the flip side." He gave her a cheeky salute and vaulted over the parapet into space. The double rope sagged but held as he disappeared into the night. After a time the tension on the rope eased.

"It's a go." His voice in her ear confirmed what her eyes saw. Her turn to step up and do or die.

In a perfect mimicry of his actions, Phoebe took her place at the parapet. A confident vault, her body kept angled against a gravity more imagined than felt, then the slide into darkness. Moving slowly at first, she quickly picked up speed. The side of the building formed out of shadow. She curled her legs and thrust out with her feet, using the resulting bounce to swing up and hook the edge of the roof. Her partner, programmed to be gallant, reached down and pulled her up beside him.

Phoebe shed her pack and knelt by the grill over the building's air shaft and quickly removed it, while he got out their equipment, all of it the latest in high-tech gadgetry. When she'd bypassed the alarm wires, they roped up again and started down the shaft, following a route laid out in her head. It was a gift, a talent, an instinct that was as much a part of her physiology as her eyes and hair and what she'd heard was her father's nose. If there was a way to get to something, a path to follow, she could find it.

Deep in the building's bowels, cutting-edge technology opened the wall they needed to access as easy as a whore spread her legs, giving them the prize they sought. They lost two minutes when a guard broke routine, but made up the time on the trip back to their starting point. Phoebe released the rope and drew it in with a sigh of relief.

"I think that was our best time yet," her companion said, the English accent giving the words more importance than they deserved.

Phoebe frowned. "If we could shave off another sixty seconds—"

The muffled shrill of her telephone, followed by the harsh whine of two computers attempting communication, cut across her words with a warning that her virtual reality game was about to be invaded.

Phoebe looked around, wondering where, from which direction, the invasion would come, but when Phagan spoke, his voice, disembodied and synthesized, came at her from the star studded night "sky."

"Playing with Steele again, Pathphinder?"

"Phagan." Phoebe touched a button on her headset, deleting the virtual Remington Steele she'd used as her partner-in-crime. She crossed virtual arms. "Coming down? Or are we playing God tonight?"

It was his favorite role, in virtual or real reality.

The darkness to her right rippled, and a figure stepped out from behind a ventilation stack. On Phagan's cue, not Phoebe's, the moon rose to light his entrance as Deputy US Marshal Samuel Gerrard from "The Fugitive."

She grinned inside her headset. Trust him to crash her B&E game with a lawman. The boy had always had a dark and wicked sense of humor.

"My enemies, and some of my friends, say I can only play Lucifer," he drawled, his voice only slightly less disembodied now that he was "earthbound."

"I'll pretend to disagree if you've cast me decently this time." Phoebe trusted Phagan with her life but not her dignity. Never with her dignity.

He walked a circle around her, his purloined visage showing a wicked appreciation for the female form. "I'm feeling benign tonight, with a taste for Meg Ryan."

"I look like Meg Ryan?"

He arched "Sam's" brows. "Do you mind?"

"Why should I? She's cute and her thighs are smaller than mine."

Phagan laughed, throwing "Sam's" head back. The faint, artificial light was kind to the craggy face and dark tumble of stolen hair. Sam seemed amazingly real—as long as Phagan kept his mouth shut. When he didn't, he sounded like the android from hell. Phagan never used his own voice. Like God, he preferred a mouthpiece.

She'd been playing his games for seven years and still couldn't put an actual face or a voice to him. Sometimes, in her real world, she'd study the faces around her, wondering if one of them belonged to him. There were things he'd said, things he did that told her he'd seen *her* more than once.

"You do it?" he asked, nodding in the direction of the building across the way.

"Despite you wanting the timing tighter than Meg Ryan's thighs."

"You needed a challenge. The last one was too easy."

"Not my fault," Phoebe said. "You're the wizard of virtual world."

He straddled a ventilation pipe, sat and flashed his stolen grin.

She smiled back, but absently. She had to tell him, but she didn't want to. She wanted to keep the past at bay, but she couldn't. It nicked her present like paper cutting skin, welling scarlet from the breach, burning like acid.

"What?"

Instead of speaking, Phoebe produced a couple of virtual cigars, handing one to him and "lighting" hers. Virtual smoke was no threat to her lungs and it gave her something to do with her hands. A wise precaution, since even in virtual world Phagan could read them like a Gypsy.

With a purloined brow cocked, he took his and lit up, blowing smoke out in a stream before asking, "We celebrating something?"

Phoebe looked at Phagan but "Sam's" cool dark stare deflected her ability to read him, even as she felt his X-ray scrutiny rake her from top to toe. She blew a series of perfect smoke circles, with a little help from the computer program, before saying as flatly as she could, "I found him."

Phagan stood up, took a drag of the cigar, then rolled the brown cylinder between his fingers as he considered her words. "You sure?"

Phoebe lowered her cigar, her hands a work of rock-steady art. "I'm sure."

Phagan turned his virtual high beams on her, waiting for more. With a vaguely frustrated sigh, she gave it to him. "He's had some work done on his face. But I'd know his eyes if he'd turned himself into a woman."

"Sam" looked thoughtful. He sent some smoke rings out to ambush hers, before asking as if it didn't matter, "Where?"

She looked at him, feeling a brief moment of real amusement take the edge off her angst. "Denver."

Phagan had Sam do surprise. "No shit? How'd we miss him?"

"He's been playing Howard Hughes recluse."

Phagan crushed out the cigar. "So how'd you spot him?"

"Apparently he's decided to come out. Caught his mug in

the newspaper. It seems—" Phoebe couldn't stop the quiver in her hands from playing out in front of Phagan, "he's almost got himself engaged to a prominent widow."

"Sam's" gaze got sharper. "Kids?"

"Two." Phoebe licked her dry lips inside the VR helmet. "Girls."

He nodded slowly. "Right. I'll contact Ollie. Make sure he's ready to move when you are."

"I'm ready." Inside the headset where he couldn't see, Phoebe's mouth curved in a smile seared by her acid past. "He made me ready."

Chapter One

One year later

"His name is Oliver Smith." Jake Kirby looked across the body at the detective, Mac something-or-other, kneeling on the other side. Jake never forgot who he was hunting or any details about them, but there were just too many cops in too many towns and he'd met most of them tracking fugitives for the US Marshals Service. "Ollie to his friends. He *was* on my least-likely-to-die-violently list."

Mac, middle-aged and showing signs of awe at working a crime scene with a Deputy US Marshal, gestured toward Ollie's face, taking care not to touch the hole punched between his bruised eyes. "Someone sure worked him over good before they killed him?"

Mac didn't ask, but Jake heard the "why" in his voice. A good question with no answer. It was on Jake's mental list right below: had the killer found what he was looking for?

Jake rose, his senses on full alert as he studied the one-room apartment that had been Ollie's last stand.

It had one official entrance, though a fire escape was visible out the lone window. Two other doors led to a closet and a bathroom, now being rummaged through by what passed for crime-scene techs in this small Montana backwater.

Shabby furniture and a clutter of dishes around the Pullman kitchen affixed to one wall looked odd sharing space with the impressively high-tech computer being dusted for prints. The smell of blood mingled with that of old food, older building and Ollie's slowly dissipating after-shave.

"What'd a geek like him do to get federal attention?" Mac asked, giving Ollie's innocuous-looking face a last glance before straightening his own fifty-something body with a grimace of pain.

"Failing to do his time for a variety of computer-related crimes and high-tech burglaries," Jake said. "He is—was—a hard man to hang on to."

"What put you on his trail?"

"He used an old alias to book his flight out of Denver. Must have been in deep trouble to make a mistake like that." Jake signaled to the tech emerging from the bathroom with various bagged toiletries, examined each bag, then frowned. "No Old Spice. So Ollie didn't live here."

"Old Spice?" Mac asked.

"Everybody has something they can't give up. Ollie's was Old Spice."

Mac gave him a skeptical look. Jake got a lot of skeptical looks, so he wasn't offended. "Smell him."

It was obvious Mac didn't want to sniff Ollie's corpse, but he didn't know how to get out of it, so he did, a look of surprise chasing distaste from his face.

"Landlord says the tenant's name was Jones. John Jones. Young guy," he offered in lieu of anything better to say as he got up and followed Jake to the kitchen area.

Jake studied the debris, looking without touching. A tech dumped the contents of the trash can out onto a plastic sheet, a tiny shower of pistachio shells caught his attention and he began sorting it into evidence bags.

"Speaking of things you can't give up." A lot of people liked pistachios, but few liked them as much as Dewey Hyatt. Did that make Hyatt the tenant or another visitor? With luck, fingerprints would tell the tale.

"I want you to compare any prints with—"

A stir in the doorway swallowed up the end of his sentence. Jake turned in time to see Bryn Bailey flash her FBI badge at the cop trying to stop her from coming in. The cop, not surprisingly, fell back. It was a common reaction to Bryn, even without the badge.

Vigorous and driven, this poster girl for FBI affirmative action was high gloss, with a near-regal beauty wrapped in a sexy black power suit that concealed her practical side. Beneath the suit and the flawless makeup was a farmer's daughter, a lass of the soil. Yeah, she wore spiked heels, but she used them like boots. Wasn't afraid to mess up her hair tackling a perp either. Not that her assignment to electronic crimes required a lot of body contact with the bad guys. Wasn't too hard on her manicure either, if the red pointed tips were any indication.

If Jake had to hunt with a "fibbie," then it might as well be Bryn. She had a good nose for following a trail and was less averse than some to following what seemed like a wild-goose chase. Couldn't relax with her, though. Anyone dumb enough to give Bryn even the slim edge of the wedge would find she'd taken a big chunk of the credit. And she'd look surprised if anyone had the guts to object.

Right now she looked annoyed.

Bryn was more than annoyed at finding Jake here before her. She crossed her arms and looked at him, fighting to stop the mixture of chagrin and resignation bubbling up her inside appearing on her outside. "Jake Kirby. Why am I not surprised?"

Bryn was tall, but Jake topped her by at least four inches, which did nothing to help her shake off the "little woman" feeling she always got around him. Maybe it was a genetic response. Or a primal one. Lean to the point of lanky, he had a graceful strength only apparent when he was in motion.

Worn blue denims and a soft white tee shirt hugged his lean and lanky body the way half the female population would like to.

Something about a guy not in uniform, she decided with an inward sigh.

As if he caught her thought, his signature charm-intensive grin spread across his absurdly young-looking face. Amusement lit eyes too blue for any woman's good and piercing enough to damn near see through lead. The nose between the eyes was straight, the full mouth below sweet in repose, wicked in response.

His tousled, light brown hair was brushed straight back from his high, broad forehead, except for a few tendrils that fell forward, adding to his little-boy-lost look. His eyes weren't lost or young though. They were old and wise. Set deep beneath run-amok brows and framed by worry lines a girl had to curl her hands into fists to resist smoothing away, they saw everything, were surprised by nothing.

His deceptive air of innocence put a smoke screen around a just-shy-of-ruthless determination. This wasn't a man who feared anything or gave up ground. He was the Marshals Service's top tracker. If he didn't get his man, no one could. Or the quarry was dead, like poor old Ollie Smith soon to be tucked into a morgue drawer.

"Let me guess," she said on a deliberate drawl, "you found him?"

Jake's shrug and quick grin was her answer. It was almost spooky the way he could feel his way to the fugitive of the hour. The guy was a born hunter. Pity the poor woman he finally set his sights on. She'd be shoeless and in the kitchen before she knew what hit her.

For an instant Bryn let herself wonder what she'd be like, this mythical woman Jake might someday hunt, might someday want enough to keep. To her annoyance, it wasn't pity she felt. It was envy.

She walked up to Ollie and looked down, firmly directing her attention to the problem at hand. His killer had saved the taxpayers a bunch of cash in court and incarceration fees, but had cost her a lead in her own investigation. Like Jake, she was hunting. "Wish I knew how you did it."

His grin got wider and whiter. His dentist must love him. "Magic," he said.

Bryn didn't grin back, but only because she wouldn't let herself, not because her mouth wasn't entirely willing to oblige him. He didn't need to be encouraged in his pain-in-the-ass behavior.

Jake looked at his watch. "You take a rocket out of DC?"

"I was already on my way." Just thinking about why took away all desire to smile. The quick, questioning arch of Jake's brow didn't improve her mood. "I got a hot tip."

Her mouth tightened as she thought about her hot tipper, the mythical and mysterious hacker known only as Phagan. It was him she hunted, though apparently not very well, or he wouldn't be sending her leads. She wouldn't allow herself to stop and think why he did that. It just made her crazy.

She saw questions in Jake's eyes and put up a do-not-ask sign in hers, then went on the attack with a subject change. "This closes the file on Ollie-as-fugitive, so why are you still here and not already after your next fugitive?" She waited a beat, then added, "And don't give me that curiosity crap."

"I am after my next fugitive," Jake said, then made her wait for who.

Obviously he hadn't been spanked enough as a child. Her eyes narrowed dangerously, so he gave her what she wanted.

"Hyatt."

"Dewey Hyatt?" Her smile was slow and loaded enough to make Mac catch his aging breath. "Maybe you are magic, Kirby."

Peter Harding stood with his hands clasped behind his back, staring out the window without really seeing the panoramic view of Denver spread out below him or the distant Rocky Mountains acting as frame. What he saw, what he always saw, was the reflection of himself.

The handsome man, flawlessly turned out in a custom-made silk suit of softest gray, was still a stranger, though a pleasing one. The hair flowing thick and sleek from a high, proud forehead, and the kindly gray eyes, were his own, though the blond hair color came from a bottle. The patrician face, newly restored to vigor by a visit to the plastic surgeon that gave him the air of a statesman, had become his own years ago. He liked to think it was the way he'd always been meant to look. He hadn't changed, just trimmed away the rough edges.

The discerning found him almost too perfect and sensed the elusive aura of a man playing a part and playing it very well. Buried deep beneath the superficial warmth of his light gray eyes was the cold heart of a completely amoral, utterly ruthless man.

Those who knew him slightly were dazzled by the charm with which nature had so generously endowed him. Got caught in the radiance of a personality that knew how to beam wide from a shallow base.

Those who knew him well fell into two camps. Those who were the fortunate beneficiaries of his schemes and those who were the victims of the ruthlessness with which he used the bounties nature had given him to get what he wanted. The lucky ones got only moderately singed by the casual contempt he had for their lives or hopes.

There were few lucky ones in his world.

Fools, all of them, in his opinion they deserved what they got. The cosmos allowed only a few winners and a lot of losers at any given moment. Fate had perfectly constructed him to be a winner. Now, after years of planning, fate had brought him within reach of achieving all he'd ever wanted.

His reflection showed neither satisfaction or guilt over his ways and means. Guilt clouded the issue, though he sometimes found it useful for others to be caught in its toils. Satisfaction would be premature. He was too careful to fall into that trap.

Impatience was his choice of the hour. He looked at his watch yet again, bit back an imprecation, and noticed the wrinkling of recently smoothed skin in his reflection in the glass. He smoothed the area with the tip of a manicured finger, enjoying the feel of almost young skin.

Amazing how easily youth was restored if you had enough money. He adjusted some wayward strands in his expensively cut hair. Defying his paternal genes, his hairline was the same as it always had been.

Nice to exceed the paternal model in every way possible.

Was the petty thief looking up from hell proud of what his genes, combined with those of a third-rate prostitute, had wrought?

Probably not.

Peter smiled, the coldly satisfied smile that few rarely saw, certainly not his soon to-be-announced fiancée. Only a fool let the quarry see the cold steel jaws of the trap ready to close with bruising force around them.

Peter was no fool.

The door opened soundlessly behind him, but he'd been watching for it and turned with concealed relief as Barrett

Stern stepped in, closing the door behind him.

Bumps and delays were all too common on the road to power, but in the past few months Peter seemed to be experiencing more of them than usual. With luck, Stern had once again removed a particularly annoying one for him.

"You're late," Peter said.

A tall man with the ability to look shorter when needed, Stern had pale hair and flat, cold eyes that looked as if light couldn't penetrate, let alone warm them. He had a thin, bland face, a thinner mouth that neither smiled nor frowned. The knack to pass almost unnoticed was a skill he'd taken pains to cultivate, content to leave the limelight to Peter. The power he sought was the kind that couldn't survive scrutiny. Like the ancient gods, he found that only the taking of life satisfied his needs.

He walked to the middle of the room and stopped, sliding his hands into the pockets of his off-the-rack pants.

"No. I'm not," Stern said, his voice flat and even.

Peter stiffened at the lack of apology in Stern's voice. Perhaps he thought that knowing where Peter's past was buried gave him a get-out-of-awe free card. He was wrong, but now wasn't the time to tell him. Only a fool poked a snake with a stick when the bloodlust was on him.

Peter dropped into his leather chair, taking care to arrange the creases of his suit for minimal wrinkling. He nodded toward one of the wing chairs in front of the desk, but Stern strolled between them instead.

This also annoyed him, but Peter didn't let that show either as he leaned back, his fingers making a steeple for his chin to rest lightly on. "I hope you have something good to report."

Stern's shoulders moved in what might have been a shrug. "He's dead. I'm not sure if he's gone."

"Did you find—"

"If he had anything, it wasn't on him. Could've been taking a pass, planning to go back later."

"How the hell did he get into the RABBIT files? He didn't have clearance. If the Feds find out—" Peter shuddered, a frown once again pulling at his refreshed skin until he realized it and stopped himself. RABBIT, a highly specialized supercomputer chip they were developing for the military, was responsible for most of the bumps plaguing him right now. Stern had warned him about getting involved with government contracts, but the money had been too good to pass up.

"How are they going to find out?" Stern shrugged, the movement made his ill-fitting jacket gape and exposed the holster at his waist. "I got his company ID. And if someone does happen to make the connection, I've erased all records of his incursions into the secure files."

Peter wasn't convinced. His instincts, the only thing he trusted, were twitching like they hadn't since the night he lost Nadine. Just thinking about her started a tic below his right eye. "We have no clue what he found or if he told anyone?"

"Nope." Stern stood quietly, unmoving except for the rhythmic flutter of his pale lashes. "I was on him as soon as the computer flagged the intrusion. Took the same flight. Followed him all the way to his bolt-hole. But I couldn't see him every minute."

"Did you question him?"

Stern stirred, a flicker of pleasure passing through his dead eyes. "He wasn't very resilient."

Peter looked away, disquieted by the sudden urge to make sure that if it became necessary, Stern died first. "Great, so we don't know who his contact was?"

Stern shrugged again. "Only thing I found in the dive was some very fancy computer equipment and a bunch of flyers."

He extracted a sheet from his inside pocket and tossed it to Peter, who opened the sheet, studied it, then frowned.

"He headed for Montana like an arrow. Why would he have flyers for a bar in Estes Park?"

Stern looked bored. "No way to know if he brought them or they were already there."

Peter crumpled the edges of the flyer, then loosened his grip, smoothing the sheet and studying it again. "Do you think it's important? Maybe you should check—"

"I've already sent one of my men. Country-western bars aren't my natural habitat."

"I guess not." Peter looked amused before worry over took him again. "Lucky you were here to see the security flag come up."

"Maybe." Stern didn't believe in luck.

"What a mess!" Peter jumped up and paced to the window.

"That's why we have a backup plan."

"I don't like the timing. We're announcing the engagement and my candidacy on Sunday."

"How is the prospective first lady?"

Peter's expression turned feral. "Eager. Her daddy not quite as much, but he'll come round when I'm governor—and the grandchildren start arriving."

Stern joined him by the window.

"Grandchildren. Interesting concept. Course, you'll have to curb your . . . appetites to make it work. The press isn't as careless as they used to be about politicians' . . . hobbies."

Peter's face lost its complacency, his gaze shifting away from Stern. "I am aware of the need for discretion."

"The question isn't do you know it, but can you do it?"

"Yes." He'd give up what he must to get Audrey and her father's political clout. If need pressed, there were ways to get

. . . sustenance on the side. "I have my memories to sustain me."

"Stick to memories and they'll be calling you Governor."

"Yes." Peter smiled. Governor. That all-important next step toward more power over lives, land, people. A different kind of lust sent an electric charge across his newly tightened skin. When that power was his, he could do whatever he wanted. And Audrey? He'd do what he wanted with her elegant body, high-born face and powerful connections. In time, after he'd properly schooled her, her life itself would be his to do with as he pleased. Her life and those of her daughters. He smiled, thinking of the smaller, perfect versions of their mother.

Were they strong enough for his love? He didn't know. He hoped so. He wanted them to be strong—though not as strong as Nadine who'd gotten away from him and Kerry Anne who almost hadn't. The surprise had been when he'd realized they were both stronger than their drunken slut of a mother who'd taken a voluntary dive down her own stairs. Two suicides in two months turned out to be too suspicious, even for the laid back small town police of his former home. Immediately after her funeral, he'd retired his Montgomery Justice identity. It was in the interim between that one and his present life as Peter Harding, that he'd met Stern, who had also been someone else.

"You slip up, Peter, you'll be getting a number and strip searched instead of sworn in," Stern said, breaking into his side trip down memory lane.

"I know what's at stake." Peter shifted irritably at the tiny cloud of old business that shadowed his vision of the future. Where was Nadine? Could she have found him? Was she the one—

"It hasn't stopped," he admitted abruptly. "I'm still getting the messages."

"He might have left something behind to foul up our computer systems. I'll check it out." Stern looked at Peter. "Unless there's something you're not telling me?"

"I got a note," Peter admitted. He unlocked a drawer and extracted a folded sheet of cheap notepaper.

Stern took the sheet and opened it. Letters cut out of a newspaper formed the words: *I know.*

"Cryptic." He was quiet for a moment. "If someone is pulling your chain—"

"How could they know to pull *that* chain?" Peter heard the rising panic of his own voice and reined it in. "How could anyone know?"

"We don't know they're pulling that chain. Relax. I made damn sure that no part of your past can be traced to this present."

"Unless it's Nadine."

Stern shrugged. "What if it is? She has no proof. The person you were is permanently missing."

"The press feed on innuendo like piranhas on flesh. All it would take is a whiff of suspicion to end my political career."

Stern turned, walked back around the desk and dropped into Peter's own chair. He stretched his feet out, his hands unnaturally still on the armrests, that look of pleasure coming back to his eyes.

"Not if I take care of her before she gets to the press. The same way you took care of her big sister."

The sun was hanging low on the horizon by the time they hauled Ollie out in his body bag. Outside the window, the low-rent district where Oliver Smith met his end looked sad under the fading August sun. Inside, the light was equally merciless as it found its way through the dirty window panes. It bumped up the smell of garlic, old deer meat, and onion and outstripped the pitiful air conditioning, putting beads of sweat on poor Mac's face. The detective was already showing stress at being caught between the immovable FBI agent and the hard-as-a-rock Deputy Marshal, Jake noted, with amused sympathy.

The techs faded away in a discreet hurry, leaving Jake to finish up with Bryn, who was seated in front of the computer. Mac went out, too, muttering something about getting them all something cold to drink.

"How long has it been since we've had a whiff of a trail on Hyatt?" Jake stood in the middle of the room, turning in a slow circle. In one corner, shoved up against the peeling green paint of the wall, was a rumpled bed, in another a lumpy chair and crooked floor lamp. But it wasn't the place he was straining to pick up on. It was the people who'd been there. Even in the most generic of settings, it was hard not to leave some traces of your personal taste behind.

He stopped turning when he got to Bryn and the sturdy desk tucked in a kind of alcove next to the closet. She'd been sitting there for what seemed an hour, like a virgin trying to make up her mind, while the crime scene slowly cleared.

"Two years, almost to the day. The Interplex Technology heist," she said.

"I remember that one. Damn near perfect piece of work. Like to meet the guys who plan their heists."

"You and half the law-enforcement agencies in the country."

Something in the way she said it triggered Jake's instincts. Jake walked over to her, propping a shoulder against the doorjamb. "It's not *one* guy, is it?"

She hesitated, then nodded. "I had my hands on one of Phagan's kids for a very short time. He let slip a nickname."

Jake arched a brow questioningly.

After another hesitation she said, "The kid called him Pathphinder. Apropos, isn't it?"

"Almost, too." *Path finder.* More modest than mastermind. And more clever, Jake mused. It was, according to the file Bryn had reluctantly shared with him, about all the FBI knew about the notorious hacker who called himself Phagan. They knew a little more about Dewey Hyatt, his second in command and the fugitive Jake now had his sights set on, and that their operation somehow involved teenage runaways. Precious little, unless Bryn was still holding out on him, which was possible, since interagency cooperation was a contradiction in terms.

"Kid could've been blowing smoke up my skirt, but it didn't feel like it," Bryn said. "As usual, Phagan spirited the kid away before I could find out more."

There was something in her voice that told Jake she'd let this particular hunt get a tad personal. Big mistake, but she already knew that. Bryn was as strict with herself as she was with any colleague. It was what made it both pleasure and pain to work with her.

"Fagan?" The question came from Mac, who had returned bearing soft drinks. He handed them out while Jake looked at Bryn for direction. She gave a slight shake of her head. No reason to make Phagan more of a legend than he already was. Besides, if the locals smelled a big fish, they'd start withholding information, hoping to make a big collar on their own. Why make it easier for Phagan to elude them? Not that he was having any trouble now.

"The thief in Oliver Twist," Jake said.

Mac rubbed his forehead as if it hurt. "Oh."

Jake hid a grin with a long, cool drink from his cup, not too surprised Mac wasn't into classic literature or musicals.

Bryn took a drink, then a deep breath, one that seemed

weighted with purpose, and turned back to the computer. Her hands hovered above the keyboard as if it were a bomb that might go off. The screen was dark, but the green cursor glowed in the lower right-hand corner.

"Anyone touch the computer while securing the scene?" Bryn asked with a reluctance that was out of character.

"No, ma'am," Mac said, "except to dust for prints."

She wriggled her fingers, like a maestro, then lowered her hands and tapped a few keys. Nothing happened. The computer wasn't going to give up its secrets that easily. She frowned fiercely. Mac shifted, dabbing at the sweat on his brow.

Jake leaned across her and picked up a plastic-wrapped sheet from the clutter of evidence bags. It was a simple flyer advertising a country-western bar called JR's, located near Estes Park, Colorado. Though Jake was assigned to DC and had an apartment there, he called Denver home. He'd been born and raised in Denver and his mom and brothers still lived there. He knew Estes, too, and, thought he remembered the bar. His family had a cabin just outside Rocky Mountain National Park. It took him a bit of thinking to pull up a memory of a log structure east of town on 34. Good music. Better beer.

The flyer was an odd thing to find so far from its home. Even odder, the series of numbers and letters written down one side.

"Any idea what this is?" he asked, distracting Bryn from her attack on the computer.

She seemed relieved at the distraction, rather than annoyed as she took it. "It's an Internet address for a MUD."

Jake blinked. "A mud?"

Bryn smiled with a decidedly superior air. "A multi-user dungeon. A place on the Internet where people meet to play games. Looks like home is in Colorado." She gave at Jake with a tense look. "Dewey and his . . . friends like to play games."

As if on cue, Jake heard a humming sound. A small airplane flew across the computer screen dragging a banner that had written on it: *You'll have to do better than that, darling.*

Bryn choked and banged on the keyboard with her fists. The airplane did fly out of sight, but it wasn't over. A small Yugo putted across the bottom of the screen with the words *Love, Phagan* on a sign on the roof.

Jake opened his mouth, but Bryn's look shriveled the words in his throat. He took a careful step back, avoiding eye contact with Mac. His elbow bumped a pile of evidence bags, starting a small avalanche that spread to the other side of the desk and continued onto the floor. He bent to pick them up.

Bryn looked at Mac, her eyes scary and her smile steely. "I don't want anyone but you near this computer, until this person," she scribbled a name on the back of her card and handed it to him, "comes to pick it up. Don't show that name to anyone. Don't tell it to anyone. You, yourself bring the guy here to pack it up, and stay with him all the way back to the airport. Understand?"

He nodded. "But . . ."

"We might still be able to pull something off the hard drive." She stood up and stepped close to him. "No mistakes. I'd hate to have to come back and rip your heart out." She stared at him for a long beat. "And eat it."

Mac gulped twice before he managed to say, "No, ma'am, I mean, yes, ma'am. Whatever you say, ma'am."

Jake started to dump the bags of evidence back onto the desk when he saw what the bags had been hiding. An answering machine, with a blinking message light.

"Looks like somebody has a message." Jake crouched

down and studied the machine, then looked at Bryn.

Bryn turned to stare. "Somebody wouldn't be that stupid, would they?"

Mac craned to see. "It wasn't doing that before."

Jake still had on surgical gloves, so he tilted the machine. Finger-printing powder fell off it in a mini-shower. He found the volume at zero on both ringer and recorder. With the volume turned up, he rewound the tape, then pushed *play*.

A tinny, metallic voice came out of the speaker.

"If you're there, pick up." A pause, then a sigh. "Call Pathphinder ASAP. And if you see Phagan, tell him the egg's in the nest—should hatch right on schedule. If we still have a schedule. You know where to reach me."

A hesitation. Then a click.

"Well, I'm damned." Bryn looked at Jake in awe. "Pathphinder is a woman."

"What was that about an egg?" Mac asked, the effort of trying to keep up written in neon across his face.

"A cuckoo's egg." She hesitated, as if she'd like to stop there, but Jake arched his eyebrows for more. "In cyberspace, an 'egg' is a computer program laid in a host machine where it will 'hatch' at some later time or from some specific action."

"Laid?" Jake frowned. "To do what?"

"Anything the Cuckoo wants. Give unauthorized access. Crash, maim or destroy. Phagan's used them to disable security systems and to download sensitive data. Like the Trojan horse, they're bad news for the 'nest' computer."

Jake nodded thoughtfully, then looked at the phone. "I wonder . . ."

He lifted the receiver and punched in the call-back code. In a few moments a phone number flashed across the digital screen and the phone was ringing. He held the phone out so Bryn and Mac could hear a voice with a decided Texas accent say, "JR's. What can I do you for?"

Jake replaced the phone without answering and then grinned at Bryn whose jaw had dropped. "That local area code is Estes Park, Colorado."

"It couldn't be that easy, could it?" she asked.

"Trust an old Colorado cowboy. If the bad guys were smart, our job would be harder." He looked at his watch. "Just enough time to catch the last flight to Denver." He grinned at Mac. "Thanks for the assist."

"No problem." The detective looked at Bryn gathering up her stuff. "No . . . problem."

Jake held the door for Bryn. "Ladies first."

She grinned, looking like the easygoing farm girl her parents had hoped for. "Let's go catch us some bad guys."

"Who was on the phone?"

Mert Mentel, lead singer in Cattle Call, slung the pay phone's receiver back on its cradle and turned to find Phoebe leaning against the office doorjamb. She leaned real good. Had the best rack in town and a waist he could span with one hand even falling down drunk. Which was the only time to make a run at the girl. Something in her brown eyes stopped him in his sober tracks. Her eyes had always been sad, like grief had a permanent home there. And her smile was usually wry, as if life were a joke only she understood.

"Dunno. They hung up."

He strolled closer because, sad or wry, she didn't seem to mind displaying her bounty. Her brief denim shorts and briefer white lace top were the perfect frame for her breasts and curving hips. Even better, the shorts left her long legs bare until all the way to her boots. Her hair was a straight fall of dark silk that curled under a stubborn chin on either side, her skin was tanned satin.

Her mouth—well, a guy could take half a day thinking of ways to kiss her mouth. Maybe longer if his big brother didn't come along and kick his ass back into the real world.

Mert sighed and reached out cautiously to smooth some of the hair back from the chin, wishing he could smooth the sad from her eyes with some hot sex. "Some asshole break his promise to call you, girl?"

Phoebe grinned up at Mert, aware of, but unaffected by, his signature Mentel charm. "Like I'd believe any man's promises. Last time I checked, *sucker* wasn't listed on my resume."

"Think I'll go kick Jesse's butt for ruining you. Or you could let me heal your broken heart." He gave her a hopeful smile.

Like those of all the Mentel boys, Mert's mouth had been made to smile and placed in a face too pretty for anyone's good. Even worse, his body was long and taut, with a vaguely designer air despite his country leanings. Blond hair tumbled halfway down his back; wicked, green eyes and a shitload of charm were given dangerous fuel by his honest worship at the shrine of the female body. A religion made easy to practice, since women loved to worship him back. The lacing of Texas in his deep, smooth voice completed a formidable arsenal.

Lucky for Phoebe, she'd received an early inoculation against the Mentel charm at the hands of his big brother, Jesse.

"I don't have a heart," Phoebe said gently. She didn't glory in knowing this. She even missed it, but before becoming "Phoebe," before this life Phagan had helped her create, she'd placed that heart in her sister's dead hands. Now it was buried with her six feet under the Georgia soil.

And there would be no resurrection until the man now known as Peter Harding paid for his crimes.

What she'd learned as Phoebe, what she'd learned from working with Phagan, made it possible for her to smile at Mert even though her nerves were stretched as tight as the strings on her guitar with worry. Just as her ears told her when her guitar was out of tune, her senses were telling her the game was out of sync.

Where was Phagan? He sometimes dropped off her cyber-map, but never so completely when a game was running. Ollie and Dewey were MIA, too, though that wasn't so unusual. A lot depended on where Phagan had them deployed.

Too bad her senses hadn't been online when she placed that phone call. Hadn't made a mistake like that since she first started playing Phagan's games. Might as well put a neon arrow in the sky, pointing to the bar. To her.

Mert's grin turned wry. The change didn't lessen its impact. "Then why not just use me for sex?"

"Because I respect you." Phoebe patted his cheek and in doing so caught sight of her watch. "Hell, look at the time."

"Don't need to with you around. Could take a whiz, though." He headed toward the john.

Phoebe, heartless but not blind, watched him walk away. He had a great butt, and a girl had to get her pleasure where she could, while she could. He disappeared into the john, leaving her to turn her attention to the upcoming set. Absently she fingered the buttons of her Daisy Mae shirt. It had only four, so she'd done up all of them. Now she wasn't so sure. The trick was to show just enough cleavage to keep attention off her face. She'd changed what she could, short of plastic surgery, but she knew he'd recognize her if he got a close enough look.

Leg, youngest Mentel and boy behind the keyboards,

poked his head in the door that separated the hallway from the bar. From under his mustache he gave her a toothpaste-ad grin.

"Your groupie's back."

Phoebe made a face. "Not Earl?"

"The one and only duke of."

"Great." She sighed. "Thanks for the heads up, even if you are enjoying it."

Leg laughed and disappeared. Smart boy.

It was a public bar. Couldn't kick out her most ardent fan. Maybe if she kept her buttons closed, he'd only drool tonight. She frowned. Who *was* Earl? He looked harmless, but she couldn't afford to assume anything. Not when she was a shining example of the hide-in-plain-sight school of thought.

She studied her cleavage. If the doughy and disgusting Earl was other than what he appeared to be, maybe she ought to make sure his blood flow headed south. She undid two buttons. The push-up bra did the rest.

Mert came back from the john still zipping his jeans. His eyebrows shot up when he saw her. "Taking show time to a new low, aren't you, girl?"

"Earl's here."

Mert grinned. "And you're gonna kill him with kindness." He studied her "kindness" with a connoisseur's eye. "What about collateral damage?"

"You'll heal," she said.

Chapter Two

Jake stopped the rented truck in front of Bryn and their small pile of luggage and jumped out. He opened the passenger door for her before tossing their luggage into the truck bed.

Bryn put her hands on her hips. "What is this?"

Jake finished stowing her laptop computer in the front on the floor before looking at her. "Transportation?"

She looked at him with one eyebrow arched.

"We're in cowboy country. What else would we drive?"

She heaved a pointed sigh before approaching the open door, where her short skirt, high heels and the truck's threshold height defeated her before she got started. She gave Jake a *now what* look. He grinned and stepped behind her. His hands gripped her waist, offering her a brief sensation of flight, then a landing on the seat. She felt color flood in her face, sent there by her pounding heart. She smoothed her skirt and collected her scattered dignity while Jake made the journey around to the driver's seat.

He slid in beside her and fired the engine, an expression of masculine pleasure lighting his eyes as the truck responded to the pressure of his foot on the gas. Bryn buckled her seat belt, then grabbed on to the armrest as they shot into the flow of traffic. Before she could assimilate the highway signs, Jake had committed them to heading south.

Jake handled the truck well. He was a confident, not reckless, driver. She just didn't like being driven. Which explained her volatile reaction to Phagan, since he was driving her crazy. With an inward shrug, she forced her feelings to the back burner, where she put all the things she couldn't control.

"Did you get a hold of your brothers?" she asked, deliberately looking away from the road.

Jake nodded. "Luke, the one with the Denver PD, is checking out the local angle with a buddy of his in Estes Park. I think I mentioned our family has a cabin near there?"

Bryn nodded, resisting the urge to tense when he changed lanes.

"And Matt, another marshal, said he'd have his computer guy check out the address of that MUD. If it is local, we should have an address by tomorrow sometime."

"Two marshals and a cop in one family?" Odd to learn Jake was a sibling. He seemed such a loner.

"Guess its in my genes." Jake pushed a hand through his hair, rumpling the surface boyishly. "Dad was a cop."

"Was?"

"Died. Line of duty." His face closed.

"I'm sorry." Bryn shifted uncomfortably. Her own parents were hale, hearty, and baffled by their daughter's law-enforcement inclinations. A regular, though rural, Ozzie and Harriet in a world of disposable marriages.

"So, what's the deal with you and Phagan?"

Bryn stiffened. "There is no deal," she lied, because she didn't know what was going on or how to explain it to herself, let alone to Jake.

She still remembered the moment she realized Phagan was doing more than feeding her leads to his unsavory targets. That she understood. His jobs were carefully targeted to maim and destroy, so of course he'd need her to clean up after him. But why would he feed her leads to where he was? It made no sense.

Then he'd started leaving her gifts, both on her desk and inside her DC apartment, places he shouldn't have access to. It was both terrifying and infuriating to do her job, to live her life, all the time wondering if he was the repairman who came to fix her television or one of the people cleaning the office. He seemed to know an extraordinary amount about her. He'd invited her to a meeting in virtual reality a few months ago. She'd been hesitant, but determined to try to smoke him out. And she'd found herself, she remembered with guilty amusement, in Ozzie and Harriet's world. All black and white and her with a fifties hair do and clothes, down to a white apron tied around her dress. But no shoes. In the kitchen.

The guy had a dark sense of humor that she was having a damn hard time not responding to.

How did he know what she had never acknowledged out loud? Terror had faded into laughter she couldn't hold in check. Phagan was a high-tech criminal whose butt she was determined to toss into jail, but he was also a benign, eager-to-please-without-getting-caught suitor with a sense of humor she secretly enjoyed. She hadn't lowered her guard, but she had grown more bold about following the clues he sent her. The idiot seemed determined to make sure she stayed on his trail and she was learning from him. She hated to admit it, but it was the truth.

How could she not like the guy a little? Wouldn't stop her from plotting his downfall, but it helped to like your work. It helped a lot.

"How about we stop to grab some grub?" Jake asked.

Grub? Boy, were they ever in cowboy country.

The lights were dim, glowing just enough to add a sheen to black satin sheets on a bed overhung with an ornate mirror. A panel slid back, revealing an expensive entertainment center. Peter scanned a row of unlabeled videos, selected one and shoved it into the machine. Drink and remote in hand, he went to the bed, made a nest with the pillows, then settled himself at its center. Before he could activate the VCR, the phone on the night stand intruded.

Muttering a curse, Peter grabbed it and took a calming breath. "Harding here."

"You alone?" Stern asked.

"Why—"

"You need to come back to the office."

"I was just going to bed."

"Tough. Get back here."

"What's wrong?"

"Not on the phone. Sure as hell not on my cell phone."

Peter cursed silently. "Fine."

He banged down the phone and stood up. This had better be worth it. He shed his elegant robe and picked up the pants he'd laid over the suit valet. Before pulling them on, he started the video, putting his clothes on as the young girl on the screen took hers off.

The music reached out the wide double doors of the log building. In a swirling haze of smoke and beer it extended a cheerful invitation to come on in and join the party. If the number of trucks crammed into the dirt parking lot was any indication, there were a lot of takers.

Jake pulled the truck into place at the end of one crooked line. He shut off the motor and studied the poorly lit exterior. It hadn't changed much since the last time he'd been here with his big brothers. The day Matt's divorce was final, Jake remembered, after a little mental time travel. They'd climbed every cliff in sight, then gotten stinking drunk. Brutal, but effective. Matt had felt so bad, it left him one way to go: up.

The people milling in and out the front door looked much the same as the clientele had then. A mix of old and young, a few tourists, some genuine cowboys on a tear ogling clusters of barely clad cowgirls, and several older couples serious about doing some dancing. Jake glanced at Bryn and found her looking uneasy.

"How—" Bryn started, stopped, then settled for gesturing toward the bar.

"We go in. We buy a couple of beers. We nose around. See if we smell anything interesting."

The bouncer chose that moment to eject two struggling figures. They staggered, took a couple of wild swings at each other, then tripped over the low lodge-pole fence that separated the parking lot from the entrance.

Her eyes widened. "O-kay."

Jake hid a grin. "But first we do something about you."

"About me? What do you mean?"

"You're too buttoned down. Lose the jacket, undo some shirt buttons and mess up your hair a bit," Jake directed. "And when you walk, do it like that." He pointed to a sassily twitching ass in tight jeans passing in front of the truck. "If our guy is in there, we don't want him thinking too much."

"No," Bryn said, "we wouldn't want that." With her teeth gritted, she made the necessary adjustments. "Better?"

Jake grinned. "Let's see that walk."

He jumped out and trotted around the truck to help her down. Was it her imagination that he'd just acquired a slight bow leg? She showed him her walk, ire adding extra oomph to the side-to-side sway of her hips. She turned to face him, letting a raised eyebrow ask the question.

"By George, I think she's got it." Jake gestured toward the open doors. "Let's go."

Good thing she hadn't been expecting high praise. She fell into step beside him, stowing female angst in a well-used compartment in her brain. Hot on the outside—despite Jake's tepid approval, she knew she was—a cold professional on the inside. She was hunting now, and she had a scent.

Her nostrils quivered. Too bad it was beer.

Jake paid their cover, then followed her to the bar that ran the length of one wall, his touch light and impersonal against her back. She pretended to sip the beer he bought her as she studied her surroundings.

The place hadn't been well designed for acoustics. Canned music blared from somewhere besides the stage, which was empty of people if not instruments. That and the sound of too many loud conversations started an ache behind her eyes as she made mental notes about the layout.

Bar to the right of the entrance. Minute stage opposite. Restroom sign over door on the left. Tables past that. Dance floor dead center and circled by milling groups of people. She noticed a short ladder that lead to a sad little balcony half way up the wall where the haze of smoke and dust was the worst, a sound and light tech hunkered over a control board.

Her survey brought her back face to face with Jake. He wiped a film of moisture off his upper lip with his sleeve, but the level of his beer hadn't changed.

"I've died and gone to hell," she muttered.

Jake hid his grin behind his beer. "Think you'll have more success with the guys than I will."

"Do you?" Bryn managed to hold back a shudder. Despite his doubts about the importance of the bar, Jake's brother, Matt, a US marshal working out of Denver, had faxed him sketchy bios he'd scraped up on the most likely suspects: the barkeep and the band members. They'd all been around for a couple of years and one of the band members, a woman named Phoebe Mentel, managed the bar. Who owned the bar was under investigation.

Jake had taken particular pleasure in telling her about the men in the band.

"Four guys—Jesse, Mert, Leg, Toes."

"Leg and Toes?"

"Fraid so." Jake had grinned. "And the woman. Same last name. Mentel. Three brothers, one cousin and one ex-wife. Bar keep's name is Chet Jones."

"Right." Oh, for the peace and quiet of the Internet. When she caught up with him, Phagan was going to pay for this. "I don't see any of them yet."

"There's one," Jake muttered, "heading to the stage. Go get 'em, tiger."

Bryn spotted the guy as he leaped the wooden barrier, picked up a guitar and started adjusting the strings. She gave a soundless sigh. She'd seen his type before. The hard part wouldn't be getting his attention. It would be losing it.

"You—" she started to say, when someone pushed past her.

"Phoebe!" The nasal voice of the man who bumped her was as grating as chalk on a blackboard. The body emitting the voice even less appealing.

A woman, apparently the Phoebe he was after, froze, then turned to face him with obvious reluctance.

"Earl." The name came out a Southern-scented sigh, one edged with irony. It suited her.

She was a bit taller than Bryn and had a flawless complexion and wonderful bones, the kind that aged well. Only a tiny frown marred the skin between her dark eyebrows. Her dark hair swept out from under the edges of her cowboy hat in smooth, dark sweep, then curled under her strong chin. Eyes the color of her hair regarded Earl with something less than enthusiasm.

"I wanted to ask you—" Earl began

"I have to get ready for the set, Earl." She softened her dismissal with a slight, though charming smile. Her husky voice had been created to stroke the pleasure centers of men, Bryn noted. Add to that her country-fresh vigor and generously curved figure, and it was no wonder Earl looked whipped.

As if she sensed Bryn's scrutiny, Phoebe's gaze swept the crowd and found Bryn watching her. She shrugged and gave Bryn a "men!" look, but there was a watchful quality behind her rueful glance. Bryn had no choice but to return her smile.

Phoebe turned to go, just as Jake moved into position behind her. She slammed into him with enough force to take him back a couple of steps and knock off her hat. Like a scene from a movie, her hands spread across his chest as she tried to catch her balance. His hands went to her waist to aid her. Gaze slammed into gaze and just for a moment, Bryn thought she saw . . . something . . . happen between them. Something electric and elemental. Then the shutters slammed down in eyes blue and brown.

She saw Jake rub the back of his neck. A red flag, to those who knew him, that the US Marshals Service's best tracker was worried.

Peter pushed open the door to his office but stopped when he found it lit only by the glow from his computer screen. "Stern?"

In the darkness Stern lit a cigarette. The red flare of the match guided Peter to Stern in the shadows.

"This better be worth dragging me out—"

Stern gestured toward the computer with the red end of his cigarette. "Someone's been messing with your kinky screen saver."

Peter stalked around the desk and dropped into his chair. The benign desk top looked normal and unthreatening. "What?"

"Just wait." Stern nudged the mouse to take the monitor out of energy saver mode.

A soft hum from the clock on the desk was the only sound that broke the silence until the screen flickered, went dark, then glowed again as a picture formed of a naked young girl sprawled on satin sheets. She rolled from her back to her stomach, then came to her knees, rocking back and forth. Sweat broke out on Peter's forehead and his loins tightened as he studied breasts too small even to jiggle from her movements.

The program featured a varied menu, but this was his favorite. The camera moved in closer and her lashes lifted. She licked red lips. "You like this, don't you?"

"Oh, yeah," he muttered, tugging at his top shirt button as she kneaded her small breasts with red-tipped fingers. She rolled onto her back again, her hands moving lower, but here the familiar sequence took a strange turn. Instead of zeroing in on her genitals, the video cam homed in on her mouth, moving in tighter and tighter until her crimson lips filled the whole screen.

"I know all about you, Peter," she said. "I know . . . all . . . about . . . you."

"What the hell—" He started up out of the chair, but Stern's hand came down on his shoulder, forcing him back down.

"She's not done."

The camera zoomed out again as she rolled back onto her stomach and gave him a sultry smile. "And soon everyone else will, too."

Then the screen went blank.

Peter looked at Stern.

He blew smoke out his mouth and nose. "Was it worth it?"

Jake rubbed the back of his neck. His other hand was wrapped around a waist so small, his fingers reached past her spine. He needed time to figure out what had just happened. He didn't get time. She was in his arms, in his face. And she smelled great. Like really fresh flowers.

Almost as tall as he was, the body brushing against his went in and out where it was supposed to and did it with extreme prejudice. Something red hugged her breasts. A brief bit of denim played second skin to her hips. Bare flesh above and below. Long legs disappearing into boots. Smooth dark hair, except for the crease from her hat. Face done up to look cheap, failing to look anything but classy. Her features were too cleanly cut, her dark eyes too intelligent. Her mouth—

Better not go down that road, Kirby.

He blinked and took a mental step back. His body wasn't responding yet.

"Sorry," Phoebe said, staring into eyes a cool blue drink of water. Eyes that gave but also took. An intriguing sleight of eyes if you had nothing to hide.

She had plenty to hide.

She spread her hands defensively across his chest, feeling heat push through the soft cotton of his shirt as she applied enough pressure to put a little air between their bodies. Instinct had her curving up the edges of her mouth and putting on her bedroom look, the way a wild thing donned protective cover. Adrenaline did a rising scale along her nerve endings as her hands did a slow slide down cotton and muscle, then dropped clear.

"I'm not." The grin he followed this with managed to be both wicked and little-boy innocent. It also packed about a thousand watts of charm.

"Phoebe?"

Earl's plaintive whine cut between them with all the delicacy of a chain saw. Instead of relief, she felt regret as their eyes broke contact. Earl had her hat in hand and a mournful expression pulled down his face.

"Thanks, Earl." She took the hat, rammed it on top of her head and adjusted the angle. The brief respite gave her confidence to look at the stranger again. "Sorry bout almost mowing you, cowboy."

"You can mow me anytime you want, Reb."

Against her design, her smile lost its provocative edge, and the shadows in her soul retreated, leaving a girl looking at guy looking at a girl.

Damn the boy was cute—looked good enough to eat, drink and be merry with.

If only—

If only every single thing in her life were different but then what? Who was she kidding? Guys came to the bar looking for a slam, bam, thank you, ma'am. Just because this one looked as if a heart wouldn't melt in his eyes didn't make it so.

She made herself turn away from his might-have-been eyes and tasty mouth, made her heart turn away from the dangerous promise of safety he gave off like after-shave. "If you boys'll excuse me, I got a set to play."

Jake watched Phoebe slip into the crowd, then looked at Earl. Dogs looked like Earl when they begged. He looked in the mirror behind the bar and saw the same expression on his face.

Not good. He'd learned to read eyes and body language, but Phoebe shape-shifted like a kaleidoscope, the changes so fast his impressions were disjointed and laced with lust. Only thing he was sure about: there was a great huge well of sadness at her center. Even when she smiled her eyes were shadowed, as if she already knew that life sucked and always would for her.

He saw Bryn watching him. It helped him find his focus. Reminded him he wasn't here to feel desire or pity. Phoebe

Mentel was connected to JR's. JR's was connected, somehow, to Phagan and Dewey Hyatt. That's all that mattered.

"Looks like we'll have to postpone further contact till after the show," Bryn said when he rejoined her.

Jake nodded, lifted his beer to take a real drink and felt a change ripple through the crowd. He looked up, turning to face the stage.

Without ceremony, the band launched into their first number, a fast-paced piece about small towns on a Saturday night that made the rowdy crowd theirs even before the chorus.

The band members were a good looking bunch of people, the guys as poster pretty as Phoebe, but it was more than that or the audience's level of intoxication, Jake decided, that lifted their competent musical rendering into something damn near mesmerizing.

It wasn't easy to hang on, to focus, with Phoebe so easy on the eye and the music pushing out thought for feeling, but after a time Jake found the group's interaction interesting enough to mute the call to the senses they sent out as they worked their way through songs, slow and fast, old and new, mixed with the occasional request.

The men were cocky, but seemed able to table ego when they changed lead singers to create the right sound. They constantly interacted with the audience to keep it pumped. Jesse, the eldest, appeared to be in charge. Phoebe stayed toward the back of the stage, so it took him a while to realize she was really the one running the show.

Throughout the set, Earl stayed front and center before the stage and danced wildly, paying bizarre homage to Phoebe with his doughy body. Sometimes he sang along, his voice both loud and bad. In his tight jeans, greenhorn boots and too new hat, he sweated profusely, the thin wisps of his hair plastered to his white skin.

Toward the end of the set, Jesse Mentel, a big, shaggy man with a huge white smile, stopped the music with a gesture. He leaned into the microphone, said with easy confidence, "Everybody having a good time?"

The audience responded with enthusiasm.

"Good enough. Time to introduce us to you. Have to before I get too drunk to remember who the hell we are." Egged on by the stamping of many feet, he took a long drink from his beer. "On keyboard—damn it, boy, where—" He turned in a listing circle, "oh, there you are. How'd you get back there? Never mind, this here's my little brother, Leg."

Leg waved from his keyboard, then did some fancy stuff on the keys. He was young, lean and blond, with a cocky mustache and matching attitude. His smile lit his green eyes and beamed good will all the way to the back of the hall.

A young woman answered its siren call. "He single?"

"Totally single and alone only when he has to be. You can leave your phone number and vital statistics in the tin cup here at the front of the stage, little darlin'."

The guys groaned, and the girls laughed.

"On bass guitar is my other little brother, Mert—who also has needs."

Mert touched his hat, his smile sweet and hopeful. His long fingers moved in an intricate riff across his guitar strings.

"On drum is my cousin, Toes. And let me assure you, ladies, he didn't get his nickname for playing drum with his feet."

Toes grinned wickedly from his place behind the drums. His hair was blond, too, and fell down his back. Like those of his cousins his eyes and his smile were blatantly come-taste-me. He flipped his hair off his face, bent over his drums, and pounded out a short, pagan, mini solo that had the women rocking and stamping up puffs of dust from the floor.

"I'll take one of him," a girl called out.

"Nothing he likes more than being taken—unless it's taking, sweet thing," Jesse assured her with a good-natured leer. He took another swig of beer, wiped his mouth and said, "I'm, uh, oh, yeah, Jesse. I sing and play a little fiddle when called for." He played a few clear notes. "All together we're Cattle Call."

"Uh, you forgot Phoebe Ann again," Toes said into his mike, giving his hair another flip.

Jesse turned to Phoebe with a start, then swept his hat off and over his heart. "Damn, girl, I'm sorry—"

"Sorriest man I know," Phoebe said, leaning into her mike.

He put his hat back on and grinned. "Ah, hell, you know I was just fooling. I couldn't never forget the shining light of Cattle Call, our lead guitarist, my wife—"

Jake's hand tightened involuntarily around his beer.

"Ex-wife," she inserted.

Jesse's grin was loaded for bear. "I keep forgetting, honey. It was such a friendly divorce."

She rested her arms on her guitar and looked reflective. "True. You got real friendly with that waitress—and I got a divorce."

The crowd whooped and hollered their delight.

Jesse rubbed the back of his neck and looked rueful. "But you still love me, don't you, darlin'?"

"Course I do, honey—now that I don't have to live with you."

"Ouch!" He threw up his hands in a mock surrender. "Lead guitar, the lovely—shrew, uh, sweetheart—Phoebe Ann."

Phoebe laughed, then bent to play her solo riff. She was good, probably better than her companions, her fingers plucking the strings with a technical precision that pleased without quite satisfying.

It was probably his imagination, Jake thought, that she seemed to hold something back. The riff was, after all, just a bit of flash to take the dull out of the introductions. But it wasn't imagination that Jesse's smile was edged with intimacy when he held out a hand to Phoebe and said, "Let's sing, girl."

She took his hand and let him draw her into the spotlight next to him, her answering smile affectionate. Her hair fell across her face when she bent over her guitar, plucking the strings with a haunting delicacy as she led off. Jesse started the vocal, his deep, soothing bass perfect for the wistful song about love spurned. At the refrain, Phoebe's voice blended neatly with Jesse's, sweetly husky, strangely familiar, as if Jake had heard her sing this song before.

On the next verse she started the vocal, her lightly Southern phrasing a pleasing underpinning to the melody line. On the dance floor, lovers leaned into each other, swaying in place amid the smoke and dust making eddies on the plank flooring.

Caught up in the thrall of her wistful stage presence, Jake didn't find Earl quite as pathetic. The music, her voice, her sad eyes, all made her performance seem personal and intimate, as if she sang only to him.

Jake turned his back to the stage, to her, and leaned on the bar. He wrapped his hand around his cold bottle and wished he could apply it to his face. Wouldn't his brother Matt hoot if he could see Jake trying not to moon over a honky-tonk singer who was also a suspect. In fact, his gut had just moved her to the head of the line.

He lifted the bottle and drank because he needed something cool and wet running down his dry throat. Behind him Phoebe started singing a song about taking it like a man.

Jake downed half the bottle, but it didn't near do the job. He set the beer down just as the bar keep thrust a plastic cup filled with electric pink fluid at him.

"I didn't order that."

"The lady bought it for you." He pointed down the bar to a barely dressed blonde. She lifted a matching cup to him and wet her pouting lips. Beside him Bryn choked. Behind him the husky sex in Phoebe's amplified voice hit him in waves. Jake swallowed and said to the keep, "What is it?"

The keep grinned. "A Hot Damn."

Jake looked at the blonde who leaned on the bar, her upper arms squeezing the sides of her breasts unto they nearly popped out of her shirt. Bryn turned away, her shoulders shaking. Phoebe repeated the refrain about taking it like man.

Jake rubbed the back of his neck and wished for a cold shower.

Phoebe left her guitar for the guys to stow and jumped off the stage, moving quickly to avoid another encounter with the incoming Earl. She ducked through a door marked *Management Only*, circling the storage room to her office. Inside, she flicked on the light, closed the door and leaned against it.

Her blood still hummed, her heart still pounded with the buzz of performing. The guys used the buzz as foreplay for sex, but she couldn't afford to let her motor get so revved that it took over her thinking and had her acting on her impulses. Celibacy kept things simple. It kept her safe. Until tonight, she'd never been tempted to change that.

She pushed away from the door and reached for her water bottle, but it was empty. *Damn.* She threw it at the trash can, circled the desk and sank onto the stool in front of a spotted mirror hanging over a small shelf. But instead of her reflection, she saw the cowboy with the high-voltage smile and might-have-been eyes.

He ought to be required to wear a bag over his head, she decided. He ought to have to register his mouth as a lethal weapon. She traced her own mouth, thinking of his. Guys shouldn't be allowed to have mouths that yummy. It wasn't as if he didn't already have the advantage in the battle of the sexes with his good-guy face and tousled dark hair. Her throat went tight with longing. Not good. She gave herself a shake.

She'd have to turn her thinking down less inflammatory paths or she was gonna burn to ash and blow clean away. *Think about the game, girl, only the game.*

It had got her through worse things than an attack of lust.

Peter's computer went dark. Having spewed its poison, it subsided back into a state of indifferent neutrality. Peter wasn't as lucky. His face ashen, he looked at Stern.

"Don't sweat it," Stern said. "If they had anything, they'd have used it by now. They're gas-lighting you to try to shake your past loose."

"*They?* Or *she?*" Peter rubbed his face. Was it possible, after all these years?

"Nadine?" Stern shrugged. "Maybe. Or could be that guy you told me Kerry Anne was dating."

"The geek. Makes sense. He was into computers big-time even way back then." Peter's expression turned ugly. "I shouldn't have let him get away."

"Shit happens." Stern crushed his cigarette out in an ashtray.

"Not to me," Peter snapped. He rubbed his face again. "Can you fix this damn computer?" Stern had a bit of geek in him, too.

He flexed his fingers. "It's only a screen saver, and you were going to get rid of it anyway, weren't you?"

Peter avoided his gaze. "Of course."

Chapter Three

The bar emptied soon after the last set ended, a whining Earl nudged out by the bar keep. Bryn homed in on Jesse, who finished stowing their equipment and headed for the door to one side of the bar. She plucked him off course with one bat of her lashes, then let him lead her through the door marked for management. This left Jake alone with the bar keep.

Jake leaned companionably on the bar and sipped his soft drink, watching the guy clean up with quick, practiced movements. When the guy moved into range, Jake held out his hand. "The name's Jake."

He got a wary look with the reluctant shake. "Chet."

"Pleased to meet you. Since I'm driving, how about a Coke for the road?"

Chet found one and shoved it toward Jake. "Two dollars."

"Thanks." Jake paid and popped the top, taking a drink before asking, "So, is JR in?"

Chet looked up. "JR isn't in much. You looking for work?"

"You got any?" Music still filtered through Jake's mind. His fingers tapped the beat on the wooden surface of the bar.

"Phoebe does all the hiring and firing."

"Really? She's the guitarist in the band, right?"

"Yeah."

"How is she to work for?"

"Phoebe's okay, but the pay isn't great. JR's a tight-fisted Texan." Chet looked morose as he polished the bar.

"What about bands? You book them?"

Chet shook his head. "JR takes care of that. He manages Cattle Call, too. When they tour, usually in the summer, he books in replacements. They've stuck close to home this year though."

Jake nodded, holding back a yawn, as he made a mental note to compare the band's past tours with Phagan heists. This kind of chat was the lifeblood of an investigation, but it was also damn boring. "I appreciate the info, man. Can I buy you a drink?"

"Sure." Chet found himself a beer. "You want anything else?"

"I'll just finish my Coke. But how about something for Phoebe? Whatever she usually drinks."

Chet looked at Jake. "You want to buy Phoebe a drink?"

"It isn't against the law, is it?"

"You gonna ask her about a job?"

"Maybe."

"She don't screw around."

Jake looked up from his wallet. "I don't screw around either."

"If I was you, I'd tell her that right away—" Chet slid a Diet Coke to Jake and took his money.

"Tell me what right away?"

Jake and Chet turned together. Phoebe stood at the end of the bar with her hands on her hips.

"That I bought you a drink." Jake popped the top on her can and held it out with a friendly smile. "Chet here seems to think that'll piss you off."

Jake knew Chet watched them, but he found that the closer Phoebe got, the harder it was to concentrate on anyone else. Her hand closed around the cold can, her fingers meshing with his for a moment. Instead of telling her he wanted a job, he stared into brown eyes that didn't give much away and said, "I really enjoyed the show."

She took the can, drank, then rubbed away the moisture

that lingered on her mouth. “Thanks.”

“Well, I’m damned.”

She looked at Chet, her eyebrows arched. “I thought you’d been saved by the blood of the Lamb.”

“Yeah, well,” he shrugged, then grinned, gesturing toward the back. “I’ll just go do something—”

“Good idea.”

Chet looked relieved as he left Jake alone with Phoebe in the echoing barn of a room.

Phoebe turned back to Jake, her eyes showing amusement against a background of sad. Did it ever go away, he wondered. She tilted her head back for another drink, the movement exposing the smooth column of her throat. That drew his eyes down to plunging cleavage framed in lace that the denim jacket she now wore did little to hide.

The air was close, still heated from the recent press of bodies, thick with smoke, and smelling of beer and sweat. He ran a finger around the neckline of his tee shirt and realized she was looking at him with question marks in her eyes.

What did she want to know? Jake narrowed his eyes, probing deep because he had a knack for reading eyes, but before he hit pay dirt, she lowered her lashes and took another drink of her soda. When she looked at him again, there was nothing to see but cool inquiry.

“So, what can I do for you, cowboy?”

“Name’s Jake Kirby.” He thrust out his hand.

“Phoebe Mentel.” Her voice was cool and she kept her hand to herself.

He wiped his on his pants and held it out again. “I’m pleased to meet you, Phoebe.”

With a laugh that shattered the cool of her face and eyes, she relented. His first thought was how right it felt when his fingers closed around hers, his second, that he was on the edge of deep trouble this time.

The sudden widening of her eyes that told him she felt it, too, only made it worse.

He'd always prided himself on being the heart-whole Kirby brother, the free-spirited marshal tracking down the bad guys, a modern-day Marshal Dillon whose Dodge City was the world. A tracker with few opportunities to stay in one place long enough to meet a Miss Kitty who would cheer him on, let alone wave him off into the next sunset.

Phoebe didn't look inclined to cheer. Retreat was wisdom but not in his job description, so he indicated a chair sitting askew by a table, mutely inviting her to join him.

Phoebe turned and straddled the chair next to the one Jake had pointed at, needing any barrier she could find to put between them. His eyes were wary, which meant he'd gotten the same jolt she did when their hands touched, but his smile was still loaded with enough wattage to take her breath away. She opened her mouth to say—what? The door behind her opened, and Jesse came out, trailing a woman. What a surprise.

"You ready to go, darlin'?" he asked, looking at his companion with a dazed expression that could have been from the beer he'd consumed, the woman or both. To Phoebe's surprise, it was the woman she'd noticed watching her earlier. Right before she ran into Jake. For some reason this made her uneasy, but a quick scrutiny found no indication that the two knew each other, and the woman seemed a natural to play bimbo to Jesse's bozo.

Phoebe hesitated, but even if the woman wanted more from Jesse than sex, she wouldn't get it from him while he was plastered. "You can go without me. I'll catch a ride with Chet when he's—"

"Or I can take you home," Jake said.

It was crazy. It was dangerous.

It was irresistible.

Phoebe liked games almost as much as Phagan, but this was one she hadn't played in a long time. It was more dangerous than B&E, but that she shouldn't be playing it only made it seem more enticing. What kind of opponent would Jake make? Was he worth the risk?

Professionally, Jake needed her to let him take her home. The personal part of him was hoping she'd say no. Her gaze locked with his. Hard as a drill bit, it mined for motive. Jake didn't flinch, but it wasn't easy. He was used to giving, rather than receiving, penetrating looks. Just when he was sure she'd bored straight through to his ulterior motive, she smiled.

"I'll catch a ride with Jake."

"Oh, yeah?" Jesse approached them with a weaving, uncertain stride, not stopping until he was in front of Jake. He leaned forward, sending a strong wave of sweat-and-beer-drenched air in Jake's direction. "Who the hell are you?"

"Jake Kirby." Jake didn't lean toward or away from the cowboy. He chose his move, his spot to hit, if Jesse turned nasty.

"He's looking for work. Jake, this is Jesse. You may have noticed him singing and getting plastered up on the stage tonight."

"Howdy." Jesse held out his hand, an intensity at the back of his blurred eyes.

"I wouldn't if I were you," Phoebe cautioned Jake. "He can chin himself with his pinkies."

Jake looked puzzled, so she added, "Rock climbing."

"Done a bit of climbing myself," Jake said and held out his hand.

Jesse tried to grab it but missed. Phoebe gave him a shove with her booted foot. "Go home and sleep it off, Jesse."

Jesse tried to grab her but missed again. Bryn moved forward, wearing a pout that looked almost real. "I thought you were taking me home, honey?"

Mert came out the office door and Phoebe turned to him with relief. "Would you drive these two?"

"I was—whoa!" Mert caught sight of Bryn. "Have we met, darlin'?"

"I don't think I'd forget meeting you," Bryn said, fluttering her lashes.

Role was the right description, Phoebe thought. Quite the performance, if you didn't look in her eyes.

Mert offered his arm, shoved his brother out the front door, then turned and said to Jake, "Mind how you go with her, mister. She's family."

Jake nodded, no sign of worry in his eyes or manner. Either he didn't consider the guys a threat or wasn't planning to hit on her, Phoebe decided. When the door closed, Phoebe said, "Sorry."

"I've got two brothers," Jake said. "Both older than me. And dedicated to keeping my ass in line."

Her smile was slow but potent. "All God's children need a goal."

Jake's laugh came natural, felt good. "Yeah," he said, "they do." Then his brain reminded him what his goal was, and he sobered.

Her eyes registered this. Her lashes flickered, turning her expression into bland and pleasant. She stood up with an abrupt movement that tipped over the chair.

"Got a bit of a performance buzz to burn off. Can we go?"

"Sure." He moved slowly around the table. She vibrated with tension, her gaze bouncing around, looking everywhere but at him. He stepped close, and she stepped back, reaching for her can of soda.

With a quick movement, Jake pulled it out of her reach. "You won't work off a buzz chugging caffeine. Come on, let's go get some food into you."

She looked startled, then grinned.

"You might regret the absence of buzz," she said with a sidelong glance as they headed for the door. "When I crash, I'm out like a light."

"You think my ego can't take a girl falling asleep on me?" he said, as he stepped past her to push open the door.

"Don't know what you can take, now do I?" She stopped for a moment, rendered briefly breathless by the fit of blue jeans across his very nice ass. She gave a little shake and stepped through the doorway, but couldn't resist murmuring her thanks for the courtesy—and the view.

"What?" Jake looked at her, as if sensing her layered emphasis.

"Nothing." She grinned. "But you'd best—feed me, Seymour."

He matched her grin as he opened the truck's passenger door for her. "Are you dangerous when you're hungry?"

She paused in the act of sliding across the car seat, leaving her long, bare legs extended for maximum viewing. He inhaled sharply, then looked up. She gave him a deliberately provocative look. "There are those who say I'm always dangerous."

Earl watched them from the shadows as they got into the truck which pulled away and turned toward town. He slid into his SUV, pushing aside his lightly snoring date. In a moment, he took off with a spurt of gravel, turning in the same direction.

"Not exactly what I had in mind when I offered you food,"

Jake said, pulling limp pastries from the convenience store's microwave oven. The pungent scent of hotdog wrapped around—without making palatable—a body of smells comprised of stale cigarette smoke, popcorn, gasoline, various body odors, wet dog and something that fell under the general heading of dirt. The mix permeated every corner of the dingy store, even the pastries Jake carried to their tiny table.

A scratchy radio dispensed a country-sounding wail into the chilled air while the middle-aged clerk desultorily turned the pages of a tattered *National Enquirer.*

"Small-town Friday night," Phoebe said, the look in her eyes equal parts amused and resigned.

He crowded the pastries onto the tabletop with her watery juice drink and his over-strong coffee, then squeezed into the seat across from her. The table, wedged between a line of self-serve soda machines and the bathrooms, put them knee to knee and damn near nose to nose. Since she had a nice nose, it wasn't a problem.

Even with tiredness and fluorescent lighting bleeding the color from her face, she gave off a wholesome, sexy vibrancy that was dangerous to someone who'd been on the go for over twenty-four hours and without feminine contact for longer than that. Bryn, being a colleague, didn't count.

He rubbed the back of his neck, hoping exhaustion was why he was having trouble routing out a pesky elemental masculine response to Phoebe Mentel. *Suspect,* he reminded himself, adding with more emphasis, *prime* suspect who could lead him to Dewey Hyatt. Just thinking about catching Hyatt helped Jake to sharpen his gaze, probing her expression for weak spots. What he found was strength in her steady gaze and in the line of her strong jaw. He'd seen unlikely people in unlikely places before, but Phoebe wasn't just an odd peg in a strange hole.

She was on the wrong peg board.

She sat on the cheap plastic bench in her long-tall-Texan getup with the natural aplomb of a royal, systematically crumbling a cardboard pastry into cardboard crumbs.

A sign she wasn't stupid.

Her body hummed like a banjo from her performance high, one booted foot tapping out a tune only she could hear while her sad, cynical eyes went over him with laser-powered thoroughness. What she concluded, she kept to herself. A sign she was smart or just had nothing to hide?

No way to know without delving into the puzzle of her mind and life further. He did wonder why he kept seeing her sitting under the spreading branches of a magnolia tree. She seemed made to wear something white and drifting, one of those wide-brimmed hats framing her face, her dark eyes slumberous with longing, her full lips parted for fine crystal instead of Styrofoam, and a big old plantation as a backdrop.

The straight line to knowledge begins with a question, so he asked, "What's a nice accent like yours doing in a place like this?"

The well-defined line of her eyebrow rose. "From where I'm sitting, cowboy, you're the one with an accent."

He acknowledged the hit with a lift of one eyebrow. "Georgia?"

The pause before she answered was just a beat too long. "Texas, actually."

"I could've of sworn I heard Georgia in your voice."

She pushed aside her mangled pastry, picked up her napkin and dabbed the edges of her mouth. "You have a good ear. My mama hailed from Georgia—moved to Texas when she married."

Nice and cool. He almost bought it. He took a cautious sip from his Styrofoam cup. "How did you end up in Colorado?"

"Colorado's got more up than Texas."

"Up?"

Jake's puzzled look shored Phoebe's shaken confidence. She smiled lazily, relaxing in her seat so that her leg brushed his long enough to maybe be an accident, maybe not. Her jacket fell open a bit. A deep breath raised and lowered her cleavage.

Nothing. Not even a quick look. She'd swear his gaze hadn't left her face since that first thorough scrutiny when they'd bumped into each other back in the bar.

"Rock climbing requires vertical terrain; otherwise it's just hiking." She moistened her lips with her tongue while her cool gaze turned back his probing one.

He swallowed, a dry sound, and rubbed the nape of his neck.

"Okay." He met her gaze and raised it a grin that curled fire in her belly and her toes in her boots. She took the charm of it on the chin, a glancing blow that nonetheless went deep, mining for a response she couldn't afford to feel. Before she could stop it, an answering smile bloomed on her mouth. That only made it worse. His grin deepened, and his blue eyes opened on his soul, giving her a quick, tantalizing peek at things she could never have.

Regret hit her next. She wasn't expecting it. She'd committed to her course and never looked back. Until today. To stop her fingers from forming fists, she grabbed her napkin and started folding it in an intricate pattern. It calmed her mind, muted despair. To distract him, she added, "And then there's the garage—"

"Garage? I thought—"

"Climbing is too expensive to support just by playing honky-tonks. The guys are stupid about girls and booze, but they can make an engine purr like a satisfied woman. So they also run a garage here in Estes Park." She finished her slightly tattered origami bird and set it between them. What could she do with her hands now?

"Everybody's gotta be good at something, I guess." He picked up the bird she'd made from the napkin and studied it, giving her a brief respite from his X-ray gaze. "Nice."

Just when she needed the knife edge of tension to keep her head clear, it dissolved, letting exhaustion rush in to fill the void. Heaviness settled around her eyes, pulling down the lids with an insistence hard to ignore. She fought a yawn and lost. When it faded, she felt boneless and kind of drifty. Made it harder to remember why she couldn't lean across the tiny table and taste his yummy mouth for herself. The guys claimed denial wasn't good for you, but that was just because denial didn't suit them.

"I can understand the climbing bit, but—" He looked puzzled. A very good look on him, Phoebe conceded, her defenses eroding faster than sand on an ocean beach. "—I thought Texans couldn't leave Texas?"

"Why not? It's just a big, flat place." She heard the words leave her mouth and tensed, waiting for God to strike her down, but He didn't have to. All He had to do was leave her in the sun of Jake's smile and wait until she melted from the inside out.

Her gaze slipped its leash, running over the lean, lanky lines of his body as a lazy heat built in her midsection. She huddled in on that warmth. She'd been cold so long, she'd almost forgotten what warm was. Her gaze continued roving. Until she ran into a big question mark in both eyes.

That cleared her head faster than a lightning bolt. She'd heard him asking Chet about the bar. If he was looking for work, why hadn't he asked one question about a job?

Past his beckoning eyes, past the uniform of worn jeans

and flannel shirt worn over his tee, beyond the relaxed air was something else, something that put him outside her world, with its rare questions and rarer confidences. The people in her world usually had something they wanted to keep in the back of the closet.

To distract him from her closeted secrets, she leaned forward and held out her hand. "My turn."

"For what?"

"Your hand. I wanna read it. Learned from my mama, during one of her rare moments of sobriety."

The tiny piece of truth came out so naturally, Phoebe almost missed it. *Phoebe*'s mama hadn't been a drunk. She hadn't lived long enough. She was mixing her real past with her fictional one. Not smart. Adrenaline entered her bloodstream in a slow but steady stream, then subsided as the question marks in Jake's eyes faded like snow in the sun of his smile.

A pity truth was so dangerous. It was so effective.

"Hand? Isn't it palms?"

"Anyone who reads just your palm is a quack—according to my mama. The palm tells only part of the story."

"Okay." He opened his hand for her viewing.

The pouting curve of his full lips started that warm stuff shooting through her blood again. It fused the tiny split in her personality, patching over the pain that tried to push out through the gap. But now she'd have to touch him.

Good move, Phoebe. The skin of her palm tingled in anticipation of—

The jangle of the bell over the door as a customer came in made them both jump. Phoebe smiled uneasily and tucked her hair behind her ear. Jake looked back her way, then, as if he knew she couldn't do it, did the touching for her.

The feel of his hand on hers sent a tiny shock of delight spiraling up her arm. It felt warm and heavy, the skin pleasantly abrasive where it brushed against hers. Phoebe let her fingers curl up around it, shivering slightly when the pads of her fingertips found skin. Her gaze lowered, a move both defensive and imperative. She wanted to see, smell—she inhaled deeply, filling her lungs with his singular scent—and hear, wanted to engage all of her senses, if only in her imagination. Her exhale came in a shaky rush.

Good thing restraint had been one of her first, hard-learned life lesson's.

Her free hand hovered over his before landing to lightly trace its narrow length. His long, strong fingers were well kept but showed no sign of pampering. The pads were softly callused, the flesh beneath firm and capable.

Her nose quivered slightly as it homed in on his scent under the smell of soap and an echo of after-shave, as if it had been awhile since he'd shaved. Going for a Don Johnson scruffy look, or just circumstances?

"What do you see?" he asked, his voice turning husky. Did that mean he felt the current running between them?

Her forefinger made a path down his ring finger, her face taking on a sultry look easy to assume with her insides doing a slow lava boil. "All sorts of things."

He cleared his throat. "Good thing I have nothing to hide."

Maybe he didn't. She explored the place on his finger where a wedding ring should be, her gaze never leaving his face. "No ring. No wife?"

What would he do with that question?

Jake swallowed dryly, wishing he'd gotten a drink with ice. "No."

For someone who was supposed to be reading his hand, she was spending a lot of time looking at his face. "Past or present."

Her low murmur could have meant anything. Each finger was touched, and turned, all surfaces tantalizingly explored. Her smoky gaze pinned him in place and stirred heat in his gut.

"This is interesting." She waited several seconds, a hundred heartbeats. "You're a hunter."

She wouldn't have felt the flinch if she hadn't been holding his hand. His brows drew together in a quick frown. "Hunter?"

She gave him a smile edged with triumph. She'd got him off guard. Good. "Hands can't hide what you've done to them."

Jake's stomach felt as if he'd taken a big drop on a roller coaster. He got a grip and asked lightly, "What—do I hunt?"

She shrugged. "Just know it's personal. And you're more driven than most."

His stomach did another drop, until he saw a swiftly veiled gleam of satisfaction in her eyes. Not magic. Just an old fashioned lie-detector test, watching his eyes with her finger on his pulse. Damn, she was good. "Driven by what?"

Her lashes lifted, her eyes meeting his. "Justice." Her fingers stroked his palm, stealing his breath. "But—"

Jake lifted a brow in a question his tight throat couldn't voice.

"There's mercy there, too. Like the horns of a dilemma."

Her gaze locked with his for a long, hot moment while Jake struggled to clear his head. With an effort, he leaned into her space, determined to turn the tables on her. "Aren't you going to tell me who I'll marry, how many children I'll have? My mom would like to know."

Her lashes hid her eyes. "Let's see."

She turned his palm up, tracing the lines inside, a sultry abrasion from a finger pad roughened by contact with guitar strings. "This is your life line. It's very long but bumpy. You take a lot of risks."

"Is that the tactful way of telling me no woman would have me?"

"That—and this." The nail of her forefinger, just long enough to be squared and serviceable, marked the place where his life line was crossed by another. "Your commitment line."

"Commitment line? I've never heard of that one."

"Really? Yours is very short."

He studied the line she indicated. It was very short. He looked up, his face just inches from hers, and chuckled. The sound emerged huskier than he liked. So far this game was a draw. "Is the divorced pot calling the unmarried kettle black?"

She leaned back with a rich and sultry laugh. "I was sixteen."

That got his attention. "Sixteen?" He shook his head. "Was it legal?"

"Don't know. Made sure the divorce was."

"How long before the waitress?" He was convinced that story was true.

"Six months, more or less. Our Jesse isn't naturally inclined toward monogamy."

"Why did you marry him?" Jake hadn't meant to ask, but their game had turned unexpectedly serious. Her eyes didn't change, her body didn't tense at the question. So why did it feel as if she'd moved away from him?

"Seemed like the thing to do at the time." *At the time.* For a moment that time weighed in against her. The girl she'd been pushed at the barrier holding her in. Jake was dangerously easy to tell things to, she'd felt it when they touched. Everything about him invited confidence, promised security, but there was no security for her. She broke contact, sitting back as far as the plastic seat would allow. "And Jesse, well, I think he confused himself with Sir Galahad, what with me being a kid and on my own and all."

For an instant he caught a glimpse of that kid in her eyes before the protective veil of her lashes dropped. He felt an unexpected distaste for his duplicity. I'm the good guy, he reminded himself. "I can understand the compulsion to play white knight."

"Yeah, well, I've learned to look out for myself." Her mouth thinned and firmed, clearly setting out a No Trespassing sign. Her eyes warned him to heed it.

He'd never been known to read posted warnings.

"Phoebe—"

"Time to head for the barn. It's past late, and I was up real early."

Her withdrawal turned into a pain deep in his gut, but he just nodded. "Sure." He slid out and helped her up. He shouldn't have, but he kept her hand for the walk to his truck. She didn't pull her hand away, but she didn't hang on either. Just accepted it. How did he know she'd had to accept a lot of things in her relatively short life?

Inside the truck, she leaned forward, her hand on the radio dial. "Do you mind?"

Jake wasn't eager for silence and nodded.

She played with the dial and soon music flowed out of the speakers, filling the silence with a country love song. She relaxed, her fingers absently picking out the chords of the song on an invisible guitar, her musky scent drifting on the cool air coming in the window.

At a light, the sound of her soft vocal added to the mix invited him to look at her. He found her face unevenly illuminated by a nearby streetlamp, her lips in the right shape for her song about shutting up and kissing.

Phoebe felt him watching and looked. The heat in his eyes stopped her in mid-hum, her lips still pursed around the words. She gave a nervous laugh and switched off the radio.

"Good song," Jake said.

"Yeah, we get a lot of requests for it." She brushed her hair back. "Light's green."

"Is it?" He let up on the brake. "I thought it was yellow."

She gave a tiny cough that might have been a laugh and said, "Turn right at the next street. It's up that rise on the right."

A single lamp gleamed behind the curtained window of a small cabin of a house. The glow from a streetlight hinted at a well-kept yard, and the porch light showed the way down a straight, neat sidewalk through trimmed grass to a blue door.

He got out and started around the truck. She didn't wait for him. He wanted to take her hand again, but it was a line he shouldn't have crossed the first time.

He walked beside to her up to the blue door, watched her dig a key out of her pocket, insert it in the lock and push open the door. When she turned to face him, an undercurrent of desire made a circuit between them.

Shut up and kiss me. He could hear the words in his head, waited to see if they'd be in her eyes when she faced him.

Phoebe wanted to kiss him so bad, her lips hurt. It made her nervous as a teenager on her first date as she stepped across the threshold and turned. In the dim glow of the porch light he looked as calm and steady as a rock.

"Thanks—for the food and the ride."

"Next time I'll do better."

Next time. She shouldn't feel a surge of pleasure. How much time could she spend getting probed by those eyes without spilling her secrets? Her brain sent down excuses, but her mouth said, "Sounds . . . good."

"Good night, Phoebe."

"Night, Jake."

While he waited, just out of reach, she backed up until she could shut him from her view. It seemed a long time before she heard the slam of the truck door, the fire of his engine, the slow fade as he drove away.

"Damn." She'd taken her share of missteps rock climbing, felt herself tumble through space, waiting for the sharp tug of the belay to stop the imperative summons of gravity. Felt the jarring collision of flesh to rock. But this—this was falling without a belay—

Course, the upside was, it wouldn't be flesh smashing into rock—

She shook her head sharply and tossed her purse onto a table. Only took a moment to shrug off her jacket. She fought with her boots in little hopping steps that took her down the short hall into the living room. The boots got kicked into a corner.

She started working at the stubborn zip of her jeans, determined to be undressed by the time she hit the bed. She needed to get unconscious, the faster the better.

There was no tingling, no sense of premonition. Just a sudden awareness of movement behind her.

She felt a hand touch her shoulder.

"Took you long enough to get home, Phoebe," Earl said.

Jake had followed his instincts into a lot of places, some dangerous, some boring, some that led nowhere, though most of the time they led him right where he needed to go. He had good instincts, accepted them as a gift from God, the same way he did the desire for hunting that Phoebe had so neatly nailed.

What kept him sniffing until he was certain there was nothing left to smell—well, that was sometimes gift, sometimes curse, depending on the situation. Fact was, he couldn't stop going forward until he got what he was after. It was the way he was. He'd put his life on the line, come close to losing it more times than he admitted to his mom, but this—*Phoebe*—was uncharted territory for him.

Not the desire, he knew about desire, knew how to channel it into less dangerous byways before it got out of hand. Now his instincts were broadcasting a warning he didn't want to hear.

He wanted *her,* not the fugitive she might lead him to. Alone in the truck, he could admit it, could admit that something about her made him want to try a different kind of hunting—the kind a man did when he met the one woman exactly right for him.

He could feel lust drawing him off the scent, beckoning him to try this new direction, despite the questions marks hovering over her. Some blanks he could fill in. Her mother was a drunk who'd probably been knocked around by her dad. She sang and played guitar in a honky-tonk band, talked tough while retaining the air of a lady. Had a good brain, great verbal skills, despite the fact she'd apparently run away from home before graduating. Married too young, divorced too young, but still on good terms with her ex.

And she managed the highly suspect JR's.

None of it added up. Yet.

Phoebe didn't lend herself to a straightforward equation, like two plus two equals four. No, she was an algorithm of unknowns, where *y* was a lot of questions and *x* stood for something he shouldn't be feeling. He was afraid the final equation could be . . . explosive.

He picked up his cell phone and punched in Matt's office

number. His brother was assigned to the Denver office of the Marshals Service and could give him access to the kind of information he needed to clear the lust out of his head.

Their different investigative styles sometimes caused friction, but that didn't stop Jake from calling when he needed help. When his brother answered, Jake asked, "Don't you ever go home to your wife?"

"She's gone until tomorrow." Matt's voice had an undertone of contentment that Jake still wasn't used to hearing coming from his tough big, brother. His marriage to the romance writer he'd been assigned to guard last year had changed Matt, Jake decided. Happiness had actually sharpened his instincts. After all, he had Dani waiting at home.

"Tomorrow is today," Jake said after glancing at the clock on the dash.

"Cut the crap, Jake. You find anything?"

Matt had been particularly derisive about Jake's lead. Figured it for a cold, dead end. He still wasn't sure what it was, but cold and dead it was not, he thought, thinking about Phoebe. "Maybe. You find anything when you ran JR's under the big microscope?"

Matt was quiet a moment. "Maybe."

Jake sighed. Matt hated being wrong. Too bad Jake had wanted him to be right this time. Because if JR's was dirty, then so was Phoebe.

"Don't be a son of a bitch, Matt. Give me what you got."

"I got nothing but suspicious indicators right now. Got my best guy hound-dogging it for you."

"Appreciate it."

"No problem. You coming in to my office tomorrow?"

"Not until the afternoon."

"What are you doing in the morning?"

"Applying for a job." Jake grinned and broke the connection.

* * * * *

Bryn pushed the door of her motel room closed and leaned against it with a sigh of relief. It would take a long, hot shower to get rid of the palm prints on various parts of her anatomy. Fortunately Jesse Mentel had been overcome by alcohol before she had to cuff him. Good thing, too. She had a feeling he'd have enjoyed it.

She flicked on the light, shuddered at the sight of the ugly little room's aging cowboy décor and headed for the bathroom. She was almost past the bed before her brain registered what her eyes had seen. The single red rose and square white envelope on her pillow.

In the space of one breath, she pulled her piece and did a fast but thorough check of the room. She wasn't surprised when she found nothing. Phagan's style was definitely hit-and-run. She sank onto the bed and eyed the envelope with equal parts ire and resignation. Phagan was getting more bold and way too romantic.

"I'm too tired for this," she wailed to the room. Instead of sympathy, the A/C kicked on, indifferent that the temperature outside had dropped too many degrees for the modified bimbo Jake had insisted she wear. She wanted to ignore the note and step under the hottest shower this dive could summon up. She wanted to tumble into bed and dream of lying on a recliner with a box of Godiva chocolates on the table and a romance novel in hand.

She picked up the envelope, opened it and two gift certificates fell out. One was for Godiva chocolates. The other for a bookstore. There was also a flyer advertising the latest Dani Gwynne romance novel. Across the bottom, Phagan had written: *TelTech, Inc.* Beneath it was a heart with an arrow through it.

With a moan, she fell back on the horseshoe patterned

bedspread and stared at the ceiling. It didn't help, so she rolled to her side and pulled the rose within reach of her nose. The rich, sweet scent drove out the stale room smell. The soft petals brushed her nose like a lover's caress and—

A sudden knock at the door sent her heart skittering into pound mode.

"Bryn?" Jake's voice was muffled but easily identified.

Bryn hastily tossed the rose and scrambled to open the door.

Jake held up a white sack.

"Followed my nose to an all-night bakery." He gently put her aside and strode into the room, stopping abruptly when he saw the rose.

"I didn't get one of those on my pillow."

"Someone has a sense of humor."

"Uh-huh." Jake took the lone chair and opened the bag. "Bagels and cream cheese. No coffee. Don't want to mess with your beauty sleep."

She sat down on the end of the bed, taking the sliced, cream-cheese smeared bagel he held out to her.

"How did it go with Jesse?" Jake took a hearty bite out of his bagel.

"He was probably an octopus in another life. Certainly has the same size brain," she said. "If he's a master thief, there's something not right in the universe. What about you?"

On the other end, Jake paused, reluctant to throw Phoebe to Bryn. Mercy wasn't exactly Bryn's strong point. On the other hand, Phoebe'd be fine if she was clean. A big, unlikely *if*.

"The lady has secrets," he admitted. He added to himself, Lots of them. "Think you can work on your own tomorrow?" He stood up, reaching the door in two strides.

Bryn looked at the note sitting on her night stand. "I think

I can manage something. What'll you be doing?"

He opened the door, then turned to face her. "Gonna apply for a job."

He was out of the room, the door closed behind, before Bryn could get out, "Why—"

"Men." She looked at the rose, then at the bagel. At least they weren't totally useless.

Chapter Four

Phoebe reacted instinctively to Earl's hand on her shoulder.

She grabbed it and in one smooth movement twisted around to face him. This turned his hand under and forced him away from her. His muffled exclamation turned to a yelp when she pushed his hand up between his shoulder blades and shoved him into the wall, using her knee to hold him there.

"You got two seconds to explain what the hell you're doing in my house," she growled into his ear.

"Damn it, girl—"

"That's not an explanation."

This violation of her space had adrenaline singing through her bloodstream in an out-of-control flood. She twisted her fingers in his hair and shoved his face into the wallboard, then went to jerk his head back for round two. Instead of his head jerking back, the hair came off in her hand.

"What the—"

"It's me! Dewey!"

"Dewey?" Her heart was pumping fight-or-flight so loud, she could hardly hear him. She stared at the wispy wig in her hand, then the tufted, full head of hair on the back of his head. "Dewey Damn Hyatt?"

She threw down the wig and stepped back, her body shuddering with a reaction that now had nowhere to go.

"In the slightly bruised flesh." He eased his arm down, flexing the fingers once before turning around. Using the wall for support, he dabbed at the red trickling out the corner of his mouth, then rubbed it between his fingers. "I guess I shouldn't have sneaked up on you."

"No kidding. You forget I don't do victim anymore?" She pushed her hair off her face with hands that shook from the surge of violence she hadn't known was in her. She didn't waste time asking how he got in. A lock hadn't been made that Dewey couldn't pop. "Let's get some ice on that."

His face and body might be Earl, but his grin was vintage Dewey, though crooked now as one side of his mouth began to puff out.

Her kitchen was a pleasantly impersonal room with carabineer wind chimes hanging above the tidy sink. Even at night, the white walls and yellow countertops appeared sunny and cheerful. Phoebe rummaged through a first-aid kit until she found a disposable ice pack and twisted it to break the seal between its chemicals.

While she waited for it to chill, Dewey began to shed his "Earl-ness," removing the prosthetic weight from around his belly, the mouth device that changed his jaw line and teeth and pulled off the bulbous nose. Flecks of the adhesive he'd used to keep it in place stayed on his skin, and he looked like a deflated clown with Earl's clothes hanging off his lean and rangy frame.

She tipped his chin toward the light and dabbed away the blood. She started to apply the pack, but Dewey took it from her, holding it gingerly to his rapidly swelling lip.

"Next time I come at you from behind, I'll wear a bell."

"Next time don't come as Earl." She straddled a chair as her knees went from fight to flop. "You been Earl all along or you just look like him for tonight?"

"If you don't know, I ain't gonna tell you." His grin widened toward unrepentant, but quickly shrank into a wince.

"You just did." She was gonna have to find a way to exact justice from his sorry hide. "What's so important you had to scare ten years off my life to tell me?"

His suddenly sober expression told her it was bad.

"Ollie's dead."

Beyond bad. She was glad she was already sitting down. "What?"

Despite her turbulent past, Phoebe and all of Phagan's young thieves were careful to avoid violence. Dewey had been known to joke that a gun added a nickel or more to your basic B&E time, but their caution had more to do with their refusal to embrace the methods of those who had afflicted them in the past. Each job, each game, was carefully designed to disarm their target covertly, electronically if possible. Their first action was usually an attempt to remove their source of income, followed by tipping off Phagan's fibbie—who they all knew by name and reputation, but not by sight.

Their success rate was remarkable, despite the fibbie's unrelenting pursuit, and had been, until now, casualty free. Until Phoebe's turn to avenge the past, until her game. She tried to pull up Ollie's picture in her head, but how could she? In their shadowy, chameleon world, reality was whatever they each decided it was. Her lips numb, Phoebe said, "Harding?"

"His pit bull, Stern, probably."

They'd done their homework on Barrett Stern before starting the game, but apparently they hadn't done it well enough.

Phoebe shook her head, rejecting the reality of his death, not Dewey's guess on who might have killed him. "This wasn't Ollie's game."

"He wanted in."

"He didn't want to die." Phoebe looked at Dewey, feeling the pain of loss from the present and the past combine inside her like the chemicals in the ice pack interacting. Phagan's first rule was never to let the past intrude on the present, but it was hard to manage when she was facing that past head on.

"He knew the risks."

Risks Phagan wouldn't let her take. The gallantry factor. No feminists in Phagan's world. That was about to change. Pain, rage, and frustration combined to form a new emotion: resolve.

"What do we do now?" she asked.

"Phagan sent me a new kid. He's pretty good. Lots of potential. He could do what Ollie was going to—"

"We're out of time. My egg is hatching as we speak. We can't push back the time-table now." She looked at him. "There's only one person who can do it. Me."

It was Dewey's turn to shake his head.

"*Yes*. I planned it. I've played it more than anyone."

"In virtual reality," Dewey objected. "It's not the same thing."

"It's my game. Harding's my target. My risk." She stood up and crossed to the refrigerator, anxious to avoid his eyes for a few minutes. They were far too penetrating and might see the deep, poisonous terror welling up from deep inside her.

"Phagan—"

She cut him off. "—will know I'm right."

"You think so?"

She turned in time to catch a slight, crooked grin turning up the side of his mouth that wasn't puffy. "I know so."

"And if he doesn't?"

"Doesn't matter." She lifted her chin. "I'm going all the way with this one." She popped the top on the soft drink she'd taken out and drank deeply.

He stood up, too. "Okay. We move on Harding's RABBIT Sunday night." He hesitated, as if he wanted to say more.

"What?"

"Phagan gave me the green light to up the ante—and the heat on Harding if you're up for it."

Phoebe tensed, powerless to stop herself. "When?"

"Harding's got his engagement party tomorrow. Rumor has it he'll be announcing his candidacy, too." He waited several seconds before adding, "I'm going to try to get you an invite. If you can you face him?"

Face him. Face Peter Harding in person. Could she do it? She was stronger than that girl who had run from him. Run from what he'd done to her sister. She could feel the roots she'd put down in Phoebe's life anchoring her on one side, while the sucking mire of the past pulled at her from the other. It was like being a schizophrenic Pandora facing that closed box, debating whether to open it.

Phagan thought she was strong enough for the game. And Phagan was always right. No reason not to believe him now. It was time she stepped onto this path and faced her demons. A layer of peace pushed back her fear.

"I've been waiting seven years to face him." Dewey didn't look convinced, so she added, "I'll do what I have to."

He flicked her cheek gently. "You always do, darling."

He hefted the spent ice pack, then tossed it into the trash and took a handful of pistachios out of his pocket. He deftly shelled them, tossing the hulls in after the ice pack.

"You staying the night?" she asked.

He shook his head. "Kevin, the new kid, isn't ready to be left alone all night." He finished his pistachios and brushed his hands down his pants, then gathered up his Earl accouterments. He hesitated, then said, "I'll beep you if—"

"I know."

When she'd let him out, she padded down the hall to her room, not expecting to sleep, but her body was wiser than her mind. It ejected thought and surrendered to the sleep it needed, sending her deep and sound until close to eight, when the sun found a space in her blinds and splayed a beam of light across her face.

For a moment she lay there listening to a robin's cheery sounds outside her window while last night's events crept back to the forefront of her mind. With a quick movement she tossed back thought and blankets, stripped off the tee shirt she'd slept in, replacing it with bike shorts and a brief top. When her hair was secured in a rubber band, she left, passing through the kitchen like a comet. She needed to clear her mind for what was ahead. Forward motion always helped her more than twisting in the wind of thought.

On the street, her feet pounded the pavement. She ran hard until halfway up the first hill, then settled into a steady rhythm. This was a dangerous time for her. That the past was stalking her future gave fuel to her run.

She had to control the game or lose it all.

Jake pulled his truck to a stop on a side street that looked down on Phoebe's house. He set the brake and studied the tidy structure in the daylight, forcing himself to wait to get out and cross the street, fighting back an unprofessional and unwelcome eagerness to see her again.

Her property was almost picture perfect, like something out of a movie, with neat flower beds outlining the house and front walk. A row of pine trees divided the approach to the garage from the tiny back yard enclosed in a picket fence. In the center was a swing set, minus the swings, with a small trampoline underneath.

Before he could puzzle out the why of that, a tingling on the back of his neck had him twisting to look down the street.

It was well worth the lost sleep, this first view of Phoebe jogging down the hill toward him with an effortless grace and a minimum of clothing. She'd pulled her dark hair back with something and it swung from side to side with each concussion of feet to ground. Her tanned body was sleek, glistening with exertion.

Without a break in stride, she vaulted the picket fence, jogged to the trampoline and used it to launch herself up until her hands closed around the crossbar of the swing set. She hung for a moment, then, with the full drag of her body on her arms, she pulled herself up in a series of chin-ups.

"Damn." It looked as if Jesse wasn't the only Mentel with a good grip. Jake resisted the urge to flex his arms as he got out and crossed the street. She was lifting a leg to hook it over the bar.

While he was still wondering how to make his presence known, Phoebe spotted him from her upside down position. He saw her hands open and swore, bounding over the fence. As he ran toward her, she tucked, pulling her legs in, trying to bring her body around. If the clearance had been an inch less, she wouldn't have made it. An inch more, her feet wouldn't have hit the tramp at an angle that sent her rebounding forward to slam into his chest.

There was time only to brace himself before she hit him dead center, knocking the wind out of his lungs and his feet out from under him. As he went backward he wrapped his arms around her and tried to relax into the collision with mother earth. It helped, but not enough.

When he could speak, he said, "Nice tackle."

She laughed breathlessly. "I'm sorry—are you all right?"

"Oh, yeah—" The words came out a bit more emphatic than he'd planned and he quickly asked, "Are *you* all right?"

"Hey, I been slammed into rock. This was much nicer."

"Yeah." Sandwiched between hard earth and her body, Jake only had to lower his gaze slightly to get an eye full. With an effort, he looked up at the clear blue sky and tried to count away temptation. He was past ten when she rolled off him.

"That better?"

He grinned. "Yes and no."

"Diplomatic."

"My mom required it of all her sons. Sometimes quite forcefully."

The thought of anyone requiring anything of Jake made Phoebe smile. As if he heard her thought, humor lit his eyes. Her gaze got hooked by his, and she sobered as pleasure bloomed in her midsection. He'd looked good in the night. He looked even better in the light.

Live it all the way or don't do it at all, Phagan was wont to say, without ever defining what *living* was, but it was now quite clear she hadn't been.

She sat up, wrapping her hands around her knees. "You ever heard that country song about the difference between lonely—and lonely for too long?"

"Yeah, I have."

"I think—" she looked at him, her gaze sliding the length of his body before returning to his face—"I been lonely for too long."

Before he could react, she jumped to her feet.

"Do you want a cup of coffee or something? I need to shower before we talk."

Talk about what, he wondered as he scrambled upright and followed her inside, led by the sway of her hips in tight shorts and by curiosity about the questions she didn't ask him. In the kitchen, she pointed out the coffee paraphernalia. "Just help yourself. I won't be long."

He took her at her word and rummaged through her cupboards, assembling the necessary items for a bad cup of coffee, since she didn't have the makings for a decent one. He spooned stale crystals into his cup and went to the sink to run some hot water. Stirring the nasty-looking brew with a spoon, he studied his surroundings. The kitchen was clean enough for the small piece of debris on the floor to stand out like a sore thumb. He knelt, felt a kick of shock when realized it was a pistachio shell.

Inside the trash were more shells, as well as a spent ice pack. He sighed, hearing the water start in the back of the house. After a pause, the flow changed from tap to shower. To get rid of his mind's inclination to ponder Phoebe in the shower, water sliding off her body, he headed down her hallway. There wasn't anything to see but an unused guest room without invading her bedroom, so he turned back. He took one sip before deciding he didn't need coffee that bad.

The other door out of her kitchen led to a living room, rustic but comfortable, the furniture light and blocky. Two crossed ice picks hung above the fireplace. Only scenery shots on the walls. No books. No magazines. No newspapers. The boots she'd worn last night were tossed in a corner, her purse on a table just inside the front entry. He walked into the room, then wheeled in a circle with his senses stretched out.

The room was almost impersonal, but still managed to exude a comfortable sense of permanence and serenity that he tried to fit into the Phagan and Dewey Hyatt setup—and couldn't.

He heard the shower shut off and turned back to the kitchen, his thoughts spinning in a kaleidoscope that wouldn't make a pattern. He almost didn't see the mark on the white wall, a few inches below eye level.

He leaned close and studied the brown flecks without touching them.

Blood.

Odd place to find it. Did explain the ice pack. Sort of. If

you had a good imagination, which he did.

He headed for the kitchen, frown between his brows and regret in his heart. Even without the lust factor, he liked her. Obvious that life had kicked her around more than a little bit, without making her bitter or mean.

Sometimes he hated his job.

Chapter Five

Phoebe stopped in the doorway of her kitchen, taking the opportunity to study Jake before he noticed her. He'd implied he was job hunting while talking to Chet, but Jake didn't look hungry enough to be job hunting. And he was too Boy Scout to be one of Harding's goons.

He reached up, making her carabineer wind chimes perform with a flick of his wrist and rational thought fled. Sunshine from the window flooded over him, finding the gold buried in his dark hair and putting shadows in the laugh lines that fanned out from his eyes. He'd exchanged last night's boots for comfortable tennis shoes but stayed with the tight jeans, tee and flannel, this time a soft blue plaid. He'd left the shirt unbuttoned, its sleeves rolled almost to the elbow, giving her an unrestricted view of every curve and hollow of his strong wrists and long-fingered hands.

Her blood warmed, as if Jake were a reflector for the sun. His chin angled her way, leaving her no time to prepare for the jolt when his blue gaze found her. He smiled, deepening the laugh lines and igniting a sultry hunger in her midsection.

"All done?" He grinned a welcome that melted her insides.

He was far too sexy to be trusted. She propped a shoulder against the doorframe, her smile emerging from the deep well of her own longing. "You aren't looking for a job, cowboy."

Did he stiffen? His grin turned crooked, but a wariness crept into his eyes.

"I never actually said I was looking for a job. That was Chet's idea."

"Chet's not too observant."

"And you are?" Jake picked up the coffee he'd made. One sip reminded him why he'd set it down in the first place.

"I try to be." She straightened, pulled open the fridge, and bent to retrieve a Diet Coke from a lower shelf.

Jake watched her snug shorts ride high, the fabric stretching over the taut cheeks of her bottom. He tried to look away but found the path of least resistance irresistible, since it let him follow the smooth, tender length of her legs. Cool air flowed out the open door, but it made no headway against heated want. He rubbed the beads of sweat from his forehead and told himself he was in serious trouble if he didn't pull himself together. Himself didn't care.

Phoebe straightened and slammed the door shut, then turned to face him as she popped the top on her can. "So tell me, why are you standing in my kitchen, not drinking my lousy coffee?"

He hesitated, his brain lacking the needed blood for a clever response. That left only a plunge into an explanation without any idea where he was going. "I could try to bullshit you with a story about being a reporter, or an author doing research—my personal favorite—or maybe a guy looking to buy a bar."

"But you won't?" The arch of one dark brow was openly skeptical.

"No." He tried to look straightforward. It was actually easier to produce an honest expression when he wasn't telling the truth. Honesty was far more nerve wracking. "I have too much respect for your intelligence to try that."

Phoebe's laugh was throaty, full of sex. "That's a good line. I can't wait to hear the rest of it."

The rest of it. Right. "Yeah, well, there isn't much more. I hate to admit it, but I'm just . . . curious."

"Curious?" The word pursed her mouth, still moist with soda.

"That's right." He gave a mental wince, but there was no going back, so he went with it. "It's the way I am. Sometimes I just wonder how things work. I mean, I've probably been in hundreds of bars since I reached the age of consent and never thought about what makes them work." He shrugged. "Then I'm in JR's last night, and it hits me. Like a bolt of lightning."

"Curiosity."

"That's it. No deep, dark secret. Just . . . curiosity."

He swallowed dryly and smiled his invitation for her to trust him into the skeptical furnace of her gaze.

The kicker was, Phoebe almost did trust him. It was just screwy enough to be true. He could simply be a curious guy. *Yeah, and I'm the president's lady.*

The look in his eyes made it easy for her. Phoebe couldn't, wouldn't, trust easily. Whatever he was, whether his interest was in her or the bar, she couldn't afford to trust him. He didn't have to be a bad guy to be dangerous to her.

She had to know and know fast, what he was after, so she straightened and stepped close to him, giving him a smoky smile. She'd played the vamp before, but this time it wasn't playing. Or maybe it was that playing didn't feel right.

"Well, curious Jake, I hate to see a man with an itch he can't scratch. So why don't you come with me today and I'll share with you the deep—" she smoothed the collar of his flannel shirt, her hands just brushing the sides of his jaw—"dark secrets of bar management. Then you won't have to be curious anymore. You'll . . . know."

Again Jake swallowed dryly. "Sounds . . . interesting."

"Oh, yeah. It's interesting all right. About as interesting as watching grass grow." She snagged a minute bit of lint from the collar of his shirt and flicked it away, knowing she'd moved past research to playing with fire. Lovely, warm fire. "That just leaves one important point to be decided."

"What's that?" His voice was husky, and his eyes had little flames at the back of them.

It looked as if she'd rubbed the right materials together. She just hoped she could control the fire.

"Whether you want to take your truck or pile in with me." She stepped back, against her own inclination and just shy of outright conflagration. "I should warn you, though, I probably won't be coming back here until . . . bed time."

For a moment he didn't have breath to answer. He tried for casual, but his smile wasn't the only thing woody. "Then I guess I'd better take my truck. I gotta run a couple of errands this afternoon."

Like get some ice to shove down his pants. Lots of it. And maybe take a couple of cold showers. He rubbed the back of his neck and wondered what he'd gotten into.

Her amusement should have taken the starch out of him, but the mischief in her eyes was contradicted by some obvious signs that he wasn't the only one popping with lust, he decided as his gaze skimmed across that part of her tee shirt lifted by curving breasts.

It felt good to look at her, but it wasn't good. She was almost certainly involved with Phagan and Hyatt. Maybe if he made that reminder his mental mantra, his body would get the message and quit sending his blood supply south.

"Fair enough." Her lashes hid her eyes. "You can follow me over and sate your curiosity."

"Yeah, well." He stepped back, putting distance that didn't help between them. "I make it a policy not to get too curious. You know what they say about curiosity and the cat."

Her face went blank, her eyes ice cool. "Yeah, I do."

It was, Jake thought grimly, more sobering than a cold shower.

Stern was still at the computer when Peter Harding let himself into the office. He looked up, surprised to see Peter standing there.

"You been here all night?" Peter asked. He surveyed Stern's unshaven chin and rumpled clothes with distaste.

"The whole network was compromised. I had to restore from the backup." That was the short version of his night but all he'd offer, since Harding wouldn't understand his pleasure at battling, and beating, whoever had altered the screen saver.

"Bet you wish you'd known about it before you killed the little bastard."

That was true, but not for the reason Harding thought. Perhaps he'd been hasty where Smith was concerned. It was satisfying to kill the good, but even more satisfying to turn them. And Smith, if he was the author these annoyances, might have been able to make RABBIT run.

Harding's intercom buzzed.

"Who else is here?" Stern asked.

"Just the guard." Harding depressed the button. "What?"

"I'm sorry to disturb you, sir, but an Agent Bailey from the FBI is asking to speak with you. What do you want me to tell her?"

"Her?" Harding looked to Stern for guidance.

Did he realize how often he did that, Stern wondered? "You'd better see her."

"Show her up," Harding said.

Stern shut off the monitor. "I'll wait next door. Leave the intercom open."

★ ★ ★ ★ ★

Phoebe unlocked the double doors of JR's, releasing the stale smell of bar nights to rush past Jake. There were no windows in the main part of the building, so the rectangle of daylight from the open door was the only illumination in the dark. Jake hesitated, but Phoebe took off her sunglasses and walked forward, the beat of her feet against the wooden floor not faltering once.

Who was she? And why was she willing to accept "curious Jake" at face value, give him carte blanche to snoop around JR's unchecked? Did she suspect him? Was she using this tour to demonstrate she had nothing to hide? Maybe she didn't have anything to hide. If she didn't, why did her face keep changing like a turning prism, until he wasn't sure what was real and what wasn't? Was she part of Phagan and Hyatt's game or someone caught in it like he was?

It was possible that Hyatt was using her to cover his trail without her knowledge. Yeah, and it was possible he was reaching for straws in a high wind. Or even worse, thinking with his dick instead of his brain.

In the middle of the room one spotlight came on, casting an almost perfect circle on the wooden floor. He pushed the door closed and took a couple of steps forward, then halted when he saw her slowly emerge from shadow, stopping at the edge of the light's heart.

"Here it is, curious Jake." Her voice was a husky, evocative echo in the big empty room. "The country bar in all its bare, tawdry glory. Go ahead and sate your . . . curiosity."

Would he take the bait, she wondered, trying to slow her wildly beating heart. It was as provocative, as dangerous as climbing without a proper belay, but Phoebe couldn't help herself. *You know what they say about cats and curiosity,* he'd said. Was it a threat? If he was dangerous, why did she feel safe around him? There was no way to know anything for sure, only her instincts to guide her on a path that even Pathphinder couldn't see the end of.

On the other side of the light she heard Jake walking toward her, his measured footsteps on the wooden floor beating the same tempo as her heart. He stopped just shy of her circle. She wanted to invite him in, to step in herself and wrap around him. She wanted to heal herself in his eyes and to warm herself against his body. She didn't dare move toward him, couldn't make herself move away from him.

All she could do was wait and see what his next move would be.

He stared at her, felt the pull behind her neutral eyes and still body. Longed to close the space that separated them and bury himself in her.

He'd felt lust before, even felt a longing for the emotional completion his brothers had found with their wives. He remembered Luke saying he'd known the first time he looked in Rosemary's eyes that his life would never be the same. At the time, he'd thought it was Luke's hormones talking. Now he understood what Luke meant. How ironic that he was feeling it for a woman he couldn't have.

He couldn't cross the line. This was business, not karma.

He looked past her with the bitter bite of regret tightening his chest and stared at the stage, where he could see the muted gleam of musical equipment. In his mind he peopled it with Phoebe and the other band members, saw them playing, their music fueled by audience excitement, felt again the strange synergy between singers and audience.

When he thought he could trust his voice, he said, "What's it like to be up there, on stage?"

"What's it like?" She hesitated, then said, "It's like . . . safe sex that feels wild and dangerous."

Heat came back like flames shooting up a flue, feeding the longing that cycled between them in unsteady bursts, trying to burn through his control.

He jerked his gaze away. He counted to twenty, mentally added an arctic wind, and managed to ask, "You ever dream of the big time when you're playing? Of a bigger audience?"

"No." She walked around the circle toward him. "I have . . . almost everything I want in the little time."

He walked away from her around the circle. "Almost?"

"If I had everything, there'd be nothing to—want."

Even in the dark he could see the bewildered pain, mingled with longing in her eyes. His control slipped, and he took a step into the circle toward her. "Phoebe—"

The door opened suddenly, and a moment later the place was flooded with light. The shadows fled, leaving the questions to linger with the dust motes in the air.

"I came to log in a load of booze," Chet said from the doorway.

For a moment longer Phoebe stared at Jake, then she turned from him and said, "I'm glad it came. I was worried we'd run out tonight."

"No fears," Chet said cheerfully.

She hesitated, then looked at Jake, her eyes showing only friendly interest. "Have you seen enough, curious Jake?"

"No." He stared back. "I'd like to see more." And understand everything, he added to himself.

"Come on then." She turned and walked away from him, the sassy sway of her ass laced with bravado.

Jake gave himself a little shake and followed, knowing in his gut that something important had just happened. He wasn't sure in what context—business or personal—it mattered. He did know he had to find out before it was too late.

Peter Harding shook hands with Agent Bailey, smiling at her with his patented charm. She smiled back. All women did. They couldn't help themselves. It had always been like that and always would be until he didn't have to play the PC game any longer, didn't have to disguise his contempt for women like this one. Women who thought they were powerful enough to play men's games.

The bitches never should have been given the vote. It was too late to turn back the clock now, but there were other ways to punish their presumption.

"I'll be in touch if and when we know more," she said, her voice brisk as she tried to pretend she was as good as a man. "Let me know if you see anything suspicious."

"I feel safe knowing you're on top of things," Peter said. He held on to her hand a little longer than he should have, squeezing it just enough to bring a satisfying flash of annoyance to her eyes. "Thank you for keeping us informed."

When she pulled away, he let her go. Let her walk away in her power suit and fuck-me heels. He waited until he heard the *ping* of the elevator before relaxing his guard. He heard Stern come back.

"She thinks we might be a target for a burglary." He laughed as he went to pour himself a drink.

Stern lit up and blew smoke, looking as amused as he was capable of.

Peter looked at his watch.

"Got a bitch to collect and people to charm. Mind the store."

Stern watched Peter saunter out like a man on top of the world. He crushed the cigarette out in the ashtray, then pulled a slip of paper from his inside pocket and unfolded it. Inside, the words hadn't changed since the last time he read them: *Knowing isn't always a good thing. Hope you have your back covered.*

Stern re-stowed the note, pulled his piece and checked it. The clip was full. He restored it to the holster and sauntered over to the bar. It might be time to reconsider his association with Peter. Harding was getting cocky, careless. That business with the FBI agent was stupid. Peter thought all women were stupid. He was wrong.

About so many things.

"There he goes." Dewey Hyatt looked away from the computer screen, which was tapped into TelTech's security system, and smiled at Kevin. "Like a lamb to the slaughter."

Kevin's grin was still wary but had the promise of great charm. He'd picked up on their basic course in hacking with admirable speed. Definitely a natural. Perhaps trust would come when the bruises his stepfather had left on his face had faded. There had been a lot of Kevins in the years since Nadine had died and there were a lot of Kevins and Karens still out there. Phagan couldn't save them all, but that didn't stop him from trying.

Dewey grabbed the phone and punched in the numbers for Phoebe's beeper. When prompted, he punched in the code that would let her know it was time for the white queen to make her move. He grabbed his coat and started to leave, but a tingling on the back of his neck made him pause.

He looked around the apartment, then at Kevin. "Think it's time to move out of here. Can you break it down while I take care of business?"

Kevin nodded, trying, like any teenager, not to look pleased. "The fallback?"

Dewey nodded. "When I'm done, I'll meet you back here to do a sweep."

A look of anxiety crossed Kevin's face. "Do you think they're on to us?"

For Kevin, Dewey knew, everyone was a *they,* with only a few *us* that he wasn't all that sure he could trust yet. He grinned. "Kev, my friend, they are always on to us, always close, but it's a game. A dance. Sometimes they lead. Most of the time we lead. If they do pick you up, we'll have you out before you have time to get used to that great jailhouse food. The trick is to stay calm and say nothing. Got it?"

The anxiety didn't leave, but Kevin nodded.

"Good." Dewey mock socked his chin. "Be gone an hour, two tops."

Jake prowled the tiny room while Phoebe sat at the desk, running figures on an adding machine. It looked normal but felt wrong.

There was no computer, no sign there'd ever been a computer there. The only other machines in the room, besides the adding machine, were the telephone and a manual typewriter. Off to one side were some file cabinets, off to the other a stool sat in front of a modest shelf which was attached to the wall beneath a substandard mirror. A row of bulbs ran along the top of the mirror and some cosmetics dotted the shelf. Next to it was a door that was probably a closet, since it was on an inside wall. On the opposite wall was a cloudy window.

She wasn't making it easy. He didn't realize he'd sighed out loud until she looked up and asked, "Disappointed in bar world?"

He grinned. "Maybe a little. You got any family besides the Mentels?"

Phoebe looked at him, felt his curiosity, but that wasn't what fueled the compulsion to be honest. She quite simply couldn't deny her sister's existence. Not now, when the game for her was running. "I . . . had a sister. She died . . . young."

"I'm sorry."

Phoebe looked down at her pencil, rolling it between her fingers. "Yeah, me too. I still miss her."

"My sister-in-law, Dani, lost a baby. She says you never get over the missing."

"She's right."

A beeper went off, and the pencil in her hand snapped. Jake groped for his pager, but found a blank screen. He looked at Phoebe.

"It's my chess partner. He's finally made a move."

"Chess?"

She shrugged. "I like games."

Jake felt his gut tighten. "Okay. But chess?"

"It's more interesting than checkers."

Jake hesitated. "I'm curious again."

"He lives in Australia. Beep is cheaper than a phone call. See." She showed him the beeper. *Queen to king's three* scrolled across the tiny screen.

Jake didn't stiffen against the kick of instinct in his gut, but it wasn't easy. His smile easy, his voice light, he asked, "How did you get an Aussie chess partner?"

"Same way I got a curious Jake. Met him here in the bar. He was in Denver for a convention a few years back."

"Oh." She played chess. She played chess with an Aussie? He felt as if he'd missed a beat and rubbed his face. "Australia. You can't play with someone closer to home?"

Phoebe tossed the beeper onto the desk and leaned back in her chair. "Sure, I could. But I have to keep taking his hand off my knee, and, besides, it makes a better story to play an Aussie."

"A better story?" Jake dropped into the chair across from

her. “You play intercontinental chess because it makes a better story?”

“According to my mama, ‘story’ is everything.”

Jake propped his elbow on the armrest, his face crinkled into cute confusion.

Phoebe grinned. “My mama wasn’t a prize, but every now and again she’d sock home an important life lesson with a story.”

“And having a better story was one of those important life lessons?”

Jake may have an ear for southern accents, Phoebe thought, but not for their idiosyncrasies. “Ever try to say, ‘don’t do that,’ to a thirteen-year-old?”

“No,” Jake admitted. “What were you doing that your mama didn’t want you to?”

She smiled. “I was in love for the first time. He was the pastor’s wild child, and I was heading for trouble. Mama took me shopping, I saw these red shoes in a window, and she had me.”

“Had you? With red shoes?”

“I was thirteen. I wanted those shoes bad. Real bad.”

“First love and red shoes. Sure, I’m getting this.”

Phoebe shook her head reprovingly. “I have to lay the thread of my story before I can draw them together, cowboy. You Yanks are so impatient.”

Jake crossed one leg over the other and relaxed in the chair. “Lay your threads, I’m patiently listening, Reb, but you’d better deliver.”

“If I don’t, I’ll buy you a drink. Now, where was I?”

“Red shoes and first love.”

“Right. Well, naturally I asked my mama for those shoes. I was sure my future happiness depended on having them on my feet ten minutes ago.” She smiled briefly at Jake and almost lost the thread of her story when he smiled back. "My mama told me that she'd buy me those shoes if I'd dump the boy."

Jake straightened. "That's cold."

"No, that's 'story.' She knew I'd break up with him sometime anyway." Jake faded away, and she was back on that hot street with her mama. "My mama smiled this smile that was part evil and part wise, then she said to me, she said, 'N—" Phoebe faltered, almost losing herself in the near slip. " '—*now*—girl, you and I know you're not gonna love this boy forever. When you're old like me and your young'uns ask you about your first love, which'll make a better story? I broke up with my first love? Or'—and she smiled again—'I gave him up for red shoes?' "

Would he understand, Phoebe wondered, as she smiled at him.

Her smile, Jake suspected, was her mama's. There was evil round the edges—and a boatload of charm.

"You took the shoes, didn't you?"

"Course I did. Mama was a drunk, but she was a smart drunk, 'cept when it came to men." She shrugged, her eyes filled with bygones that weren't really gone.

"Great story," Jake said.

"My mama had her moments." For an instant sadness almost overwhelmed her. There were so few of those happy moments kicking around her memory, it had been easy to push them into the deep, dark recesses of her mind. Was it the game that was bringing them bubbling to the surface, or was Jake somehow the catalyst, opening up her personal Pandora's box by making her feel again?

Because she couldn't help it, she looked at him and found him looking at her. Was that the same longing she felt, peeking out of his eyes, or was she projecting what she wanted, needed, to see? There was no way to know with this liquid fire creeping through her veins, turning her whole body languid with longing.

She tried to fight it by getting up. She pushed back her chair and started around the desk with some papers in her hand. She should have stayed put. The room wasn't big enough. There wasn't enough space left to spit, let alone breathe, on the other side of her desk. He was so close, her horizon was completely filled with his blue eyes and wide shoulders.

A move, any move, and her mouth would be against his. And the chiseled, pouty curve was more tempting than a puff pastry. Her mouth strained toward him, but she reined it in. The only outward sign of her struggle was a slight tremor that lit new fires in those heady blue depths. She wasn't too proud to retreat, so she stepped back.

"I should run my errands," he said, a husky edge to his voice. "See you back here tonight?"

The question sounded more important than was allowed, than was safe. She didn't know who he was or what he wanted, but he couldn't have it. She couldn't give it. There was only the game.

She nodded without breaking the lock he had on her eyes. He didn't move, despite his stated intention. The moment stretched out until she was certain she was going to burst into flame or climb over the desk and throw herself at his chest. Then a knock on the door broke passion's link. She dropped into her chair like something air had been let out of and shuffled the papers from one side of her desk to the other.

Without waiting for a response a big man opened the door opened and slouched in the frame.

"You Phoebe?"

"Yes."

"I'm looking for a job."

She had to glance at Jake then. Needed to see the answering gleam of laughter light his eyes more than she needed air to breathe. She made herself look away, made herself look at the intruder. His beefy profile and mean eyes made him easy to place in Harding's column. No surprise he hadn't gone for the subtle approach. This was a bar.

"Got nothing right now." She hooked her thumbs in the pockets of her shorts. "You can leave your name and number and—"

"I'll just check back." His mean eyes did the guy thing over her assets. Phoebe didn't flinch. She was used to it.

Jake wasn't. He had to rein in the urge to punch the guy's mean lights out, even as he assessed the subtle change that had come over Phoebe. Her demeanor had lost all softness or warmth. No quarter visible.

The man looked at Jake and stiffened, his narrow eyes thinning to malevolent pinpoints. Jake didn't know him, but he could tell the man was a con.

And that the con knew him for a Fed.

Chapter Six

Out in the hall, Billy Books cussed silently. Stern hadn't warned him there'd be a Fed in with the broad. That would cost him.

He saw the pay phone, looked both ways, then with his back to the wall, he dialed Stern's cell phone number. It was gonna cost him big time.

Seated at a borrowed desk in the local Bureau field office, Bryn was going through reports, hoping they'd take the bad taste out of her mouth from her visit to TelTech. It galled her that the law forced her to be on the side of someone so subtly scummy. She'd use him to catch Phagan, but she'd make damn sure she found his nasty secret and took him out, too.

An agent cleared his throat nervously and Bryn realized she was scowling. She used a red tipped finger to mark her place in a report, before looking up at him. "Yes, what is it?"

"I think we got ourselves a laundering op running out of that bar you asked me to check out."

"Really?" Bryn gave him the nod to sit down. Resting her elbows on the pile of reports, she applied pressure to her temples.

Once seated, he leaned forward, using his hands to emphasize his points. "It's got all the markers. A complex trail of dummy corporations leading to more dummy corporations, dead or MIA directors." He shrugged. "Sure as hell haven't found a JR anywhere in the mix."

Bryn frowned. "Local PD says he's a big-deal Texan."

"More like a big-deal invisible man. I'm betting it's an ID built on a grave. Vintage Phagan work. Missed on our first, quick check on them."

"You running background checks on the employees?"

He nodded.

"Good." She rubbed between her eyebrows, noting absently that she needed to pluck. "Keep digging. Find me the pot of gold at the end of the rainbow. ASAP."

"You want I should put someone in the bar?"

She hesitated, then shook her head. "Jake Kirby's already in. So far he's cooperating. Let's not muddy the waters."

"Right." He left, but Bryn didn't go back to her reading. The reports were dull stuff for whirling thoughts to light on. Phagan was there, a shadowy figure just out of her reach.

What was he up to now? Where did an obscure country bar fit into his plans? Was this one of his crumbs, leading her where he wanted her to go? Or a clever diversion planned to keep her attention away from his real objective? Or was its discovery, like Ollie's death, just another piece of bad luck, one Phagan was hoping she wouldn't notice?

Please, let it be door number three.

Phoebe headed for her SUV, while her thoughts circled uneasily around the summons from Dewey.

Queen to king's three.

How did she feel about it? Was she really ready to face her sister's murderer?

For answers to these and other questions, stay tuned to this brain, she thought, with a wry calm that surprised her. Somehow she'd expected to feel more. This was it.

Closure time. She shined a light inside her head and found no sign of triumph and plenty of fear.

It had been seven years, but some things wouldn't have

changed. He'd still be a dirty fighter, a mean survivor, and a dangerous adversary.

Obviously Stern had found the flyers when he killed Ollie and Harding had moved to get his gnarly guy in to check out the bar. Though he hadn't sent his best man, Phoebe noted as she spotted without seeming to, the beefy goon lying in wait across the road, only partially shielded by trees.

Hard to know whether to be insulted or relieved.

She slid behind the wheel and fired the engine, her wheel-spinning start sending a wave of gravel flying out from beneath her tires all the way to the paved road. She turned toward town, noting without surprise the man's truck sliding into place at a barely discreet distance behind her.

Halfway to town, Jake's truck popped up behind the tail.

"Who are you following, curious Jake? Me or him?"

She'd noticed how quickly he'd smelled what was rotten in the guy's Denmark, but what had the guy smelled about Jake? They hadn't circled each other snarling, but there'd been a hair-raising tension crackling between them. The explanation that fit best was that Jake was some kind of a cop. But what kind? He didn't act like any cop Phoebe knew, despite her long association with the less-than-law-abiding Phagan.

Of course, this deal with Harding was the first time Phagan had let her so close to the action. Other than a couple of new recruits, Phoebe was the only one in Phagan's little gang without a record for even a small infraction. Never even got a speeding ticket, though she'd bantered with one of the local cops prior to his marriage a couple of years ago. Well, the search for light and knowledge about Jake Kirby would have to wait until after she jerked Harding's chain. Which meant she had to lose both the tail and the tail's tail.

She passed into the outskirts of Estes Park and prepared for the first turn, automatically checking her rearview before moving over. Both tail and Jake moved over, taking the turn with her. She took several more turns, random ones now, and the truck followed, with dumb, dogged persistence, letting her lead him astray.

"Guys, any other day I'd enjoy this." Now was not a good time to be lead car in a three-car parade. She lifted the armrest between the seats where her car phone nestled out of sight and punched in a phone number, then left it on speaker, because she didn't want her quarry to see her making a call that might give away the surprise.

"Estes Park Police Department."

"Is that you Honk?"

"Well, as I live and breathe, Phoebe Ann?"

"The one and only, darlin'."

"What can the Estes Park PD's finest do for you?"

"What you do so well, Honk. Arrest someone."

"Damn." Jake watched the patrol car with lights flashing come between him and Phoebe's tail. Phoebe's SUV turned a corner. Jake hesitated only briefly before deciding to stick with her tail and not with her. He pulled into the curb well back but with a good view of the truck.

The officer slid out of his cruiser and approached the truck alertly. The driver got out, his hands visible. He'd done this scene before. The officer said something. The man protested. The cop went to the rear of the truck, kicked out a tail light, then pointed to it.

A setup. Damn. Jake hated it when a lead got busted. He shifted into drive and pulled around the two stopped cars. As he passed, the guy took a swing at the cop. Jake's last view as he rounded a bend was of him spread-eagle on the ground getting cuffed. Phoebe's work was nice, though. He had a feeling she'd be one hell of a chess opponent.

★ ★ ★ ★ ★

When Jake didn't follow her, Phoebe took a few random turns to make sure she really was clear, then got back on course. Jake, she admitted freely, wasn't the only one who was curious. And, she admitted, not quite so freely, her curiosity wasn't nearly as impersonal as she would have liked it to be.

Jake could have noticed the guy's interest and followed to protect her, but just because he was her enemy's enemy didn't make him her friend or mitigate the very real threat he could be to her and her friends. It was one thing if it was just her at risk but it wasn't.

Her loyalty belonged to Kerry Anne first, her friends second, and the game they were running next, with her hormones lagging a distant last. She couldn't let herself get distracted by Jake, not right now. He wasn't, she could tell, going to go away, and not because she was spinning his hormonal wheels. He had a law-abiding interest in their game, probably because of her stupid phone call to Phagan's last apartment in Montana.

She pulled into the parking lot in front of an office bearing a brass plate with uninformative inscription, *Smith's* and stared ahead without seeing it. She was on the tightrope. There was no going back just because a curious stranger with a cute ass was swinging in and out of her view.

She gave herself a firm shake and climbed out. This was not a good time to lose her concentration, not when she was about to face *him*. She let herself in, locking the door—and all thoughts of anything but her next step—behind her. The door secured, she passed through the silent office with its skeleton furniture without turning on any lights until she came to a bathroom with a lighted vanity set up in one corner. A cabinet held the basic bathroom necessities, with a locked closet next to it.

Phoebe dug out her keys and opened the closet, revealing a small wardrobe and a theater-style make up set up, complete with wigs and prosthetics.

She thumbed through the clothes on the rod until she found the item she needed. Along with the red shoes she'd mentioned to Jake and Kerry Anne's photo was Kerry's white high school graduation dress. Kerry had given it to her the day she left for college. Those three things were all she'd brought with her to her new life. Had she known that someday this moment would come? Had the subconscious "path finder" been able to see this far ahead and anticipate this moment?

She fingered the soft white organdy, releasing a faint whiff of Kerry Anne's flower scent, and a host of memories, into the air around her. Phoebe lifted the sleeve to her cheek and closed her eyes, letting the whirlwind of the past engulf her in its part-pleasure, part-pain embrace.

Their mama had been an incipient drunk before Montgomery Justice, the man now known as Peter Harding, entered their lives. Phoebe had wondered what he saw in their mama back then. Mama had been Junior League, but her drinking had made sure her daughter's weren't invited to join. Now, when it was too late, she knew what he'd seen, what he wanted. Had her mama known, too, at the end? Had she accidentally fallen down those stairs like the newspaper said? Or had Justice finished his work of destruction and simply moved on, thinking he'd left the past behind?

"He's wrong, Kerry," Phoebe said, the dress as soft against her cheek as Kerry's hand had been the day she died. "Neither of us can escape our past."

Her internal tightrope gave a quiver that almost tumbled her off, but Phoebe managed to steady herself, inside and out. She took out Kerry's picture and propped it on the mirror's ledge, pretending she couldn't see the cracks to the past that showed in her eyes and in the tension around her mouth.

Moving slowly, steadily, she began the process of remaking herself in the picture's image, taking care not to look down, pretending she didn't notice the chasm opening at her feet.

As Kerry Anne began to edge out Phoebe, apprehension was edged out, too. By the time she was ready for the contact lenses, her hands were steady enough to insert them. Kerry's eyes were blue and had always been true. She'd died trying to be true to her little sister. Now her little sister would be true to her.

The outward changes she was making seeped inward, changing her walk, the way she used her hands. Memory gave her back her sister, or maybe Kerry Anne's gentle spirit invaded Phoebe's soul, to aid her this one last time.

She smiled her sister's smile, then took that image with her as she left, to keep at bay the other image of her sister. The one with slashed wrists and blood spreading across white tile.

Outside she got into a small car and turned it toward Denver where Dewey waited for her.

Stern's cell phone buzzed discreetly. "Mr. Stern?" Billy's voice was muffled. "I got a problem."

Stern gave a silent sigh. Billy had been Harding's uninspired pick for their team. As usual, Stern was the one who'd have to fix the mess it was causing. "It's not your job to have problems, just to collect information."

"Can't do nothing if you don't bail me." Billy sounded sulky and a bit threatening.

A tiny crease appeared between Stern's eyes. He didn't like being threatened. By anyone. "Bail you?"

"I got stopped by a local yokel. Claimed I had a taillight out, but I know the bastard kicked it hisself."

"Why would a broken taillight require bail?"

"It don't." Feet-shuffling was audible despite background noise. "Bail's for punching the hick cop."

"I'm glad you kept your head." Sarcasm was wasted on Billy, but Stern used it to vent his own frustration. "What did you find out about the bar?"

"You gonna bail me?"

"If you give me what I want."

"The manager's a woman—Phoebe I think they said. Foxy—could get my rocks off on her, I'll tell you—"

"I'm not interested in who—or what—gets you hard." Stern kept his voice even with an effort. "How did you give yourself away?"

"I didn't do nothing. I asked her about a job, and she told me she didn't have no openings. I did the nice and left, then waited for her to come out. Was following her when I got copped by the brownie."

"Not the information I was looking for."

"It could be her."

Stern could tell by the man's voice there was more.

"Give it all or you'll need protection from *me*."

"She had heat with her. Not a local lame-ass. A Fed." Billy didn't have to tell him the Fed had made him. Sounded as if half the town had made him.

"You just made bail."

Stern rang off without adding that Billy's employment was going to end very soon.

"Okay, I got it." Jake wrote down the MUD address Matt had gotten him, then eased the drifting car back into his lane. Good thing Bryn wasn't with him or there'd be a coup d'etat initiated on the driver. "Tell Sebastian thanks for me, Matt. I'm just outside Denver now. Gonna go check it out before I come in."

"Bryn and I'll meet you outside the building," Matt said.

"You don't—"

"I don't care if they are computer geeks, you're not going in without backup. Now wait for me."

"Yes, big brother."

"You wait or I'll kick your ass."

"Kiss my—" Before Jake could finish, Matt broke the connection. Jake grinned as he stowed the phone, then keyed the address into his laptop, his fingers tapping the steering wheel until a map came up. He was close. That was good, gave him reconnoiter time before Matt and the troops got there.

Peter Harding felt like a god as he looked out the window at the gathering below. This was it. This was the beginning of his rule, his first step into Denver society as Audrey's fiancé. The day he declared for governor with her powerful father standing behind him. They didn't know it yet, but they were there for him. It was as it should be, as it was always meant to be. He was destined to be supported by lesser lives, to absorb their strength to power his own.

How he'd hated the years of hiding, the sneaking around like some common criminal. He wasn't meant to live in shadow. Now, today, he was stepping into the light. True, it was borrowed light from Audrey's father, but that wouldn't be for long. Power was fluid, a liquid-gold energy that continuously sought the one most qualified to wield it. He was that person.

Norma Jean Beauleigh and her daughters had been a mistake. He could admit that now. He'd let himself be sucked in by the small perfection of Kerry Anne and Nadine. He hadn't learned to take the long view back then.

A small tremor of unease disturbed the surface of his satisfaction at the thought of Nadine. She had to be the one sending the notes and now the black rose that had come this morning in the box that was supposed to hold his white lapel rose. But if it was her, why had it taken her so long to act? Had she, like he, been consolidating her power?

His first reaction had been to cancel today's event. What if she showed up at the party? Stern, in that damned enigmatic way of his, said he hoped she would.

Now that he was here, he hoped she did, too. How could he fear her when he was at the apex of his power? There was no way a mere woman could take it away from him. No way in hell. He stroked the black rose pinned to his lapel and smiled. Behind him the door opened. Reflected in the window, he could see Audrey, dressed in the trappings of her father's wealth.

"Are you ready, darling?" she asked.

He smiled before he turned to face her. "Oh, yes."

Jake pulled his truck to a stop across the street from the apartment building and checked it against the address Matt had given him. It matched, so he got out and looked around. It was a quiet street, sort of middle-class. Clean, but the trees were on the scraggly side. Looked like they could use water. Still, it was a long way from the low-life place in Montana.

No sign of Matt or Bryn. He looked up, but the angle was wrong for him to see anything but the sun reflecting on the windows of the apartment. All the buildings within the immediate area were similar, but the apartment house to the right of this one was a twin, right down to the trim around the windows. A narrow alley separated them. Both walls had fire escapes snaking down the sides and fire doors across from each other. It got Jake thinking. He decided to check out the non-MUD building, just for the heck of it. He had a few minutes to kill. If the buildings were identical on the outside, chances were, they were identical on the inside, too. He could get a feel for the layout without tipping his hand to anyone who might be inhabiting the apartment they were interested in. And have a chat with the super.

Dewey was waiting for Phoebe next to a sleek black limousine. Phoebe shook her head, Dewey was a character, but he was a character with style.

She parked her car in the mall lot next to him and got out, feeling Kerry's dress drop softly into place, feeling Kerry all around her as she walked toward him. With each step the soft fabric whispered against her calves like echoes from the past, soothing her fear and shoring up her resolve.

"I'd never have known it was you," Dewey said, his eyes hidden behind mirrored glasses. His voice was flat, almost too flat. Was he worried about her? That must be it, because he hadn't known Kerry. It was Phagan who'd known Kerry, who'd talked her into running away with him. Who'd lost her when she insisted on bringing her little sister along, too. If only—

Phoebe cut that thought off at the knees.

"Harding's gonna shit a brick when he sees you."

"I hope so." Phoebe smiled her sister's smile as she slid into the limo through the door Dewey held open for her. She leaned back, not thinking about what was ahead. Not just yet. Right now was for her and Kerry.

As if he sensed this, Dewey didn't speak either, just directed the driver to take them to the country club. He did take her hand in a comforting grip. She held on and let the past engulf her.

Jake was sitting on the stoop sipping a soft drink when Matt and Bryn arrived with some local uniforms.

Matt climbed out of one of the cars—the driver's seat of course—and looked at his little brother. He had a powerful, stocky body and blunt, weathered features that his marriage had softened slightly. As always, he reminded Jake of their dad.

Jake finished his drink and tossed it into a street-side rubbish bin. "Took you long enough."

"Got caught in some traffic." Matt looked tense, but compared to Bryn he was positively mellow.

Bryn was giving off tension vibes like a hot sidewalk. Being a wise man, Jake refrained from commenting on anything but the job at hand. When they'd deployed the local men outside the building, he led Bryn and Matt inside to the elevator.

Phoebe moved through the crowd like a ghost, sliding between clusters of rich, smart people like a will-o-the-wisp. At some level her senses were on alert for a sign of Harding or his goon, Barrett Stern, but it was hard to feel real when no one even acknowledged her presence in this gathering of the powerful and moneyed of Denver.

It was like being split into pieces. Kerry Anne was in full and firm control of Phoebe's outside, but inside, who she was now and who she'd been wrestled like twin babies in a womb. A gateway to the past had been opened. Her demons were out of the box and couldn't be sent back because she needed them to make the game happen. She just hoped she could control them. The stakes were high. If she lost this one, she lost big, she lost it all, she lost without hope of recovery.

This wasn't a news flash. She'd known the risks when she signed on to the game. What she hadn't anticipated was meeting Jake. He was a wild card in their game, who, totally against her will, made her wild with longing for a life outside the game. Meeting him had introduced a bitter regret to the emotions seething below the surface of the Kerry Anne façade. It was like adding propane to a flame, turning it bright, hot and dangerously unstable. Unstable was not the way she wanted to be for her first meeting with her sister's murderer.

She found a leafy bower near a small artificial lake and sank down onto the decorative bench. There was one person she could summon right now, one identity that would bind them together into a cohesive whole.

Pathphinder.

With the thought came the path she needed to follow, step by careful step. She sighed, feeling the tension give way to purpose. She, they—all the people she'd been in the last seven years—would do what was necessary. No matter what the cost. No matter what she would never have because of it.

She stood up, but before she could turn around, she heard his laugh behind her. It was charming, even infectious. Only those who truly knew him heard the edge of evil buried in its heart.

She turned slowly and found him standing in the full sun with the black rose on his lapel. Light loved him, though he didn't love it. He fooled it, as he did most people, with his easy, addictive charm. Like taking a drug, being around him was intoxicating at first. Only when it was too late did you realize the pleasure of his company was a soul-destroying poison.

She actually took a step back as her flight instinct overcame her fight. Then she saw him smile down at the two little girls standing next to a woman who was obviously their mother. He touched the older child, his eyelids drooping in pleasure, then lifted his glass and drank.

It was at that moment he saw her.

★ ★ ★ ★ ★

"Here it is," Bryn said, stopping outside a solid wood door just around the corner from the elevator.

"Guns and badges?" Matt asked.

Jake shook his head. "These guys pack pocket protectors, not guns."

Bryn hesitated, then nodded her agreement, but she kept her hand on her weapon.

"Ollie Smith's death might have changed that." Matt stepped to one side of door jamb with his hand also on his gun.

Jake took the other side, then knocked on the door. "Might already be an empty hole—" He stopped at the sound of movement from inside. Someone fumbled with the lock, then the door opened a crack, the safely chain still on. A young, scared face peered out.

"Yes?"

"I'm Jake Kirby, US Marshals Service." He held up his badge, shifting his weight to put his shoulder against the door, a precaution that immediately proved wise when the kid tried to slam the door.

Matt saw it coming and shoved his foot into the opening to help Jake, giving a grunt of pain when the door crunched into his foot. "Damn. I hate nice neighborhoods. The doors are too damn heavy." He slammed his shoulder into the door and this time it gave as far as the chain would allow.

"He's running." Jake pulled his gun, stepped back, and kicked the door. The chain snapped and the door popped open.

"Cover me," Matt said. He went in sideways, with his body turned to present the smallest target, with Jake and Bryn on his heels. Moving fast but carefully, they fanned out. Jake took the kitchen and almost immediately found the rear exit swinging on its hinges.

"He went out the back!" Jake yelled. "I'm heading down."

As he went out, he heard Matt shouting instructions into his radio. Out in the hall, Jake looked down the flight of stairs, then turned and headed for the elevator. He had his own idea of where the kid would come out.

Peter Harding couldn't believe what he was seeing. Kerry Anne Beauleigh, standing in a flower and leaf frame? Could it be? The dress. He remembered it. Graduation. In a rare moment of sobriety, Norma Jean had taken her to pick it out. The girl had looked magical in it. Hopeful, ready to fly free. She hadn't known yet that she'd never be free. Not until he'd explained her options to her. Her eyes—they looked at him now with the same expression she'd had that night.

Wide, shocked. Accusing. Defiant even as her blood dripped her life onto the white tile. He'd left her for Nadine to find, so she'd know what would happen to her if she defied him. Instead, she'd run away.

His hands curled into fists as a red mist formed before his eyes. It had to be Nadine. Kerry Anne was dead. He'd watched them wheel her lifeless, naked body away. Made all the arrangements to put her in the ground since Norma Jean was, as usual, too drunk to cope.

"Peter? Are you all right?" Audrey's face came between him and Kerry Anne.

"I'm fine." He lifted his arm to shove her out of the way, but someone grabbed it, the fingers biting into his flesh like a vise.

"You've cut your hand," Stern said, interposing himself between Harding and Audrey.

Harding looked down, saw blood and drink dripping onto the broken shards of glass. Pieces of the glass still cut into his palm, but he felt no pain there.

"Looks like you had a cracked glass." Stern spoke again. His eyes told Harding to pull it together.

Harding took a shaky breath, realized his heart was pounding like a piston. He licked his lips. Stern shoved a glass of water into his good hand and lifted it to his mouth. Harding drank, then pushed it away.

"I thought I saw . . . an old friend. You should . . . bring her to me."

"I will, when I'm sure you're all right," Stern said. He stepped aside for Audrey.

In control was what he meant. Harding managed a reassuring look for her. "Sorry, darling. Those . . . flowers over there reminded me of my . . . mother's funeral."

Behind Audrey's back, Stern's eyes told him it was a good save.

Tears filled her eyes as she took his hand in hers. "You're bleeding."

Her touch, combined with the smell of his own blood, was intoxicating. He could feel the power, the violence rise within him. Could imagine his fist smashing into her face. Blood spurting from her mouth and nose. Seeing the look in her eyes change from love to fear—

"We'd better find a first-aid kit," Stern said, breaking into his thoughts with a firm voice and a vice-like grip. "Perhaps Mrs. Dilmont could hold down the fort with your guests until we get you taken care of?"

The only thing Peter wanted to take care of was business. As if Stern sensed it, his grip on his arm tightened until Harding winced.

"I know you don't want to leave your *guests* alone for long."

"No, I don't." Now he could feel the throbbing pain radiating from the cut. Could feel the warm, wet slide of blood across his skin. He managed a smile that was almost normal for Audrey, helped on by the watchful stare of her powerful father a short distance away. "I won't be long."

As he turned away, he looked toward the bower. It was empty.

He waited until they were out of range to hiss, "Find her."

"When you're in control."

Normally he'd hang on to these feelings, then take it to the red-light district and find a prostitute to pound on, but he couldn't do that right now either. Not with the glare of publicity shining on him. He had to hold it in, keep it all on a leash. He could do this. He could. He was in control. Not even his passions would master him. He was stronger than all of them. And Kerry Anne, or whoever the hell she was, would soon find out how dangerous it was to play games with him.

The kid—his name was Roger, but he carried ID that said his name was Kevin—cautiously opened the door to laundry room. Heated air that smelled of bleach surged into the stairwell. He could hear the murmur of the dryer off to one side, broken by the occasional thump of something heavy hitting metal.

The sounds of pursuit had turned away at the first floor, heading out into the street. He slipped across the room, past the slowly spinning clothes and through the doorway to the storage area. He counted cages, stopping at the fourth one to insert a key into a padlock. It took only a moment to move the boxes within aside and expose the door just where Dewey had said it would be. He leaned against the wall to catch his breath as relief took the flight out of his legs.

He'd wanted to trust Dewey, wanted to believe his life could be different, but he'd been fed the "We'll keep you from your step dad" line before. He'd gone through the system, done what he was told, then been delivered back to his mom by the same people who'd promised to help him. Each time they'd told him it would be better this time. And it just got worse. He'd run away once before, but they'd caught him.

Then he'd happened onto Phagan's web site, while cruising around on the school computer so he wouldn't have to go home. A few e-mails later, he had a bus ticket and a destination. He kept waiting for the other shoe to drop. For Phagan's gang to turn out to be some kind of male prostitution ring or something but Dewey hadn't laid a hand on him. Had given him a key to lock his bedroom, in fact.

So far, Dewey had been real cool. He'd almost begun to believe this could work. Then the Feds banged on the door. Well, first thing Dewey had taught him was where and how to retreat. He slipped through the door and pulled the boxes back into place behind him as best he could, feeling as clever as the fox he'd chosen to follow.

Bet the Feds didn't expect this, he gloated, his mind moving ahead to the next thing Dewey had told him to do if this happened. He'd taken careful mental notes because there was no way in hell he was ever going back home. He'd die first.

From where he sat, getting his hand bandaged by a doctor friend of Audrey's father, Harding couldn't see the gathering, couldn't see Kerry Anne. She had to be flesh because he didn't believe in phantoms. He'd feel more at ease, though, when Stern got his hands on her. Not that Stern made any effort to do so. He'd been staring out that window since they came inside.

"Why don't you get back to the party? As you can see, I'm in good hands."

Stern turned to look at him, his gaze both assessing and probing. It was also annoyed, though only someone who knew him very well would know it. His normal expression was stone, cold rock.

"I have such a good view here, I thought I'd take a minute to look for our friend. So far no sign of her."

Was he telling the truth? Peter couldn't tell.

Stern wasn't telling the truth, of course and he could tell from Harding's expression that he suspected but didn't dare ask. Hadn't the asshole learned by now that it was always better to let the quarry come to you? Let her find what she was looking for, then pounce.

Stern didn't sigh as he turned back to the window, because it wasn't his style. There was no question Harding was behaving oddly. What was it about this Nadine that pushed his buttons? She'd been clever so far, poking and prodding him from a safe distance, but she had made a mistake today. Never pull a tiger's tail in person. Even the caged ones could be dangerous.

Behind him the doctor said, "There, that should hold, though you should go in and get a tetanus shot on Monday."

"Thank you."

Stern waited for Harding to join him, then heard his indrawn breath as they saw their "phantom" at the same moment. Approaching Audrey Dilmont. She'd chosen a good place to apply pressure. Clever girl but not clever enough.

"Get her." Harding started to clench his hands, but a sharp stab of pain reminded him why he shouldn't as he forcibly relaxed his fingers and waited for Stern to move to intercept. He had to keep her away from Audrey. And her beautiful little girls. He would not let the bitch ruin this for him. He needed their innocence like a junkie needed coke. It was his reality, his imperative, his life-giving air. There was no fighting it, he could only postpone it for a time. That time was running out.

Instead of following Stern, he stepped out onto the balcony. He was right above them. He could see Audrey's smile, see the question in her eyes as "Kerry Anne" stopped her.

"These are your daughters?" she asked in a rich Southern accent he'd thought lost in time and the warm, wet ground of Georgia. The rich timbre of it carried him back to those sultry nights when she'd been his—

"Amy and Simone." Audrey's voice, filled with the pride of a mother, was a cold shower on his hot memories. He saw his girls give brief, shy curtseys. So polite. So obedient. Just the way he liked them.

If Audrey could see the phantom, then she was flesh and bone that could be bruised and broken. He spotted Stern trying to work his way through a sudden flow of people heading for the refreshment tables. Picked a hell of a time to start serving food.

"Getting a new stepfather. How exciting." She was obscured by some damn tree. The branches hung between him and her, but he could see its leaves brush her cheek as she knelt in front of the little girls and smiled the smile he'd never thought to see again.

"Peter adores them, and they adore him," Audrey said.

"I'll bet he does," she said. "I heard he likes the young."

Kevin was relieved when the door opened under his hand, releasing him from the dark tunnel running between the buildings. It was only fear of what was behind him that had kept him walking forward in black darkness. He was surprised to find the matching storeroom dark, but it was lighter than the tunnel he'd left, thanks to a row of windows just at street level, and he moved forward without hesitation.

He eased around another set of boxes and unlocked this last gate. Once it was locked again, he turned to leave, but a hand clamped down on his shoulder, and a gun barrel was placed against his side.

"Gotcha," a voice said.

Chapter Seven

When Jake brought a handcuffed Kevin out the door of the other building, he saw a worried-looking Matt lower his radio.

Matt glared at him, then raised his radio to say, "Jake's got him. Get a forensics team over here ASAP." He looked at his brother with a noticeable lack of enthusiasm as Bryn came out the front door. "How the hell did you do it?"

Before Jake could answer him, Bryn said, "Let me guess. Magic?"

Jake grinned. "Let's take him back inside while we secure the premises."

Bryn signaled to a couple of men, who hustled the kid inside.

"Don't feed me that magic crap," Matt said. "How did you do it?"

"Talked to the super while I was waiting for you." Jake shrugged. "Told me there used to be a tunnel between the buildings, so I checked it out. When the kid bolted, I figured that's where he was headed."

"In other words, pure dumb luck," Matt said with a big brother's scorn.

"You wish." Jake held the door open before following him and Bryn inside.

Phoebe saw Barrett Stern pushing his way toward her. Above, Harding watched from the balcony, nursing his bandaged hand. Her work here was done. She blew Harding a kiss and saw him flinch. He'd always hated to be thwarted. It was his Achilles' heel, the pressure point they planned to jab over and over until he betrayed himself and gave them the game.

She'd have to gloat later though. The game would be over if Stern got his hands on her. He was covering ground quickly, despite the sudden surge toward the now-ready refreshment table. Phoebe picked up her pace, counting off the distance to the clubhouse in footsteps and heartbeats. There was always risk when you pulled the tiger's tail, but she didn't intend to be counted out just yet.

She passed through the door with quick thanks and a smile to the someone who might have been the attorney general of the state—who held the door for her and let it swing in Stern's face. The combination of gallantry and rudeness gave her just enough time to duck into the ladies' room ahead of his reaching hand. A couple of shocked women kept Stern from following her inside.

She made a face at him over their shoulders before the door swung closed, then ducked into a stall and started shedding Kerry Anne. Under Kerry's drifting dress she wore a sleek beige number that hugged her body like another skin. Out of a pocket came a bag that she stuffed the dress into. The wig she tossed down behind the toilet. The blue contacts came out. She peeled the white surface off her shoes, turning them beige to match the dress. She made sure no sign of the dress was poking out of the bag, fluffed her hair, and stepped out.

Three chattering women preceded her out the door where Stern waited, his thinning patience apparent in the chilling of his eyes. He didn't give Phoebe a second glance as she passed. In a moment she was outside. The limo pulled forward and Dewey opened the door for her. She pulled the door closed behind her and answered the questioning lift of his brows with a shrug and a smile.

"Any problems?"

"Nothing I couldn't handle." She didn't quite meet his glance and kept her hands pressed against the seat. Her heart was pounding, which made them tremble. It wasn't fear. There'd been no time for fear. It was pure adrenaline pumping through her veins. "He was wearing our rose on his lapel."

"And he sliced his hand open when he squeezed his glass too hard."

Phoebe twisted in the seat to stare at Dewey. "You just had to watch, didn't you?"

"Performance art is nothing without an audience, darling. Brava." He clapped three times, but his eyes looked worried. "He's a lot more unstable than I realized."

"The guy likes little girls, beating women and killing them. Exactly what made you think *stable* was a word that even remotely applied to him?"

Dewey grinned. "I guess it was that whole running-for-governor scenario. I mean, you sort of assume some level of stability, even factoring in the politician mentality."

"In other words, you didn't really think about it."

His grin was crooked. "Like you, I try not to."

She looked away. "Yeah. Well, what happens next?"

"You go back to your strumming and wailing, and I go help Kevin move. I'm having intimations of impending discovery."

Phoebe looked down the street as they turned the corner and saw the cop-filled block ahead. "I think your intimations were a little late."

"Damn."

"How bad are we screwed?"

"Hard to say. Kev's new to the game, but he doesn't want to go home. He'll hold, for a while anyway."

"So, he'll need a lawyer."

Dewey nodded. "Cold-hearted bitch or warmhearted public defender?"

Phoebe studied the truck mingling with the cop cars. There were lots like it, but not with the same tag as Jake's. "Cold-hearted bitch."

"Something in black?"

"With a touch of red."

Matt found Jake sitting in the kitchen of the apartment staring at three ice packs in evidence bags lined up in a row on the table as if they held the answer to some cosmic, universal question.

He looked up when Matt came in. "Everything all right?"

"Who knows." Matt picked one pack up by the corner. It slid limply to the bottom of the plastic bag. "Looks like somebody had a run-in with a door—or a fist."

"Yup."

Matt waited for more. When he didn't get it, he added, "So?"

"Look at this." Jake shoved the trash can toward him.

Matt looked inside. "Someone likes pistachios." He hesitated, then said again, "So?"

"Hyatt loves the things."

"Prints?"

"Everywhere." He turned back to the ice packs and rubbed his chin. "With a little luck, some will match Hyatt's." For expediency, Jake had brought a copy with him for comparison on site.

Matt stared at his brother. "I can keep trying to dig it out of you. I could pound it out of you. Or you could just tell me."

Jake looked up and grinned. "Sorry. I thought you could still read my mind. You always seemed to know when I was going out the window."

"That's 'cause Mom could read your mind and tipped me off."

Jake arched his brows. "Well, I'll be—"

"Do I need to get Mom in here to save your ass from me?" Matt snapped. He jerked a chair around and straddled it.

"Sorry. It's just, this morning I saw an ice pack and pistachios in Phoebe Mentel's kitchen." Jake shrugged. "Could be a coincidence."

Matt snorted.

The fingerprint tech stuck his head around the corner and said, "We got a match. It's your guy."

Jake looked at his brother.

Matt stood up and paced away, then turned back to his brother. "You'll need more than an ice pack and a few shells to get a search warrant on her place, but I'll concede, you got yourself an honest-to-goodness lead." He picked up one of the bags again and shook his head ruefully. "Damn, maybe you are magic."

It was a handsome admission, but Jake wasn't elated. He didn't want to be magic where Phoebe was concerned. She was gutsy and sweet in a prickly cactus kind of way. Put together in a very un-cactus kind of way. This wasn't the first time he'd felt attracted to a suspect or had regrets at taking one down. But it was the first time it felt like a betrayal. As if he were joining league with whoever had put the sad in her eyes. He didn't want to be the one to add another nail to her unhappiness coffin.

"You okay?" Matt broke into Jake's reverie.

Jake pulled out his grin and tried to shake away the ache in his chest that had the same insistence as a tooth going bad. "Sure. Heard anything about the kid's ID yet?"

Kevin's ID looked authentic but was probably more bogus than a hooker's orgasm—and would take longer than one to unmask if Phagan was running true to form.

"Not yet. I got Alice checking it out."

Jake nodded. "How's the kid doing?"

"He should be about to piss his pants," Matt said, easing the swinging door open so they could study him.

"Looks pretty cool to me," Jake observed. "Maybe he doesn't know he's been harboring and abetting a federal fugitive." Jake grinned. "Let's go tell him."

Matt gestured through the door. "After you, Mr. Magic."

Kevin watched the two Marshals approach and braced for the encounter. *Stick to the script,* he reminded himself, even as he felt sweat slick his body.

The two men stopped in front of him. He had to look a long way up to see their faces and found them filled with a detached pity. They didn't speak, just stood there looking down at him. Kevin fought a compulsion to fill the silence himself.

Don't speak until spoken to. Dewey's voice in his head, coaching him, gave him the courage to return their stares without speaking. Behind his back, he flexed his cuffed hands and reminded himself they didn't know his real name. As long as they didn't have that, they couldn't send him home.

When the silence was two beats past unbearable, the one called Matt asked, "Why'd you run, kid?"

"You can't question me without a lawyer. I know my rights." He tightened his lips against the other protests that wanted to leak out. *Keep your cool. You can't incriminate yourself if you keep your cool.* "You should read me my rights."

The one called Jake rubbed his chin, then sat down opposite Kevin, his elbows propped on his knees. In his hand was one of the ice packs Dewey had used to take down the swelling on his mouth.

"Ran into a wall," he'd joked, his grin more crooked than usual.

"What was his name?" Kevin had shot back.

"You'd be surprised." Dewey's smile had been amused enough to make him really curious.

The one called Bryn, the FBI agent, broke in on his thoughts with a hard insistence, "We don't have to read you your rights until we start questioning you."

Kevin frowned at this deviation from the script. "He asked me a question." His nerves were jumping like a grasshopper, and his voice tried to follow their lead. He made a valiant try to smooth it out, but puberty was against him, too.

"Well," Matt said, "there are questions, and there are *questions*."

"We're just making friendly conversation," Jake chimed in. He smiled as he tossed the ice pack up and down. Up and down.

Kevin tried not to follow the hypnotic motion, but it was like trying to stop the tide.

"You can join in or not, whatever you want," Jake added, snatching the ice pack out of the air and standing with a quick movement that made Kevin's heart leap in fear.

The three of them stared at him, their eyes relentless and unblinking. He could smell himself, smell his own fear, but he was cold, too, shuddering cold. In the silence, he heard the air conditioning switch on, working against him, too. He gritted his teeth when they showed signs of chattering but couldn't stop the shudders from shaking him and the couch he sat on.

"What—no, that would be a question," Jake said. He looked at Matt. "Never realized how hard it is to not ask a question."

Both men settled down on either side of him and gave him friendly smiles that didn't warm or remove fear. Kevin tried to relax, too, but it was hard to get comfortable with his hands cuffed behind him and his body jerking on its own rhythm. The need to shift, to move, to speak, grew in direct contrast to the utter stillness of the three of them as they stared at him.

"Let's just read him his rights, and then we can ask him whatever we want," Bryn said, looking at him like something she'd like to slice up and eat with salt.

"Not without a lawyer!" Kevin said before he could stop himself. To his annoyance his voice broke on *lawyer,* making him sound like a kid. He hunched into the couch and glared at them.

Jake leaned back, relaxing into the cushions, now tipping the ice pack from one side of the evidence bag to the other, as if the wet mass was somehow critical to life on earth or something.

Matt frowned and rubbed his chin. "I don't know. I kind of like to know who I'm reading and talking to before I do the rights reading."

Kevin was trying to figure out what this meant when the bag slipped from Jake's hands, thudding softly against the carpeted floor. Kevin jumped, heart and body. His insides twisted with the need to do something, anything but just sit there.

They'll try to do a good cop, bad cop on you. Try to get you to trust one of them. The nice one is as much your enemy as the mean one.

Jake shrugged. "Matt's got a point, Bryn. Wouldn't want to give a lawyer a loophole to slide him through. Kid's so puny, it wouldn't have to be a big loophole."

"So," Bryn asked, "what's your name, kid?"

"You know my name!" The ID was his Achilles' heel and Kevin couldn't stop the words bursting out. "You got my ID!"

"This?" Jake held up Kevin's wallet, open to his license.

Kevin nodded and Jake held it out, as if comparing the photo with the real person. "It's nice work. Almost looks real."

"Almost—it *is* real! You—" Kevin swallowed the words, his cuffed hands clenched in support of his fight for control. This wasn't supposed to happen.

"We know you're not Kevin Jones any more than I'm Barney Google with the googly eyes," Matt said, rising to stand over him with his arms crossed over his powerful chest, the same way his mom's new husband did before he popped him one.

Kevin cowered against the couch, waiting for the blow to fall.

"That's goo-goo-googly eyes," Jake corrected Matt with utter sobriety.

"Really?" Matt looked at his brother. "You sure?"

"As sure as I am this is crap," Jake said, tossing the wallet onto the coffee table in front of Kevin.

The wallet flopped open, the ID photo staring up at him. *Kevin Jones* it said. *Your name for now,* Dewey had said. *Roger's gone forever. Going forward won't always be easy, but you never have to go back. Trust me. They are always on our heels, but if you hang on, we'll be there to bail you out.*

Kevin looked at Jake, then at Matt. In both faces he found no mercy, but some pity. He looked at Bryn and found no mercy in her face or her eyes. She leaned forward. "We don't want you. We just want Hyatt. Give him to us and you can go home."

Home. When hell froze over he'd let them send him home. Now he knew who he trusted and who he didn't.

"I want a lawyer."

Jake sat back with a sigh. They'd almost had him. He'd seen it in the kid's eyes. Until Bryn mentioned home. He studied him, noticing now that he was looking for it, the almost faded bruises on his face.

Damn it.

Through the window of the interrogation room, Matt and Jake watched Kevin pace around the small room. He looked nervous, but resolute.

Matt looked at Jake, one brow cocked. "What's scarier than we are?"

Jake rubbed the back of his neck. "Home?"

"Damn." Matt looked less than thrilled.

"No kidding." Jake leaned against the wooden frame of the one-way glass. The kid was probably newly inducted into Phagan's operation. Jake explained to Matt that besides thieving, Phagan also ran an extensive underground operation that helped runaways the way society was supposed to. This inspired an almost fanatical loyalty and made the kids impossible to turn. All they had to offer them was a trip into foster care or a return to their nightmare.

"So the only way to crack him is to be worse than whoever was beating him?" Matt asked, sounding rightly uncomfortable. "Great."

"If we wait for Bryn," Jake said wryly, "she can do bad Fed for us."

He heard a cough behind him. They turned around.

"Neither of you," Bryn said, "were spanked enough when you were little, were you?"

Jake grinned. "I'm not spanked enough now."

He could see her struggle, but she did manage to hold back an answering grin.

"Take it on the road, or let's go crack the kid before Phagan sends in a lawyer to—"

Before Bryn got her hand on the doorknob, Jake saw his biggest brother, Luke. He was an older version of Matt, more weathered, but a tad softer. Not that Jake spent much time comparing his brothers. How could he when next to Luke was a . . . woman. No, he thought, dazed. Make that a *woman.*

Dressed in sexy, slinky black, she sliced through air and space like a weapon, wearing heels so high she should have needed oxygen. Her dark hair swung on either side of green eyes and a mouth so red it almost made his eyes bleed just looking at it.

"Kid's lawyer," Luke said, trying not to laugh.

She was close enough now for Jake to see that she had nothing on under the power-suit jacket. He almost went up on his toes to confirm this, but his toes lacked the needed stiffness, which was all concentrated in one central place in his body.

Jake knew he needed to say something, anything, but nothing sprang to mind except "Damn!" Couldn't say that out loud. Actually, he wasn't sure he could say anything at all. The moisture in his throat and eyes went right up in the smoke of her gaze. Nothing he could do to get it back. He just felt lucky his eyes didn't fall out and roll across the floor, where she could impale them with her heels.

He sort of knew that Bryn was staring at him, but that didn't stop his jaw from dropping or his tongue from trying to fall out the opening. When the lawyer passed him, he turned in concert with his brothers and watched her move through the door to the interrogation room.

The kid looked as shocked as Jake felt, but at least the glass provided Jake with a small measure of protection—enough for his power of speech to return anyway, he thought, rubbing the back of his neck. At least he was hoping it would return.

"I'd like to be a fly on the wall in there," Matt said, not quite flattening himself against the glass but not far from it.

"That wall." Luke pointed to the one that would give the best view of the lawyer's impressive cleavage.

Jake laughed and found it helped clear his head. Bryn's frown further boosted the process. "What I'd like to know," he said, "is how she knew the kid needed a lawyer when he hasn't made his call or even been formally charged yet?"

That got Matt and Luke's attention, but Bryn was the one with the answer.

"Classic Phagan maneuver. We gotta find a way to block bail or we'll never see the kid again."

Matt and Luke paused in their gawking to give Bryn politely incredulous looks. Her answering smile lacked humor.

"Trust me. This guy could make the Statue of Liberty disappear," she said.

Luke rubbed his face and scowled at the oblivious lawyer through the glass. "Like to help you take this Phagan bastard and his gang down. Hate people who prey on abused kids."

Jake felt his defenses come up at his brother's words, but before he could speak in Phoebe's possible defense Bryn said with more than a hint of defensiveness in her own voice, "He doesn't exactly prey on them. At least, not the way you're thinking."

Both Jake's brothers turned to stare at her as if they couldn't quite believe what they were hearing. They were so much alike, that it was almost spooky.

Bryn was still staring at Kevin and his lawyer, so she didn't know she was in trouble yet. "You're thinking he's like Fagan in Oliver Twist but it's not like that at all. He also, well, helps them."

The silence that followed these words seeped into her distraction and alerted her too late to the danger. With lifted chin she turned to face their amusement.

"Are you saying," Luke asked, "he's a *good* thief?"

She stared at him for a long moment before replying with tight annoyance, "Of course not. But, well, he does get these kids in school, he finds them places to live, helps them become . . . useful citizens." The polite incredulity in his brothers faces slowed her down some, Jake noted with an inward grin. "At least, that's what the word on the street is. His actual . . . band . . . of thieves is a very small, very limited . . . group. And their targets are not even close to being upstanding citizens."

She kept her chin up and gave them a cold stare, then turned back to the window, leaving Jake to grin at his brothers.

"Actually,"—Jake offered a bit of support, since he happened to agree with her—"their targets are downright gnarly."

"And if," Luke asked, "we figure out who their current target is here, we have to protect them?"

Jake nodded, noting out of the corner of his eye that Bryn started to say something, but then stopped. He made a mental note to probe this later, when they were alone.

"Well, that sucks."

Jake nodded again.

"Maybe we shouldn't try so hard here?"

Matt shook his head as if he couldn't quite believe their attitude. "If we identify their target, how about we take him out ourselves?" He pointed his hard gaze at Luke, then at Jake before asking, "I supposed you've tried to infiltrate?"

"Of course." This question put Bryn back on more comfortable ground. "But we couldn't come up with a cover deeper than Phagan could penetrate. We even tried using actual runaways."

"What happened?" Luke asked.

Bryn compressed her lips into a grim line, then opened

them far enough to admit, "He turned them. He has a reputation for being quite the . . . charmer."

It was obvious to a blind man that this was touchy ground for Bryn, and neither Jake nor his brothers were blind. As one they all gave silent whistles and turned to the far more fruitful activity of pondering the wickedly attractive lawyer in the interrogation room, who now had Kevin grinning like an idiot.

Phoebe closed her briefcase and stood up to leave. When the curtain of her hair swung forward to cover her face, she told Kevin, "They'll move you to juvvie after I get done with them. Hang tight. We'll have you out of there before they can spoil your palate."

Kevin stood up and wiped his hand on the side of his ragged jeans before taking the hand she held out to him. "Uh, thanks."

His voice cracked in the middle, but Phoebe pretended not to notice. She'd stayed longer with Kevin than she'd planned to, because of a mix of pity for his obvious terror and her own self preservation. She'd needed the time to achieve internal equilibrium again. She could feel Jake watching her through the one-way window. Cold-hearted bitch had definitely been the right choice.

It had been quite a shock to come face to face with him, especially so close on the heels of running into his brother the DPD cop. Jeez, looked like the whole family was into law enforcement, though she still wasn't sure exactly what Jake was. She sure knew how to pick a guy to lust after. If Phagan ever found out, there'd be no virtual reality peace for her ever again.

She gave Kevin's clammy hand one last, comforting squeeze, squared her shoulders and turned to face her problem. At least she'd soon know exactly what he was and what she was up against.

The impact of Jake's gaze was every bit as unnerving as she'd expected it to be. To avoid direct eye contact, she pulled out fake business cards and handed them around.

"He's got nothing to say," Phoebe said in a clipped northeastern accent that she'd picked up on a gig with the band many years ago, "and you'd better move him to juvenile detention or your asses are grass. I feel certain that you'll charge him within the required time?"

With smiles that were half dazed, half admiring, and one that was very bitter, the three men and one woman handed her their cards.

Luke signaled to a uniform. "Move the kid to juvenile," he directed, then turned back to Phoebe. "You'll be the first to know when we file charges, ma'am."

"Thank you." She turned and found Jake looking at her, a frown between his wild-boy brows. Time to get the heck out of Dodge before he figured out what puzzled him. It took all her control not to let any sign of recognition light her glassy green eyes. Her fingers gripped the handle of the briefcase so tightly that her arm ached. Turning away from him was like breaking free of gravity. She didn't lose the force of his pull until she was outside.

Dewey was waiting, but she wished he wasn't. She needed time and some space to regroup. During that Maine gig, where she'd acquired the accent, she'd taken an early-morning walk down to the wild, rocky shoreline. The wind roaring in from the sea had almost knocked her back on her heels. She'd dug in and taken the buffeting until she was tired enough to sleep again.

That's how she felt now, only this time the wind wasn't coming from just one direction. It was hard to dig in her heels against this multi-directional buffeting. Her instinct was to hit the ground and hope it all would pass her by, but that instinct had to be suppressed. She'd brought this on herself by trailing her cloak in front of Harding. As always, there was no retreating, only forward until some kind of ending was reached. Then it wouldn't matter what happened.

She felt the sun's light hit her without giving warmth. She missed warm, missed the warm she'd felt around Jake. There was tonight, she reminded herself. He was meeting her at the bar. It wasn't wise to look forward to it, now that she knew he was a federal marshal. Course, if she'd been wise, she wouldn't be getting into a limo next to a thief.

This made her smile as she climbed in beside Dewey.

"I take it things went well?"

"He'll hold," Phoebe said. "But he's made some interesting new friends." She handed him the business cards she'd collected. She should tell him about Jake, but she didn't think she could without giving away more than she was ready to.

Dewey studied the cards, his eyebrows arching like rising half-moons. "Impressive. Kev's definitely hit the big time."

"The woman and this guy," she tapped Jake's card, careful to keep her voice neutral, "were at the bar last night. You may have noticed them, too. She left with Jesse and he was my ride."

Dewey made a face. "The flyers. Phagan thought he got them all. He won't be happy to know he didn't."

"I called Phagan from the pay phone in the hall. I know better."

"Hey, hounds have been closer than this. Don't sweat it. Just do what you do best. Find us our next step forward."

The next step? She frowned. Their game was picking up the pace. She could feel it the same way she felt an avalanche coming. They needed to move faster or they'd get buried. "You got your phone with you? I need to call Phagan."

He pulled it out of his jacket pocket and pushed the power button, then gave it a shake. "Guess I let the battery run down. Sorry."

Phoebe leaned forward and opened the glass between them and the driver. "Pull over here and wait."

She slid out, leaving Dewey alone in the car. He pulled the door to and watched her walk over to the pay phone, her walk hitting somewhere between the bitch lawyer and Phoebe. She fed it coins, punched in the number and a few seconds later his cell phone rang. Sometimes he thought he should just tell Phoebe he was Phagan. But, he reminded himself, it protected them both. As long as she didn't know who he was, she wouldn't have to choose between her freedom and his if the Feds picked her up.

He fitted a voice synthesizer over the mouth of the phone and then pushed Send.

"Yeah."

"The missing one returns," Phoebe said, her voice sardonic and relieved. "Jeez, Phagan, things are popping here. Not a good time to go AWOL."

"There's never a good time to go AWOL, darlin'," he said, grinning when he saw her shake her head.

She leaned against the side of the phone booth and rubbed her face, her wry smile briefly lighting her face.

"What you gonna do about it?"

"I think we need to move up the timetable." They'd planned to hit TelTech the night before Harding was due to turn RABBIT over to the military, shooting for maximum embarrassment, but she could tell in her gut that things weren't going to hold together until then.

"When?"

"Tomorrow. I think we need to move tomorrow."

"Okay. You want to tell Dewey or should I?"

"He's waiting for me in the car." She hesitated, then added with sudden mischief, "I met your Fed. You know, she's more likely to kick your ass than jump your bones."

She hung up before he could bite back. He quickly stowed the phone. "Smart-ass. I knew you'd figure that out." He sighed. "Wish you weren't likely to be right about my Fed."

He leaned forward and told the driver, "Find me a flower shop."

Phoebe heard him as she scrambled back in beside him. "Don't tell me you're in love, too?" she asked, sliding in next to him and closing the door. "You and Phagan will have to start a club."

He grinned. "I won't. And we won't." He leaned back. "So what did Phagan say?"

Chapter Eight

Jake stared after the lawyer, his instincts screaming a message he didn't quite understand. Or maybe he didn't want to understand. Because what he was feeling just wasn't possible, was it?

Behind him he heard Bryn saying, "Somebody check this name and address. See if she's local. If she's not—" She didn't have to spell it out for them. If her ID was bogus, she was a link to Phagan, however tenuous. "Check this card she gave me. You should be able to get her thumb and index. Also, check here where she touched the door knob, the table and the chair she pulled out and sat in. Get me a good set of latent prints and I'll buy you a round at the local bar. Get me a real name to go with them and I'll have your child."

Jake heard their chuckles but from far away as his brain played with the pieces of the puzzle, trying to find a pattern. The bar. The game seemed to be shifting to Denver, but he still felt JR's was important. Or did he just want to keep his promise to meet Phoebe there later? Wasn't like him to lose his focus in the middle of the hunt. Or was his focus getting clouded? It was obvious someone besides him was interested in the bar. Could it be someone sent by Phagan's current target?

Okay. Phagan targeted people who hurt kids. If past patterns were any indication, it wasn't enough to just hurt them. He'd want his target to know who was after him and why. Not too surprisingly and on the advice of their lawyers, Phagan's past targets weren't talking about their experiences with him. No information available on whether Phagan engaged in a little judicious gas lighting prior to the main move. If he were Phagan, it's what he'd do, even if an alert target was harder to move on.

Just thinking about Phoebe's being involved in something so dangerous sent cold chills down Jake's back.

Queen to king's three.

Her beeper message abruptly came back to his mind, this time weighted with more significance. Was it really a chess move, or a call to some other action? There'd been no chess set at her office and he hadn't seen one at her house this morning.

If the king were the target . . .

The queen was a key piece.

Was this *Phoebe's* game? Or was she Phagan's Pathphinder? Damn.

Their initial investigation on Phoebe Mentel had turned up no sign of criminal priors, but that didn't mean much. With Phagan involved, Phoebe wouldn't be her real name. In the Phagan band's past priors there was no hint of a woman. Despite their care and obvious expertise, the FBI had picked up Dewey Hyatt, Ollie Smith and a couple of the runaway kids. Hadn't managed to hang on to them, but they had been picked up. If Phoebe was Pathphinder, as he was beginning to suspect more and more, then it was possible that her role was that of planner, strategist, not active participant.

Until now.

She was one tough lady, but she wasn't superwoman. He could feel the heat, the subdued rumble of trouble about to blow out of control, more trouble than even she could manage. That's what his gut was telling him, and he always trusted his gut.

"What you gonna do?" Matt asked him.

"Heading back to JR's and keep a close eye on the lady singer. She's gonna make a move soon and I plan to be there when she does."

A pat down for his keys helped him avoid his brother's eyes. He found the keys halfway through a long pause. Nothing for it but to look up. Some things couldn't be avoided. His brother's eyes were among those things.

"What?" he asked, resenting the fact that his brother could still make him feel defensive and about fifteen years old.

"What's going on?" Matt asked.

"What's always going on—the hunt."

"Just the hunt?"

Jake met his brother's probe squarely. "Just the hunt."

It wasn't a lie. Even if he felt something for Phoebe, there was nothing he could do about it except follow the rules. Jake followed the rules. Always.

"Call me," Matt ordered.

"It'll be late. Don't think Dani would appreciate the wee-small wake up," Jake said in lieu of agreement as he headed out the door.

"Call me."

Jake stopped, his shoulders rising in a sigh as big as Phoebe's Texas. He looked back. "You're worse than Mom."

"That's 'cause I'm bigger and meaner."

He had a point. Jake grinned. "I'll call you."

He waited until his back was to his brother to mentally add, *when I'm damn good and ready*. He tossed his keys up and neatly caught them coming down. A pretty policewoman coming into the building smiled back at him.

Jake held the door for her, then promptly forgot her as his thoughts turned once more to Phoebe and JR's. Those thoughts were as twisted as the road back to Estes Park, and like some bizarre version of a Monopoly game where all moves led to jail, with the Get-Out-Of-Jail-Free cards in the hot hands of Bryn Bailey—who was never generous in passing them out.

Bryn hadn't said much about her investigative efforts today but he had a feeling she had a good lead to Phagan's target but didn't want to talk about it, either in the police station or in front of his brothers. He'd dig it out of her later.

Jake turned his truck into the parking lot at JR's, surprised to find Phoebe's SUV missing. It was well past the time for the band's sound check. It didn't seem like her to be late.

Inside JR's he found two Mentel boys hunkered down in front of the bar nursing a couple of beers. The other two were hanging from the ceiling with climbing gear.

Jake had known guys like that, climbers who just weren't comfortable unless they were suspended over something. Once again, Jake was struck by what a pretty group of boys they were. No wonder girls flocked around them like buzzards to a carcass.

All four returned Jake's examination with varying degrees of interest, ranging from the outright bored to the mildly curious.

"You seen Phoebe Ann?" her ex-husband asked Jake. "Ain't like her to be late for a sound check."

Jake shook his head. Worry took a big bite of his gut and held on like a pit bull. Maybe he should have stayed on her tail instead of following the con. "Not since this morning."

The one called Toes lowered a bag to his cousin at the bar, drawing it back up when it held a couple of beers. "Think she headed into Denver," he said. "Something about needing strings for her guitar."

So she had been in Denver today. Trouble was, he couldn't see how she could have pulled off what he suspected she'd pulled off. How she could change herself that much?

How she could face him down in the freaking police station without even a flicker of nerves? It didn't seem possible. So far the prints Bryn had collected had turned up a big, fat negative match with Bryn's Phagan gang files but it would take several days to get a definitive answer back from the national database.

Leg spun himself in a slow circle, snagging one of the beers as he went by. "One of the amps is acting up, too."

Their comments reinforced his initial impression that Phoebe was the linchpin that held this group together. The insight aroused his professional interest as much as her earthy sensuality aroused his body.

"Wouldn't she call if she was running late?"

From the doorway, Phoebe watched the guys look at each other. Finally, Mert said, "Dunno. We're usually the ones who are late."

"Well, that's surely God's truth," she said. She stared at the waiting men, holding herself erect with an effort. She was both glad and sad to see that Jake had beaten her here. She'd wanted to see him as bad as she needed air, but not yet. Not without some time to put Phoebe back together. She'd been too many people today. She felt fragmented, her hold on Phoebe uncertain and fragile.

With the lights behind him, Jake's eyes were in shadow, but the light still managed to find all that buried gold in his hair, then slide forward to stroke some of that gold along the strong, smooth jaw line. It also threw into sharp relief the strength and grace of his body.

Longing slid through her veins, a semi-painful tingle of life returning to a sleeping limb. Why him? Why was he the one to make her feel what she shouldn't?

For a brief instant the fog in her head cleared and Pathphinder got a clear view of the two courses available to her. One, bright and enticing, leading directly to Jake. One, dark and dangerous, leading away from him forever.

Only the choice was an illusion. She was already on Phagan's path, and there was no way to leave it. There was no way to get to him from where she was. Her choice, if she could call it that, had been made long before this day, this time, this longing. She'd see this game to its finish and then disappear into Phagan's shadow world again, leaving even her memories behind. If she survived.

She lifted her chin, straightened her back and walked toward Jake, but she was really walking away from him. It hurt more than she'd expected, but her mind, her body was already adapting to the loss and the pain.

She'd had plenty of practice.

With Jake's gaze on her, she dug deep for resolve and approached him.

Jake let her come to him, noting with concern the brittle quality that hadn't been there earlier. It put his senses on alert as she stopped, her gaze meeting his for a long moment that put the heat on under his heart.

"You all right?"

She nodded, then looked at the guys. "It's late. Let's get this over with."

"You're a hard woman," Mert grumbled good-naturedly as he lowered himself from his piton perch.

"You got that right," she said, sounding as if she were passing sentence on herself.

It didn't take them long to get their instruments ready, once a broken guitar string had been replaced and the amp fiddled with. Jake noted the store logo on the bag Phoebe pulled the replacement string from—it was in Denver—even as he admired the comfortable confidence with which she mobilized her boys. Chet came in with his radio on, playing a

Wynona Judd song. He quickly turned it off, but the band picked up the tune, and turned it into their warm up song. The segue was smooth between radio and real life. Too smooth. Close his eyes and he couldn't tell the difference between Phoebe and Judd. The band switched gears, and it happened again. This time she sounded like Martina McBride. In quick succession she crossed a wide range of the voice spectrum of female singers. It was uncanny. It was . . . enlightening, and made him feel a lot less crazy about suspecting Phoebe of being Pathphinder.

They stopped to let Jesse work on his C-string, and Jake knew he had to probe a bit. "Is it just me," he asked, carrying his soft drink closer to their tiny stage, "or did you just sound like Martina McBride?"

Phoebe's head came up, like that of a wild thing scenting danger, but her eyes showed no fear, no emotion, when Toes grinned and said, "Our Phoebe is a first-rate mime."

Leg looked up from his keyboard. Jesse shook his head sadly as he explained, "Kid's young."

Toes looked around. "What?"

"A mime," explained Mert, "is what Phoebe almost slugged in New Orleans that time."

Jake looked at Phoebe, who shrugged and smiled. "He made an obscene gesture," she explained.

"Oh." Toes looked crestfallen. "So what's Phoebe?"

"I think," Jake said, holding Phoebe's gaze with his, "the word you're looking for is mimic. Phoebe's a very . . . good . . . mimic."

Phoebe smiled, her eyes neither denying nor confirming his suspicion. "Only very good? You're a tough critic."

Jake managed a slight grin, but inside he was wishing everything were completely different. Next to her, Jesse's long-fingered hands pulled a gentle ballad from the strings of his guitar. The others filled in the holes, loosing love's lament into the big, empty hall.

Phoebe tried to resist the song's invitation to give in to feeling and failed miserably. With a fatalistic shrug, she put down her instrument and leaped lightly from the stage, landing a few feet from Jake. There was harm in it, but not too much, what with the guys watching her every move. Of their own volition, her feet started her toward him. The closer she got, the more fluid she felt. The pain melted away, leaving only anticipation. She wanted to be in his arms. She had to be in his arms or die. It was as simple as that. She had to clear the huskiness from her throat before she could get the words out. "Dance with me, curious Jake."

Jake's throat went dry at the husky-voiced invitation. She stood motionless, but the air around her pulsed with an ancient, unmistakable need.

"I never get to dance," she said.

It would have been easier to stop breathing than say no. He couldn't do either, so he held out his hand, felt his breath catch as her fingers meshed with his, her other hand settling on his shoulder like a pigeon come home. He pulled her closer, leaving a single important inch between their bodies to salve his conscience as his hand cupped her waist, half on cotton, half on skin left bare by her brief top.

It felt right to have her in his arms. Like she'd always belonged there.

They began a shuffle that could be taken for dancing by someone on drugs. No one led. No one followed. He didn't look at her. Knew she wasn't looking at him.

As the song wound toward a climax, he couldn't stop his gaze from doing a slow slide in her direction. He breathed in her scent, felt her body heat arc that single inch that separated them. His gaze found hers, dark with longing. On some level his brain registered that his nostrils were smelling a lingering trace of expensive lawyer mixed with her usual clean scent. Another link in the evidence chain toward her, but he didn't care. His arms were full of woman. The right woman. The only woman, he was afraid, for him.

The music died away. They stopped shuffling. He stared at her, wanting to say something, but before he could think of anything, her lashes drooped, shutting her longing from his view. She stepped back, her hand sliding free of his.

He wanted to hold on, to pull her back. He didn't.

"You out there, Phoebe?" Jesse asked, trying to peer past the footlights to their shadows.

"Yeah, I'm here." She turned and walked away from Jake.

He wasn't sure what was worse—that she could do it or that he could let her.

Stern stood staring into the dark, smoking and thinking, while behind him Harding argued with someone on the phone. The smoke soothed as he mulled the situation.

The sun was setting over the city and, it seemed, on Harding. It was becoming increasingly obvious that he wasn't going to be able to hold it together. It was a pity. He had the right stuff to be a serious contender in the political power game. Charm, ruthlessness, native wit and "vision." A pity he had that dark side that so many of the bright ones seemed cursed with.

Power, real power, was a balancing act that required the holder to never let one factor overwhelm the others. Once balance was gone, a long fall was inevitable.

Stern had done well with Harding, but he wasn't about to go down with him. Not for something as stupid as a sexual addiction the asshole couldn't control. Not to mention the nasty temper.

Behind him Harding slung the phone back onto its cradle with a mumbled curse. Stern turned and found him sprawled in his chair looking like a sulky teenager.

"So, Billy thinks the woman could be Nadine?" Harding asked.

Stern nodded, lifting the cigarette and inhaling deeply.

"Go get her. I want . . . to see her with my own eyes. Be sure. This time I want to be sure she won't ever be a problem again."

Sure, that's why he wanted to see her. And I'm blind, deaf and stupid. Stern stubbed out his cigarette. Smoke spiraled up from the stub where an A/C current caught it and dispersed it—not unlike the chilling reality bringing his association with Harding to an end. He'd bring the girl back, not because Harding wanted her, but because, by messing with Harding, she'd messed with him. No one messed with him without paying a price. Harding would settle part of the bill. And when Harding finished with the girl, she would beg him to kill her.

He would. Eventually.

He headed for the door, feeling an odd sense of anticipation at the coming meeting. Been a long time since he'd had an adversary this talented. Should be an interesting encounter.

"Stern?"

Stern stopped at the door but didn't look back. He knew what was coming.

"No more waiting. We go tomorrow night."

We? Stern bit back a pointed reminder that Harding would be sitting it out safely on the sidelines. Asshole already knew how Stern felt about pushing up the timing, so there was no point in arguing it further.

As if Stern *was* arguing with him, Harding said, "I never

did like the idea of having RABBIT get grabbed the night before we were supposed to turn it over. General Hadley's sure to smell a rat."

"You think a couple of days is going to affect his sense of smell?" Stern turned, shoving his hands in the pockets of his ill-made suit. He could pull his guys together, but they wouldn't like doing it as a rush job any more than he did. "Bromfield might still get the damn thing to work."

"No," Harding shook his head. "He won't. He's as big an idiot as the others. Make him disappear. He knows too much."

"People who know things *are* dangerous."

Harding looked sharply at Stern. Stern met his with a look kept carefully blank, before spinning on his heels and striding out.

Harding waited until he heard the distant swish of the elevator before saying softly to himself, "Yes, they are, my . . . friend."

Did Stern think he hadn't noticed the way he'd been watching him? Or the vibrations of unease between them? He hadn't gotten this far by not knowing when to trust. And when not to.

He unlocked a drawer of his desk and pulled out a hand gun. He checked the clip, making sure it was full, then shoved it back into place and returned the gun in the drawer.

"People who know things are very dangerous, my . . . friend."

Now that she was committed to making the move on TelTech, Phoebe was aware that her life as Phoebe Mentel could be counted in hours. Twenty-four, to be exact.

With sharpened clarity, she picked up her guitar and looked out at the foot-stomping, hand-clapping patrons waiting for the first twanging note. She couldn't call them friends—she couldn't have friends—but they were familiar strangers who had been a part of her life for several years. She would miss them, and she would miss her guys. She would miss singing with them, climbing with them, laughing with them, even fending off their occasional advances. They'd made her feel real when grief had left her hollow and wanting. They'd filled her with their buoyant life force and let her hide in their shadows. They'd been her family, and it grieved her to leave them without explanation or farewell. They deserved better, but they couldn't know anything and would never understand if they did. The Feds on her tail would come down on them hard but would eventually have to admit the guys didn't know anything and let them go. As long as none of them hit anyone.

Did she dare give them a hint, a warning not to lose it? It worried her, wondering how they would manage without her, but they would learn. Even if she did stay, she wouldn't be around to help them anyway. She'd be in jail. And, knowing them, they'd try to bust her out and end up behind bars, too.

And then there was Jake.

She didn't want to look at him through jail bars. For the brief now, she could see him across the sea of heads, see him watching her from the bar. When he caught her gaze, he lifted his can in a discreet toast. It hurt to think of never seeing him again. She didn't know how it had happened that he'd come to matter so much, but there was nothing to be done now but live with it.

She'd had lots of practice at living with things.

Leg gave her a discreet nudge and she realized the guys were all looking at her, wondering why she didn't start the set. She gave the nod for the last time, and they launched into their opening number, her fingers flying across the strings with angst-driven precision. Luckily the song was fast enough and loud enough to make thinking damn near impossible. After a time, the music smoothed over the rough edges and carried her along. It was easier to ride the sound, to ride the surface. Just this once, she took the easy way. Hey, there was no one to tell her she couldn't. Besides, it wouldn't last. Nothing seemed to, except maybe the pain. That outlasted everything.

Other than a brief run during the last set to bring back Chinese food, Jake watched the whole show from his seat at the bar. Chet didn't push him to buy drinks, as if sensing that something bigger than drinks was on the line. There was an air of finality about Phoebe that no one but Jake seemed aware of.

She was getting ready to move, to act. But on what? All night he sat discarding plans to stop her from going so heedlessly into the danger zone. He knew in his gut that he didn't have the power to stop her. God probably couldn't stop her, he decided. She was one hell of a woman.

He knew he was losing her, either to the shadow world or to jail. It might be a body blow he couldn't recover from. There were, he believed, people who were meant to be together. Like his mom and dad. Like Matt and Dani. Like Luke and his Rosemary that he'd lost to cancer. A perfect fit was rare in this world of disposable marriages. If you found your perfect fit, you sure as hell didn't let her go.

Just his tough luck to find his perfect match singing in a honky-tonk and involved in some kind of high-tech heist on some rich asshole who might be under observation by Bryn and her FBI cronies. If Bryn did know the target, as he suspected, then she had a good chance of catching Phoebe in the act. Captivity would, he knew for sure, be hell for her, a hell she might not survive. If the sad in her eyes were any indication, life had already given her some good, hard kicks. Did it have to administer the final, soul-killing blow? Did he have to watch?

The music called him from his dark thoughts. She'd never played better. Somehow he knew that, though his days with her could be counted in the single digits. No one left the bar until the final note sounded, and then they left in reluctant bunches. Jake waited until the stage and room were clear to commandeer a table for the Chinese food. He spread it out and then took a chair where he could watch for her. He didn't have a lot of memories to take with him into the future. No sense passing up even one.

"It won't be long now," Stern said. With his two best guys, Harley and Farley Hicks, he sat in his car in the shadows cast by two huge evergreens, watching as the full parking lot emptied until only two vehicles were left. The SUV, he knew, belonged to Phoebe Mentel, who might or might not be Nadine. The other was the Fed's truck. He didn't like messing with a Fed, but when you were already screwing over the military, it seemed nit-picking to worry about it.

He didn't mention it to his boys, though. The thought of a death sentence if they got caught might mess with their aim.

A bag crackled as Farley stowed it, wiped his hands on his polyester pants and checked his weapon. Farley was a large man, partly because of his passion for junk food and partly because of his gene pool. His father had been a pro wrestler who married his mother after she whipped his ass in a mud-wrestling ring. Evidently his family liked to be dominated, which made him the natural choice for lieutenant in Stern's private army.

His brother, Harley, was his younger duplicate in everything but IQ, which made him a good soldier. Harley finished a bottle of Yahoo and got out his gun.

Stern screwed a silencer onto the end of his. "There's a rear entrance and one window on the right. Farley, you take the back door. Harley, you get the window. There'll be one guy with her. Take him out, but not the girl. We need the girl alive." He checked the clip before adding, "Bruising is optional."

Phoebe found Jake waiting for her by a table cluttered with distinctive white cartons. The odors of the evening retreated in the face of his personal, oh-so-male scent which filled her nostrils and her insides with painful desire.

"I hope you like Chinese," Jake said. His voice was husky, as if they were already ripping each other's clothes off.

The vision was so real, for a moment she wondered if she'd acted on it.

"What's not to like?" She cleared her head before she said, "Let me lock up."

Her looking had to last a lifetime, so she walked backward reaching behind her to snap the lock into place and reduce the lighting to one beam on the table and Jake. In the shadows, she let her eyes be hungry and longing, then reined it in for the walk back to him. At least she thought she'd reined it in, but the closer she got to him, the more her body throbbed for him, for the painful peace of passion acted on. She wanted him so badly it hurt like a sore tooth *not* to do something.

She stopped on the opposite side of the table. If somebody didn't do something—

Somebody did.

In the heated silence, they both heard the sound of a silenced gun fired into the flimsy front door lock.

Chapter Nine

Passion exited abruptly as Jake's training took over. Before the sound of the lock breaking faded away, he had his gun out and was taking aim at the light. Phoebe shook her head. "Wait."

She was right. No reason to warn the intruders they were armed.

"Is there another way out of here?"

Before she could answer, they heard glass shatter from the direction of her office, followed almost immediately by the sound of the back door being kicked open.

"This way," she said, heading for the dubious cover of the bar.

The front door gave just as they reached the bar. Jake crouched down beside Phoebe and realized she was still one step ahead of him when she opened a panel to reveal the breaker box. He only had time to grin at her before she took out the lights. That left only a triangle of light just inside the door.

"Phone's dead," she said, her lips against his ear.

"I've got a cell phone."

"Let's find some better cover first."

She was right, behind the bar was the first place anyone would look for them.

"We could use another gun."

"As much fun as it would be to be in a shoot-out at JR's bar with you, I think we can do this with less mess."

"They'll have the exits covered."

"Not this one." She shifted closer, until he could feel her

body against his. "You said you can climb?"

His eyes were adjusting to the pitch black. Now he could see her outline against the reflection from a row of bottles. He nodded, wondering if she could see the movement.

She could. She'd always been able to see like a cat in the dark. Despite this highly useful skill, Phagan had refused to let her participate in their real heists—until now.

She touched his arm, then followed it down until she found his hand, their fingers meshing like yin and yang. It touched her that he didn't hesitate to follow where she led. Not many men would have, particularly when it became apparent she was leading him into a corner.

It was too dark to see her but he felt the warmth from her body when she stopped.

Behind them, the search was heating up. Flashlights flickered in the back rooms, coming closer. She took Jake's hand and placed it against the log wall, urging him forward until he could feel the junction of the logs. "We can climb up to the support beams and get out the roof access panel."

Jake started climbing. She was glad he didn't waste time with any ladies-first crap. The guy knew his stuff, knew he'd be in a better position to provide cover above her than below. As soon as he was higher than her head, Phoebe started up, too, the path a familiar one for her. She'd raced the guys up every corner in this room. Most of the time she'd won. She made the beam before two flashlights stabbed white light into the main room. The intruders found the bar. Footsteps moved that way, separating to cover both ends.

She tapped Jake's arm and pointed toward the center of the ceiling where all the beams came together. It wasn't a perfect path—they'd be moving toward danger and if they were heard, they'd be exposed and vulnerable—but it was better than the inevitable shoot-out. Jake nodded, gesturing for her to go first.

Phoebe had walked this beam at least a hundred times, but never without light. She wished she'd had time to take off her boots. She did better when she could feel the surface with her feet. It was slow going, trying to place her boots squarely without making a sound. She sensed, more than heard, Jake following her.

They were halfway to the center when the hunters below went quiet. Phoebe and Jake froze, too. Phoebe halted her breath, then let it out slow and easy. Time for a distraction. She patted down her pockets. Empty.

"Where the hell did they go?" a male *I'm-in-charge* voice asked.

"Dunno. Thought they'd be behind the bar. Only cover in the whole room."

"Maybe they slipped past us in the dark," a third voice spoke.

All three voices came from the same general area—almost directly under them. That helped the odds a bit. Jake tried to recall how far the drop was, estimated how far they'd climbed and came up with something definitely in the leg-breaking range.

"I wonder . . ." the in-charge guy said.

One of the lights started to track toward the rafters. Jake sighted his gun along the light, but before he could shoot, he heard a soft *ping* in the direction of the doorway. All three figures did a stampede in that direction, making just enough noise for Phoebe to say softly, "Button."

Jake chuckled.

"Farley, you go out the back. Harley, you take the front. Do a circuit of the outside and check their vehicles. I'll check the office again. If we come up empty, head for the car and we'll get the hell out of here."

They sounded as if they knew they'd lost, but Phoebe

didn't start moving again until they were well out of range. Careful *and* clever.

In short order they were beneath the panel. Phoebe popped it open, Jake helped her push it up, then gave her boost up onto the roof. She lowered the panel quietly and soon he was beside her on the sharply peaked roof. They lowered the panel back into place.

"You come up here often?" Jake whispered. It felt good to be out in the fresh air. The towering pines cast a long shadow on their position, so there was little fear their silhouettes would be visible against the waning moon. He followed her to the peak and peered over, careful to keep low as normal night noises got lost in the sounds of the search. Finally they heard a motor start and tires spinning against gravel.

The car moved out from the cover of the trees, but when Phoebe had thrown the breaker, she shut off the big parking lot lights, too, so there was no way to see the color or a plate.

"I couldn't tell," Jake said softly. "Did they all leave?"

"I think so," Phoebe said. "Saw at least two for sure."

"How—" Jake began.

She rolled onto her back, tucked her hands behind her head and gave him her toe-curling smile. She looked as relaxed as if she were on her own bed instead of the steeply peaked roof. "Ate a lot of carrots as a kid."

Jake laughed, even as he fought back the urge to just kiss the girl. He rolled over, careful not to make contact, and stared up at the night sky, where the moon was fading as fast as his self-control. Maybe if he didn't look at her, he could do this.

"Another story?"

Her chuckle was husky and bedroom soft. "No stories tonight, curious Jake. I'm too tired, and—"

She stopped, but her mind finished the thought. She was

too curious about what would happen if she just rolled toward him. But if she breached the wall, broke the rules, she'd be breaking faith with herself and Kerry Anne, not to mention Phagan, who had loved Kerry, too. Kerry Anne had sacrificed more than her life for her little sister, more than any sister should have to sacrifice for anyone.

She hated bringing the poison of the past into this moment, but she needed it to keep her from making that roll Jake's way. It was almost Harding's moment of reckoning, and she couldn't sell that for a roll on a roof, no matter how enticing the guy.

She was an outlaw, he was a lawman, and even Pathphinder couldn't find a way between them.

Jake sighed, but not so she could hear him. Not good for a suspect to know her pursuer was in coyote position, howling for the damn, impossible moon. Her breathing was soft but even, almost contented. Maybe she was just glad to be alive. Maybe it was his ego telling him she was glad to be with him. Maybe.

He didn't know how long he'd have stayed there, staring at the stars and listening to her breathe, if his cell phone hadn't rung. Her sigh matched his almost perfectly. He turned his head to look at her and found she'd done the same. Her smile was wry now, her eyes sad.

"Guess you should call the cops when you're done."

Jake nodded, then sat up and pushed the button to take the call.

Bryn felt oddly cheerful as she came out of the dingy motel bathroom trying to dry her hair with a towel that was too small and too wet. She finally gave it up as a bad job and tossed the towel back into the bathroom. She could let her hair air dry while she watched a little TV or did some work on her laptop. She was too restless to sleep.

She was trying to decide between television and work when she saw two roses wrapped in green paper and ribbon lying on her bed next to a box.

The thought of Phagan's being in the room while she was naked in the shower sent her adrenalin soaring. She wanted to scream and kick things, since *he* was no longer here to kick. Because she was a grownup and a professional, she opened the box instead. Inside she found a virtual reality headset and gloves, as well as a note with an Internet address on it.

She examined the gear, which, though obviously home-made was better even than the last set Phagan had given her.

"Damn," she said, sinking down on the bed, "the guy is *good*."

Though her trust surprised and dismayed her, she tried on the gear. It was a perfect fit. She went to her laptop. It was easy to connect. She logged on to the Internet and then typed in the address Phagan had given her. She opened and prepped her online search program so she could run it when Phagan appeared, then put on the head set.

After a moment in the dark, she found herself in a pleasant little park around a gently gushing fountain with a statue of Venus, the goddess of love in the center. She almost turned around and left then, but curiosity and her desire to get Phagan kept her there. She walked around the fountain and found a bench with a single rose lying on it. When she picked up the flower, a mariachi band appeared out of the park's greenery, playing and singing a Spanish love song.

Bryn chuckled. At least this time he'd let her keep her shoes on and stay out of the kitchen. She sat down to enjoy the music until Phagan showed his virtual face. When he did, she'd track his ass back to his hiding place, kick it up over his ears and throw it into jail.

She brushed the rose across her mouth, inhaling deeply. Almost smelled real, but he couldn't be *that* good. She had to be picking up the smell of the roses he'd left in her room.

Unnoticed, Dewey approached from the other side of the fountain. Bryn was smiling, so he figured she must be plotting his demise. He knew he'd tried her patience, when what he wanted was to win her heart.

Nothing like falling for the impossible dream. After Kerry Anne died, he'd really thought he would never feel anything again. He sure as hell hadn't expected to feel something for a women he could never, ever have. Talk about unlucky in love.

He didn't feel guilty about his feelings for Bryn. Kerry Anne wouldn't have expected a permanent state of mourning from him. Mostly he felt stupid. Only emotion he seemed to arouse in Bryn was rage. Of course, she was magnificent in a rage. He grinned, remembering the first time he'd been caught by the FBI. Maybe he shouldn't have made a pass at her, but hell, he'd been handcuffed. Not like he'd grabbed her ass or something. He'd simply told her he'd like to kiss her. He hadn't actually done it.

She still hadn't noticed him, so he took a minute more to enjoy her rare—to him—smile. It was a great smile. No matter how hard she tried to look efficient and tough as nails, she stayed all woman.

He was taking a big risk meeting her like this, but he couldn't seem to stop himself. As soon as she saw him, she'd start trying to track him, and she was good enough to do it if he wasn't careful. Too bad he stopped being careful as soon as he got around her. As Phoebe liked to put it, he was thinking with his southern brain.

Bryn's smile narrowed to a scowl, and he knew he'd been spotted. He deleted the band and walked around the fountain toward her as she rose to meet him. She'd be starting her search program. He started his clock, too.

"Phagan." He'd come as Mr. Green Jeans this time and she wanted to chuckle, but she refused to let him see any sign of softening. If he was this bold when he thought she hated him, what would he do if realized he was making headway? Because the sad fact was, he was making headway. Not that anything could come of it, but how could she resist a man who was her intellectual equal? Who seemed to like her tough side as much as her soft side? Who wasn't afraid of her?

He ambled closer, carrying a rake, of all things. He realized it and looked around for a place to put it, then settled for making it disappear.

"Evening—" He looked around and realized that in their VR it was day and changed day to night. "Hi."

She should be patient and let him engage in small talk. The longer she could keep him with her, the better chance she had of tracking his location, but she'd never been a patient person. "What?"

Mr. Green Jeans grinned. "You don't like games, do you?"

"No, I don't." She turned away from him and made herself take a couple of deep breaths. On her VR screen a little timer showed her that she needed to keep him talking for three minutes to have him. She turned around. It was more than she could do to smile at him, but she did sit down. Let him think he was in control. "Nice little park, though. Does it have a real counterpart anywhere?"

He joined her on the bench but didn't crowd her. "It's sort of like one I saw in New Orleans a few years ago. I liked New Orleans."

Liked. Past tense. But maybe she could backtrack and—

"You're going to miss the here and now, Bryn," he said, breaking into her thoughts.

"It's Agent Bailey—"

"You called me by my first name," he pointed out, giving her a smile that seemed less Mr. Green Jeans and more something—or someone—else. Had his real smile broken through VR?

"You only have one name that you've shared with me," Bryn said. The time was down to sixty seconds and falling. She rose and stepped away from him. "I don't know why I came. I always end up talking in circles with you."

"You came to catch me," he said, standing up behind her. He gently turned her to face him. He'd changed, but she didn't think he was showing his true face.

"And why did you come?" she asked.

"To tell you I'm not your enemy. But—"

He stopped. The clock was almost run.

"But," she prompted. Thirty seconds. . . .

"Believe me when I say, my enemy is your enemy. Be careful."

"You're not the good guy, you know. If you'd just—"

"Turn myself in? You'd cut me a deal?"

She hesitated, then nodded. "In exchange for information I'd—"

"Could I be your partner?" He gave her such a hopeful look, she dang near nodded.

Her frustration surge. A red mist obscured the timer. "When hell freezes over!"

His grin was a warning, but his hand was quicker than her eye. He vanished and the landscape turned into his version of hell. Frozen over.

She ripped off the head set and threw it against the wall to stop herself from moaning long and loud. The clock on her search had stopped at one second.

Phoebe's cop friend, Honk, did a good job of securing the

crime scene, but it still took an hour before she was seated beside Jake in his truck driving to town. Phoebe left her SUV there in front of the bar. She wouldn't be needing it again. At first light, which was about an hour from now, Dewey would be picking her up. They were hitting TelTech tonight, and once the game was played, Phoebe Mentel would vanish, never to be reborn. Somewhere Phagan was probably already working on her new identity.

She didn't talk and Jake didn't seem inclined to chat either, until he reached the turn to her house. He braked and looked at her.

"Is it possible they went to your house . . ."

The same thought had occurred to her. Even if there was no threat at home, she didn't want to see the place again. It was something else she had to give up. If the weight of things and wants got too heavy, she might not be able to break free.

"Maybe." Dread was a dead weight on her chest that made even that one word a labor to say.

"I'll bet they have a free room where I'm staying." He seemed as relieved as she was that he didn't have to drop her off right away, but the trip to his motel kept them together only a few more minutes. Estes Park wasn't that big.

When the truck stopped outside the office, she turned to him. "You don't—"

"I'll wait," Jake said. All night if need be. Probably wasn't going to get any sleep tonight anyway. She got out, moving stiffly, as if she'd aged in the last couple of hours. He knew there were things he should do, but he sat there staring through the plate glass window at her profile as she arranged for a room. Only when she came out did he get out of the truck.

In silence they walked to her room, both of them looking everywhere but at each other. Bryn had the room next to her, and he had the one after that. The thought of Bryn stuck in the middle made him smile.

"What?" Phoebe asked.

"Nothing." He shrugged.

A silence.

"I'm just down here, if—" He stopped. "I'm sorry about the Chinese food."

"Tacky of them to take it."

"Might help your cop friend catch them. If he waits an hour and then stakes out that convenience store."

Phoebe chuckled. "Maybe." She hesitated. "Thanks."

It sounded more like good-bye, but he just nodded. "If you need—"

She looked at him then, regret written large in her eyes. "I—"

Can't. She didn't say it, but he knew that's what she meant. Words crowded in his throat, but all that came out was, "I know."

She was almost too tired to do it, but she did. She turned her back on him and opened the door. There was nothing left to say, so when she'd stepped through, she smiled, then slowly shut the door between them.

Jake stood there, trying to summon the energy to walk away. He was tired in a way he'd never been before. This was losing tired. And he wasn't used to feeling it.

He rubbed the back of his neck, then touched the closed door, spreading his fingers against the cool surface. Pretended that she was doing the same thing on the other side.

Only she wasn't. And he shouldn't be.

He sighed, turned and went back to the office. Inside, the clerk was starting to drift off to sleep again behind the counter. He showed her his badge. "The lady who just checked in? She makes any calls, you let me know immediately."

The clerk glanced down at the switchboard. "She's dialing right now." She wrote down the number and handed it to Jake. He waited until the light on the panel went out, then dialed the same number. After one ring a male voice said, "Video rentals."

Jake hesitated, then said, "Sorry, wrong number."

Jake dialed his cell phone again, as he left the office. "I got a phone number I need an address for." At Phoebe's door he hesitated, then moved on to Bryn's and knocked. Before she answered, he had an address.

"Saddle up. I think I've got Dewey Hyatt's address."

She nodded, shut the door in his face, then, it seemed, almost immediately opened it again. Course, he could have nodded off. He was that tired. He handed her the keys to the truck.

"You'd better drive." Last thing he saw before he nodded off was her pleased smile as she fired up the engine.

Chapter Ten

Phoebe closed the door between her and Jake, her fingers spreading across the cool surface as if sheer longing could push it and her through to the other side to him. In her mind, he was doing the same thing. When she heard him leave, his footsteps headed back toward the office instead of his room, she let her arm drop to her side.

Lightheaded and adrift, she reached for the phone he'd already be moving to monitor and dialed. She'd give him something and protect her knight.

Queen to king with a check and mate in sight.

When Dewey answered, he seemed to understand she wasn't in the mood to chat and arranged where to meet her. He had to drive from Denver, so she had time, too much time, before he could come. Too much time to linger at this intersection between past, present and future.

She sat on the edge of the bed and listened as Jake came back. Did he hesitate outside her door? Then he was past her and knocking on the next. Phagan's FBI agent. It appeared her feint had worked. It was the logical move for him to make, since his job was pursuing fugitives like Dewey. Phagan's fibbie would probably go, too, since she'd figure Dewey could lead her to Phagan. A neat little game of move and counter move with cold, hard logic controlling the board.

After a time, she heard both of them get into Jake's truck, his engine fire, then pull away. Good old logic that left the queen standing alone.

She looked around. Some palace. The room was shabby and sad, the thick air resistant to being anything but stale. It was the kind of place that made her want to leave.

It was inevitable, she supposed with a weary sigh, that the past would creep in now. Intersections were for reflection and assessment. They weren't intersections if you didn't stop to think, to choose. Or to at least remember why you'd chosen the present course.

She wasn't a dewy-eyed innocent. Her stepfather had made sure of that. But she hadn't known everything, merely felt it on a subconscious level. It was only later, when it was too late, that she'd put all the pieces together.

Things like his footsteps in the night. He'd come and look in on her, but it didn't make her feel safe or watched over. Some deep instinct had her pretending she was asleep until he closed the door and moved on to Kerry's room. She'd be asleep before he walked past again, but some nights, too many nights, muffled sobs dominated her nightmares.

With adult clarity, she knew she'd been too young at the time to cope with what she knew on that subconscious level, but reasoning couldn't stop her from feeling she should have done something. She'd spoken the truth when she said that Peter Harding liked the young. Her blessing and her burden was that her sister's sacrifice had saved her from Harding's attentions. Kerry Anne had made a bargain with the devil that she kept even after she left for college.

Back then, Phoebe had wondered, when any wondering could breach her burgeoning adolescence, why Kerry Anne came home every weekend when it was clear she hated it and hated him. Only when it was too late did she comprehend the full horror of her Kerry's existence and what she'd sacrificed to protect her little sister.

Somehow, some way Kerry had realized he was getting ready to break his unholy bargain with her. The last visit before her death, she'd warned Nadine to prepare herself to leave. She didn't give many details to Nadine, just that they were going to disappear with the help of her boyfriend, Phagan, but did warn her to travel light.

In the end, all she took were the shoes, the dress and the picture of Kerry Anne. That's all that wasn't tainted by him, by the gratitude and slavish obedience he demanded from his stepdaughters.

Phoebe rolled onto her back and faced her greatest fear. Had she been the one to give away Kerry's plans? Had Montgomery Justice somehow picked up on or sensed her secret hope to get away from him? Had she been the accidental cause of her sister's death?

The weight of not knowing almost broke her. She opened the doors, let herself remember that night she'd come home and found her sister dying on the bathroom floor, her wrists slashed almost to the bone in an apparent suicide.

She had turned to go call for help, but Kerry Anne called her back. Her blood was everywhere by then. She'd had to kneel in it to lift Kerry's head onto her lap, to get close enough to her blue lips to hear her whispered words.

"He did this, didn't he?" Nadine had sobbed.

Kerry had nodded weakly. "You . . . have to leave . . . nothing . . . to stop . . . him now."

She hadn't understood what Kerry Anne meant. Not then, God forgive her. Or maybe He'd been showing mercy and kept her from understanding everything then. Full knowledge might have had her joining her sister on the tile.

Kerry told her where there was some money, not much, but enough to catch a bus and gave her Phagan's phone number, with a warning not to call him until she was clear. And Phagan had sent Dewey to her. He'd helped her disappear. Helped her find a new name, a new life with the Mentels. Later, after her marriage to Jesse ended, he'd sent

Dewey to her again with a plan for justice, not just for her but for other runaways.

It had been enough to keep her focused until she met Jake.

The kicker was, Kerry Anne wouldn't condemn her for turning aside. She'd probably welcome it. She hadn't given her body or her life so that Phoebe could spend hers in a quest for justice.

Phoebe got up and faced the lousy motel mirror. Looked into her own eyes and told her demons, "All she ever wanted was for me to be happy. I'm the one who can't forgive or forget. I can't forgive myself." She gave a harsh laugh, one that was exceedingly short on happy and broke in the middle. "I'm sorry, Kerry, but how can I seize my freedom, knowing he's free to do it again?"

It wasn't just about Kerry Anne. Not anymore. It was about his new fiancé and her two little girls. Maybe there'd been others during those years he'd disappeared, too? Maybe she wouldn't succeed. Maybe he would kill her. Maybe Jake would stop her before she checkmated Harding, but she still had to try. It's what Kerry Anne would have done if he hadn't killed her.

She felt . . . like weeping, she realized with a shock of surprise. She hadn't cried, not once, since her tears had mingled with Kerry's blood. Crying might help ease the knot around her heart, but she didn't have time. And she sure as hell wasn't going to face Dewey with red eyes and nose.

She took a shaky breath, then another. After the third, it was a little easier. She looked around and realized she'd come to the motel with nothing, not even a toothbrush, that she needed to take with her. There was nothing to hold her here or hold her down except her own longings.

She left the key in her room, pulled the door closed, then slipped down the walk, heading away from the lighted office.

When she reached the road, she kept walking. If she put one foot in front of the other, eventually she'd get to where she was supposed to meet Dewey. If she didn't, well, nothing she could do about it.

The sun was just topping the mountains when Jake and Bryn got to the address his contact in the DPD had given him. Bryn had nudged Jake awake when they reached to the outskirts of Denver so, she said, he could help her watch for street signs. Jake had his own opinion about why she woke him up. She probably didn't want him groggy when they went in.

Too bad. He was gonna be groggy. He'd slept just long enough to feel like complete crap. He rubbed his face, fingering the day's growth of beard turning his chin the texture of sand paper. His eyes felt as if they were filled with sand, and his head felt thick and stupid, as if his brain had been replaced with a slug of cement.

Even worse was the feeling that he'd let himself be distracted by lust and pity into making the wrong move. Logic said it was his job to go after Dewey Hyatt, but his gut was saying the queen, Phoebe, was where the action was or where it would be. Hyatt was probably long gone, and Phoebe would be, too, by the time they got back. If he hadn't been so tired, he'd have never let himself be outmaneuvered so neatly. He'd probably lost Phoebe, too, but just to make sure, he dialed up the Estes PD and asked them to go to the motel, pick up Phoebe and hold her for questioning.

Surprised and not altogether pleased, Honk reluctantly agreed. He finished his call as Bryn stopped the truck, looked at the house, then at him.

"This is a waste of time, isn't it?" she said.

"Probably."

Her sigh was huge and frustrated. "Do you think they'll

call it off, wait until we get tired of waiting for them to do something and then move in again?"

Jake frowned, trying to get past cement and activate some actual thinking. Without looking at Bryn, he said, "Phagan's been sending you leads, hasn't he?"

The pause before she answered was brittle. "Yes."

"They won't fall back. They're going to finish this. I just wish—" He stopped.

"Wish what?" Bryn sounded ready to boil.

"I wish I could figure out why Phagan wants us, or at least you, in the game this early on." He looked at Bryn in time to see her blush. It was charming. No question. And Phagan might have a romantic interest there, but that still didn't explain what he was about to do or why he'd put his people at risk, particularly Phoebe. It made no sense. Trying to figure it out made his head hurt, so he gave it up for now. "Let's get some crime scene people in to toss this place and then—"

"What?"

"Well, we squeeze Phoebe Mentel, if by some miracle Honk does find her, and let's have her place tossed, too. We should have enough for a warrant now. I'm sure he was there the other night, so his prints will be, too. If we link her to Hyatt, then we'll have cause to hold her if—"

A very big, very unlikely if, Jake conceded. She wouldn't be there. And this time just following the scent wasn't going to work. She was too good at laying down false trails. He'd have to keep his eye on the whole board, try to anticipate all the moves, not just the next move. If he wanted to catch her. *If.*

He bit back a groan as he unfolded his body from the passenger side of the truck and followed Bryn inside.

There shouldn't be an *if* in his head. He needed to bury his personal feelings fast and deep. Beyond want was personal honor. Law enforcement wasn't just a job he got paid to do.

It was a personal trust he'd never betrayed before. It didn't matter how sad the lady's eyes were or how enticing the lady's mouth. The situation sucked, no question about it, but a lot of things did.

The address was in a modest, middle-class neighborhood, a corner lot that made half a gateway to a quiet cul-de-sac still slumbering in the slowly building morning light. On this Saturday morning most of the lawns still had newspapers lying on their lawns and the shades drawn on the windows. The sun hadn't had time to burn away the chill, the rich scent of green from the air, or the dew giving a jewel-like patina to the landscape.

In the distance Jake could hear the buzz of a mower, like a small plane coming and going, and he caught a glimpse of a jogger working off last night's supper, but otherwise there was no one outside to see them approach the house.

No car in the driveway or the garage, he noted as they split up to cover the front and back doors, confirming his feeling that they were already too late. Bryn rang, the sound echoing through the interior of the house. Jake knocked halfheartedly, then sagged against the railing while Bryn kicked in the front door. She was the one who was the most pissed, and he didn't have the energy to kick a hole in a paper sack. When she let him in, it was obvious the king—Jake wasn't sure who was white and who was black in this game—had already moved to a new square, leaving nothing behind but a single red rose on the scrubbed top of the kitchen table. Somehow he knew it was the rose that put sparks in Bryn's eyes. He was more interested in the small pile of pistachio shells in the garbage can.

Jake had enough strength to dial his phone, so he was the one who called in Denver's official crime-scene techs. That done, they returned to the truck and headed back to Estes Park. Jake stretched back out as best he could in the passenger side, sparing a brief thought to a wish that he could be beamed to his destination with a little help from Scottie before sleep claimed him again.

Phoebe woke around noon feeling like she'd been chewed up and pooped over a cliff. It had only been a few hours since she said goodbye to Jake, but it felt longer. After they got to their new place in seedy section of Denver, Dewey had insisted she try to sleep for a couple of hours. To her surprise, she had dropped off almost immediately, but now that a mental open season had been declared on her past, it was running amok through her dreams. She'd waded through blood and dodged Peter Harding for most of the night. And those were the good dreams. She struggled free of sheets she wasn't sure were clean and headed straight for the shower.

It was almost as bad as her dreams. Dewey had chosen their new digs for anonymity, not amenities or décor. To call it gnarly was to imply it had at some time been gnarl-less.

The single window was so crusted with dirt light couldn't penetrate it, which was actually a positive thing since the small pane of glass looked out on an alley that was a home for the fund-free and displaced. A lone light bulb struggled to produce minimal wattage, which was also probably a plus. It was better not to know how not clean the green tile was as she stepped under the languid stream of tepid water. After a time, the water warmed up enough to fog the mirror over the sink.

Phoebe dried herself, then wrapped the towel around her hair and faced the mirror. Between fog and age, the mirror reflected her in pieces.

Through a glass darkly.

She didn't know where the phrase came from, but it seemed to fit the here, the now, her present reality. Hadn't she lived her life in pieces? In the shadows? Didn't she reinvent herself almost daily as the game demanded? Wasn't she about to do so again? Even without help from the mirror, she was able to turn her brown eyes blue with the contacts Dewey had picked up for her. She released her hair from the towel, the wet ends starting a chain reaction of tiny chills where they touched her bare skin. She rubbed the strands until most of the water was in the towel, then dragged a comb through section by section until the tangles were gone. The bag Dewey had packed yielded a pair of salon scissors as well as some sassy, sexy lingerie.

She discovered she could still smile, even ankle-deep in angst-ville.

With a comb, she separated out a section of hair. The scissors sliced smooth and deep, releasing damp pieces to fall to her shoulders. They slid down her body where they curled into dark question marks against the green tile.

When she was surrounded by them, she stopped and fingered the butchered ends. Amazing how it changed her look. The old chess queen Phoebe was dead. Long live—damn, she couldn't remember the new name.

She dug out the new driver's license. Polly?

She wasn't surprised when the bag also gave up a shirt in parrot colors of green and yellow to go with the ragged blue shorts. And some temporary dye for her hair. Or should she call it her plume? Under wooden clogs that hinted at a perch, she found the glue-on fingernails. Long, curved. Like claws.

Polly didn't want a cracker. She wanted to kick Dewey's ass.

Their warrant secured, Jake watched the crime scene

techs go through Phoebe's house, waiting for confirmation of what he already suspected. It came quickly. Dewey Hyatt had been here. And Phoebe's prints matched the kid's lawyer's prints on every point. Apparently, he was doomed to recognize her no matter what she turned herself into. This was his new reality. He'd become a homing beacon for a thief.

When the frenzy slowed, he walked through the house, going where he hadn't gone before. Odd to feel like an intruder in a place so personally impersonal. In a strange way, her restraint in decorating said more about her than a thousand knickknacks, photos and papers would have. He'd seen her extraordinary self-control. Sensed how single-minded and stubborn she was, that she wouldn't give up or give ground unless forced to. That she kept her own counsel and played to win. Obviously it didn't matter to her that this game she was playing with Hyatt and Phagan was dangerous and that she wouldn't be coming back, dead or alive. He was convinced that she didn't necessarily like it, but she accepted the rules of her game and played them to win. That, like him, she did what she had to do.

Just as he had to play by his rules, because they were a matter of ethics and the law. He chose to follow those rules because he knew he couldn't sleep with the enemy and keep his integrity. That's what he'd told himself last night when his body had been screaming to take that step toward her and find ease in her body for the burning in his gut. He'd turned away and reduced the burn to a sullen smolder.

And if he had it to do again? In the cold light of day, his choice seemed more bitter than wise. If she came back to him, if he found her again, he'd step across that threshold. He'd cross that line. He'd take her and at least have the memory to warm him on the long, lonely nights. He'd—

Do the same thing he'd done last night. He'd do what

he'd taken an oath to do. Who he was and what he believed in were fixed points in a shifting world of grays and compromises. He couldn't stop being who he was any more than Phoebe could stop being what she was. Sometime in the past, their lives had committed them to different paths, to a course that made them adversaries, not allies. If either of them shifted ground, they'd stop being *them*. So they'd lose either way.

He went outside to the truck. It was a relief when Bryn joined him. He didn't dare think hot thoughts around her, though she was looking as ragged as he felt. Something was going on there, but he didn't feel up to finding out. He sure as hell didn't want her probing his secrets and was pretty sure that—as in the sense that the sun would probably rise tomorrow—that she didn't want him probing hers.

"I think we have enough for an arrest warrant—if we can find her. She didn't leave much of herself behind," she said.

"Then it might be better to start with, wanted for questioning. I hate to over-play our hand."

"If we can match her voice on the answering machine and ID her as Pathphinder, she's ours," Bryn said.

"Lots of *ifs*," Jake pointed out. "Let's let them finish here and head back to Denver. That's where the action will be. If you think your tip on TelTech is a good one?"

"Who the hell knows? So far the owner, Peter Harding, looks squeaky clean and yet he smells to high heaven. Of course, that could be because he pissed me off. Obviously has woman-in-power issues."

Jake held the door of the truck for her, then got into the driver's seat but didn't start the motor. He realized he was facing the street that Phoebe had run down just yesterday and felt regret take a big bite out of his concentration.

"If we can find out who Phoebe Mentel really is, it might

clear up something. Maybe Harding is lurking in her past somewhere," Bryn said.

"She told me she married Mentel when she was sixteen," Jake said slowly, "and that her mother was a drunk. She's obviously one of Phagan's runaways."

"That could just be her cover story—"

Jake shook his head. "I don't think so. It had the ring of truth about it. She also mentioned a sister who died."

Bryn frowned. "According to our info, Phoebe doesn't have siblings. Interesting she'd make a mistake like that. She doesn't strike me as someone who makes mistakes."

Jake frowned, remembering that day in her office. There'd been something in the way she said it, as if she couldn't not say it. "I could be wrong, but I think the sister is the key to her involvement with Phagan."

"My guy is still digging. Hopefully he'll find what's rotten if Harding *is* Phagan's next target. On paper, he appears to be an upstanding guy. Hell, he's making a run for governor. Be a stupid move if he's got a big old skeleton in his closet."

"You'd think. Wouldn't be the first politician to think he could outrun his past though. Or Harding could be a smoke screen Phagan's putting up." Jake turned the key and put the truck in gear. "If we're watching TelTech, he and his gang could happily make their move on someone else. No way in hell we could cover all possible targets in the area. No way we could even identify them."

The one consistency in the Phagan profile was that there was no consistency, except the evil his targets had done in the past.

Bryn bit back a denial that Phagan would deceive her. The truth was, she didn't know what Phagan would do. Perhaps his careful lead feeding had been meant only to build trust so that she would blindly follow his lead. Except she'd never blindly go anywhere. Phagan had to know that about her. Hell, the guy knew she liked to read romance novels. Even her mother didn't know that. "He didn't have to tell us anything. And"—she cleared the defensiveness from her voice, before finishing evenly—"it tracks with his profile to lead law enforcement to clean up after him. He seems to have a remarkable grasp of the law and just what we need to nail his targets, once he's done with them. It's one of his more . . . annoying characteristics."

"One?" Jake's innocuous question invited confidences that she found she wanted to give. But would Jake respect her in the morning?

"If there's something going on with this guy . . ." Jake added, gently.

She watched Jake point the truck toward Denver, then flick on the speed control. He looked so relaxed, so in control of his life and his feelings, her defensive feelings came back up in a rush.

"There's nothing going on that I can't handle."

"No one said you couldn't handle anything."

She made herself relax, but the words still wanted to stick in her throat. "His behavior has been . . . unorthodox." She rubbed her face, so she wouldn't have to look at him. "Hell, this is so embarrassing! He's sort of . . . seems to have . . . a kind of . . . crush on me."

The relief of sharing her secret was immediate and overwhelming, followed almost immediately by horror that it was out. She stole a look at Jake and found him looking thoughtful, not amused. Smart guy.

"He's obviously a man of taste and good sense."

"And?" she prompted.

"Has he been stalking you?"

"*Stalking* isn't exactly what I'd call it."

"Would *courting* be more accurate?"

She nodded without looking at him. "He's given me gifts. Small things."

"The rose in your room and at the house?"

She nodded. "Gift certificates to things he knows I like. Nothing big. I don't use them, of course. Except . . . he built me a VR headset so we could meet. I did use that. He's good. Very good. And very careful."

"If he's leaving you roses, then he's in the area." That was interesting. Jake had gotten the impression that Phagan pulled his strings from a safe, or a maybe a lofty distance was more accurate. "Phagan must be someone you've met at some point . . ."

"I've racked my brain trying to figure out who it could be. I meet so many people in my work." Bryn rubbed her head as if it hurt. "He could be someone I've questioned, or the guy who washes my car or cuts my hair. No way to know without cracking his network."

"No wonder you're frustrated. Every time you leave home, you'd be wondering," Jake said. It was a wonder she hadn't crashed like a hard drive under that kind of pressure. Of course, he'd always known she was a tough cookie, and yet Phagan seemed to have made some headway in his courtship. Kind of funny, when he thought about it. He and Bryn were caught on the horns of the same dilemma.

So why wasn't he smiling?

Chapter Eleven

From the doorway Dewey watched Phoebe sorting through their equipment for tonight. She obviously hadn't heard him come in and the shutters that usually masked the expression in her eyes were not in place. He stepped back outside, feeling like an intruder. Her sadness could have been because the game was bringing back memories of Kerry Anne, but Dewey had a feeling the past was just the icing on her misery cake. Her past was old, and the wounding in her eyes was new, the bleeding fresh and painful to see.

He leaned against the wall, feeling the weight of the responsibility Kerry Anne had left him with when she'd entrusted her little sister to his care. Feeling a sense of failure. Though Phoebe hadn't known it, her need had saved him, given his grief a channel. He need had kept him from giving in to his own grief at losing Kerry Anne, his own sense of helplessness at the time.

"I've been a poor guardian, Kerry," he whispered. "I saved her life, but at what cost? She's not happy. I thought . . ."

What had he thought? That committing them both to avenging Kerry's death would make them happy? But he hadn't thought. He'd felt. They'd both been lost in their feelings of rage and horror. Not a good place to be making life decisions from. He hadn't been much more than a kid himself—expert at computers, not life—and still reeling from the things Kerry had just told him about her life of hell with her stepfather.

He rubbed his face, feeling the horror of that moment sweep through him again. He'd known that sorrow had a permanent home inside Kerry Anne, but not why. He'd hope that his love was the key to driving it out. That whatever her burden was, he could remove it.

If he hadn't placed that anonymous call to the authorities, would Kerry Anne still be alive? In his innocence, he hadn't realized how connected Montgomery Justice was. Now Dewey knew just how good Justice was at finding who could help him and who could hurt him. And how effectively he neutralized opposition. Dewey's report had disappeared or been buried deep in the system and Kerry Anne's death had been ruled a suicide before her body was in the ground. A few weeks later, their mama had taken a drunken tumble down the stairs and a "grief stricken" Justice had left the area.

In the end, all Dewey did for Kerry Anne was save to Nadine from Justice's intentions. He'd gotten her a brand new life, then deluded himself into believing that vengeance was the road to healing for them both. He'd healed nothing and cost her a life with her marshal. Way to go, Dewey. What are you going to do for your next trick?

He'd made a royal mess of things, but the game was running. They had to deal with that right now. Maybe after . . .

He opened and closed the door, noisily this time. When Phoebe looked up, the shutters were firmly in place in her now baby blues.

"Kevin okay?" she asked.

Dewey nodded. "He's on his way to Idaho. Seems he likes potatoes."

He knelt down beside her and started stowing the equipment she'd finished checking. They worked without talking, then headed for the kitchen. Phoebe sat at the table with a diet soda while Dewey heated up some soup and made sandwiches. When he was seated across from her, she picked up a sandwich half, then set it down again.

"You okay?" he asked, crumbling crackers into the steaming soup.

"Do you remember when we met?" She looked at him, but he could tell she was seeing the past, that night when he'd found her huddled in a corner of the park where she'd spent hours until he came trying to screw up the courage to slash her wrists with a rusty razor she'd found under a bench. Kerry's blood was still splattered on her clothes, though there were signs she'd taken the time to wash her hands and face before boarding the bus to the next town. Her eyes were wide and filled with the horror of it. She'd looked up at him, her face and eyes swollen from crying.

"Are you Phagan?" she'd asked, her voice hoarse with unrestrained grief.

The four years he had on her had shrunk to nothing with his own grief and horror and near paralyzing guilt. He'd wanted to sit down beside her and cry with her. Wanted to take the razor and end his own pain of losing Kerry. Her need of him was terrifying, but too insistent to walk away from.

To this day, he wasn't sure why he'd shaken his head and offered his real name, not his Internet handle. "I'm Dewey. Dewey Hyatt. A friend of Phagan's."

"I remember," he said now.

"Stupid question. Sorry." She picked up some crackers and crumbled them into her soup, letting them trickle through her fingers in a tiny yellow shower.

"You having second thoughts?"

"I can't seem to stop remembering. I spent all these years not letting myself remember any of it. Being Phoebe, who didn't have that past. Living Phoebe's life completely, the way Phagan said to. But now, I can't . . ." She picked up a spoon, stirred the crackers into the broth, then set it down.

"If she hadn't come back for me—"

"Don't go there, honey."

"She was free."

"Not as long as you were still there with him." Did she know, he wondered. Did she know the full horror of what Kerry had endured? He saw her lashes lift and knew she did.

"That's why she came back. Because I was there and he . . . made her . . ."

"Don't do this to yourself. What Kerry did was because she loved you. She'd have done anything for you." He pretended to look out the dirty window. "She didn't die so you could live your life drowning in guilt. She did it so you could be free of him."

Phoebe's smile was wry and sad. "I let her down again. I'm not free of him."

Phoebe hadn't let Kerry down. He had. He'd promised to take care of her and her little sister. He'd taken care of them all right. Kerry Anne was dead and Nadine was condemned to a shadow life without love or joy or—

"Let's just go. Cut our losses and get out of here—"

Phoebe shook her head. "Don't you see? It's not just about me or Kerry Anne anymore. Those two little girls. They're us all over again. It has to stop. I won't be free of him until he can't hurt them or anyone. We can't just right the wrongs that are easy. We have to right the wrongs we find. We've already lost our lives. We can't go back or pretend this never happened. We'll know. We'll always know. And if we don't finish it, all we've lost will be for nothing. He'll have won the past *and* the future."

He pulled some pistachios out of his pocket and cracked them. Instead of eating the meat, he said, "Do you . . . like that marshal?"

"Does it matter?" She shoved back her chair.

"Yeah, it matters." He stood up and leaned on the table, holding her gaze with his. "I'm sorry."

"You don't have to be." Her smile was resigned. "You, Phagan, me—we made a choice seven years ago. Choices have consequences. Good and bad consequences. You make the choice, but you don't get to decide the outcome. That's the deal. No fair to whine about it now. Let's just make sure it was worth it." She stood up. "What say we go kick some butt?" She smiled. It wasn't much of a smile, but it hadn't been much of a day.

Dewey grinned. "Sounds like a plan."

The after-hours office was somewhat quieter than the eight-to-five office, but bad guys punched their fellow man, not the clock, so the office never completely stood down. The lighting had gone from wide area to localized, putting pockets of shadow between the door Jake and Bryn entered and the desk where Matt waited for them.

As Jake followed Bryn in an indirect beeline around desks and other obstacles, he couldn't help thinking the lighting was like their case. A few spots of light, a lot of dark, with nothing to tell them what mattered and what didn't but an imprecise blend of experience and instinct.

Matt was looking out the window at the night city but turned at their approach. Tiredness cut deep tracks around his eyes, but he still gave off enough energy to light the city and most of the suburbs. Just looking at him made Jake feel tired. He ought to send Matt's wife, Dani, some flowers or something for living with his big brother.

When they were in range, Matt gestured for them to follow him. "Got my people waiting in the conference room. Time to bang our heads and ideas together and see what falls out."

Jake exchanged a look with Bryn but followed her and Matt to a room short on people and long on food debris. Matt's people were Alice, Riggs and his computer expert, Sebastian.

Alice Kerne was an attractive black woman in designer jeans and silk blouse. Her crisp intelligence, common sense and ability to see the humor in any situation made her a good foil for Matt. Toby Riggs, on the other hand, was anything but crisp. He was always rumpled and always eating. His strength lay in filtering through minutia to find small, significant leads. Sebastian was the comic relief on the team with his stand-up shock of bright red hair and perpetually surprised expression. Like Hyatt, he'd been a hacker in his younger days. He'd been caught, then recruited by the Feds.

If Bryn felt intimidated by being the only representative of the FBI, it didn't show. She took a seat next to Alice and helped herself to a doughnut.

Jake got them both coffee, then took a position at one end of the table and sipped the bitter brew, his gaze following Matt as he strode to the other end and looked down his nose at Jake. His look said in no uncertain terms that Jake was on Matt's turf, even if this was Jake's case.

Jake briefly considered taking on Matt, then decided he didn't have the energy for it and sat down. He wasn't too tired to assume a provocative slouch though. Out of the corner of his eye he saw Bryn and Alice exchange looks, their respective lips twitching. Riggs had his eyes closed, so he missed the testosterone byplay. Sebastian was hunched over the computer next to a printer spitting out pages.

"Had a good day?" Matt asked, crossing his arms and propping a shoulder against the wall behind him.

Bryn said her piece, minus Phagan's stalking/courtship, then handed off to Jake. He rubbed the back of his neck, then took his turn. His information didn't seem nearly enough for how many miles he'd traveled and how tired he was.

Matt dropped into a chair about halfway through their report, shoving fast food containers out of the way, so he could beat a tempo on the tabletop that didn't stop until they did. He nudged Riggs with his foot. "Let's put an APB out, have people watching the airport, trains and buses. Though if they're as good as you say, it'll be about as useful as pissing in the wind."

Riggs yawned and stretched, then shuffled out the door. There was something laid back about Riggs in motion, something hypnotic.

Jake felt his eyes start to close.

"So, what now?" Matt's barked question brought him back with a jerk.

Judging by the weight of his eyelids, it was going to be a damn long night. His thoughts spun in a sleep spiral, until . . .

"Runaways." Jake wasn't sure he'd said it a loud, until he saw everyone looking at him. The word hung in the silence while he took a drink of coffee. The caffeine partly peeled back the fog inhabiting his head. "Need to look at reported runaways seven to ten years back."

Bryn frowned. Alice looked thoughtful. Matt looked . . . blank.

"Runaway reports?"

Jake nodded.

"From where?" Matt asked.

Where? He frowned, then, like a gift, heard in his mind Phoebe's voice saying, "Mama hailed from Georgia . . ." He straightened. "Georgia. Let's focus on Georgia. If that doesn't work, well, we'll figure something out."

"You want a two to three *year's* worth of runaway reports for the state of Georgia?"

"Just the ones for females in the fourteen to sixteen age range," Jake clarified as his thoughts began to sharpen. "We need a *why* before we can be sure *who* their target is. If Teltech is in the bulls-eye, we need to find out what they're after."

"I have a feeling you don't have enough time before this case goes hot to go through that many files. I'm not sure you've got that much *life* left." Matt looked at Jake as though he'd lost it.

Jake didn't blame him. He agreed with him, but since he'd said it, he'd stick with it for now. This whole case was a peeling back of layer after layer to find . . . what? Was it an artichoke with something substantial at its heart? Or an onion with a lot of layers, and nothing at the center but a bad smell?

"We'd need to narrow the search more than by gender and age," Alice said, giving Jake an apologetic look for coming on Matt's side. "Can you isolate a year? A city? A town?"

"I wonder if we could find the record of Phoebe's marriage to Jesse Mentel? That might helps us narrow down the time frame. She said she was sixteen when she married him. And cross match with deaths? See if we can turn up the dead sister?"

"What makes you so sure Georgia is even our state?" Bryn asked. "It's obvious she's able to put on and take off an accent pretty much at will."

"My mentioning Georgia made her jumpy as an addict. She was very anxious to turn my attention to Texas. And we've got to commit to something. No time to second-guess ourselves," Jake pointed out.

"That's true. I'll go see what I can shake out of the system. Probably won't be a lot tonight." Alice started to leave, then stopped. "I almost forgot. This came for you." She handed a manila envelope to Bryn.

Bryn examined it. "No postage. No messenger stamp. How did it come?"

Alice shrugged. "No clue. It just showed up in the interoffice mail basket."

Bryn opened the clasp and flap and pulled out a newspaper clipping. Jake got up and leaned over her shoulder. It was a photograph, obviously taken at a funeral. The mourners hid the coffin but not the hearse parked to one side. The caption, if there had been one, was gone. The clipping was old and grainy, the faces no more than gray blurs against the paler blur of sky.

"Hold on, Alice. I think we just got our break."

"Can we scan and enhance this?" Bryn tapped the photo. "There's a plate on that hearse."

Jake looked across the table at Matt and felt a guilty pang when he saw Matt rubbing his face. He was keeping the old boy up late. He looked at Sebastian. "Can you do it, Sebastian, so Matt can go home to his wife?"

Matt gave Jake his deadly look, the one that promised retribution later. "If our helpful informant is really being helpful. Any idea who sent this?"

Bryn and Jake exchanged quick looks. Jake, not about to tell his brother the lovesick hacker story, shrugged. Bryn did, too. Then they both had to endure a long and pointed examination from Matt before he finally said, "I see."

Lucky for them, Sebastian was both good and fast. He soon had the photograph scanned onto his screen and a few keystrokes later, they had the plate number to the point they could read it. Sebastian hit 'print.' When it was free of the machine, Bryn snatched it and went off with Alice to track it down.

Jake stayed by Sebastian. "Let's see if you can clear up the faces a bit. I'd like to see if I recognize any of our mourners."

* * * * *

Peter Harding paced back and forth in front of Stern, wearing a track in the expensive carpet in his living room. He couldn't seem to stop himself, even in the face of Stern's barely concealed contempt.

"They're digging into my past! I can feel it. What if—"

"There is no 'what if.' Peter Harding's life is squeaky clean all the way to birth and back."

"*His* past. What if they find someone who knew him before—" Harding didn't finish the sentence. Even the walls seemed like his enemy tonight.

"You survived a top-secret military clearance investigation." Stern sounded bored with the subject. He stalked to the liquor cabinet and poured Harding a stiff drink, shoving it into his hand, forcing him to stop and drink it. "Pull yourself together. We'll do what we've always done. Deal with what happens as it happens. Do what we must to get what we want. Now—" He straightened Harding's shirt collar, then his tie. "Don't you have an alibi to take care of?"

Harding stared at him for a long moment before slowly nodding. "I'll be with Audrey, when, if—"

Stern nodded. "I'll call you when it's done."

Chapter Twelve

"My, my." Dewey turned as Phoebe came out the alley entrance in her black jump suit. "My, *my*." He walked a circle around her. "I thought I'd seen everything you have to offer, but I can see I was *so* wrong."

Phoebe looked him up, then down. "And I can see you overestimated what you have to offer."

"Ouch. Guess I should have packed . . . socks."

Phoebe chuckled, happy to feel her pre-Jake rhythm returning as they went into action. "The way these things fit, I don't think it would have helped."

How Phagan had gotten his hands on some CIA jump suits was anybody's guess. The suits were, according to Dewey, obscenely high tech and known in spy circles as "chameleon," because they were capable of merging with any dark background. The fabric was light as air, could warm or cool as needed, and was as flexible as—and fit like—skin. If they performed as billed, they'd even the odds with the heat sensors Harding had securing the perimeter around his building.

In addition to their satellite-link capable laptop, Phagan had also provided them with headsets that were not only night-vision capable, but also had tiny receivers that let them receive the signal from the laptop and display it on a tiny screen.

She and Dewey had spent the afternoon in VR, playing the game over and over until each move was as natural to them as breathing. They were as ready as they would ever be.

Taking it to reality was different, and more intense, Phoebe realized as Dewey drove the van to their sortie point. She used the time to securely pack all her identities put

Pathphinder in a mental box, which she locked and tossed away the key to. If she survived the op, she could always pick the lock and figure out who the hell she was going to be, though she was sure of one thing: "Polly" would be shed as quickly as reasonably possible.

Dewey parked the van under cover of trees a short distance from TelTech. They pulled on the hoods that attached to their jump suits, completely covering their heads. Eye holes were all they needed, since the fabric was light enough to breathe through.

He unloaded their packs while Phoebe used the laptop and the "egg" she and Ollie had planted in the system to access TelTech's security cameras.

Now she could see what the guards were seeing, and, thanks to a tiny camera Ollie had planted in the A/C duct in the security office to track the guards movements during her planning phase, she could also see the guards.

Once the headsets were activated, the same picture would be beamed to hers, which was also connected to a keypad, using tiny wires embedded in the jump suit. She strapped on the keypad, plugged it in, then put the headset on over the snug fitting hood and connected it, too.

With the keypad active, she could also capture, record and replay as needed. So not only could she see what she needed to, corridor by corridor, she could also control what the security guards saw as she and Dewey made their drive toward the RABBIT's hole dug deep in the bowels of TelTech. It was all very cool.

She tested the controls, navigating her way through the various cameras, saving the hidden camera until last. "That's some camera Ollie installed. I can practically see the dandruff on their heads."

Dewey jumped out the back of the van, which had a local

news station logo stenciled on both sides, grunting as he hefted his pack, constructed from the same material as their suits, onto his back. He looked at his watch. "Ready?"

Phoebe left the laptop running, it was their link to their egg—and hopped out after him. They locked up, activated the anti-theft system, then began hiking through the woods that surrounded TelTech on three sides. Beyond the trees, TelTech and RABBIT waited, framed by mountains and a waning moon.

Jake leaned against the wall next to the fax machine, watching as the Kerry Anne Beauleigh's police file emerged one slow page a time. The license plate in the newspaper photo had led to the Valdosta, Georgia funeral home that had handled her funeral. Jake had called and rousted the owner out of bed without compunction. Despite the intervening years, the man had been able to identify the family in the photo Jake faxed him. His information had led to a call to the local PD and to the pages printing so slowly Jake could read the sheets and hand them off to Bryn, then take a short nap while waiting for the next one to appear.

Jake stirred as a picture started to emerge. What looked like a girl in a school uniform, one of those one-shot, all purpose pictures done at the beginning of the school year. The generic background framed the jaw line now coming into view, a jaw as familiar to him as his own, despite the short time he'd known Phoebe. The nose was next, then finally her eyes, still shadowed, still sad.

Had she ever been happy? The sheet fell free of the machine. There was writing across the top. Nadine Beauleigh. 15. Went missing day of sister's suicide.

Nadine? Nadine. Jake tried the name out in his head. It rubbed wrong, but he had no doubt this was Phoebe's face,

Phoebe's past. Phoebe's sorrow. Somewhere in the pile of pages was the key to the present, the why, the where and the who. He hunted through the sheets for the autopsy report and sat down to read it again.

"Nervous?" Dewey's voice was tinny inside the headset.

"No." Phoebe didn't look at him, because there was nothing to see. Their gear rendered them virtually invisible in the shadow cast by a ragged line of fir trees.

She wasn't lying. Their night-vision goggles made reality more VR than VR. None of it seemed real. It was just another game in a long line of games. Or maybe choreographed dance was a better description.

There was no perimeter fence, but the building was well defended against intrusion. Even with Ollie's inside information, TelTech had been Pathphinder's most difficult challenge. The landscaping was both beautiful and functional. Each shrub and tree hid heat sensors or security cameras. Triggered heat sensors activated big lights and alarms. The camera images came up on the guard's display on a random basis. Using their "egg," Phoebe had programmed a more intrusion-friendly randomness into the sequence, and they'd soon know if their high tech suits worked. She'd also programmed in a warning if one of the guards suddenly decided to pull up the view from a particular camera.

Harding had lavished his greatest attention on interior security, with the most sophisticated of equipment protecting the laboratory where his RABBIT's hole was. Thanks to Phagan, they had more than the chameleon suits. He'd also provided an impressive array of electronic assistance, all of which had performed perfectly in VR. Time to see if it all worked in the real world.

Inside the headset, a digital stopwatch fed them the time

available for each part of their "dance."

"Get ready . . ." she said, waiting for it to hit zero. Three . . . two . . . one . . . "Go!"

Dewey took point, with Phoebe on his six. They started across the sculpted lawn, using the shadows around shrubs and trees to mask their movements from any watchers. In her viewfinder, the guards showed no sign of alarm. The suits had muted their body heat. Soon the woods were behind them, the side of the building looming dark and high.

Still performing their dance in perfect synchronization, they pulled out rocket launchers, aimed and fired at the roof. Dark strands shot upward. When hers stopped playing out, Phoebe pulled the rope until it held firm. She had her harness on and quickly attached the lift motor, then her harness, using a carabineer. She checked the connection, activated the motor and began to rise, with Dewey slightly ahead of her.

She used the time to check the guard's station and found them watching the Broncos on television. Her digital stopwatch indicated they were slightly ahead of schedule.

Dewey reached the roof ahead of her, scrambled over the edge, then helped her up. They shed their packs, and Phoebe went to work on the alarm wires around the ventilation shaft.

"God bless the CIA," she murmured, giving Dewey the thumbs up to crack the grill when she was done. Still ahead of schedule, Dewey settled the electric winch over the opening and roped up for the descent.

"Wish it would happen," Phoebe said.

"What?" Dewey, his legs dangling over nothing, lifted the night goggles and looked at her.

"Whatever's going to go wrong."

"Try to be less optimistic, darling."

Phoebe couldn't see his grin, but she heard it in his voice. He repositioned his goggles and started his descent. Phoebe checked the guards one last time before starting down, as that feeling of someone walking over her grave got stronger.

Stern paused to light a cigarette—and to study the desolate street—before entering the rundown garage. Inside he found Billy and two other men pitching pennies by a dark car that wasn't as ramshackle as it appeared to be. The enclosed place was fetid and stuffy. Underpinning the acrid stench of sweat were a variety of petroleum-based scents, stale and fresh cigarette smoke and . . . Cheetos?

He turned toward the smell and found Farley munching out of a bag of the bright orange puffs. Farley, Harley and the other three men were to lead the assault on TelTech tonight, but only Farley and Harley were . . . scheduled to return with RABBIT. They were the only ones Stern trusted to keep their mouths shut. Since Farley had inside help, he could have walked in and out of TelTech with his eyes closed, but that wouldn't look good on the six o'clock news.

Appearances were everything in politics.

Stern took a last puff of his cig, then dropped it onto the gritty cement and ground it out with his shoe. Interesting that he felt so much more comfortable here, with Farley and his doomed goons, than in Harding's lofty office. Even more interesting that he'd worked so hard to get away from places like this. He'd hooked his life to Harding's ruthlessly rising star and never looked back.

Until now.

He'd seen and recognized the look in Harding's eyes. Trust was gone. Perhaps his boss had been receiving notes like the ones being sent to him? Someone was sowing the seeds of distrust. Someone was succeeding. An uneasy truce was in place until the RABBIT problem was taken care of, but after? Only one of them would be left standing. Harding had never been one to take prisoners.

"Your men ready?" he asked Farley.

Farley tossed the empty bag into a greasy barrel, grabbing an even greasier rag to wipe the orange residue from his hands. "You guys ready?"

They shuffled into what passed for a line.

"When do we get paid?" Billy asked, appointing himself spokesman for the group.

"Like always," Stern said. "When the job is done." He walked toward Billy, not stopping until Billy took a step back. "And done . . . right." He looked at Farley. "Hit the road."

Farley met Stern's eyes until ten seconds had ticked away, then moved toward the car. His men in black followed.

From an air conditioning grill, Phoebe watched the guard finish his round and head for the elevator with the eagerness of a horse heading for the barn. Phoebe wasn't surprised. The Broncos game was heating up nicely. An unexpected bonus. They'd picked up almost five extra minutes thanks to the home team.

Using her keypad, Phoebe created a film loop of the empty hall, then nodded at Dewey. In short order they were moving toward the second-to-the-last barrier between them and RABBIT. Dewey attached the device to the keypad that operated the lock and popped open the door.

Inside, Phoebe headed straight for the row of state-of-the-art research and development computers, offering up a silent prayer that Ollie had finished his work here before he died. If he hadn't, she wouldn't be able to get into RABBIT's data files. Dewey was on the safe before Phoebe could sit down and start the boot-up. Other than the computers, the room was oddly barren, as if the occupants had already moved on to other things.

She checked the guards again, noticing that the camera was recording them for some reason. No time to worry about it now, and it wouldn't hurt anything. Maybe she and Dewey could watch the game later. It was in the final quarter with the Broncos still ahead.

"We've picked up six minutes."

"I'll be done in three," Dewey said.

They went in quietly, their weapons camouflaged by cleaning equipment. Farley and Harley stayed in the rear, using the other men as cover from the surveillance cameras. A guard strolled out to meet them, his attention still drawn toward the office blaring with the sounds of the Broncos game.

The guard had a heartbeat to realize they weren't the regular cleaning crew before Billy took him out with a silenced gun. The men moved into the office and took out the other guards quickly and quietly.

Farley stopped by the first guard and picked up his weapon before he followed them in. Two shots and Billy was down.

The other two men didn't blink. They'd already been told that Billy wasn't supposed to come back from the job. They hadn't heard about their own demise. Harley used another guard's gun on them, then dropped the weapon by the guard's body. Farley returned his gun to its dead owner while Harley found the security tapes and removed them.

Farley dialed Stern on his cell phone. "The building is ours." He hung up without waiting for an answer and followed his brother to the elevators.

"I'm in." The safe door swung open with a soft *swish*.

"So am I." Phoebe looked up from the terminal. "I'll be

done downloading data in five. Then I'll activate the virus." She looked at her watch. "We're still ahead of schedule and—"

She stopped as something odd in the security office caught her attention.

"Houston, we have our problem."

"Cops?" Dewey swept everything in the safe into his pack, closed the door and spun the dial.

"I wish." A few keystrokes pulled the camera up on her monitor so Dewey could see what she was seeing.

"Crap! Do you think they're headed here, and what do we do about it if they are?"

Phoebe didn't answer. Her mind was racing, exploring various options, searching for the path out of the maze. "First"—even as she spoke, she was typing again, tapping into the security terminal inside the tomb that had been the security office—"let's get the cops involved." She activated the silent alarm.

"Okay." Dewey didn't sound thrilled by her action, but he didn't argue. "Though you might have waited for your data download to get done."

"Oh yeah. Three minutes." She pulled up the camera in the elevator the two guys were coming up on. "And they'll be here in two minutes unless . . ." It seemed to take a long time to get into the elevator controls while Dewey counted off the floors.

"Five . . . six . . . seven . . . we're next."

"I'm in." Just as eight lit up on their panel, she managed to stop the doors from opening. "I think I'll leave them there for the cops."

"It would be poetic justice." Dewey's chuckle was absent-minded. "Download?"

"Done. Virus uploading." In the monitor, the two men were punching buttons and trying to pry open the door. One pulled out a crowbar. "Uh, oh. They don't want to wait. We're done. Disconnect."

Dewey removed the satellite uplink from the computer, while Phoebe tossed her gear back into her pack.

"Up or down?"

"Up."

"You killed all the elevators, didn't you?"

"Didn't have time to be selective."

They were at the stairwell door when Phoebe heard a shout. She looked back and saw that the two men had managed to force a crack in the elevator door. The one not holding the crowbar reached for his gun. Phoebe didn't wait to see what he'd do with it. She slid into the stairwell a bare inch ahead of Dewey and started up the steps.

"You just had to pull the tiger's tail, didn't you?" Dewey said, the words panting out between the sound of their feet slapping the concrete stairs. They had rounded the last flight when the echoing sound of pursuit reached their ears.

The police file was depressing reading. According to the autopsy report, Kerry Anne Beauleigh had been pregnant and nearly flunking out of university when she apparently slit her wrists. The report assumed it was someone at school who'd gotten her pregnant. It theorized that she'd returned home despondent over that someone's rejection and killed herself. The assumption: Nadine had come home and found her dead—her bloody fingerprints had been all over the bathroom and her bedroom—and taken off "in a fit of grief." The sisters had been close, and Nadine had been having problems at school, too. The file also noted that their mother had been "sickly" and unable to supervise the girls closely. No mention of where she'd been when Kerry Anne slit her wrists, but the stepfather, Montgomery Justice, had been playing cards with his hunting buddies—one of whom was the doctor who performed the autopsy.

Mama was a drunk.

The report had a sanitized feel, not exactly covering up but not telling the whole truth. On Monday, he'd call both schools and see what he could turn up. Now that they'd matched Nadine's fingerprints to Phoebe's, they'd have no trouble getting the necessary warrants.

Matt had left muttering something about shaking the dew off his lily. He came back on a run. "Silent alarm at TelTech. Police are responding."

So Bryn's source had played it straight. Jake silently cursed. He hadn't expected them to move this fast and only put together a surveillance plan a few hours ago. They'd all agreed it could safely be implemented tomorrow night at the earliest, since the owner, Peter Harding, had been alerted to a possible threat.

"So are we." Jake was up and heading for the door before the words were completely out. "Bryn know?"

"Alice is paging her." Matt checked his weapon and grabbed his suit jacket as they passed his chair on the way to the door. He shrugged it on while they waited for the elevator, which seemed to take a long time, then a longer time to work its way to the ground.

Alice and Bryn were waiting in the car for them with the motor running. Alice didn't wait for Jake to shut his door before she put the pedal to the metal.

Dewey didn't waste time finessing the roof access door, just kicked it open and followed Phoebe through, then turned, hunting for something to block the door with. There was always something available in the movies, but not for them. He could hear the labored, pounding footsteps of their unlawful pursuers and the distant wail of sirens approaching.

"You just had to call the cops, didn't you?" Dewey muttered as he followed her to the edge and helped her set up the rocket launcher and their last length of rope. She fired it, and he quickly secured it on their end.

Phoebe attached two handles and hopped onto the edge, her feet dangling over nothing.

Dewey helped her slip her pack back on. "You know I hate going out like this."

"Pretend we're astronauts and our rocket is about to blow." Phoebe grabbed the first set of handles. "Because we're not, but it is."

"No shit."

"Don't wait until I'm down or your ass is grass."

"I'll shake you off if I—"

"Just do it!" She went over the side, rushing through the cold air toward the dark stand of trees. No chance either of them would have a neat, or pain-free, landing this time. She was almost there when she heard a shout. The rope bounced violently from Dewey's additional weight. Her legs swung up over her head, breaking her grip. She experienced a brief sensation of out-of-control flight before she crashed into a tree.

His gun out, Farley raced to the edge where the shadow had gone over and looked down. He could see the rope bouncing, but no sign of anyone on it. It was like the guy was invisible or something.

"Where they'd go?" Harley asked.

"Down, I guess. Should we go after them?"

"I'm not going down that rope." Harley peered over the edge, then flinched back. "Long falls don't agree with me."

Farley opened his mouth to agree, but before he could speak he realized what he was hearing. Sirens. Getting closer. "Oh, shit." He looked at the rope, then his hands. "This is gonna hurt."

"It doesn't have to." Harley ripped off one of his sleeves from the shoulder and looped it over the rope, then double wrapped his hands. He sat on the edge of the building, took a deep breath and launched himself into the void.

Sometimes Harley reminded Farley why he kept him around. Farley quickly followed suit. Might have been better to wait to see how his brother fared, he realized, when he saw flames spurt out from under Harley's shirt where it met the rope.

Chapter Thirteen

When Jake and the others arrived at TelTech, the police were still sweeping the building. The buzzing morass of official activity outside didn't prepare them for the eerie silence inside. No one knew where to turn on lights, so their flashlights joined a dozen other dancing, flickering beams around the dead. Added to this was a sick feeling in the pit of Jake's stomach at the violence.

Had Phoebe participated in this carnage? It didn't seem possible that she or Dewey Hyatt could have done this. He hadn't known Phoebe long, but he'd tracked Dewey off and on for years. Until Ollie's recent demise, never once had there been any sign of violence. And Phoebe? Did he want her to be guiltless? Was that blinding his judgment?

"This isn't right." Bryn slashed her beam back and forth over the scene as if it was a sword that could cut out the sight. "This isn't their style." Her lights stopped on the three guys not in uniform. "Who are these guys?"

"That one asked Phoebe for a job in her bar and then got himself arrested. Estes PD could probably ID him."

Bryn looked interested, but he could tell she didn't know what it meant either.

Before Bryn could respond, Luke joined them. "They took the security tape with them." He rubbed his face wearily. "I knew one of the guards. He was retired PD. Wife, kids, grandkids."

Jake shoved his hands through his hair, the sick feeling growing until it started up his throat. Be embarrassing if he had to puke his guts. Hadn't done that since his first serial killing crime scene—a killer who was into torture. He swallowed hard and took a couple of deep breaths.

"Do we know what exactly they were after?" Bryn asked.

Luke shook his head. "We're waiting for the owner and," —he consulted his notebook—"some guy named Barrett Stern, who's in charge of security, to get here."

"Hate to be him," Jake observed, glad for the change of subject.

Luke shook his head. "What a mess."

"And yet . . ." Bryn did another sweep with her light. ". . . not."

"What do you mean?" Luke asked, his frown deepening as he did his own sweep.

"No bullet holes in the walls. Both sides appear to have had remarkably good aim during a pitched gunfight." She showed them the walls with her light.

Jake looked at Luke. "Downright amazing."

Luke nodded thoughtfully. "Downright."

"Phoebe? Come on, girl, snap out of it."

The voice was Dewey's, but he seemed to be a long way away. Between her and him was this throbbing pain that seemed greatest, but not limited to her head. There was also a sense of motion, as if they were bouncing forward. A metallic creak and downward lurch vibrated through all her pain zones and narrowed the gap between them. "Don't make me take you to the hospital, girl."

A jerked stop, another creak, then she felt her hand taken and patted. Something cold and wet on her face. She crawled up out of the fog and opened her eyes. Dewey loomed over her, two worry lines cutting deep furrows between his eyebrows.

"What happened?"

"I bounced you off the rope."

"Oh." Memory returned in painful chunks. She touched her head. "I hit a branch or something." She took the cool rag he'd used on her brow and applied it to the swelling lump. "What happened to those guys who were after us?"

Dewey grinned. "They had a rough ride. Tried to slide down after us and caught the rope on fire. Last I saw, they were limping off into the night."

Phoebe grinned. It didn't hurt, so she decided to sit up. That did hurt. A lot. But it didn't kill her, so she didn't stop. "How's our hornet's nest?"

"Nicely stirred. Want to take a look?"

"Wouldn't miss it." Phoebe tried out her arms and legs. They worked. "I'll change while you drive."

Dewey scrambled back into the driver's seat but looked back to say, "Make sure you clean off the blood."

Phoebe grabbed a mirror. There was indeed blood, a thin line creeping down her temple toward her jaw. Not to mention a lip getting fatter and a shiner in the making.

"Great."

Dewey grinned. "There's an ice pack in the first-aid kit."

He put the van in gear and turned it toward TelTech and their hornet's nest.

Hornet's nest was a serious understatement, Phoebe decided. She'd think they couldn't get any more officials inside and then some more would come. Then the military. FBI. US Marshals. It was a regular law-enforcement-rich zone. Enough to make a lady thief and her accomplice a little nervous.

"What's taking him so long?" Dewey had started doing lame magic tricks with a pencil—when he wasn't using it as a drumstick against the dash. Phoebe was about ready to shove it up his nose, when a murmur of sound and the beginnings of new activity outside the van distracted her.

Light from the rising sun began a slow creep across the scene as Peter Harding's limousine nosed into the melee. It was immediately surrounded by the moderate mob of press who had been shivering over steaming cups of coffee in the predawn cold.

Exhilaration at having achieved their first objective filtered a fine clarity over the scene for Phoebe. It was as if all her senses had been heightened and expanded until she could see not only what was apparent but also what was hidden.

Because of her messy landing, Dewey suggested she play camera man and hide her bruises behind a camcorder. She climbed out and did a slow camera sweep of the crowd as Harding emerged from his car and was immediately mobbed. Stern came around and tried to clear him a path with something less than courtesy. Phoebe hung back, going for the long view, while Dewey, as "reporter," joined the pack. As Harding topped the steps, his face loomed in her tiny horizon. She used her zoom to frame his face and record the moment of her triumph. His mouth moved, but she couldn't pick up his answers over the questions bombarding him from every side. She tightened her focus to just his eyes and felt a jolt, a sudden panic she couldn't explain.

He looked exactly as he should, exactly like any man would who'd just been burgled. So why was a cold dread spreading out from her midsection? She stayed with him until he disappeared inside, then slowly lowered the camera and slipped into the rear of their van to wait for Dewey.

What was wrong with the picture?

She stowed the camera and scrambled forward, about the climb into the passenger seat when she saw Jake come out TelTech's door, flanked by his brothers. She shrank back, but not so far she couldn't see him. He looked sad, tired . . .

worried. About her? She tried to hope not, but she wasn't that noble. She wanted him to be worried about her. She wasn't quite ready to cut that tie, to forget this past. Maybe she knew she never would. It went deep, she realized, as deep as her sister's loss. He mattered. He . . . mattered.

She leaned her cheek against the cool plastic of the seat. "Oh, Jake." His name came out on a soul-deep sigh. As if he heard her, or felt her presence, she saw him stop. His gaze swept the crowd. She shrank back into the shadows, her heart pounding with bitter regret. He was never hers. She couldn't lose what she didn't have, could she?

"Something wrong?" Matt asked.

Jake rubbed his face to avoid answering the question. How could he explain the feeling that Phoebe was out there somewhere, watching the chaos she'd wrought? How to explain it when he didn't believe she'd been responsible for the carnage inside? He felt like Jekyll and Hyde. Convinced that she and Hyatt were responsible for the run on TelTech but not the deaths. It was crazy. Insane. Madness.

Now he knew how Alice had felt falling down that rabbit's hole. He needed quiet and a big pot of coffee while he sorted through the chaos, but all he was going to get was the coffee.

Maybe—he had a sudden, chilling thought—he'd never feel peace again. What if the huge rip in his heart never healed? What if the marshal never got over the lady outlaw?

It would be dang ironic, he decided, trying to lighten his mental mood. It didn't help much, but any improvement was welcome. As was any interruption. With a sense of reprieve, he met the approaching crime-scene tech halfway.

"What you got?" Jake asked.

"Their egress point."

Must have started his life as a lawyer, Jake decided as he

followed the tech around the building. With the sun peeking over the mountains, there was enough light to see the rope hanging limply from the roof. The tech held up the burned end for Jake to see. "Rough landing. I'll bet that wasn't part of the plan."

Jake frowned. Another wrong note. Phagan and Hyatt's ops were meticulously planned, right down to any surprises. "Where's the other end?"

The tech led Jake to a stand of trees where the other end of the rope trailed from a rather battered tree. Jake picked up this burned end, but he was studying the broken branches. "Looks like someone made it down before the rope burned through. Any footprints?"

"We got two sets heading toward the road. Tire tracks toward the highway. And at least one set, maybe two, heading off into the hills. No sign of transportation in that direction yet."

Jake frowned. "We got a stolen cleaning van in the parking lot out front. I wonder why they split up and . . ." Why two cars? If they were planning to come out this direction, which the get-away vehicle seemed to indicate, then why the messy landing? Surely they'd have prepared for it?

Jake straightened. It was almost as if they were dealing with two separate events. But that was crazy. Or wishful thinking. If he peopled TelTech with two sets of thieves, that let Phoebe and her cohorts off the hook for murder.

He saw Luke crossing the lawn with Bryn and knew it would take more than gut feelings for him to let Phoebe off the hook for this. He'd need hard proof. Facts, not fancies. When the pair got close enough for him to read their eyes, he could see neither looked particular happy, and an air of tension clogged the air around them.

"What?" Jake asked, giving them both a wary glance beforc looking to Bryn for enlightenment.

"This just doesn't add up," Bryn said, her voice tight and tense.

"To?" Jake prompted, ignoring a frustrated sigh from his brother.

"A Phagan op." She massaged her temples, either because they hurt or to clear her thoughts.

Or maybe both, Jake thought wryly. Either way, he understood. His head hurt and his brain did, too. Iron bands squeezing inside and out.

"It's like—" she began.

"—we're dealing with two different operations?" Jake finished when she didn't.

She gave him a relieved nod. "That or our perps were a couple of Jekyll and Hydes."

"Do we know what they got?" Jake asked.

Luke answered this one. "Some kind of super-chip and all relevant research files. A total wipe-out. Folks were pretty closemouthed but did admit that it was something in development for the military and due to be turned over in a few days. All very hush-hush and very, very bad it's gone missing."

"Not something you'd want to go missing so close to announcing your candidacy for governor," Bryn said. "That part of the crime scene, the research lab, is pristine. Clean as a whistle. No indication of how they got into the room, let alone how they able to log on to the computers. From what we can tell, the files were downloaded to someplace off site, then a virus was introduced. And the one scientist who held all the pieces of the chip puzzle seems to have disappeared."

Luke looked thoughtful. "That ought to up the street value on the chip."

"If Phagan did this hit, it probably won't show up on any

market, local or worldwide. He uses the non-cash take for leverage against his target." Bryn's frown was puzzled. "I just wish we could connect Harding to Nadine Beuleigh. So far, he's still squeaky clean. He thinks his scientist is the one who stole it, because he's gone missing. Said something about the instability of genius."

"You said they never go in shooting," Luke said, "but we've got four dead guards and a missing genius." He looked at Jake, his shoulders rising in a frustrated shrug. "What put you on to TelTech in the first place?"

"I got a tip," Bryn said, with obvious reluctance.

"Reliable source?"

"Has been up to now." Bryn looked at Jake, not at Luke, warning him to keep his mouth shut.

As if Luke sensed the holding back, his face turned grim. He opened his mouth, but before he could ask, they heard Matt's voice on Luke's radio. "Get in here. You gotta see this."

Back inside TelTech, they stood back until the last bagged body was rolled out, then entered the security office. The row of televisions that had been monitoring activity in the various hallways and offices were all playing the same picture, so they didn't have to crowd around one monitor to see.

The time/date stamp in the upper right-hand corner of the picture showed it was taken at two a.m. The silent alarm had gone off at 2:08 a.m., according to the security company. On the monitor, Jake saw the guards watching the Broncos game on the television in the corner, putting the angle it was shot from in the opposite upper corner.

Jake looked up and saw a tech removing the A/C grill from that area and returned his attention to the last few moments of the guards' lives. When it was over, he inhaled shakily. It had been a particularly nasty little scene.

He looked at Bryn. Maybe it was just the lighting that took all the color from her face. "How does it feel to be right?"

"Not as good as you'd think," she said, managing a wan smile. "How come I keep thinking this was an inside job?"

"And who the hell captured the feed?" This from Matt. "And how? Why are they sending it to us now?"

"Yeah, and where's it coming from?" Luke asked.

"Probably some kind of satellite uplink that's been planted in the computer. We'll need to open it up," Bryn said. She stopped, then asked, "Are we capturing this?"

There was a concerted leap to get a tape into the machine before the scene started a new loop. Jake stepped back from the group, his thoughts suddenly jumping in a new direction. He looked up as the tech pulled the grill away, revealing the camera secreted there.

Without stopping to think about it, Jake stepped around the tech until he was in full view of the camera and stared into it, as certain Phoebe was looking at him as he was that his chest had just gone too tight to breathe.

"Let me help you," he mouthed.

Phoebe stared at Jake like a deer caught in the headlights. He knew she was there and watching him. Dang, he was good. Too good.

"Let me help you," he was saying. Willing her with his eyes to listen and respond.

Damn it, she wanted to, more than she wanted to destroy Peter Harding. She stared at him, unable and unwilling to look away until the busy tech cut her connection with the room. She sat back with a sigh, reaching out to cut her uplink. They were bound to look for it next. It wouldn't be easy, because Ollie did good work, but they would find it and attempt to track it back to them. That would take them on a trip around the world, but they say travel is broadening. She would have grinned but for the feeling Jake was still watching her.

Let me help you.

This was pathetic. She'd now joined Phagan in feeding the Feds leads. This was beyond pathetic. It was dangerous. She hadn't even planned it, just acted on an impulse she couldn't explain. Well, maybe she could. It would put more pressure on Harding, even if he hadn't been the one to send in the thieves. The whole thing screamed *inside job,* so somebody on the inside was dirty, and it might as well be him.

That crime scene had to be confusing as hell. She couldn't resist a slight grin at the thought. Lucky for her she'd accidentally recorded the shooting. She had no desire to be the object of a murder manhunt. Okay, so maybe she also didn't want Jake to think she was a killer or involved with killers.

Of course, he should know that. They all should. How long had Phagan been operating without a whiff of violence?

No one at TelTech would be able to hang the deaths around their shoulders either, since she had RABBIT and the tape recording. If nothing else, that would seriously muddy the waters.

She pushed her chair back and paid a visit to the well-stocked mini-bar. Dewey had moved them from dirtiest dive to the honeymoon suite of Denver's finest hotel, thank goodness. The amusing part? TelTech was picking up the tab. Dewey had found a corporate credit card in the safe with the chip.

She popped the top of a Coke and drank. Wiped her mouth with the back of her hand while her thoughts did lazy circles inside her head, eventually bringing her around to the question of who inside TelTech had been trying to steal RABBIT. Or was that why?

She went around the heart-shaped bed, walking across a carpet of palest pink, and picked up the chip Dewey had removed from the safe. Lifted it to the light. It looked ordinary. Innocuous. Unremarkable.

What exactly was RABBIT? Ollie had died before he could tell them what it was. What precisely was it supposed to do that made it so valuable to Harding?

She tossed it up in the air, caught it neatly. Maybe it was time she found out.

Peter Harding closed his office door with a sigh of relief. Talk about the hounds of hell. The press wasn't going to go easy on him. Stern went straight for the bar and poured them both scotch, straight up. He handed Peter his and drank deeply from the glass he kept. Then he strolled over to the window and looked out.

Peter knew he would survive it. He had to. No, he was meant to. The storm would pass, and his troubles would be over, because RABBIT was gone. He tossed back half the glass, feeling the warm liquor rush into his bloodstream. "So far so good. When will your guys contact you?" Harding dropped into a chair, put his feet up on the desk, and held the glass up in a silent toast.

"I told them not to contact me for twenty-four hours, unless something went wrong. Just in case." Stern turned from the window. "We may have a problem."

"What?" He didn't want to hear about problems, not now, when it was almost over.

"My guys weren't planning to bail off the roof. There are other indications that someone else was here."

"What indications?" Stern just couldn't admit Harding's plan had worked perfectly. How like him to try to rain on his parade.

"Who set off the silent alarm?"

"I thought your guys were planning to do that when they were done."

"The alarm was tripped just after two. The timetable didn't allow for it until nearly two-thirty. They would have been in the elevator when it tripped. And, no, they weren't early. They couldn't have been. I was with them until one forty-five." He frowned. "That's why it took me so long to get here."

Peter got up and joined him at the window. Far below him, officials swarmed in and out of his building. Soon he'd have to talk to General Hadley about his lost RABBIT. It wasn't going to be pleasant, but it would get less so if RABBIT turned up on the foreign market. "If our guys don't have it, then where is it?"

There was a knock at the door, then that FBI bitch, Bailey—or something like that—stuck her head in.

"If you have time, there's something we'd like you to look at, sir."

Harding didn't look at Stern, he just nodded and followed her out and down, down, down to the security office with Stern on his heels. He entered the room and found himself facing three men waiting for him, something oddly similar in the way they all looked at him.

"Gentlemen?" Dealing with low level functionaries was familiar ground for him. He could feel his balance return as he returned their gazes with a practiced, worried one.

"This is Deputy US Marshal Jake Kirby," the woman said, pointing to a lanky man sprawled in a chair in front of the row of consoles. Kirby nodded at him. "And this is his brother, also a US Marshal, Matt Kirby."

Peter shook hands with him, tested his grip and found it as formidable as his hard gaze. "Marshal."

"And this is their brother, Detective Luke Kirby of the Denver Police Department."

"Quite the family affair, gentlemen," Peter said, allowing himself a slight smile. "This is my director of security, Barrett Stern. Have you found who stole my chip?"

"Well"—Jake turned to the console and punched some buttons—"we've made a good start."

Peter turned to the console, watched it flicker, then come alive. Saw the office, saw the guards. Saw them die.

He didn't have to pretend to be shocked. "I need—"

He couldn't breathe, couldn't get the words out. Stern pulled a chair forward and shoved him down into it. "Put your head between your knees."

Peter didn't argue. He needed a few moments out of sight of the barrage of eyes. Needed time to think. He didn't get it. Above him, he heard one of the men ask, "Who do you think put that camera in that vent, sir?"

Chapter Fourteen

The rattle of a key in the lock gave Jake and his brothers a short heads up that Mom was home. Jake felt a rush of relief. Mom was home. He'd missed her more than he realized since his transfer to DC.

"Well."

Jake looked up from the bowl of her soup he'd been dozing over and waited for her scrutiny to make its way to him. He looked, he'd been told, like his mother, where his brothers were near carbon copies of their dad. Jake didn't see it himself, except maybe in the eyebrows; hers tended to run amok, too, and he had her blue eyes.

She was tall and thin, almost as tall as Jake, with a narrow, clever face and hair that had turned gray when their father died. She'd been sad for a long time, but that had finally given way to acceptance and a serenity that became her sons' anchor in the years that followed. Lately, she'd also acquired a sparkle that Jake had attributed to Matt's marriage, until Luke burst his bubble with the news she was seeing someone. A buddy of their dad's.

It wasn't exactly an elephant in the room, but it was something Jake was still getting used to. He didn't begrudge her happiness. She'd worn black for Dad long enough. It was just hard to think of your mom in the dating zone. Which, judging by the flush in her cheeks and the softened line of her lips that tipped up in a slight smile, she'd just returned from.

The vestiges of her smile didn't survive her scrutiny of her sons. The three of them did, Jake had to concede, look pretty hashed. No sleep last night, followed by a long, hellish day, had put new lines in all their faces and deepened the ones already there.

"Dani must be out of town. Or you're afraid to wake her." Debra Kirby's gaze summoned Matt from the counter supporting him up. He gave her a kiss and a hug. Luke didn't wait for her gaze to find him. He planted a kiss on her opposing cheek the same time as Matt, then dropped into a chair and gave her his I'm-the-good son smile. The slight lift of her brow erased it.

Jake felt her high beams find him but was too tired to protect or defend his secrets. Limbs heavy, he pushed back his chair, rounded the table and lifted her into a hearty, desperately needed hug. If Mom couldn't make it better, then no one could.

"About time you showed up here," she scolded. Her arms and clean scent enfolded him in a wave of comfort. Before she let him go she patted him down for injuries, then framed his face with her hands.

Jake set her down. "Sorry, mom. Been—"

"—working. I know." Their gazes met and he saw hers widen slightly, then narrow into two X-rays. "Just like I know you'll find time to tell me what's been happening with you."

"Cross my heart." He knew he'd gotten off lightly, mostly because his brothers were there. She'd dig out his secret, but not in front of his brothers, not until she was sure it was common knowledge. If he had his way, this particular secret never would be common knowledge. He dropped back into his chair, exhaustion a dead weight dragging him down. "After I've had some shut-eye."

A shower came on over their heads, and her eyebrows shot up.

"It's Jake's FBI agent," Luke explained. "We made up the bed in the guest room for her."

"How domestic of you." Jake felt his mom's gaze swing his way again, question marks like neon signs in her eyes. Was this who'd put the sad in her baby boy's eyes, they asked him.

Jake gave her a silent no, then let his upper lids go back to ground zero against his lowers. More than anything, he wanted to fall onto his old bed upstairs. But he wasn't sure he could make it up the stairs, let alone down the hall to his boyhood bedroom, one that now did double duty as a sewing room. His mom didn't leave shrines to the past in her house.

"Want me to drop you off, Luke?" he heard Matt say, his voice wavering in and out as tired began to win the battle for Jake's body.

"Thanks." Jake heard the scrape of chairs being pushed back. "But let's get our baby bro up to his room. Doesn't look like he's gonna make it."

His brothers' voices, got farther and farther away. The sensation of being manhandled barely registered before tired took him down into a deep, dark well.

Phoebe woke face down on a pink rug amid scattered sheets of computer paper. She rolled onto her back and saw Dewey kneeling next to her. He smelled, she noted groggily, like roses.

It wasn't a great way to wake up. To make matters worse, she'd stiffened up, first from her collision with the tree, and then from falling asleep on the floor. She could see herself in the mirror over the heart-shaped bed. She'd managed to ice away the shiner but now had a strange looking rose pattern creased into her cheek from the carpet.

Dewey, wise man that he was, moved back a safe distance before he grinned at her. "What the hell happened here?"

Phoebe managed to sit up, though it felt as if she was

breaking bones to do it. She looked around because she had no idea what he was talking about.

Coke cans, chip and candy wrappers, mingled with the print-outs of RABBIT research data. The television screen was giving off a white-noise buzz, and a tape protruded from the video player. Pieces of memory drifted to the front of her mind, then whole chunks, until she remembered.

"Oh, yeah." Not remembering had been so much better. "I've been finding out about RABBIT. What it does. What it doesn't do. Like . . . work."

She leaned against the bed and rubbed her imprinted cheek, hoping to speed its return to normal.

Dewey dropped down beside her. "What are you talking about?"

"Harding's little chip is a piece of crap."

"What?"

"It doesn't work. That's why those guys were there. To steal it before other people found out it doesn't work, too."

He stared at her, his jaw slack, but there were indications in his eyes that he was attempting to assimilate what she was saying. He held up the morning newspaper.

"He wouldn't. Not when he's running for governor."

"Apparently he had no choice. Losing it being preferable to, say, jail?"

"No way. He wouldn't be that stupid, would he?"

"Maybe the billions of dollars he took from the government to develop RABBIT gave him a false sense of security. Thanks to Ollie, I've got the real tests and the falsified ones Harding used to keep the money flowing his way. But it was all going to come out when he turned it over if his RABBIT didn't disappear into the night."

"Billions, huh? Well, that could make a man stupid. What tipped you off?"

She crawled through the debris to the video player, pushed in the tape and started it. The television screen cleared, turned black, then filled with the scene outside TelTech the night before. "Look at this."

The tape she'd shot of Harding appeared on the screen. She froze the frame on the close-up. "Look at him."

Dewey looked. "What?"

"Look at his eyes." Phoebe sank back on her heels, fighting off the feeling of being sucked back in time. That was the way he'd looked when he punished them. Sorrow on the surface, pleasure underneath.

Dewey leaned in, then looked at her. "I see what you mean."

"He's why those guys were there. He had to have RABBIT to disappear." She rubbed her face. "And, clever little thieves that we are, we did the bastard a favor by grabbing it. If we give it back, turn this stuff over to the Feds, he can claim we faked the data and ruined his chip. Who's going to believe the nasty little thieves?"

Dewey processed this and finally sighed. "Well, that's pretty damn ironic."

Phoebe chuckled, then leaned her head on his shoulder. "That, my friend, is a serious understatement."

Despite the early hour, Harding poured drinks for them both. He left Stern's on the bar and carried his to the window. Stern left the drink where it was and walked over next to him. This wasn't the time to cloud his wits with liquor, especially if Harding was inclined to play the fool.

Outside the window, Harding's landscaping was tidy and controlled. The shrubs and flowers lined up like soldiers on review. Even the fountain spouted water in regimented bursts. Just the way Harding liked it. The view and the liquor smoothed the stress from Harding's face, blurring the façade and giving a brief glimpse of the evil that lurked beneath. He craved control, fed on it; like a junkie, he had to have his fix at regular intervals or he spun out of control.

In the years since their mutual darkness had drawn them together, Stern had made sure Harding had his fixes, had fed his addiction judiciously, kept him in control. Looking at him now, he wondered why he'd bothered. It was obvious that the addiction would never really be under control, just occasionally forced into remission.

The fool was happy now because he thought the threat was over. Whoever was gas-lighting him was good. And knew him well. Knew where and when to apply the pressure. It was hard to believe that a terrorized fifteen-year-old girl had managed to grow into someone clever enough for this kind of game. At first she'd mildly interested Stern, then she'd begun to annoy him. Now, well, even he could appreciate a job well done.

She'd reminded him of something he'd forgotten. Drive, don't be driven.

He'd let himself be distracted putting out fires. Reacting instead of acting. He'd gotten lazy, almost sloppy. He should know better. His perfect, middle-class father had taught him to keep an eye on the details, but never lose the long view. He'd kept track of everything but his only son. By the time he'd realized it, Stern had already chosen his long view.

Everyone had to choose light or dark. Some, like Harding, chose dark to hide their own evil. Others, like Stern, just liked the dark. Like Batman. It was his natural element, the place where he belonged. He liked danger. He liked killing. There was something fascinating about watching a life slip away. Where did it go? Was there a soul in those bodies? Or was it just over? Sometimes he thought he could see the soul leave, if the life he took had been lived in the light. When the innocent died, he believed in souls, but the feeling didn't last.

Unlike Harding, he didn't seek out victims, but he didn't turn aside when circumstances delivered them to him either. It was all in the details, and someday he'd know. One way or another, he'd know.

"Farley doesn't have RABBIT," he said, taking out a cigarette and lighting up to avoid seeing Harding's histrionics.

To his surprise, Harding said calmly, "So, what? As long as it's gone."

"And if it's offered for sale?" Stern blew a cloud of smoke in Harding's direction because he knew it annoyed him. "Be a pity if rumors came back to bite you on the ass." That got a reaction from him.

Harding headed for the decanter and slopped more into his glass. When he'd downed half of it, he aimed for the couch, stumbling slightly as the liquor went to his head. He rubbed his face. "How do we get it back? We have no idea who did it, do we?"

"No." Stern strolled behind the bar and poured himself a cup of coffee. "Farley says their faces were completely covered. I do have contacts in certain areas. They'll be watching for it to come onto the market, and they'll notify me if it does." He stubbed out the cigarette. A tiny spiral of smoke rose from the ashtray, circling his arm like a snake. "There is another possibility."

"What?"

"What if it was the same people who've been gas-lighting you?"

"I hadn't thought of that." Harding frowned, obviously having trouble coordinating his drink-saturated brain to grapple with the problem intelligently.

"If they try to expose it, we can dump the whole mess onto their shoulders. Who's to say what happened to it while it was out of our control?" Stern said.

Harding looked startled, then smiled, lifting the glass in a mock toast. "Yeah. Who's to say?" But before he drank, he asked, "If it is them, how do we find them?"

Stern smiled. "If they did this to get at you, we won't have to find them. They'll come to us."

Phoebe stretched out amid the papers, her hands crossed behind her head, and stared at the ceiling, feeling oddly resigned. They'd tried. They'd failed. Shit happens.

"Is it check and mate, Pathphinder?" Dewey asked. He'd stretched out beside her, but on his side, with his head resting on his hand.

She tried to clear her thoughts, to see the board, the game, but for the first time, she couldn't. She shook her head slowly. "I don't know. Pathphinder seems to be in shock."

"We need to fall back. Take some time to regroup. You've been working too hard if you can't see the game. And we need to get the heck out of Dodge. It's getting real hot here. Never seen the Feds try so hard to find two losers."

Phoebe grinned. "If you're trying to prick my pride by calling me a loser, it's not working." She sat up. "But you're right. We've been here too long. We need to move."

Without warning her flight-or-fight instinct kicked into high. She'd never been psychic, but right then, she'd swear she heard the howling of the hounds getting closer. She started grabbing all the papers within arm's reach and stuffing them into a briefcase.

Maybe Dewey heard the dogs, too. He started packing up their equipment with his usual swift efficiency. He had done this before.

"We'll have to split up," he said. "I'll write down my new beeper number for you. Your new beeper's on the desk."

"That where you've been?"

"That and arranging transportation for us. Something that will match our new lives."

Phoebe couldn't wait to see what kind of car he thought went with Polly. Or maybe she could. "Did you ever wish you could get out of the game? Live a normal life with a little woman somewhere?"

"Yeah." Dewey stopped, his eyes shifting from the immediate to a distant view.

What did he want, she wondered. Or was it who? There was so little that she knew about him.

"How did you get over it?" she asked, because it was all she could ask. The rest of his life wasn't her business.

He looked at her then, his gaze direct and sad. "I didn't. We can't. If we get over it, we risk becoming like them—like Harding and the others. We risk forgetting why we do it and just do it because we can." He gave her a crooked grin. "It's not as if you don't know about power and corruption."

"More than I want to." It was almost funny. She'd been thinking they were into avenging wrongs, but that wasn't the whole story. It was also about power. About taking it from those who had too much and giving it to those who had lived too long without it.

Dewey was right. She needed to just get on with it.

She picked up the chip. "It's too bad . . ."

"What's too bad?" Dewey asked.

"That *we* can't get it to work." She tossed it up in the air and caught it, then tossed it to Dewey. He snagged it and gave her a slow grin.

"Pathphinder?"

Jake could feel his mom watching him as he ate the breakfast she'd prepared for him and for Bryn—who had gulped hers and bolted out the door as if his mother's domesticity scared her.

Jake smiled. His favorite waffles, eggs, bacon, served with screaming hot coffee and ice cold milk weren't meant to be bolted but enjoyed. He ate until he couldn't manage one bite more. He pushed the plate away with a sigh of satisfaction. It didn't cure what ailed him but did make him feel he could deal with it.

"Thanks, Mom." He wiped his mouth on the paper towel she handed him. "That was great." He looked at his watch, started to rise, then made the mistake of making eye contact. He sank slowly back into the chair. "What?"

Her eyebrows rose.

"I'm fine! Really." The silence was insistent. "I'll be fine. This is just a tough case." He tried to get up again. Made it upright, but that was it.

She took a drink of her coffee, then asked, "What's her name?"

He rubbed the back of his neck. What was her name? His gut told him it was Nadine, but she'd always be Phoebe to him. He sighed. "I don't know."

"How much trouble is she in?"

"More than I can prove." He rubbed his index finger along the edge of the paper towel, remembering how she'd made her napkin into an origami bird. Was she already flying away from him?

"And what you can prove?"

"Harboring. Aiding and abetting, if—" He stopped. What was her next move? How did she plan to use RABBIT? If she had it. He could see the board but not the pieces. He was playing her game in the dark.

"If?" His mom's voice was soft.

"If I can find her. Her . . . associates tend to disappear."

Her hand covered his. “Which is worse, Jake? The thought of not seeing her again? Or having to arrest her when you do?”

Jake’s smile was a miserable effort. “I wish I knew.”

He turned toward her, into arms that circled him with comfort.

“If it’s meant to be, it’ll work out. If it’s not, you’ll just have to find a way to get over it.”

“And if I can’t?” He closed his eyes, felt her fingers stroke his hair.

“Then you learn to live with it.” She framed his face with her hands. “There are joys and sorrows in this life. You can’t escape either. You do your duty and you just keep going.”

She knew all about sorrow. She’d kept going after Dad died and kept them going, too. He managed a grin. “I know.” He looked at his watch again. “And that’s what I need to do—get going.”

He gave her a last hug. “Thanks, Mom.”

She patted his cheek. “If you do find her, I’d like to meet her. She must be something to put the squeeze on your heart.”

“Oh, she’s something all right.” Jake rubbed the back of his neck. Boy, was she something. Something a guy didn’t get over easily. Or fast. He headed out the door, feeling a little lighter of heart. It still ached, but was no longer dragging him down. He was just getting into the truck when his cell phone shrilled a call to action.

“Yeah?”

“Jake? Riggs here. Hey, man, Matt had me tracking down phone numbers of all calls made from the bar and the house. I found one you might want to have someone check out.”

“Give me the address,” Jake said, propping the phone between shoulder and ear and grabbing his pen and notebook.

“It’s called Smith’s. Part of a strip mall in Estes Park.”

Riggs gave him the address. "I called around, tried to find out who they were or what they did and came up a total blank. Landlord doesn't know what they do but thinks it's something to do with computers. The name on the lease is a bogus. I called it probable cause, and a judge agreed. I got a warrant. How do you want it handled?"

Jake sat for a moment, thinking. Logic said, assign it to someone in the Estes Park PD. No reason for Phoebe to be there. She was going forward with her game, not backtracking.

"I'll take it," he said. His brain was telling him it was a waste of time, but his gut was twitching. He followed his gut and put his truck into gear. He'd pick up the warrant and head for Estes Park.

Phoebe drove past *Smith's*, looking for signs it was under surveillance and finding none. Okay, so they hadn't found the number on her phone bill yet, but they would. Then someone would come. This setup was the kind of lead that Phagan's fibbie/love would sell her firstborn for.

She pulled into the rear, since the orange, green and yellow piece of shit Dewey had gotten her to drive would stand out like a sore thumb in the parking lot out front and her clothes didn't match the car. She'd passed on the Polly clothes and hair paint for a black sheath and heels. She wished she could have passed on the car.

Inside she started a wipe/delete on the hard drives of the VR setup in the back room where she'd planned the TelTech heist. There weren't a lot of papers lying around, since Phagan didn't believe in paper trails, but what there was, she fed into the shredder, all the while keeping an eye on the security monitors.

The emergency wipe was about half done when she saw Jake's truck pull to a stop out in front.

Chapter Fifteen

Jake had to jiggle the key the landlord had given him in the lock before the front door gave. The lock felt stiff, as if it wasn't often used. To reinforce this impression, the door gave a protesting squeak as it swung closed behind him. Inside, the light that filtered through imperfect blinds was thick with dust motes as it dimly revealed what looked like an ordinary office. A lesser desk near the front door seemed to be for reception purposes, with several desks of better quality lined up behind. Phones, computers, and filing cabinets completed the picture of a business enterprise, though there was no indication what that enterprise was supposed to be.

He pulled on protective gloves and adjusted one set of blinds to let in more light. The air was stale, and—Jake swiped a finger across a slat—a layer of dust coated everything in sight. Did this mean it was a cold trail? The call had been made two weeks ago. He didn't have statistics on dust accumulation, only personal experience to go by. He'd been gone from his apartment in DC for a month or more and hadn't had this much dust to take care of.

He walked around the reception desk and sat down. Opened a few drawers, all empty. Tried the phone. It didn't work. The computer monitor wasn't connected to anything, and when he touched it lightly, it fell off the desk. And bounced.

Jake picked it up. Cardboard. Designed to fool the casual observer. Did that make this place a front, and, if so, for what? The rent wasn't huge, but it wasn't peanuts either. If this was part of the Phagan setup, what role had it played?

Well, whatever purpose this place had served, this fake office wasn't going to cough up anything but dust bunnies. Maybe the prize was in one of the back rooms. He got up and headed for the doorway.

That's when he heard a toilet flush.

He had his gun out and was in the hallway when the door opened. Light spilled into the corridor, just short of where he stood, painting a familiar, leggy outline onto the floor at his feet. He followed it up to the source, but before his eyes got to her, his senses already knew who it was.

Phoebe.

"Jake? What are you doing here?" She looked genuinely surprised to see him and not at all alarmed.

"I could ask you the same thing." His eyes drank her in. She was wearing something black and slinky that lightly hugged her body everywhere that mattered, then stopped well above her knees, leaving plenty of leg. He didn't know a pair of black heels could be that sexy, but there'd been a lot he didn't know before he met her.

She leaned against the jamb and crossed her legs like a teenager on the porch with her first beau.

"Just taking care of a little business." Her tongue traced a moist path around her lips. "And you?"

"The same." He heard the hoarseness in his voice and cleared it. "You . . . cut your hair."

She reached up and touched the sheared ends, something that could be uncertainty flashing in her eyes. "It's . . . cooler."

Her eyes were deep, sad pools threatening to drown his sense of duty. Her scent turned the stale air sweet and his thoughts thick and slow.

"It's . . . nice. It suits you."

Her smile was quick and pleased but slightly shy.

As if to make sure no blood got to his brain, his collar

turned into a noose. He tugged at it, but it didn't help. What he needed was water. Cold water. Applied everywhere. He rubbed the back his neck, fighting for control. When he reached the point of tenuous control, as if she knew the exact moment when questions began to rise above the lust, she asked, "How did you get in? We're closed, you know."

That cleared his head. He holstered the gun he'd almost forgotten he was holding. Stripped off the gloves and stuck them in his jacket pocket. "I . . . have a warrant to search the premises."

Her eyebrows arched. She did surprised very well. "All you had to do was ask, curious Jake."

"I didn't think you were around to ask. I thought—"

"What did you think?"

"That you'd left."

"Without saying goodbye?" She stepped toward him. "I wouldn't do that."

"I thought we had said goodbye. At the motel the other night. It sounded like good bye."

"Things . . . aren't always what they seem."

He licked his lips. "No, they aren't."

She took a glove, hanging part way out of his pocket and examined it. "Afraid you'll catch something? I promise I'm not contagious."

But she was. Jake swallowed dryly as she stuffed the glove back into his pocket, real slow, as if she expected him to stop her. He knew he should stop her, but it would be easier to stop breathing than stop her from touching him.

He didn't decide to touch her. His hands acted on their own, sliding around the back of her neck, the short, silky ends of her hair stroking his skin as he bent toward her parted mouth. His heart jumped, then settled into a hard but steady rhythm.

It was as if he'd waited his whole life for this moment.

Phoebe didn't, couldn't, close her eyes or look away. She needed to see him. See what he was feeling pass through his eyes each moment that was left to her. This time, this kiss had to last her a lifetime. There'd be no one after him. How could there be anyone but the lawman for this outlaw?

His scent reached her before his mouth did. It filled her senses, heady and clean, like mountain air first thing in the morning. A pulse beat frantically against her hand. The feel of his skin was a delight all its own. She could have spent the whole day just absorbing it, feeling the wonder of his skin against her.

But her mouth, her impatient mouth had waited forever to taste his. She arched onto her toes, eager to close the last millimeter between them. Her head spun with longing as his breath mingled with hers.

Had she thought there was anything she wouldn't give this man? This other half of her soul? She felt surrender stealing through her body in a hot rush. Maybe she could trust him with it all . . .

She wasn't ready when he jerked her back and felt his bitter, betrayed gaze rake across her.

"What are you hiding, Phoebe? What's really going on here?"

Her chest hurt with the need for air, for him. There was no room for thinking or even planning. Only one bitter reality. She'd never know his kiss. She'd never know what it was like to be his. She closed her eyes against him. Against the longing to beg him to take her back into his arms. There was pride inside her somewhere. She had to find it.

He gave her no time. "This way, I think."

He pulled her toward the door with a faint light showing under it and shoved it open. Fumbled for and found the light switch. Saw the status of the wipe on the computer monitor. It was close to the end of the bar but not there yet.

Without missing a beat, he found the power cord and yanked it from the wall.

His chest heaved once, then he turned and looked at her. Her eyes were blank, neutral, as if her soul had fled to that deep, dark place where her sorrow lived. He'd done the right thing, but it didn't feel right. He could hear his mom's voice in his head, "You do your duty and you just keep going."

He looked at the row of dark monitors, saw a VR helmet and gloves lying on the desktop, several CPU towers and a couple of printers. "It looks like you could run the world from here."

"I almost did."

This wasn't about him, but he still felt the bitter bite of betrayal, the pain of the knife burying itself in his back. He'd had no reason to trust her, certainly no right to expect anything from her except deceit, but he had. Damn it, he had.

"What now, Phoebe? Or should I call you Nadine?"

Chapter Sixteen

Peter Harding climbed into the rear of his limo and found Stern waiting for him in the richly appointed interior. He stretched his long legs out with a sigh of satisfaction, enjoying the faint vibration of the automobile's leashed power underneath him. Like him, this car was damn near invincible. It had been made by the same company that supplied the President's vehicles. No one could get in or out unless he wanted them to.

Stern gave a warning look toward the open partition that separated them from the driver. "The police have a suspect in custody. They want us to come in."

"Okay." Harding tensed. This wasn't part of the plan. "The police station, Jim."

The driver nodded and put the car into motion. Stern closed the partition and added, "They want to put her in a lineup for our . . . edification and possible identification."

"Her?" Harding felt a sharp bite of excitement. If it was Nadine . . .

"Her. And under no circumstances will you give any sign that you recognize her, Harding. Under—No—Circumstances. We don't want her cutting any deals with the Feds, now, do we?"

"What do you have in mind?"

"She'll need a good lawyer. We get her one, then get her bailed out. My boys pick her up and—"

"And bring her to me!" Harding felt his loins tighten as he thought about having Nadine back in his power, where she was supposed to be. Where she was meant to be. He'd teach her a lesson she wouldn't forget again.

"This is not the time for that. Not while you're in the press spotlight. Let it go. Let her be the one you didn't get. I'll make sure she disappears after I find out who and where her partner is. Once they are dead and buried, so is RABBIT." For a moment anticipation gleamed in Stern's dead eyes.

"I have to be sure it's her," Harding insisted. Damn Stern just wanted her for himself. The asshole liked a challenge. Well, he wasn't getting this one. Nadine was his. "I'll be careful. But I get her first. When I'm through, you'll have no problem convincing her to talk. She'll do what she's told, just like she used to." He looked at Stern. "You can get your jollies off her partner, but I get her."

Stern shrugged, but Harding could tell he was annoyed. For once, he wasn't sure Stern would do as he was told. He thought again about the anonymous note he'd received, warning him about secrets and people who knew them. It was a pity, because Stern had served him well, but maybe it was time to bury his secrets. Permanently.

Being booked wasn't the worst thing that had ever happened to Phoebe, but it came in a close second. The worst part was the loss of control, the loss of her personal power. It brought back echoes of her past and threatened her steely grip on the present. Only pride—and Bryn Bailey's watchful gaze—kept her from breaking down while being strip searched and then deloused. She donned her jail garb with outward nonchalance, pleased and surprised at how steady her hands were, all the while wondering if she'd ever be free of the smell of the delousing solution, wondering if her own scent would ever return.

The female uniform who'd done the search held the door open, but that door would only take her to another cage, a different level of confinement. Phoebe paused in the doorway, feeling the barrage of law-abiding Kirby eyes hit her. Felt like more than three guys. The trio sure packed a personality wallop.

She lifted her chin and drawled in her most Southern accent, "Interesting experience. Kinda brought back memories of my wedding night. Also brief but thorough."

She heard a muffled choke from Jake's brother, Luke, and couldn't resist looking his way. He was trying hard not to smile. She winked at him before letting Bryn prod her into an austere interrogation room. Bryn indicated a chair across from the court-appointed lawyer and left the room, but Phoebe knew she and the Kirbies three would be watching through the mirror affixed to the wall. She chose the one chair that put her back to the mirror, then reversed the chair's position and straddled it. With her elbows propped on the straight, battered back, she clasped her hands to keep them from trembling or twitching.

This was Pathphinder's most difficult game. The board was obscured, her pieces scattered, and she was facing a public defender who looked as if he was about to wet his pants.

Dewey would have come on the run and played a better lawyer, but that was likely what Phagan's fibbie was hoping he'd do. She had to protect her knight. She didn't have that many pieces to play.

"I'm Calvin. Calvin Dobbs, Miss . . . er . . ." His voice wavered up and down several octaves and his glasses slid to the end of his nose, dislodging a bead of sweat that had been hovering there. It dropped off the peak, then ran down to rest in the indention above his upper lip.

"You call me whatever you'd like to, Calvin. I'm very flexible." Phoebe smiled at him, but that only seemed to throw him into further disarray. "Have you ever done this before?"

He gave her a panicked nod that could have meant yes or no. "Your charge sheet says your name is Nadine Beauleigh. Also known as Phoebe Mentel." He looked up, his Adam's apple bobbing frantically against the pale skin of his long neck.

Phoebe sighed and gave him a sad and soulful look. "Is it a crime to change your name?"

"Um, no." He stared at her as if mesmerized. "Um, is there anyone who can . . . verify . . . your identity?" He switched his pen nervously from hand to hand.

If the guy had any more nervous habits, he wouldn't be able to get anything done. Phoebe slid her chair toward him, so that she was positioned between him and the mirror, took the pen and wrote a number on the inside cover of the file. "Call this number and punch in nine-one-one, then your number. Can you do that for me, Calvin?"

"Of . . . course." He took out his cell phone and dialed the number. When he'd managed it without too much shaking, Phoebe relaxed back in her chair. Now Dewey would know she'd been picked up, but that she didn't need a lawyer.

Calvin's fingers tapped against the tabletop until he stopped himself by curling them into fists. "Now about these charges . . ."

"I am, of course, completely innocent." She gave him her most innocent look, batting her eyelashes a couple of times for emphasis.

"Right." He wrote *completely innocent* on the sheet, his handwriting blocky and labored, like that of a first grader taking a spelling test.

She wished Jake were in here. He'd get a kick out of Calvin. Couldn't be a coincidence she'd gotten such a totally lame lawyer. It appeared that Bryn intended to play as dirty as she could get away with.

"Is there anything I can get you?" Calvin asked. "Anyone else you want me to contact?"

"I wouldn't mind something to read. And cigarettes?"

"Cigarettes? You don't look like—"

"I heard they're just like money in prison."

His smile was surprisingly sweet. Good teeth, too. Calvin had lots of unrealized potential, Phoebe decided.

"I don't think you'll be in here long enough for that. As soon as you're arraigned, we'll have you out on bail—"

Before he could finish, the door opened. Bryn stepped into the room. "We need your client to participate in a lineup for the owner of TelTech."

Phoebe could feel her stomach muscles tighten and forced herself to relax. Peter Harding couldn't touch her while she was in jail. Wow, she thought as she followed Bryn out, who'd have thought there could be an upside to getting your butt tossed in jail?

Jake stood in shadow to one side, positioned to watch Peter Harding and his side-kick during the lineup. If he was Phoebe's past, her and Phagan's current target, he wanted to know it. He heard the shuffle of movement as the five women came out and formed a ragged line on the other side of the one-way glass. Harding licked his lips, his gaze moving along the row, stopping for a long moment on Phoebe before moving on.

"Turn to the right," Luke directed the women through a mike.

Again Harding's gaze traveled the row. It didn't stop at Phoebe, but it came back to her. He licked his lips again, and Jake saw sweat pop up on Harding's upper lip. Jake's skin crawled. The guy had a definite kink. No question.

"Now to the left," Luke said. "See anyone you recognize, sir?"

Jake saw him look at Phoebe one last time, then at Luke. He shook his head.

"Sorry."

He's lying. Jake knew it even before he saw Harding watch Phoebe file out with the others. So why not finger her? Dumb question. If he was her target, he'd have a lot to hide. But what part of Phoebe's past was he involved in? Research had revealed that all of Phagan's other targets had a family connection of some kind to one of his runaways, but this guy, while old enough to be Phoebe's stepfather, didn't remotely resemble the descriptions of Montgomery Justice. Maybe they needed to cast the net wider, look at her schoolteachers and others from her past.

Harding started to leave. Jake stepped into his path. He was convinced Harding was Phagan and Phoebe's target and decided to play a new card, one he'd been holding back. "Could you look at this picture, sir?" Jake pulled a mug shot of Oliver Smith out of his inside pocket. "You ever seen this man?"

Harding took the picture with an odd air of reluctance and studied it. "I'm not . . . sure . . ." He licked his lips again, but this time it was an obviously nervous movement.

Stern took the photo, studied it, then handed it back to Jake. "He worked at TelTech for about three months. Then one day last week he didn't show up for work."

"I'll need the exact day," Jake said.

"I'd have to check his personnel file."

"We'll need a look at that file," Bryn said, inserting herself into the conversation.

"Our files are confidential and—" Harding began.

"He's dead. I don't think he'll care," Jake said. Neither man looked surprised. Stern looked like a guy who might get his jollies pounding faces. Jake was already looking in to his past, but he'd look harder now.

"I'll see that it's sent over," Stern said. "Will there be anything else?"

"No." Jake watched them leave, oddly relieved to have them gone. There was something off, something definitely wrong about the pair. No question Stern was running interference for his boss.

"Lovely pair, aren't they?" Bryn asked.

"You don't like them?"

She made a face. "I don't like them, and I don't like that I can't find what they're hiding. Did you see Harding staring at our girl?"

Jake nodded. "You're so sure they are hiding something?" he asked, curious to get Bryn's take.

"Oh, yeah. Guys like that, they can't help it. I just haven't found the right rock to look under yet." She sighed in frustration. "And I might not, without Little Miss Larceny. If we don't open her up—" She looked at Luke. "You monitoring her?"

Jake looked at his brother, too, noticing Luke didn't look too happy.

"Of course I am, but I'm not sure this is such a good idea—"

"What's not a good idea?" Jake asked. He looked at Bryn. "What's going on?"

Her expression hovered between defiant and guilty. "We haven't got much time until she's out on bail. Once she's out, she's gone."

"*What* have you done?" he asked Luke.

Luke's look was apologetic. "We put Phoebe in with Holly the Horror."

"What the hell?" Jake didn't have to ask why Holly was a horror. Every jail had a prisoner who could be counted on to make life rough for the newly incarcerated. "Have you lost your minds?"

Bryn bristled like an outraged hen. "It's a proven technique for softening up—"

"Explain to me how putting someone who was probably abused into running away from home into an abusive situation is going to soften her up?" He got in her face. "From where I'm standing, it just makes us abusers, too."

Her mouth worked for a moment as she struggled for control. "I didn't think of that."

"Next time you have a plan for *my* collar, have the professional courtesy to run it past me first." He saw red spots of rage bloom on her cheeks, but he didn't give a damn. He whirled on his brother. "Get her out of there. Put her in federal holding. Alone. Now. And I want her watched all the time. No one—I mean *no one*—goes near her without my permission."

Luke raised his hands in surrender. "I'm on it."

Jake saw more than surrender in his brother's eyes. He also saw questions sprouting like weeds. Jake didn't have answers. Well, he didn't have good answers for why he was so pissed off. At least not answers he wanted to share with his big brother. Life was hard enough without Luke and Matt knowing he'd gotten emotionally involved with a perp.

"Chill, little brother," Luke said, stirring the still-hot embers. "No one's going to let your . . . collar . . . get hurt."

Jake's hands curled into fists. He turned and stalked out before he took a swing at his brother. He'd lose that one, since Luke topped him in height and weight. That left Bryn, but, even pissed to hell and back, he knew better than to hit a woman. Maybe he ought to hire Holly to kick her ass.

Phoebe knew something was up before she reached the

cell in the local, not federal, section of the jail. When the cop opened the door, the hair on the back of her neck rose in warning. She stepped far enough through the door so he could close it, but no farther.

"Be nice to the new girl, Holly," the cop said with a smirk before strolling off.

Phoebe heard a low growl from the shadows of the lower bunk. The bed creaked, then groaned as Holly rolled over and got up.

She was big and beautiful. Magnificent. Tall and formed like an Amazon, she had a rioting mop of red hair and hard purple eyes. Her lush body strained every seam of the drab prison garb. The pointed red tips of lethal-looking nails fanned across her hips as she surveyed Phoebe with a distinct lack of welcome.

Phoebe had a feeling Holly's "nice" wouldn't be pleasant.

"You must have pissed somebody off, honey, 'cause that asshole knows I hate sharing. And I really hate getting woke up from my beauty sleep."

"I guess that means you're going to try to kick my ass." Phoebe spread her feet and softened her knees, her body tensed to respond to any sudden movement.

"No, honey, it means I *am* going to kick your ass." Holly clearly didn't think it would be a problem.

"It may not be as easy as you think. You're gonna get bruised, too." Phoebe met her suddenly narrowing gaze squarely. "Unless . . ."

"Unless what?"

"I don't see why we should give the cops what *they* want. And getting all bloody and bruised? Besides being messy, it's boring."

"Boring?" A touch of amusement softened Holly's hard eyes. "Getting pounded on is boring?"

Phoebe shrugged. At least she'd succeeded in piquing Holly's interest. "Let's just say I prefer the unpredictable."

Holly circled to Phoebe's left. Phoebe turned, keeping them face to face.

"And unpredictable would be . . . ?"

Phoebe extended her hands, empty palms up. Turned them over, did a small flourish and turned them back. A small harmonica was now in one hand.

Holly looked surprised. "They let you bring that in here?"

Phoebe shook her head.

"How did you get it through the search?"

Phoebe grinned. "Magic." She made the harmonica disappear, then reappear.

Holly laughed, a rich, rolling sound that echoed around the jail, bouncing off the arid walls in diminishing volleys before dying away. "I like you. What did you say your name was?"

"My friends call me Phoebe." Phoebe played her get-out-of-ass-kicking-free card. "I'm betting you have a hell of a fine voice. What say we kick their asses instead of ours?" She lifted the harmonica to just short of her mouth and smiled hopefully at Holly.

"No wonder they wanted me to kick your ass." Holly's eyes weighed her in the balance, then she smiled. "What the hell. No reason to break a nail for those assholes."

She sat down. "What can you play on that thing?"

"Anything you can sing." Phoebe sat on the commode and played a scale, then launched into an intro for "Amazing Grace." She was right. When Holly came in on cue, she had a hell of a voice.

Chapter Seventeen

Jake waited until he'd cooled down before heading for the jail. He found Luke and Bryn watching a closed-circuit monitor.

"What?"

Without answering, Luke pointed at the screen. Jake stepped around him and saw Phoebe in a cell with another woman.

"Why haven't you moved her?"

"We were waiting until they finished *Wild Thing.*" Luke grinned at his brother.

Jake did a double take. "Is that a harmonica?"

Bryn's expression was classically conflicted, with equal parts rage and laughter. She managed to control her twitching lips long enough to say, "Looks like the poor little abused girl can take care of herself." She rubbed her temples. "Sure like to know how she got that thing past us."

Jake grinned. "Magic?"

Luke gave Jake an amused, pointed look. "It's obvious she has a highly disruptive influence on *everyone* she comes into contact with."

Jake rubbed the back of his neck, saw Bryn and Luke watching him do it and lowered his hand. "How about you get her out of there before she gets too comfortable, Luke, while Bryn and I figure out a new approach?"

"You sure know how to take the fun out of things," Luke grumbled good-humoredly as he left. Something told Jake he'd be back, though, with more questions for his little brother. Behind the humor had been a boatload of worry.

Bryn crossed her arms and leaned against the console. "Works for me. What are you thinking?"

Jake turned his back on the console and Phoebe. He couldn't think while looking at her. "They go after their targets mainly to expose their nasty secrets, right?"

"That appears to be their priority." She sighed internally. It was hard to hate Phagan. She was reluctant to admit it, but she was worried about him. She hadn't heard from him since Phoebe got picked up and had had no flowers, chocolate, or romance novels from him either.

Jake's stopping that disk wipe had seemed like a major coup. To her deep chagrin, she had been relieved when Matt's computer guru found nothing. Chasing Phagan was like trying to take down Robin Hood. She was getting damn tired of being on the side of legal slime like she suspected Peter Harding to be. She hadn't gone into law enforcement to protect his ilk.

"So, if we can't beat her, why not join her? We offer her a deal in exchange for what she knows about Harding, Hyatt and Phagan."

"She won't give up Phagan. If he's on the table, she won't deal." The conviction in her voice startled her. What was wrong with her? She'd been hunting Phagan for five years. Here was her chance to get him, and she was backing off? "And I'm betting she won't rat on Hyatt either. If she is Pathphinder, they've got to be tighter than these shoes I wish I wasn't wearing."

She grimaced and eased them off to give her feet a short break. It took away any height advantage she had with Jake, but he didn't seem to notice.

He was frowning into the distance. "You're probably right. Course, if they are tight, Hyatt will make some kind of move to help her. We should start with the whole package.

The real question is, can you make a deal that doesn't include Phagan?"

"If she returns RABBIT, I might make it work with my people. What about you?"

Jake's smile had an edge to it that made her uneasy, though she couldn't say why.

"I've got a few ideas that should make it palatable to my side," he said. "I just need some maneuvering room, so I can make it look as if I'm giving ground."

"Okay." She gave him a minute to enlighten her, but he didn't bite. She sighed. "You want me with you when you make the offer? She doesn't like me."

Jake grinned. "Phoebe doesn't like much. If you don't mind, I think I should go in alone, at least the first time." He looked at his watch. "The clock is ticking. We'll let her simmer a bit while we get approval. Let me know ASAP."

Bryn nodded. She wanted to ask him if he was going to be okay, but she knew he would. He just might not be the same. He was hiding it well, but Phoebe had changed him somehow. He'd lost his little-boy-having-an-adventure aura. Was more serious, more . . . sad. It wouldn't change what he'd do. She knew he'd do what he had to. But at what price?

She sighed. What price would they both pay before this was over?

Stern passed Harding's secretary, his glance flicking over her long enough to see her slight grimace warning him all was not well in the inner sanctum. He wasn't surprised to find the room dark, the curtains shut against the world slipping from Harding's control.

He heard the clink of ice in a glass and turned away from the desk. As his eyes adjusted to the lack of light, he saw Harding stretched out on the couch, his tie loosened, his mouth drooping in a petulant pout. On the bar, the brandy decanter was nearly empty. On the floor next to him his glass lay on its side, the melting ice dripping onto the carpet.

He knew that Harding stood on the thin edge between madness and sanity. Had wondered what—or maybe it was who—would push him over that edge? If Harding could have mastered his lust for controlling women he could have directed it toward the accumulation of money and power over many lives. Nothing could have stopped him. Without his rather glaring Achilles' heel where women and girls were concerned, he could have had the Presidency one day. All great men were both shadow and light, but if they weren't careful, what they did in the shadows, could overcome the light.

It had been a wasted effort to erase his past. He'd brought it with him. If it hadn't been Nadine, it would have been someone else. You couldn't have the kind of tastes Harding had without something being exposed. The Feds were looking hard now. They'd find something. They usually did once they'd gotten a scent.

Maybe, just maybe, he could contain the threat Nadine and her cohorts posed. He'd come too far to throw it all away. But he wasn't going down with Harding. Not because the asshole who wanted to control the world couldn't control himself.

He punched the intercom. "Get hot coffee in here. Lots of it."

Harding stirred and opened his eyes. "Where you been?" His speech was slurred and thick, but then he seemed to shake it off. "Do you have her?"

"It takes time to set up something like this without leaving a trail. I've got Farley arranging for a lawyer. If the cops check, it'll look like they were all in it together." He'd made sure he didn't mention to the boys that they'd been captured on film or they'd both be long gone. He needed them alive just long enough to help solidify the frame. A pity they'd have to die. He rather liked Farley. As much as he could like anyone. "They won't arraign her until they have to."

"What if she makes a deal?"

"Then we're screwed. They've got her in isolation. No one can get at her. My man inside laughed when I asked him to try."

"I pay good money to—"

"There isn't enough money in anyone's bank account to change his mind. She's under constant surveillance. He's greedy, not stupid."

The secretary brought in the coffee and hurried out. She knew her boss's temper when drunk and had no desire to hang around. Stern poured him a cup and ordered him to drink it, then poured him another.

"Get your head clear. Think. She knows she'll get bail. She's got no record. The Feds can scream all they want about flight risk, but all they got on her is aiding and abetting. Not nearly enough to convince a judge to deny bail. Not with a good lawyer crying foul. She's proved she's not stupid." Unlike you, he added to himself. "She'll sit tight because she wants you."

"She wants me." Harding smiled, his eyes glazing. "And I want her." He looked up at Stern. "You have to get her for me."

"Get sober and call your fiancée. She's been leaving messages for you."

It was definitely time to . . . sever . . . his relationship with Harding, Stern realized. He'd help Harding finish his game because he wasn't going to let some twit of a girl beat Barrett Stern. But that was all he'd do for the man. He headed for the door without looking back.

"Call me if you hear anything!" Harding called after him, wincing when Stern slammed the door. Stern was getting too cocky. "Asshole," he muttered, setting down the coffee cup now that he was alone.

"I totally agree," a voice said from the darkness in the direction of his desk.

His desk chair swivelled around until he could see someone sitting in it. Whoever it was reached forward and turned on the desk lamp. Harding winced again as the light stabbed into eyes. His brandy-sodden brain gave a painful lurch as he tried to remember if they'd said anything incriminating.

"Who the hell are you?" Harding struggled to his feet and started toward the desk and his gun, until he got close enough to see his gun trained on him. "What do you want?"

"World peace, an end to hunger, and clean air to breathe," Dewey said. "But I'll settle for being obscenely wealthy." He got up, gesturing with the gun toward the recently vacated couch. "Better sit down while we talk. I don't like picking drunks up off the floor."

Harding wanted to object, but even drunk, he knew better than to argue with a gun. "How did you get in here?"

"I have my ways." Dewey perched on the edge of the desk. "As, apparently, do you. You're quite the villain, aren't you?"

"What do you mean?" Harding rubbed his face with his hand, feeling the lines that fear was carving into his brow, but too panicked to do anything about them.

"Come, come, Harding. Your RABBIT don't run. It don't even totter. It's beyond the dud zone. I suppose that's why you tried to have it stolen. Only I beat you to it."

"It was you." Harding threw a quick look at the door. Stern had picked a hell of time to leave, he thought bitterly.

They'll come to us, he says, then leaves him alone and unprotected. He downed the coffee. Had to get his head clear. The surge of caffeine gave him a brief burst of clarity. "You'll have a hard time proving you're not the one who fucked it up."

"The thought did occur to me." Dewey studied him long enough to make Harding nervous. "What would you say if I told you I have a working prototype?"

"I don't believe you. You couldn't—"

"I had a feeling you'd say that. Do you think I'd be here if I couldn't prove I have a chip that works better than the Energizer Bunny?" Dewey walked over to the bar and helped himself to a dash of Harding's best brandy. "I'm sure even in your impaired condition you can see the benefit to your political aspirations if you recover your RABBIT and it actually works."

Harding licked his lips. "What's the catch?"

"I told you. I want to be obscenely wealthy. And not in jail." He went back to the desk and keyed up the computer, then turned the screen so Harding could see it. "I want half of the money you've got stashed in these Swiss bank accounts. I'll give you a number to transfer half my money to. When I verify you have completed the transaction, I'll meet you here with proof your RABBIT runs."

"How do I know you won't take the money and run?"

"Because you'll have Nadine. I get her back—*unharmed*—and the other half of the money when I deliver your chip." Dewey walked up to Harding. "What do you want more, Harding? To be governor? Or Nadine?"

"I want them both."

Dewey was smiling, but his gaze was chilling. "Nobody gets everything they want." The look in his eyes had Harding tugging at his tie. "Take me, for instance. I want you dead for killing Kerry Anne Beauleigh. I want you to die slowly, the way she did. Your blood drip, drip, dripping out of your body. Your life fading slowly away and you have to try to explain to your maker why you were such a miserable bastard. I want you to be as afraid as she was when she died."

Harding was finally stone-cold sober. Looking death in the eyes did that. He stared, afraid to move or speak. Slowly the deadly look faded to one more neutral.

"Since I don't get what I want, you don't either. We'll just call this one a draw and go our separate ways. You get your life, minus some cash, and we get ours, plus some cash." He ran a finger the length of the gun. "Of course, if you renege in any way or try to alter our deal by a single penny, I will kill you. I'd consider it a privilege to go to jail for ridding the world of the likes of you."

"I need to think about it."

"I wouldn't think too long. I'm sure the Feds will offer Nadine a sweet deal for returning the chip. And she's liable to turn over both versions to lighten her sentence." Dewey headed for the door but stopped before opening it. "I wouldn't mention this to your goon, Stern."

"Why not?" Harding struggled to his feet.

"You didn't ask where I got my working prototype. You didn't think *I* got it working, did you?"

Before Harding could respond, the man was gone, pulling the door closed behind him.

Stern. He'd had a working prototype all along? Why? Why would he do this to him? Of course! He wanted the power for himself. The bastard. Well, he'd find out what happened to those who screwed Peter Harding over. He'd find out. And then he'd be dead. Very dead.

Stern had a finally honed sense of danger. It had served him well for many years. It led him to those who could help him and away from those who were against him. Harding would be a challenge to neutralize. He was a public figure. The challenge would be taking him out while implicating him in the theft, then getting away clear and clean. Stern was also a semipublic figure. If a shadow could be considered public.

He'd gone to his office after leaving Harding wallowing in his own fears, but his sense of unease grew too strong for confinement. He needed to be out, where he'd have a clear sight line ahead of him and his back protected.

He let himself out the private entrance, where no cameras monitored his comings and goings, and crossed to his car. Inside, he shoved the key into the ignition, but before he could turn it, he felt something cold against his neck. Something long experience told him was the barrel of a gun.

Without moving a muscle, he looked in the rearview mirror.

"Put your hands where I can see them," Dewey said, digging the gun harder into Stern's neck for emphasis. "Slowly and carefully. I'm a little jumpy, and this has a hair trigger."

Stern was no fool. He did as he was told. "Who the hell are you?"

"I'm the man who's going to make you very rich," Dewey said.

"I'm already very rich," Stern said, wondering how he could distract him.

"Not this rich."

"Okay. I'll bite," Stern said. "How are you going to do it?"

"By delivering RABBIT to you."

Stern jerked, but couldn't quite repress a smile. "RABBIT?"

"Let me clarify that. The one that works."

That got his attention. "I don't think I understand you . . ."

"Oh, you understand me all right. At least halfway. You

knew that chip in the research lab was worthless. You just didn't know about the one that worked. The one Harding had stowed in his personal safe."

A pause. "What makes you think I didn't know about it?"

"Call it a gut instinct." Dewey rubbed the barrel on Stern's neck. "Do we talk? Or shall I fade away and let your chips fall where they may?"

Stern stared at him in the mirror. Did the little jackass really think he could take him on and live? He'd find out what happened to people who screwed with Barrett Stern. As would Harding. "We talk."

Jake had enjoyed the family dinner, as much as he could enjoy anything. His mom's roast had been better, even better than his memory of it, the talk lively. He'd been to Matt and Dani's wedding, but this was his first chance to see the couple together in a post-nuptial setting. In an out-of-the-loop way, he'd been amused to think of his tough-minded big brother getting snagged by a romance writer who was afraid of heights. He was surprised to find he liked her and that she wasn't at all what he'd expected. Although he couldn't have said exactly what he'd expected a romance writer to be. She seemed to have Luke, who called her Louise, wrapped around her pinkie right next to Matt. Mom liked her, too, he could tell, suddenly feeling like an outsider.

When Dani'd announced she and Matt were expecting an addition to the Kirby clan, the reunion turned into a celebration. Jake was delighted for Matt. His big brother deserved to be happy. He'd become harder, more distant after the collapse of his first marriage. He'd always wanted kids, and Jake knew Dani had lost her first child in an accident. They deserved this happy ending and even happier beginning.

It wasn't their fault Jake's life was spinning off-center, that there'd be no happy ending for his . . . hell, he couldn't even call it a romance. Some heavy breathing, one near kiss and a bunch of might-have-beens did not a romance make. He felt like the specter at the feast and slipped outside to keep from casting his personal pall over the proceedings. Hell, had he stooped so low he was jealous of his brother? If this was what love did to you, he wanted no part of it.

He looked back toward the house, where his mom was telling Dani what kind of baby Matt had been. This couldn't be love. That stuff inside the house was love. Love was joy, not pain. All he had now was only lust, proximity. It had to be. It would fade. He'd move on and get on with his life.

He heard the screen door slam and saw Dani strolling toward him like someone out to enjoy the night. She was, Jake decided, a beautiful woman, though not in the way most people rated beauty. She was a quiet mountain meadow, as opposed to the Grand Canyon. Her coloring was soft, but there was strength of character in the rounded curve of her jaw. Her steady gaze was that of someone who had seen sorrow and come to terms with it.

"It's nice out here," she said softly. She leaned against the fence and stared up at the sky. "I always vow I'm going to learn more about the stars, but I always forget."

"Too many things, not enough time," Jake said, feeling his insides begin to smooth out. No wonder Matt looked as if he'd found the mother lode when he had her to come home to every night.

There was a short, companionable silence, one filled with only the soft sounds of the night, the murmur of his mom's voice directing the cleanup of the dinner debris and the hum of a distant car passing.

Jake sighed. "I'm really happy for you and Matt," he said.

"I know." She turned, her eyes reflective and almost sad. "When Meggie . . . died, I avoided being around children." Her smile flickered briefly in the dark. "I'd drive blocks out of my way so I wouldn't have to pass any schools." She rested her arms on the fence as she stared skyward. "It wasn't that I begrudged other people their children, their joy. I just . . . couldn't bear to see it. It made my loss seem bigger. More raw."

"How did you get over it?"

"I didn't. I thought I had, but I was just moving too fast for the pain to completely overwhelm me. It wasn't until I got stopped in my tracks by the little incident last year—"

Jake grinned at her calling being kidnaped by a nut case and almost tossed off a mountaintop a "little incident."

"—that I realized it. It took almost dying to make me realize how much I wanted to live, even in a world without my daughter. There isn't a day that goes by that I don't miss her, but I've made my peace with the pain. Learned to live with it, like a lousy roommate." Her smile was wry, but soft. "One thing I know for sure, the shadow of her death makes the . . . light I've found with Matt that much sweeter. Because of the sorrow, the joy is . . ."

Her hand spread across her stomach in a gesture both protective and loving. He saw unshed tears glittering in her eyes and felt his throat tighten.

"Let's just say I'm trying to not run from life." There was a long, peaceful pause, then she asked, "What's she like?"

"How did you know?"

Her laugh was soft but kind. "I'm a romance writer. If I couldn't sense unrequited love in the air, I'd be a disgrace to my profession."

Jake chuckled, surprised that he could. "You'd like her, I think. And she'd like you but probably wouldn't admit it."

He rubbed the back of his neck. “Getting her to admit anything is damn near impossible.”

“Is she the one you have in custody?”

Jake nodded. “Mom says if it’s meant to be, it will be.”

“You don’t believe her?”

“It’s not that.” He shoved his hands into the pockets of his jeans and scowled at the future.

“You want it to be but don’t see how it can?”

“You’re good.”

“I’m a romance writer. I have to be.” She slid her arm through his and started him back toward the house. “Does she feel the same about you?”

“I think so, but—”

“No buts.” She stopped, forcing him to look at her. “You’re a fixer, like Matt, so this is driving you nuts. My advice, for what it’s worth is, you do your job and let love find the way.”

Right. He managed to smile at her, as if she’d helped, as they started up the steps. “Okay.”

She laughed. “You don’t believe me. Let me ask you a question then. How did you catch her? Matt didn’t seem too optimistic about that prospect yesterday.”

Jake stopped halfway up. “You know, that’s a good question.”

An offhand comment Sebastian had made while securing the computers at *Smith’s* came back to him now. “I wonder why she didn’t phone in the wipe?” he’d asked, as he unplugged the computers from the phone line.

At the time, Jake had assumed there’d been physical evidence she needed to destroy and let the comment pass, but why hadn’t she done that before the heist? So far Sebastian hadn’t found anything on the drive. It was almost as if it had already been wiped. Matt had put someone on to piecing together her few shredded papers and hadn't found anything of interest there either. If she was Pathphinder, how had she made such a rookie mistake?

"A . . . very good question."

"Maybe she's trying to find a way to you."

Or, it was part of the plan?

"Matt is luckier than he deserves." He grabbed Dani and quickly kissed her on the mouth.

The screen door opened, framing Matt in the opening. "When you're through kissing my wife, I'd like to take her home."

Jake grinned. "I'm almost done." He kissed her again, this time on the cheek. "Thanks."

She patted his cheek. "I can't wait to meet her."

Jake rubbed the back of his neck. Maybe romance writers couldn't help being optimistic.

Chapter Eighteen

It seemed like a long time since the cell door had slid closed behind her with a final-sounding *clang*. She wouldn't be here for long, her mind said, but her heart wasn't so sure. She was alone in this part of the jail. There were no sounds besides her own breathing. No window to the outside world, no way to track time or assess its passing after being stripped of her belongings and all contact with the outside world.

Of course they wanted her to be anxious. She was more likely to make a mistake if she was on edge. They didn't have much time to crack her before she was out on bail.

Despite the unrelenting stare of the surveillance camera, she wasn't as uncomfortable as she'd expected to be. It was kind of a relief to be alone, her options narrowed to so few and nothing to do. Nothing she could do. Wouldn't be too great for the long haul to have her world narrowed to three walls and a row of bars, but right now the breathing space was nice. There was nothing to distract her. Certainly nothing to remind her of anything familiar.

She was tired, she realized, and not just in the physical sense. Her soul was weary, too. She stretched out on the narrow iron bed, the odor of the same disinfectant they'd used on her engulfing her. *Would it hurt them to add a little lemon scent to it?*

At some point she fell asleep, her dreams spent in a fruitless search for a coat. When she woke and found she was chilled, she knew why. The orange jumpsuit, besides not being even close to her color, wasn't warm. A coarse blanket was folded at the foot of the bed, so she wrapped up in it, feeling the first stab of homesickness for her lost house in Estes Park.

To her surprise, they hadn't taken her harmonica, so she pulled it out. It seemed natural to do, since she didn't smoke—the only other logical solitary prison activity. Sad, plaintive tunes suited her surroundings, suited her new role as prisoner, she thought wryly. Something to put her in the right mood.

She didn't try to think or plan. Planning would come later, when she had a better sense of what moves had been made by the other players in the game while she slept. Right now she didn't care. Drifting from song to song, she felt suspended in time, in space, even in identity. Who was she?

She didn't know and wasn't sure she cared. That was for later, too. She'd been so many different people, she didn't know who to be now. As if her soul had been set adrift. Or maybe—she paused in her song—she was like a chemical ice pack, waiting to be twisted, waiting for all the people she'd been to mix into someone entirely new.

She liked that idea. Why not blend all the whos she'd been? The past, the present, all the roles she'd played in all their games? Maybe when this was over she could put all those pieces together and be a single, whole person. Maybe, just maybe, she could lay her burden down and have, if not a real life, something that looked and felt real if not examined too closely.

Someplace warm. She wrapped the blanket more tightly around her and tried to think of warm things. Like how hot it felt up there on the tiny stage at JR's when she was performing.

She'd miss being Phoebe. Miss the bar, the guys, the music. If she left Phoebe behind, would she also lose her feelings for Jake? What she felt with him, for him, made her feel more alive than she'd ever felt. She didn't want to go back to her former dormant state.

In playing the game, in keeping her distance, she hadn't lost touch only with other people. She'd lost touch with herself. In a way, she'd given her stepfather a partial victory. She didn't know the psychology of his need for power over her and Kerry Anne, his need to destroy lives, but her gut was telling her that if she retreated from these feelings, he'd win, even if they managed to take him down.

Love, she was coming to understand, could heal even as it hurt. That's what Kerry Anne had been trying to tell her the night she died, but the girl Phoebe had been hadn't understood. Maybe she couldn't have understood without meeting Jake. Maybe love's lessons could only be learned in its furnace?

And maybe she was heading just a tad too far into the philosophical zone? At this rate, she'd be a pathetic puddle of pure angst by the time they made their move.

Time to lighten up.

She played a jazzy riff, then stopped when she felt him watching her.

She looked up. He wasn't alone. A couple of guards were with him. One had two chairs, one a small table and another what looked like bags of . . . Chinese food? She held back a grin. The boy did not know when to give up.

Jake saw her half grin as he signaled for the guard to open the door, then waited outside until the table was set up. The guard locked him in with her. A sudden case of stage fright held him by the door, but she looked so ordinary, so innocently pleased as she got up to investigate the cartons of food, he relaxed.

"I didn't even realize I was hungry." She smiled. As soon as her gaze met his, a current of heat did an end run around his resolve before he could close the circuit. His first thought was, he was glad his back was to the camera and the people at its other end. His second was, this was going to be much harder than he'd expected it to be. His third, had he really expected anything to do with Phoebe to be easy?

He returned her smile, holding back as much of himself as he could. He sat down opposite her and watched her help herself to the sweet and sour pork. She chose chopsticks instead of the plastic fork, wielding them expertly.

"Am I allowed to know what time it is?"

Jake looked at his watch, even though he knew exactly what time it was and how many hours he had left. "It's after midnight."

"No wonder I'm awake. I'm usually singing right about now." She tried her drink. "Diet Coke. You remembered." Her lashes lifted, and for a moment something intimate arced between them.

"Yes. It's a gift, or a curse. Haven't decided which. It's useful in my line of work. It's the little details, unnoticed habits, things people can't give up, that trip them up."

"So if I wanted to say, disappear, I should probably give up Diet Coke?"

"If you don't want to get caught."

She looked thoughtful but didn't say anything more until she pushed the carton back and patted her tummy.

"That was great, thanks." The spark of mischief in her eyes gave him a brief warning the games were about to begin. "Interesting interrogation technique."

"What?" Jake cleared the debris, setting it on the floor by the table.

"Let the suspect get rest and food." She propped her elbows on the table. Her accent getting more Southern. "You trying to kill me with kindness, cowboy?"

Jake grinned, gave a half shrug. "I knew the typical wouldn't work with you, *Reb*."

She laughed, a throaty sound that sent quivers through his mid-section. Knowing he was being watched by Bryn and others, kept his blood supply moving up instead of down.

With a smooth motion, she got up, reversed her chair and straddled it. She did that, Jake had noticed, when she was on the defensive.

"Are we waiting for Calvin to join us? You weren't going to question me without my lawyer present, were you?"

"I'm not going to question you at all." Her eyebrows shot up. Seems he'd finally managed to surprise her. "This little session is completely off the record."

He turned toward the camera and made a slicing motion across his throat. After a pause, the red light went out.

"Interesting opening gambit, cowboy. Unexpected. *Curious*." Her smile was all mischief, reminding him of that morning in her kitchen.

It was a good diversionary tactic. He'd been more than curious in her kitchen. His mouth twitched with a suppressed grin as he took a file folder out of the briefcase he'd brought with him and laid it on the tabletop.

"I'll begin with a broad outline of what I know."

"The facts, just the facts, ma'am?" She propped her chin on her elbows and gave him her attention with a look that shouldn't have made his toes curl in his shoes. "By all means, put the rest of your pieces in play—or would that be cards on the table? Are we playing chess or poker?"

"Might be blind man's bluff." This was either a brilliant strategy or the dumbest thing he'd ever done. Or both.

The lift of one eyebrow acknowledged the hit. A slight nod gave him tacit permission to begin.

"You were born Nadine Beauleigh, formerly of Valdosta,

Georgia. We were able to match your fingerprints with a set done at a mall, in one of those protect-our-kids-from-abduction booths. Possibly the same day you choose the red shoes over that boy?"

If she could lob personal-moment bombs, then so could he, although he wasn't immune to the collateral effects of them. What would she choose today? Would he be able to reach her? Her eyes gave away nothing, though a tiny pulse beat in her neck.

"When you ran away from home following the suicide,"—her eyelashes flickered at this—"of your sister, Kerry Anne, your stepfather, Montgomery Justice, turned over your prints. Your mother took a fatal tumble down some stairs not long after, and Montgomery Justice seems to have dropped off the face of the earth."

He paused, but she didn't fill the silence, just stared at him as if what he was saying, while interesting, had nothing to do with her.

"We found Dewey Hyatt's fingerprints in your home and at *Smith's*, where you were apprehended."

For a moment, he thought she might speak. He admired her control. He knew the flaws in his case as well as she did. Suspicions without proof were just sound and fury.

He moved on, detailing the links they'd made between her and Dewey Hyatt. Why he believed they'd both been present during the heist at TelTech. Touched on areas of investigation he believed were vulnerable for her, like the answering machine tape they'd taken from Ollie Smith's crime scene.

"You're Pathphinder, Phagan's strategist." He watched her for a long count, then said, "We could probably uncover all your secrets, given enough time and attention. You haven't been under the big microscope yet. Once you are, there's no turning back. If we put the time and resources into investigating you, we will press charges on anything we turn up. And we'll make them stick. This could be the beginning of a long incarceration."

"I'm not a lawyer, but—"

"—you've played one," Jake inserted.

Her gaze met his without flinching, but it did narrow to wary. "Which makes me think you're being overly optimistic about your chances of linking me to anything substantial."

"We could find out." He waited a long beat, then said, "Or . . ."

Against her will, Phoebe felt her curiosity rise. There was danger in listening to him, because she wanted a way out.

"What if I told you that you're not our . . . primary interest?"

She arched her brows. "I don't know whether to be pleased or offended." She'd been expecting this and knew her next line. "What—or is it a who—do you want?"

"What and who." Jake relaxed in his chair, giving her plenty of space. "You'll have to give RABBIT back, of course."

"Rabbit?"

He ignored this. "And you'll have to be debriefed on Phagan and Hyatt, tell us what you know about their organization. Tell us if you know where they are."

This she also expected. Her freedom for theirs. Some choice.

"And we want Harding—or whoever it is you're after at TelTech."

She hadn't been expecting that.

"We're not stupid, Phoebe." She noticed he didn't call her Nadine. "We know what you've been doing. Believe it or not, we are the good guys. If it is Harding, if he's done something to you or someone you know, it needs to come out.

Not only has he been working on a sensitive military contract, he's making a run for governor." He gave her a crooked grin. "Call it the public's right to know."

"I can't see that the public cares or wants to know what their leaders are up to in private." Phoebe felt bitterness slip her leash for a moment. She reined it in. "Is that it?"

"You will, of course, cease and desist all illegal activities. If you work with us, I think we can arrange a sentence that doesn't include jail time. You'd probably have to do some community service." He hesitated, as if he wanted to say more, but didn't.

She didn't know why, but she had a feeling that what he hadn't said was the one thing she wanted to hear.

"I don't know, cowboy. Your deal seems pretty lopsided. Lot of maybes there. And, frankly, I think I could get a suspended on what you've got, with a good lawyer and a bit of remorse." She fluttered her eyelashes.

"But you might not get Harding. The game will be over for you." He hesitated again, then said, "People with your skills are in demand in law enforcement. It's not uncommon for, say, really good hackers to be . . . recruited after being caught. I can't promise anything, but Internet criminals are tough to catch. Why not try justice on the right side for a while? Come out of the shadows?"

This she hadn't expected either. Before she could stop it, hope tried to get a foothold in her heart. He was good. Dangling a bright and shining new world in front of her *and* the offer to help her take out Harding. All she had to do to get it was betray the two men who'd saved her life seven years ago.

He must have a real high opinion of her integrity.

If only he understood the irony. She didn't know *where* Dewey was. Didn't know Phagan's real name or location. And once he got word she'd been taken, no information she had would lead to him. He'd already have moved to make sure of that. As for Montgomery Justice a.k.a. Peter Harding, she knew *what* he'd done to her sister, but any physical evidence—as well as Justice's face—were lost in the past.

That left RABBIT. Yeah, that piece of crap would buy her a bright, new future.

She was cool, but Jake could see her inward struggle playing out in her eyes.

Do your job, and let love find the way. He'd given her a chance, now she had to have the courage to take it.

"If I were this . . . Pathphinder,"—she smiled slightly as if the notion amused her—"do you seriously think I could, or would, betray my friends? For . . . any reason?"

It was the opening he'd been waiting for. Her hand, the one not gripping the chair back, trembled slightly before she could pull it out of sight. Poor baby. He wanted to take her in his arms and tell her it was going to be all right. That she wasn't alone anymore. He was there and he'd always be there for her, but she had to help him.

"I have to have something . . ."

"I can't give you what I don't have."

Her voice resonated with certainty. He frowned. What was she trying to tell him? She didn't have RABBIT? Had the other thieves beaten them to it? Damn, he was tired of move and countermove. Why couldn't she just tell him?

"Then why are you here?"

A pause. "Because you arrested me?"

"You let yourself get caught, Phoebe. What is it you want from me?"

Harding wanted a drink more than he wanted a girl. He couldn't have either. Not tonight. He needed to keep his wits about him. Couldn't afford to let his guard down now or

Stern would take him out. Damn the man. He wasn't going to win this one. No one screwed his pooch and got away with it.

He rubbed his aching head, realized his hand was shaking. He was used to telling others what to do and having them do it. He was a leader, a director of events, not some stupid peon. Stern was already suspicious. He'd seen it in his eyes when they ran into each other outside the building.

"Any action?" Stern had asked.

Harding had shrugged, all the while wanting to leap on the man and pound his face to a bloody pulp. Only no one pounded Stern. Not without immobilizing him first. He'd have to take him out quick. Shoot him in the back. Or drug him?

Harding liked that idea. A quick kill was no fun. Gloating was half the pleasure of a kill. Kerry Anne had taught him that. He really needed to show Stern who had the power. He'd gone too long without a fix.

Stern had taken away everything. His women. His videos. Even tried to keep Nadine for himself. He'd pay for it. Oh, yes. First Stern. Then Nadine.

Nadine. He stretched out on the bed and thought about Nadine.

It was almost as good as a video. Almost.

He wasn't sure he could give her up, even for the chip.

Dewey hunched over the computer screen in the tiny room he'd rented on the dark side of town. It was small and austere as a sort of penance for Phoebe's current incarceration. Until she was free, no five-star hotels for him.

He'd been typing for so many hours the tips of his fingers were numb. He gave them a shake, then rubbed his eyes. It didn't help the blurring, but he didn't stop. He didn't have time to stop. The illusion had to be perfect or they were dead.

Might be dead anyway, but he didn't want it to be because of faulty work on his part.

Harding was balanced on the knife edge of sanity. It showed in the trembling of his hands, in the twitch in one cheek and in the expression in his eyes. Dewey wasn't sure any illusion would be enough to get them clear. There were too many variables without solutions in this last play of their rapidly unraveling game.

Harding was obsessed with Nadine. Who knew if she'd survive until Dewey could get her clear? Would Harding be able to choose his chip and his political career over his obsession with her? Dewey wasn't sure the bastard was thinking clearly enough to choose anything. If it were his call to make, Phoebe would be long gone from this place. But it wasn't. As she'd pointed out, it was her game, her risk. He just hoped to hell that Harding did what he should, not what he wanted. Though it was nice to know their gas-lighting had worked so well. But what a time to be effective.

Then there was Bryn, who could throw a spanner into the works by getting Phoebe's bail denied. It was a long shot, but Bryn was good at delivering long shots. If the authorities managed to hang on to her, he'd have to deal himself in to get her out. He was not letting Kerry's little sister rot in jail protecting his sorry ass.

And then there was Phoebe. If Harding was balanced on the knife's edge, well, she was balancing on top of him. Worse, she was on the hop, acting on instinct instead of brain waves. In a way he understood why. She wanted to get Harding, but she also wanted it to be over. So did he. Kerry's death had weighed heavily a long time. Retreat wasn't an option. They'd given too much of their lives to this moment to stop now. The cat was in the pigeons; fur and feathers were flying.

Some things you didn't walk away from. Sometimes you could only do or die. Be nice if the odds were a little more even, but, what the hell, if they failed, their lives wouldn't be worth living anyway.

He looked at his watch. Time to give Harding's chain another jerk. He dialed his number, waited for Harding to answer, then said, "Tick, tock, tick, tock. What do you think Nadine's saying to the feds about you right now? Maybe they're digging around in your past even as we speak? Ooh, I wonder what they'll . . . dig up?"

Stern didn't sleep well, so he wasn't happy when his phone rang after three a.m. Even less happy to hear Harding's voice in his ear.

"I got the call."

Stern sat up and rubbed his face.

"You there?"

"I'm here," Stern said. "Where?"

"My office. Five o'clock tomorrow. He wants Nadine there for the exchange."

Stern frowned. Awfully confident of him. Of course, he thought he had a friend on the inside. It was almost too easy. "I'll arrange security. Once the girl is out—"

"I want to be there."

"Not smart. If the Feds are tailing her—"

"Arrange a bait and switch. I need to talk to her."

Stern bit back what he wanted to say to the asshole and gritted out, "Talk to her? About what?"

"Old times."

He'd known that killing her wouldn't be enough for Harding. It never had been. It was stupid, but so was screwing over his right-hand man. Before tomorrow was over, Harding would be smarter. And then he'd be dead.

"I'll see what I can do," Stern said. It didn't really matter in what shape the girl arrived. By then it would be too late for complaints from his new "partner." The man had been moderately clever, but clever wasn't enough. You had to be invulnerable, too. Obviously he was attached to Nadine. That was his weakness and it would be his downfall.

Stern looked at his Spartan surroundings with detached amusement. He didn't care about the money. Not really. He just liked to win. Any way he could.

He lay back in the bed, his arms behind his head, reviewing the various moves planned by his opponents, planning his countermoves and looking forward to a day that promised many deaths. Maybe *the* death, the one that answered his question.

Do men have souls?

After that first night at Jake's mom's, Bryn had opted for a hotel room. His mama's eyes were a tad too penetrating for comfort, and this way she'd be easier for Phagan to contact. Not because she was missing his gifts, of course. She was just interested in any leads he might be inclined to share.

She hadn't gotten either since her move to the hotel. That wasn't the reason she was tossing and turning in her bed though. She had too much to think about. What had transpired during Jake's off-the-record meeting with Phoebe Mentel? All Jake had said was, "She's considering our offer," before trotting off to his mom's.

She'd been tempted to pay Phoebe a visit but was still licking her wounds over the "Holly the Horror" incident. Not her finest hour, she had to admit as she punched up her pillow and tried to quiet her mind. Phagan had taught her well.

Phagan. What was she going to do about him? Assuming

she could do anything about him. Here, alone in the dark, she could admit she was worried about him. He'd never let this much time pass before without some kind of contact. He played a dangerous game, and no one was invincible. If he'd formed a partnership for his run on TelTech, he hadn't chosen well. That scene of cold-blooded murder had been playing over and over in her head, along with the question, had Phagan been part of the violence?

She knew in her gut he was in this mess somewhere. Unless he was dead.

She'd studied the faces in the crime-scene photos, but none of them seemed right for the man she thought she knew. Or she didn't want them to be right. She wanted Phagan to be the bad-boy-champion myth he'd created for himself. He'd wormed himself into her thoughts, maybe even into her heart. If the bastard was just another scummy bad guy, well, the fool was one role she really hated to play. Love and hate were two sides of the same coin, and she hadn't liked finding out she had a heart. Hadn't liked it one bit.

She rolled onto her stomach. It was hopeless. Even if they did meet, she'd have to toss his butt in jail. She punched the pillow again. At least she'd know where he was.

She sagged into the pillow, forcing her thoughts off the maze, but they shattered when her cell phone shrilled a summons. A brief fumble across the night stand, then she had it.

"Bailey."

"Did I wake you?" The voice was muffled, husky.

"If this is an obscene phone call—"

"Much as I'd like to talk dirty with you, this is business, darlin'."

"Phagan?" It was as if her thoughts had summoned him. It was a bit creepy and yet comforting, too.

"Afraid so."

She sank back against the pillows, clutching the phone like a lifeline. Their first real-life contact. And she felt as uncertain as a teenager. Jeez, Louise.

Before she could check herself, she asked, "Where've you been?"

"Here and there. Don't tell me you've been worried about my sorry ass?" He sounded pleased.

To her own surprise she said, "Actually, I have. There were a lot of bodies at TelTech. You usually pick your partners better than that."

Silence. She'd surprised him. She smiled, feeling the balance of power between them shift slightly her way.

He chuckled. "You're my only outside partner, darlin'."

The cheeky devil. Why did he have to be on the wrong side of the law? She sighed. "I wish—"

"I know." He got quiet, then said, "I need your help."

Bryn sat up. "You need *my* help?"

"Stay online tomorrow, and be ready to move."

"Okay." She wanted to ask more but knew he wouldn't give it to her.

"You'll know what to do with it when you get it." Another pause. "Sleep well . . ."

His last words were muffled. Had he added *my love* at the end?

It was probably better not to know. She settled back against the pillows with a sigh. What was he up to now? A thousand questions without answers started trekking through her brain. It was going to be a long, sleepless night.

Chapter Nineteen

The day began quietly. The sun rose, spilling warm light on another August day, but as the time for Phoebe's bail hearing approached, distant thunder rumbled a warning that a storm was moving in. Dark clouds clung to the mountains, then were torn free, pushed by a front that seemed intent on driving them toward the city.

Jake turned his back on the window and the storm. His team, most of it on loan from Matt, who had been called away on a minor emergency, awaited the call to action. "Does everyone know what they're supposed to do?"

Riggs and a young, pony-tailed boy named Henry, both in black jumpsuits and SWAT-type gear, gave him a thumbs up. Because of his youth, Henry's was a tad more enthusiastic than Riggs'. A huge tad.

Jake almost didn't recognize Alice without her upscale suit and heels. She looked up from checking her gun clip to give him a short nod.

Sebastian, manning Bryn's laptop with its satellite uplink, gave him an over-the-shoulder wave. He had a small-boy air of fascination as he made his screen flicker with some computer game. His guns blazing, he grabbed a swig from his Yahoo bottle.

If Matt hadn't assured him the man was good at what he did . . .

Jake looked at Bryn. "I wish we knew what your boy was up to."

"You, me and a cast of thousands." Bryn shrugged. "If he does intend to bring us in this early, I'm guessing things aren't going exactly as planned."

"Or this is exactly what he planned." Jake rubbed the back of his neck. This op was more like a maze than a chess match. He'd think he had it figured out, then go around a corner and run straight into a brick wall.

"Let's just hope our plan works and we don't have to rely on Phagan to stay in the game."

Jake looked at Luke. "Your men ready?"

Luke had offered his best men to tail Phoebe, since they needed faces not already familiar to Harding or her for this part of the op.

"My guys and the transponder are standing by. They'll tag the car's bumper before it pulls out." Luke was all serious cop, as if he knew the stakes on this op were more than the lives of a couple of charming thieves. "We won't lose her."

Jake knew they'd do their best. He just hoped their best would be good enough. There were too many variables for absolutes. "I wish we could wire her," he muttered.

Bryn arched her eyebrows. "Only if we sedated her. And then I think she'd notice." She got up and walked to the window, then turned to look at Jake, her voice sympathetic. "She knows the risks better than we do, Jake. If that hasn't stopped her, we sure as hell won't."

"I know." He rubbed the back of his neck again, but it didn't help. Pain was a vise gripping his head and gnawing inroads on his stomach. Would Phoebe fight as hard for her life as he was? Who knew what horrors lurked in her past? Further information had surfaced about her past. He knew she'd been in the emergency room because of a "tumble" down some stairs. The doctor had reported the fall to Social Services, but the report had disappeared, never to be investigated. No wonder she had trouble trusting the system. How deep were her wounds? How strong was her will to live once she'd achieved her goal?

Only time would tell. He looked at his watch. Time was passing, but too slowly. He looked out the window. Looked like the storm would arrive about the same time she was released.

Phoebe was allowed to change into her own clothes, the black dress and heels, for the arraignment hearing. Looked as though no one wanted to get in the way of her speedy release. Nice that everyone was being so accommodating, and just when she'd decided jail wasn't so bad. Calvin had vanished, replaced by a smarmy snake who had probably slithered out from under a rock near Harding's. Harding was reacting as expected, which should be comforting but somehow wasn't.

The man he'd once been had been predictable only up to a point. She remembered one occasion when she'd thought she'd had him figured out. He'd broken her arm during that beating. The only time she'd had to go to the emergency room. He'd told the ER nurse that she'd taken a tumble down the stairs. Usually he was too careful to leave such visible evidence. Though she'd denied getting beaten, the doctor had told her someone would come to investigate her injuries, but no one did. Then, like now, Harding had powerful friends.

The hearing proceeded to its expected conclusion. All she had to do was say "not guilty" at the right moment. She was escorted out of the courtroom, sent through the system and then released with her personal items in a large yellow envelope.

The lawyer kept checking his watch, as if he had somewhere else to go, but when Phoebe suggested she didn't need him, he did a bad impression of helpful. Which meant he had orders to escort her to somewhere. No sign of Jake or Phagan's fibbie. She hadn't really expected a big sendoff, but it would have been nice to see him again, just in case. . . .

She shook off that thought. Only a fool went into battle expecting to lose. Of course, she also reminded herself that Harding's weakness was his belief in his own infallibility. He was convinced he was destined for greatness and that gave him the right to do whatever he wanted along the way. It was time for him to get a huge dose of reality, one involving incarceration.

"It's raining," the lawyer said.

It was indeed, coming down in sheets, cleaning the stale from the air. They needed the rain, she thought, then had to remind herself she wasn't part of "they" anymore. She didn't need anything but an end to the game.

"Afraid to get wet?" She pushed open the door. Despite the dark clouds, Phoebe felt like a mole emerging into light. The wet slap of drops against her face felt good. She turned her face skyward and laughed.

The lawyer grabbed her arm. "Your ride is over there."

Across the street, a limo waited at the curb. The lawyer pushed her toward it, but a Moonie, or a Moonie's first cousin, stepped into her path.

"Beware the world's end," he said, handing her a pamphlet and a small rose pin. His eyes looked suspiciously like Dewey's.

"I will." She pinned the rose to her lapel. The lawyer grabbed the pamphlet, studied it briefly, and then stuffed it into his pocket. He shoved Dewey out of their way and pushed Phoebe toward the waiting car.

As they crossed the street, she identified at least two cops in street clothes doing a great imitation of hurrying through the rain. One dropped something by the limo just as the lawyer opened the door. He bent out of sight, then was up and moving down the street again.

Very smooth.

The lawyer gave her a pointed nudge. "Get in, damn it. I'm getting soaked."

She scrambled inside and the door shut. Water dripped down her face, blurring the features of the man waiting inside.

"Nadine." His voice was smooth and cold, like a tomb waiting to be filled. "I've been looking forward to meeting you."

She heard the scrape of a match, then saw a blurry flare as it connected with the end of a cigarette. She rubbed the water out of her eyes and saw Barrett Stern, his eyes a dead zone that watched her through a haze of smoke. He had a gun, but that wasn't what made him dangerous. It was the vacuum where his soul should be. Unlike Harding, who killed because it made him feel powerful, this man killed to fill himself. He was a ghost who kept trying to warm himself with a fire he'd never feel. His emptiness was a gray mist that crept out from him and wrapped its icy chill around Phoebe, trying to blanket her hope with despair.

The doors locked, trapping her inside with him. He tapped on the window that separated them from the driver, and the limo moved forward with an un-limo-like jerk.

The game, she realized as her body turned to ice, was a lot different when it was played in real time.

The difference between living or dying.

It was a relief to be moving, to be doing something. This kind of stress Jake could handle. The rain was a pain in the ass, but they'd manage. It's what they did. All his anxieties, his fears, his worries vanished as training, and a rush of adrenaline, took point.

Luke was coordinating their movements from command central, since his men would be playing tag with the limo. He had four teams of men—code-named dogs Blue, Red, Yellow and Green—whose job it would be to keep the limo in sight.

Riggs and Henry were down on the street with a small squad from SWAT, on hold for a target to move on and probably still arguing the merits of The Grateful Dead. Four other squads were stationed in possible target sectors, to give Luke as much flexibility and speedy response time as they reasonably could.

Jake, Alice and Bryn lifted off in a chopper with radio station markings, hoping they'd look as if they were watching traffic, not tailing the limo. They'd be Luke's eyes in the sky and play backup for any team that got tangled in traffic.

Sebastian was still playing shoot-the-hell-out-of-fake people on Bryn's laptop, trying to beat her top score. Jake hoped the guy would notice if or when Phagan made contact.

On a small map, Jake traced the limo's movements with his finger, while their pilot did the same in the air. Wherever they were going, it wasn't toward TelTech. Each turn was taking them farther and farther away. They'd dug deep into Harding's holdings and turned up a warehouse owned by a subsidiary of TelTech, but they weren't heading toward that or Harding's house. It wasn't unexpected. If Phagan had set up some kind of a meet with Harding and Phoebe, he'd most likely pick a public place, where Harding's threat would be minimized.

While he listened to Luke and his dogs radio traffic, Jake studied the surrounding area, trying to figure out possible destinations. "Something's wrong. There's nothing in this area that's right for a meet," he shouted to Bryn. Before she could respond, Blue Dog reported, "Dog pound, I've lost visual. I repeat, I've lost visual."

"Have you lost signal, Blue Dog?" Luke asked.

"Negative. Signal is strong. Our stray is not moving."

"I can't see them either," Alice yelled. "They went under

that overpass, but haven't come out yet."

"I count four," Phoebe said. When Stern arched a thin blonde eyebrow, she added, "Cops. Following us."

Something that might be amusement flickered in his eyes. "It won't be a problem much longer. We get out here. Keep low—don't draw attention to yourself. It wasn't my idea to keep you alive this long."

She nodded, and he released the lock. She slid out, doing as she was told. She could have ditched him—he wouldn't risk shooting at her in front of so many witnesses and with cop hounds so close on their ass—but that wasn't part of her plan. They dodged a few cars and scrambled into the rear of an unmarked white van parked up on the curb out of sight.

When the light changed, the van driver pulled away from the limo and the hounds. As they emerged from the shadow of the overpass, she recognized the driver. He was one of the TelTech shooters. He didn't turn in the direction of TelTech but in the direction of Harding's warehouse.

No big surprise Harding didn't intend to do as he'd been told.

"This isn't smart."

"No shit."

"But you have a plan."

Stern's smile had a feral quality. "I always have a plan."

"Anybody got a visual?" Anxiety sharpened Luke's voice.

"I got 'em. The light stopped them, but they're moving again," Red Dog said.

More time, more turns. Where the hell were they heading? Jake wondered, once again comparing their route to possible outcomes on the map. They'd avoided the freeway and residential areas and were now traveling through a business suburb. Jake's gut was telling him something was very wrong.

"We got a turn signal," Green Dog said. "This may be it." He gave them the address. "Looks like some kind of limo company. What do you want us to do?"

Limo company?

"Move in," Luke ordered after a brief hesitation, "but do not fire unless fired upon. Repeat. Do not fire unless fired upon."

"We joining the party?" the pilot asked.

Jake hesitated, then shook his head. "Hold position." It seemed to take a long time for the dogs to report, "It's a bust, Dog Pound. Repeat, it's a bust. Limo is empty."

Bryn looked at him. "Now what?"

Jake tapped a spot on the map. "Let's check out this warehouse."

Through the windshield of the van, Phoebe, sitting in the back, caught the occasional glimpse of warehouses. From the passenger seat, Stern kept his gun pointed at her. As far as she could tell, he hadn't blinked. The van passed through warehouse doors, then stopped so abruptly, if she hadn't been seated, she'd have taken a nasty tumble.

Without a seat belt, Stern wasn't so lucky. He slammed into the dash, the gun flying out of his hand. Before he could recover, the van's driver had pulled an Uzi from under the seat and pointed it at him. The rear doors were opened by the second shooter, also holding an Uzi.

Stern played it cool. Actually, very cold.

"Farley?" he said.

Phoebe was glad she wasn't on the receiving end of his look.

Farley didn't appear to like it either. He looked distinctly uneasy as he tightened his grip on the Uzi and shifted but held his ground. "Sorry, boss. Got a better offer from Mr. Harding."

It seemed Dewey's plan to sow the seeds of discord had worked. Would it help her situation now or make it worse?

"You do not want me for an enemy," Stern said. Though he hadn't moved, he had the look of a tiger about to spring on his prey.

Farley noticed it, too. "Harley!"

Harley came around and opened the door on Stern's side, gesturing with the Uzi for him to get out. If it weren't for the hardware, the pair of gunmen would have looked comical. Both had potato-shaped bodies, narrow on top, then widening to hips atop legs that looked too short. Farley had a Cheetos bag poking out of the pocket of his ratty jacket. Harley appeared to prefer Ding Dongs.

Stern got out. Harley gave him a wide, respectful berth, almost dancing on his toes with anxiety.

"I make a bad enemy," Stern added.

"You won't have time to be a bad enemy, boss," Harley said. "You're gonna be deep-sixed ASAP. Sorry."

He sort of looked like he meant it.

Stern's cold gaze hammered Harley long enough to make him take a step back and take a better grip on the Uzi.

"You chose the wrong side."

Farley looked at Phoebe. "You, too. Get out, and keep your hands where I can see 'em."

Phoebe did as she was told. This was it. This was the moment she'd planned for, worked toward for the last seven years. Well, not exactly this moment. In her imagination, she, not Farley and Harley had been holding the Uzi.

There was no sign of Harding, but she felt his presence. Though the warehouse appeared to be standard issue in size and level of dirt, with a temperature that hovered between stuffy and stale, evil pervaded the structure. What wasn't standard issue were the spotlights and video cameras arrayed around a metal-framed double bed. The bedspread was leopard skin, and various implements of bondage were scattered around it in a way that some might consider artistic.

While Harley covered them, Farley patted both of them down, then nudged them toward center stage. Harley secured Phoebe to a metal folding chair using a pair of the ominously plentiful handcuffs. Stern was prodded toward the bed but balked when Farley told him to lie down on it.

"Mr. Harding doesn't much care what shape you're in, boss," Farley said apologetically. While Harley kept him covered, Farley raised the gun butt. After a stare-down that left Farley looking hammered, Stern lay down and allowed his hands and feet to be cuffed to the four corners of the bed.

Phoebe found herself in the odd situation of feeling sympathy for a murderer. He'd probably killed Ollie, she reminded herself, but it didn't help. This wasn't about who he was or what he'd done. This was about what she was. And what she didn't want to become.

"I think I like your plan better," she said to Stern.

"It's not over yet," he said, with enough menace to turn Farley white as a sheet.

"Go get Mr. Harding, Harley." Farley licked his lips, looking over his shoulder. Phoebe noticed that Harley gave Stern a wide berth as he headed for a door to a partitioned area off to one side.

"You do know why Harding wants him dead, don't you?" Phoebe figured now was as good a time as any to stir the waters a bit more. "He knows too much." She waited a beat, then added, "And now you do, too."

"Ain't like that." Farley's bravado was too sweaty to be convincing.

Stern flicked Phoebe a look that might have had respect in it. "Harding's running for governor. He can't afford to let you live now that you know about this place."

"Trying to sow the seeds of discord among my men, Stern?" Harding strolled out of the shadows.

Phoebe watched him come. Here and now melted away, leaving the past rushing in to fill its place. He'd changed his face, but he couldn't change who and what he was. It showed in the way he walked and in the satisfaction gleaming from his hungry eyes. He thought he was the alpha dog, and it showed. The charm was gone. This was the reality behind the myth. He hid his evil well, but like the lava lurking beneath the earth's crust, it had to break through to relieve the pressure on his dark soul.

"Try to take being replaced,"—he gave Farley and Harley his most reassuring smile—"with a little dignity, Stern. You know I only punish those who betray me."

"You'll never be governor, Harding," Stern said. "You're going to die today."

"I will be whatever I want to be. It is my destiny. It is my right." He looked down on him. "I knew I had the capacity for great power, and now I am in full possession of it. I was never meant to be bound by the petty restrictions of lesser people." He tested the handcuff that held Stern's wrist against the headboard. "They feel my power, they are drawn to it like moths to a flame. They will overlook its dark manifestations because they need it. They need me."

"When this gets out—"

"It won't. You might call this the final performance of my little theater of the real. You first. Then Nadine."

Phoebe could feel his gaze shift her way, felt the chill of his evil reaching out to wrap around her as he walked toward her. They'd come full circle. The past had met the present. It was hard to feel other than powerless while shackled to a chair. *I'm not alone.* Her spirit reached out to Dewey. To Jake. *Don't give up on me.*

"Nadine." Harding sighed, something beyond satisfaction entering his gaze. "My how you've grown." His gaze traveled down her body like slime oozing from a pit.

"And you've become addicted to clichés." It was dangerous to poke a snake. She could see how close he was to losing it. She still knew the signs. But now, like then, she couldn't give him her submission. "Not that you ever were very original."

He stopped, his gaze promising punishment. "Why aren't her feet secured?" he snapped.

"Afraid the little girl can kick?" Phoebe taunted.

Harding waited until her legs were secured, then pulled a chair in front of her and sat down. His knees rubbed against her first. He leaned toward her, his gaze raking up her body. His breathing sped up as he flexed his hands, then lowered them to her knees.

Her body flinched. She couldn't help it. He smiled, then gripped until she had to bite her lower lip to keep from crying out. Her soul retreated from him because her body couldn't. She used her eyes to deflect him and defy him. He'd never gotten total submission from her. Not then, and he wouldn't now. If it was her only victory today, she wouldn't give it to him. She wouldn't.

His hands slid down to her feet, removing the black heels she'd been wearing when Jake arrested her. He looked at them, then smiled. "We'll save these. I might need them later."

His eyes reminded her what he could do with a high heel and a bare back as his hands started back up over her knees. Under the edge of the black dress, he stopped.

"You wearing a wire, Nadine?" he asked.

He kneaded and pinched the flesh on the inside of her legs. It took all her control not to respond in any way.

"If I am wired, you won't find it by groping me. My friends get their equipment from the same place as the CIA."

Rage flared in his eyes. He dug his nails into her flesh, leaving red crescents on her bare skin.

"Careful, Nadine. You know how I feel about disrespect. We have a couple of hours to get . . . reacquainted before the meet with your partner. I'd hate to spend too much of it going over . . . old ground. There's so much new ground to cover."

He ran his hand up under her dress, fingering the edge of her panties. He retreated, then went up again. Her body jerked, and he smiled. *I can do anything I want and you can't stop me,* his eyes told her as his hands finally retreated.

He rose, his eyes strangely lit as he cupped her chin, forcing her face up. She knew what was coming and rode out the slaps, first one side, then the other. A blood trail, warm and thick, formed on either side of her mouth.

"Think about it, Nadine. This can be pleasant,"—he stroked her breast—"or hard." He pinched her nipple, his gasp of pleasure coming on top of her gasp of pain. "Think about it very carefully, while I take care of some new business." He pushed the chair back, but before he left, he grabbed her chin and held her immobile while he licked the blood off her mouth, first one side, then the other. He whispered in her ear, "Yum. You taste good, Nadine, much better than Kerry Anne."

He straightened. "Will you be as good as her?"

"Go to hell."

"We'll see who goes to hell today."

She didn't see the punch coming. The blow snapped her head back and turned everything black. When her vision cleared, Harding was standing by Stern.

"I'd like to take care of you myself, Barrett, but the video's worth more if Lily does you. And it will be so educational for Nadine. I'll sit next to her and enlighten her on her options and the consequences of defying me." He turned to Harley and Farley, who were both looking queasy. "Get those cameras going and—"

The ring of a phone cut across his instructions. Annoyed, he signaled to Farley, who was nearest the office, to answer it. "Take a message."

In a minute Farley was back. "Wouldn't leave a message. Said you better come to the phone if you want your rabbit."

With a muttered curse, Harding left them. Both Harley and Farley looked relieved as they mopped their sweaty brows.

"Who's Lily?" Harley croaked. He looked a little green around the gills. He turned and bumped a tray of what looked like surgical instruments.

"Lily?" Stern smiled. "You don't want to meet Lily. But you will."

From the office they heard the phone slam back into the cradle. Harding emerged, his face a thundercloud. "It seems we'll have to postpone our business here for a short time." He frowned. "Put her in the van and drive North. Take your cell phone, make sure it's charged. Wait for instructions."

Farley nodded and went to work on Phoebe's cuffs. Harley nodded toward Stern. "What about him?"

Harding hesitated. "Leave him. This won't take long. We'll deal with him when we get back. It'll give him time to ponder the error of his ways."

Phoebe waited until they'd were driving away from Harding to say to the two men, "I hope you've both got strong stomachs."

Harley turned a deeper shade of green, Farley once again paled white as a sheet.

The rain was letting up when Jake, Alice and Bryn cautiously approached the warehouse. Weapons out, Jake signaled for Alice to stay where she was. Bryn went right. Jake went left. There were no windows, but Jake rounded a corner and found a door standing ajar.

Policy dictated he wait for Bryn to back him up, but Jake was sick of waiting. He nudged the door open just wide enough for him to slip through, then stopped so his eyes could adjust to the dim interior.

Ahead of him, dirty skylights cast uneven light in a line down the center. He rounded a partition that could have been an office and saw a sight that stopped him in his tracks.

"Jake? Where are you?" Bryn's voice came softly through the radio earpiece.

"I'm inside."

"Without backup? Are you nuts?"

"Trust me when I say there is no threat here." Despite this reassurance, he did a quick recon of the area, with his gun out, the barrel pointed slightly down. Only then did he approach the bed and its gagged, manacled, and very naked occupant. Around him, among some very interesting bondage equipment, were the tattered remains of what were probably his clothes.

Jake picked up a piece and examined it. It appeared to have been cut off. Possibly with the knife stuck in the mattress between the poor man's bare thighs.

"Do you require assistance?" Jake asked, trying not to grin.

He gave Jake an eye-rolling, "Are you shitting me?" look.

Jake removed the gag, then looked around for the keys to the handcuffs.

"What happened?" He heard Bryn and Alice coming in and grabbed a piece of shirt, tossing it over the man's family jewels, which weren't exactly doing him proud.

Farley looked glum. "An unfortunate error in judgment."

Chapter Twenty

Phoebe hoped she'd done the right thing to help Farley convince Harley that Farley should go back and release Stern. Both of them agreed Harding wasn't what they'd expected, but Harley thought it was too late to change back to Stern's camp. That Farley hadn't called seemed to indicate Harley had been right. A pity right didn't seem to be much comfort, Phoebe thought as Harley wiped his sweaty brow again. If Farley had freed Stern, Harley was now squarely in the very nasty, very dangerous middle. She just hoped it would help things break their way. They could use a break right now.

While Harley drove and sweated and muttered, Phoebe went to work on her handcuffs. They'd secured her hands in front, a lucky miscalculation for her. It didn't seem to be their day for making good decisions.

Keeping a wary eye on wild-eyed Harley, Phoebe unpinned the rose Dewey had given her and put it to use. The small snick of the handcuff lock releasing came at the same moment Harley's cell phone rang. They both jumped at the sound.

Phoebe met Harley's gaze in the rearview mirror.

He rubbed his face, his hand shaking, then picked up the phone. "Y-y-yes?" He listened for a moment. "Okay. Sure . . . Fine. Everything's fine." He looked at her again, perplexity written large on his face. "He wants me to take you to the TelTech parking lot."

"Better do what he says." When he wasn't looking, Phoebe pinned the rose to the inside of her waistband. Just in case. Then she positioned the cuffs so she appeared to be secured.

She leaned back, getting as comfortable as the metal panels would allow. So, she'd been right to think Harding would choose his own turf for the meet. It was obvious he thought he could get RABBIT and keep her, which meant he intended to pop Dewey as soon as he turned over the chip. She thought about the warehouse, the bed and the things around that bed. If Harding succeeded, Dewey would be the lucky one.

She tried to wet her dry throat with a painful swallow. Well, they'd just have to make sure Harding didn't get his way. Or die trying.

The offices and halls of TelTech were deserted when Harding let himself in. He'd realized earlier that it was pointless to continue operations while the theft was being investigated. The security office was empty, with crime-scene tape still strung across the doorway.

The silence, broken only by the sound of his footsteps on the marble floor of the entryway, calmed the agitation brought on by seeing Nadine. This was his turf, the seat of his power, his kingdom. This building, this life, he'd built from the near ruin of the old. He'd learned much in the years since Nadine had escaped him. His tastes, his passions, had been refined to near perfection, as she would soon learn.

She would die this night, but not until she'd completely and totally submitted to his will. As he rose in the elevator, his longing to be with her rose, too. He was almost willing to turn aside from RABBIT, from all this, to finish what she'd run from all those years ago.

Almost.

Patience, he reminded himself. No woman was worth losing a working prototype of RABBIT. With it, his power would grow. Nadine was an interlude—a turning the page on the old to bring on the new—not the main event. Besides, she was older now, good only to prove his power absolute. For the main event, there was the power of the governor's mansion and Audrey's money and connections.

And her daughters. Her lovely . . . young daughters.

He smiled as he unlocked the door to his office and went in for this last act—though not the last scene—of his old life. The smile disappeared when he saw Nadine's partner waiting for him. Sitting in his chair.

"You took your sweet time," Dewey said. "I was getting ready to call the general."

"Where's RABBIT?" Harding's hands curled into fists in the pockets of his expensive suit. This young man needed to be taught a lesson before he died. Lily was going to get very lucky this night.

"Safe." Dewey stood up and gestured for Harding to take his seat. "And ready to show off for . . . daddy . . . after you prove Phoebe is all right."

"She's fine." Harding walked around his desk and sank into the chair without taking his gaze off Dewey. "If you don't have it on you, how the hell am I supposed to know it works?"

"I've rigged a remote camera for you." Dewey pointed toward Harding's computer. Some kind of headgear and a pair of odd looking gloves had been connected to it. "It's not that I don't trust you—well, actually, that's not true. I don't trust you any more than you trust me. Creates some interesting difficulties, but we'll deal with those as we come to them." He rubbed his hands together. "First, I see with my own eyes that Phoebe is alive and well, then I give you a demonstration of RABBIT's capabilities."

Dewey could tell Harding wasn't happy, but it wasn't part of the plan to make him happy, so he didn't waste any worry about it. All his worry was for Phoebe. He could see Harding was in a state of creepy excitement. Just being in the same room with the guy made his skin crawl. He never should have let Phoebe do this. Harding was seriously unstable.

Harding shrugged, a slight twitch forming below one eye as he pulled the phone toward him and dialed. "Get her out, and have her look up." Harding covered the mouthpiece with his hand. "Look out the window."

Careful to keep one eye on Harding, Dewey did as he was told. Two people stood by a white van, but they were too far away to be sure. "That could be anyone out there."

Harding gave an exasperated sigh, opened a drawer and handed him a pair of binoculars. Dewey didn't ask what they were doing in his desk drawer. Knowing what he knew of Harding, he didn't want to know.

He adjusted the focus until the woman's face sharpened into Phoebe's. She looked tense, the strain obvious, and her mouth looked bruised and puffy. Dewey lowered the binoculars, pulled the gun out of his jacket and pointed it at Harding. "You hit her, you bastard. I could kill you now, and your goon down there couldn't help you."

"If he doesn't see me come out that door in fifteen minutes, he has orders to kill her." Harding's shrug was arrogant, his triumph obvious. "You're right. Our mistrust is quite mutual. I suggest we get on with our business or a couple of slaps won't be the worst thing that happens to Nadine."

He thinks he controls the board, Dewey thought, fighting his way back to calm. Well, we'll see who controls what. He picked up the headgear and handed it to Harding.

"You put this on your head, your hands in the gloves," Dewey said. "When you're ready, I'll activate the remote connection."

Harding picked up the headset, examining it for a long moment before fitting it over his head. Dewey allowed himself a silent sigh of relief.

"I'm ready."

Dewey briefly crossed his fingers, then hit Enter on the keyboard.

"What am I seeing?"

"You're inside the vehicle RABBIT is controlling. I've programmed it to drive an obstacle course, choosing the best possible route for itself. It will go through it once, calculating the variables, then go through it again. Artificial, intelligent automation. Just what the military ordered."

Dewey looked at his watch, then started the program.

"This is . . . impressive," Harding said. "I can't believe that bastard Stern hid it from me."

"You shouldn't have believed it," Stern said from the private doorway. His cold gaze and his gun were both pointed at Dewey.

Harding ripped off the gloves, then the headset. "What the hell—"

"That should be *who the hell* and the answer would be *him*. And Nadine, of course." He nudged the door wider. "Bring her in, Harley."

Harley did, pushing her in ahead of him with a terrified look at Stern."That'll be all," Stern said, then shot Harley twice in the heart.

Harley fell at Phoebe's feet, his eyes, wide and shocked, stared at her for a small eternity before awareness faded. She'd seen the man kill as indifferently as he was killed, but that didn't stop her from feeling an odd sense of loss, even some guilt. Maybe there was something to that *every man's death diminishes me* quote. Or the realization it was her game that took him out. He wasn't a game piece being casually bumped off the board. That this hadn't been part of the plan was no excuse.

"Drop your gun, or she's next," Stern said to Dewey, turning the barrel toward Phoebe.

Dewey started to lay it on the desk, but Stern shook his head sharply. "On the floor. Kick it toward the door."

"Stern." Harding smiled and started toward him.

"Don't even start." Stern turned the weapon on Harding. "Sit."

"What are you doing? They set us up to—"

"And you bought it. I don't forgive. Or forget." With his free hand, he pulled out a crumpled pack of cigarettes, extracted one and lit up, his cold, steady gaze never faltering or showing distraction. He didn't even blink when the smoke curled up around his head. "You two, sit. There and there."

He indicated the couch near the bar for Dewey and the chair in front of the desk for Phoebe. Divide and conquer. It was a good strategy.

He hooked one leg over a bar stool, resting his gun hand on the elevated knee as he studied the remaining players with an air of leashed menace that was increased, not lessened by his relaxed stance.

"I'm afraid I'm not up to speed on what's going down here. I was . . . tied up." His cold gaze found Harding, whose angry look had faded to ashen. "Someone enlighten me."

Phoebe exchanged a look with Dewey. "What do you want to know?"

Stern took a long, slow drag on his cigarette, then blew it out. Through the smoke he studied her. "I had a feeling you were pulling the strings on this little game. With your past knowledge, you'd know right where and when to apply pressure, wouldn't you?" He ground the cigarette out in the ashtray before he added, "Let's start with your cards on the table."

"I don't—" Phoebe started.

"The handcuffs. I notice the rose is no longer adorning your lovely breast. Why don't you put the flower on the desk and secure those cuffs for me."

Phoebe unpinned the rose from her waistband and put it on the desk, a tiny spot of red that looked like a drop of blood on the wide, dark expanse. Phoebe secured her handcuffs with an audible *click*.

She'd underestimated Barrett Stern, failed to research him thoroughly. He wasn't Harding's knight, he was the far more powerful queen, though he probably wouldn't appreciate the description.

It was a relief when his gaze moved off her and onto Harding.

"Now you." Stern pulled another set of handcuffs out of his pocket. "So thoughtful of you to make sure I had a plentiful supply of these. Around the wrists and through the arm of your chair." He tossed them at Harding. "Though I thought we agreed you'd get rid of them. You should have listened to me."

With a venomous look at Stern, Harding looped the cuffs through the arm and then snapped them around his wrists.

"And now you," he turned his gaze on Dewey. "What the hell is your name?" He tossed Dewey some cuffs.

"Hyatt. Dewey Hyatt," he muttered, snapping the cuffs around his wrists.

Stern stared at him, his look assessing. "I think I need you to be secured a bit more than that." From his pocket he pulled out yet another set of cuffs. "One to your wrist, the other around that bookshelf behind you."

The snap of the cuff sounded final in a silence broken only by Harding's agitated breathing. With Dewey secured, Stern relaxed enough to pour himself a drink. It in one hand, gun steady in the other, he approached Phoebe, his feet sinking silently into the expensive carpet. She needed a move, the next move, but her mind was blank, her gaze locked with his like she was the cobra and he was the snake charmer.

He stopped and studied her, something sexual flickering very briefly in his dead eyes. Her skin crawled, but she had to consider using it. She didn't have a lot of options just now. Only she couldn't. She just couldn't.

She gave Dewey a quick, apologetic look and got an uncomfortable thumbs up as an answer. Okay. She took a deep breath. She'd play this scene as herself, whoever that was.

He sat down in the chair next to Phoebe's and drank without taking his gaze off her. She didn't look away, even though it was like a glimpse into hell.

"So, Nadine—or should I call you Phoebe?"

"I haven't been Nadine for a long time."

"Okay. Phoebe." He drank again, a slight, very slight frown between his pale brows. "You . . . intrigue me."

This wasn't good.

"You're not going to obsess on me, too, are you? Doesn't seem like your style."

Stern smiled, one that was almost attractive. "No, it's not my style." The smile faded. "But you do present a . . . problem for me. Unlike these two, who tried to screw me over and failed . . ." He tossed back the last of his drink, then fixed her with a curious stare. ". . . you . . . didn't. Farley gave you all the credit for his change of heart when I left him in my place at the warehouse."

"Well, no need to get warm and fuzzy," Phoebe muttered, answering Dewey's incredulous look with a slight shrug. "I just didn't want to see anyone tortured to death. It wasn't personal."

His smile flickered again in the empty expanse of his face. "That doesn't change the fact that my only reason for killing you is what you know about me." He studied her dispassionately. "You appear to have an agile and devious mind. I'll be rebuilding my organization. I could use someone like you."

It seemed to be her week for job offers. Talk about *déjà vu*.

"You're only interested in my mind?"

His gaze traveled down her body, then back up to meet hers.

"Of course."

"Well, as tempting as that is, I think I'll pass." Would he take no for an answer?

"Don't worry. Unlike our friend here, I prefer my women cooperative." He stood up. "Are you sure?" His gaze found hers, with regret and something else almost warming his eyes. They looked at her now, tempting her to give in to him. To survive.

Her body, her cowardly body, urged her to do it. It wasn't love, but it was life. Life, any life, was better than dead.

Only her brain knew it wasn't true. She'd had "any" life. Lest she forget, she looked at that life, that past, sitting across the desk from her.

"I'm sure."

"All right then." He stood up. "That brings us to the question of RABBIT." He looked at Dewey. "I'd like to believe you got it to work, but it stretches my credulity a little too far."

"I just saw it working, on that helmet thing. We can still do this, Stern," Harding said. "We can have it all."

"What did he see?"

Dewey looked at Phoebe.

"Tell him the truth," she said.

"VR smoke and mirrors. The chip is and always was crap."

Harding slumped in his chair, the ugliness of his soul now visible on his face.

"That's what I thought." Stern's gaze slid toward Phoebe again. "It's a pity you didn't limit your adventures in VR to video games for teens." He frowned, his gaze moving from Phoebe to Harding to Dewey, then back to Phoebe. "Normally I'd go from left to right around the room, because I like to be orderly, but for you—" He gave Phoebe a slight smile, "I'll kill Harding first."

Harding gasped as the barrel of the gun swung his way.

"You wanted revenge," Stern said to her.

"I wanted justice," she said.

"There he is. Montgomery Justice." In quick succession, he fired three times, the shots so close together they sounded like one. He looked at Phoebe.

Check and mate. Just like that, it was over. Harding was dead. This hadn't been the plan, but the world was better for it. No question. She could lay her burden down. Die in peace. It didn't matter now because it was over.

"Was it as good for you as it was for me?" Stern sounded far away, at least a light year or two.

Only it did matter. She wanted to live, not die. She wanted to turn her devious brain to the problem of how to bridge the gap between a larcenous lady and the law-abiding US Marshal.

Stern leaned over her, trapping her in the seat, not just with his body but with the menace he gave off like after shave. He brought the gun up. "Last chance to change your mind, before it's splattered all over this expensive chair."

He might like her a little, but he liked killing more. She could see the anticipation in his eyes. Distantly, she knew Dewey was shouting, trying to break free of his bonds. For her, there was only this man. This gun.

"I don't suppose you'd believe me if I told you this whole

scene was being beamed to the cops and they're surrounding the place as we speak?"

"No."

"I didn't think so."

His finger tightened on the trigger.

She jerked up with her cuffed hands. Knocked the hand holding the gun up. Then she kicked him, low and hard. He doubled over, presenting his chin. She kicked that, and he staggered back, sprawling across the desk.

Too bad he'd managed to hang on to the gun. The barrel started to swing toward her as a stream of profanities poured out his mouth. The office doors burst open.

"Don't move!"

For the space of one heart beat, Stern looked at Phoebe and she knew he was going to move. That he wanted to die. Why? Her mouth shaped the question, but it didn't come out. Then it didn't matter. He started to bring his gun around.

Guns coughed at him from two directions. His body jerked one way, then the other, as bullets from both directions found him. He stopped, almost suspended in time, then fell back across the wide, dark desk.

He looked surprised. Blood trickled from his mouth onto the desk as he looked at her.

"I . . . have a . . . soul." He tried to touch something only he could see, then his hand fell back to his side. Awareness faded from his eyes.

The room filled as men and woman in black swarmed in like flies. Bryn approached Dewey.

"Where's your weapon?"

"What?"

She unlocked one set of cuffs, so he could lower his arms, but not the other set securing him. Smart lady. "Your gun. You had a gun."

"Oh. That." He looked around. "It's there. On the floor by that plant."

An agent closer to it picked it up and handed it to Bryn. She hefted it, examined it, then looked at Dewey. "A water gun? You took on these guys with a water gun?"

His grin came slow and was a little ragged around the edges. "I'm not into violence. Besides, a gun can add a nickel or more to your time in stir."

Tension rushed out of Phoebe, replaced by giggles bubbling up from inside. They were alive. It was over. Jake crouched in front of her, launching a different kind of tension.

"You took your sweet time getting here," she said.

Jake's chest heaved with the breath he was still trying to catch. They'd been at the warehouse when the call came. Bryn and Alice had been subduing Lily. He'd been staring at Phoebe's shoes—on a tray next to scalpels. He could still hear the shock in Sebastian's voice when the security monitors from TelTech suddenly overrode his game, could still hear his play-by-play of the action coming at him through his earpiece as they rushed across the city.

"Some things—" His breathing was starting to slow, but his heart didn't know it. Looking at her sent it into overdrive. "—take a little longer than others. How the hell did you manage to stay alive?"

"Magic." She grinned. It was crooked and slightly puffy, but most definitely a grin.

Chapter Twenty-one

"I don't think Phagan's fibbie trusts us," Phoebe said, holding an ice pack to her sore mouth. She had good reason for her belief. Before bustling off to manage the crime scene, Bryn had attached them to the van like a couple of lost dogs on a short leash. To add insult to injury, the handcuffs, which looked suspiciously like some she'd seen in Harding's creep show, were of the bondage variety with long thin chains between the steel bracelets. Bryn also didn't appear to trust the hordes of armed police milling around. Or she was seriously overestimating Phoebe and Dewey. Phoebe rattled the chain looped through the door handle. "Does she think we're a couple of Houdinis? I really don't know what Phagan sees in her."

Not that Phoebe had spent any time looking at Bryn. She couldn't take her eyes off Jake. It was interesting to see him in this light, even if it was waning with the day. Black was definitely his color, she decided with a sigh, right up there with tight jeans, tees and soft flannel. The fibbie didn't realize Phoebe didn't want to run away. Life was going to separate her from Jake soon enough. Jake would go back to catching bad guys, and Phoebe would go to jail without passing Go or collecting any money. Probably minus the harmonica, too.

"She's not so bad," Dewey said, interrupting her descent into the angst zone. "Not her fault she has to do her job."

Something in his voice, an odd note of defensiveness, distracted her attention from Jake. She looked at him and found him gazing at Bryn in a decidedly wistful way. A decidedly lustful way. Surely he didn't have the hots for her, too . . .

It was as if someone took the blinders off her brain and let her see the years, not the way Phagan had wanted her to see it, but the way they were. Phagan was Dewey. Or Dewey was Phagan. She'd been blind not to see it before.

Her first reaction was to be pissed. Didn't he trust her? She ought to kick his ass, except it looked as if Bryn was going to do it for her. Anger faded. They were both going to be thoroughly punished for their sins. Didn't need to punish each other. Not that she was going to pass up the opportunity to pull his chain a bit.

"I guess she's not so bad."

Dewey twitched, then looked at her, wariness replacing sick-puppy in his eyes. "Phagan seems to think so." He shuffled his feet like a small boy caught with his hand in the cookie jar.

"To each his own." Phoebe gave him a bland smile, but it didn't last. It seemed neither one of them was going to get what they wanted. "Sorry about all this. Not my best plan."

With a jangle of chains, Dewey crossed his arms and leaned against the side of the van. "I figure the worst we'll get is a couple million hours of community service."

"In what reality?" She frowned. "You weren't planning to put Phagan on the table to save my ass, were you? Because I won't let you."

"Oh, ye of little faith." He rattled his chains as he adjusted his tie. "Here they come. Let me do the talking."

"Dewey . . ."

"Trust me." His eyes reminded her they'd done this same scene all those years ago. "Full circle, girl. Let me close the last, little bit."

"Dewey, I can't—"

"Just . . . trust me. I promise, it will be all right. For you.

For Kerry Anne. Even for me. Promise me you'll let me handle this?"

The last thing she meant to do was nod, but she did. She'd been giving in to Dewey for a long time. She was going to stop now?

Long gold rays from the setting sun stretched across the parking lot to light Jake and Bryn's way toward Phoebe and Dewey Hyatt. It wasn't over, Jake knew, not by a long shot. Phoebe was up to her beautiful eyes in deep trouble, and as far as he could tell, the only way out was over Phagan's hide—something she'd already made very clear wouldn't happen.

The light was wrong to see their faces, but their body language was serious. When Hyatt put his arm around Phoebe, Jake's gut clenched. What if he had imagined the attraction? Or she'd been playing him for a fool? What if—

Jake stepped into partial shadow and saw Phoebe's eyes. He felt her gaze pierce his soul and he knew she hadn't been playing him—but she hadn't any more hope of a happy ending than he did.

Bryn halted in front of them, her hands on her hips. "Are you ready to play let's-make-a-deal, kids?"

Dewey could have been uncomfortable. Bryn sat on one side of him. Jake Kirby was on the other. They were both looking at him as if they thought they could cut their way into his head just by staring. He could have been freaked by it, but, truth was, he was happy to have Bryn looking at him, happy to be in the same room with her under any circumstances.

She looked damn cute in her little black jump suit. He'd follow her to hell and back, and not just because she had a great ass. Too bad she wanted to kick his to hell and leave him there. After he gave her Phagan.

It was an interesting problem. He could easily give her Phagan, and he'd do it in a heartbeat if he thought it would get him what he wanted. Dewey Hyatt had room to negotiate. Phagan—well she'd put him in a box and throw the key into the middle of the ocean. Then do the dance of joy.

It might, he admitted, have been a bad idea to kick her anthill so repeatedly. She was at full swarm right now. Cute, but definitely ready to bite.

He saw her and Kirby look at each other. Saw her give him a slight nod. So Kirby was taking the lead. That was probably good. His Bryn had a hasty temper. The marshal seemed able to keep his cool—when Phoebe wasn't around.

The marshal looked at him, his gaze almost penetrating enough to make him squirm.

"You're in serious need of a deal, Hyatt," he said. "Problem is, you've only got one thing we want."

"Phagan," Bryn said, an odd note to her voice that Dewey hadn't heard before.

"You don't want RABBIT?" He feigned surprise.

"We know it's crap. Phoebe told me," Jake said.

"Well, it was crap when we took it," Dewey admitted. "A serious setback at first. But you can't keep a good thief down." He gave Bryn a cheeky grin and watched color run up her face like lava up a volcano.

"Are you saying . . ." Jake pulled his attention away from Bryn.

With a sigh, Dewey let him.

"I got it working?" Dewey leaned back in his chair. "Yes, sir. And I figure if you won't deal, the military will. It's truly a sweet little item."

That got their attention. Was that . . . relief . . . in Bryn's baby blues? A tiny crack in the iron lady's defenses? Hot damn. Dewey waited for a long beat, then said, "I think I'm ready to play let's-make-a-deal if you are?"

He thought Bryn choked, but she covered it up with a cough. She was fast on her pointed heels.

It seemed to Phoebe that she'd been in the tiny interrogation room for hours, but once again she had no way to clock the passing time. Unlike the one she'd been in before, this one didn't have a one-way window or mirror. Just a sliding panel over a barred window in the door and another barred window to the outside world. Maybe, she wondered uneasily, it was the one they put people in when they planned to kick their butt.

She tried sitting down, tried pacing, seriously considered banging on the door, but she had a little pride left, so she settled for leaning against the grubby wall and staring through the bars at the even grubbier alley and the tiny patch of night sky showing between two tall buildings. The ice pack had lost its chill, so she tossed it onto the table.

Full circle. The past had met the present. Her dead were finally at peace. Now only the future remained to be sorted out, though it seemed obvious what was ahead for her. It was kind of ironic that Harding had escaped the incarceration now lying in wait for her and Dewey. She'd always meant for him to do time, to be as powerless as the people he'd hurt, to feel the full horror of what he'd dished out.

Stern had thought she was looking for revenge, but it had always been about justice—the difference between night and day. She'd spent her time in the night. There were times when she'd fantasized about killing Harding, even slowly torturing him to death. She'd lost her taste for that long before her little visit to his warehouse of horrors. She felt a sense of peace, knowing this. He'd shaped her life, but she'd never *be-*

come him. She lived in the day, not the night.

Jake quietly opened the door and stood watching her, remembering the first night he'd seen her. She seemed so far away, he didn't know what to do, or even who she was. Phoebe or Nadine? Or someone else now that her quest was over?

"I don't know what to call you."

She turned. "Retired?" Her grin was pure Phoebe.

Relief almost took out his knees. He needed to see Phoebe. Needed some of Phoebe to hang around. "I'm glad to hear it."

She grabbed the back of the chair. Jake didn't know why, but it seemed important what she did next. She hesitated, then pulled it out and sat down. Her gaze was steady, her expression neutral and oddly distant as she looked up at him, as if there were a barrier between them.

"What happens now?"

Jake sat down, too, spreading his hands on the battered tabletop to keep from reaching out for her. She seemed so fragile, sitting there waiting for the storm to break over her head, and yet strong, too. Submissive, yet not. Her strength was gathered in close, her spirit braced and ready for whatever would come. She knew she would endure. She knew she would survive. She'd learned how the hard way.

She amazed him. And she scared the hell out of him, because he wanted her to need him as much he needed her. Could she? She'd been alone so long, would she know how? Did she even want to try?

"We're working out the details of the deal," Jake said. "That was quite the bombshell Hyatt dropped." Did she tense? Why? "I take it you didn't know he'd gotten RABBIT to run?"

"No. I thought—"

"He'd have to give up Phagan?"

"I hoped he wouldn't," Phoebe admitted. Her eyelashes covered her expression. "Were . . . people . . . pretty upset?"

Jake grinned. "Just between you and me? I think Bryn was a little relieved."

Her lashes lifted at that. Her smile spread across her face like the sun rising over a mountain. The sight of it stole his wits. She'd smiled before, but, he realized, she'd always held something back. This one held nothing back.

"Cool." The smile faded, but the warmth lingered. "So he gets his suspended sentence and the million hours of community service?"

Jake didn't answer, because he wasn't sure he could keep the edge out of his voice. Hyatt had had so many years with Phoebe, years of intimacy. He knew things about her Jake never would.

He realized she was looking at him, a tiny frown between her brows and a question in her eyes. "He was more concerned about what would happen to you, though I suspect he'll get whatever he wants from the military." He hesitated. "He cares about you."

"I have been fortunate in my *friends*." Her voice turned very Southern. "And the kindness of strangers."

He chuckled, feeling the tightness in his gut ease. The past was the past. It was her future he was interested in.

"I was able to get you temporarily released into my custody," he said. "If that's not acceptable, I can make other arrangements for you. It's your choice." When she didn't immediately respond, he added, "You can't go back to Estes Park yet, not until the deal is completely worked out." He hesitated, then added, "I called my mom. She's making up the guest room for you. If you want it."

"Your mom?" Her eyes opened wide, and for the first time she looked alarmed.

"She told me that when I found you she wanted to meet you." He grinned. "I always try to do what my mom says."

She smiled back, but the alarm didn't fade from her eyes.

"I can also offer a personal meeting with an honest-to-goodness romance writer as an extra incentive. My sister-in-law is Dani Gwynne, and she's eager to meet you, too. On the downside, well, you've already met my brothers."

Phoebe looked down at her hands, realized she was twisting them in her lap. Just because he was taking her home to meet his family didn't, couldn't, mean anything. Put your hope back in the box and lock it up, girl.

"Do they know I'm a thief?" Jake's hand covered hers, and she realized it was what she'd been waiting for. Delight coursed up her arm and heat. Her libido was obviously really easy to please.

"You're not a thief." Jake sounded defensive. "You're—"

"A thief. A person who conspired to steal things."

"It's what you were, not what you are." He rubbed the back of his neck. "And, yes, they know. They're fine with it, okay?"

"Okay." But it wasn't. They weren't fine with it. She could tell he was worried about what they'd do. Maybe not his mom, though Phoebe couldn't figure out why the woman wouldn't be frantic. For sure his brothers would be upset. They'd know what associating with her could do to his career.

What was that scripture? *Charity never faileth. It seeketh not its own.* It seemed she was learning all her lessons about love on the fly. She loved Jake, but while her love wouldn't fail, it also wouldn't seek its own. If she had to break her own heart, she would not suck Jake into the morass of her bad choices.

"Give me a few minutes to get your paperwork done and we'll go."

Chapter Twenty-two

Phoebe woke late the next morning, surprised and a little unsettled by how deeply she'd slept. Normally, when she woke with her nerves jumping like beans, she'd go jog to clear her thoughts and settle down, but she wasn't sure she could leave. What were the rules of being in Jake's custody?

She stretched and sighed, then sat up and looked around. She'd been too tired last night to do more than absorb the fact that Jake looked like his mother and that Debra Kirby was a kind person who was worried about her son.

The room she'd showed Phoebe to was cheerful and neat. It could even be called quaint. The furniture was western and rustic, the curtains at the window white and lace. The wall by the bed was a family photo album of the-Kirby-boys-grow-up. Jake was easy to identify, because his hair was lighter than his brothers' and his smile hadn't changed much with the passing years.

Seeing the pictures put him in a different context, made her realize what a small part of his life she was. A minute or two in years of experiences. It wasn't just the law and the unlawful part. In the time it took him to go to the prom with a pretty blonde and receive his high school diploma, she'd begun and ended a marriage. He'd attended college and graduated with honors while she'd refined her grand-larceny skills. When she wasn't buying booze for the bar or shaking her booty in smoky honky-tonks across the country.

Forget Venus and Mars, she and Jake inhabited different galaxies.

Usually she tried to avoid normal people, normal lives, because they only reminded her how screwed up her life was. She shouldn't have come here. Shouldn't have given in to the temptation. This wasn't a house. It was a home. A place where people who loved each other lived and laughed and helped each other through their hard times.

Which made it not like any house she'd ever been in.

The differences went way beyond the comfy furniture and cheery curtains at the windows. Her furniture wasn't quite as nice as Debra Kirby's, but that wasn't what made this a home. No, it was the way the house felt, the way she felt being in it.

Her house gave nothing away. It shut out. It hid from.

This place, this room, was wide open, welcoming. Even to a thief.

Debra had left a thick yellow towel and washcloth on the wooden rocking chair. Also an unopened toothbrush and a new tube of toothpaste. Fresh flowers on the dresser. A dish of candy and a couple of romance novels on the night stand. One a Dani Gwynne, the other a Kelly Kerwin.

Such small things, but each one said, you're our guest. We want you to be comfortable while you're here.

She couldn't remember ever being a guest. She felt like an alien who'd wandered out of her galaxy. *Company manners, baby* she could almost hear her former Junior League mama say, her voice a drunken slur.

Did she even remember what company manners were? Their family standards, and social position, had been sliding long before Montgomery Justice appeared on the horizon.

She pushed her covers back and slid out, her feet settling on a rag rug put there to protect bare feet from the chill of hardwood floors. When she stood up, she noticed a suitcase sitting on a small chest. Inside were clothes from her house, her life as Phoebe. Jake must have arranged for them.

Her chest felt tight and kind of hurt, where there'd been no feeling at all for so long. She rubbed her chest, but it still hurt. A lump formed in her throat and tried to turn into . . . tears?

No way. She didn't cry. Sure as shooting, she was not going down those stairs and facing Jake and his family with red eyes. She would not use tears to sue for pity or acceptance.

She'd go down looking—she picked up a pair of shorts—like a bar slut. There was nothing in the case, in Phoebe's life, that went with this house. Nothing in there even remotely normal. Maybe she'd just stay upstairs.

She dropped the shorts. Who was she trying to fool anyway? A change of clothes wouldn't make her any less a thief, wouldn't change what she was or what she'd done. Sure as hell wouldn't bridge the space and time that separated her from Jake. She should have stayed in jail. At least there she could see the bars, knew her place and what to expect.

There were two windows in this corner guest room—no bars, but there might as well have been. Her past still had her trapped, cornered. She abandoned the suitcase for a window, choosing the one looking out on the backyard.

A mature garden occupied one corner, its formerly neat rows overrun by nature's abundance. Flowers circled the fence with cheerful abandon, and a tall cottonwood provided shade for a cozy wooden deck. Among the leaves of the cottonwood, she could see the weathered remnants of a tree house. It wasn't hard to imagine this yard peopled with small boys, two dark, one light. Or Jake's son . . .

Don't go there.

She heard a car door slam and turned to the other window. It gave her a glimpse of a small piece of the street. Enough to see Matt and Luke emerge from a car with a woman she presumed was Matt's wife, the romance writer. Phoebe liked the look of her. She was what her mama used to call a lady. Kind face, nice smile. Matt wore a thunder cloud face. Luke looked more worried, than angry.

She had a good idea what had put those looks on their faces, even before pieces of what they were saying made it as far as her ears.

". . . can't believe . . . that stupid . . ."

"Maybe . . . not as bad . . . it sounds . . ."

The slamming of the front door cut off their words. Apparently they'd found out their little brother had brought a thief home to dinner.

It's not as if she hadn't known she wouldn't be welcome here. Because she had. She knew what she was. Just because the room was welcoming didn't mean the people were.

She looked at the suitcase.

Live it all the way or don't live it at all.

Jake heard his brothers' voices downstairs before the shower went on in Phoebe's bedroom and drowned them out. He thought about the first time he'd waited for her to shower. The things he'd thought. The things he'd done. The moves and counter-moves that had brought them to . . . his mom's.

Dani had been right. He'd done his job, and love was finding a way. Unless his brothers screwed things up for him, which it sounded like they planned to.

He tossed his wet towel and pulled on skivs, then jeans. Better go down and calm his brothers before Phoebe made an appearance. He just wished he'd had a chance to talk to mom alone before they got here. He wasn't sure how she felt about the situation.

He padded downstairs without bothering with shoes, his

hand gliding down the banister the way his butt used to. He lived in DC, but this was home. The shower went off over his head. She'd reach for the towel to capture and contain the water sliding down her bare skin . . .

"Jake?" A voice splintered his hot thoughts with a dash of Mom. "Is that you?"

Time to face the music.

"Can you leave us alone, Mom?" Matt asked, grimly. "And you, too, Dani."

Or the firing squad.

Inside the kitchen, he found Matt looking like a storm over Long's Peak. Luke, in keeping with his more easygoing nature, just looked worried. Dani and his mom were facing Matt down with crossed arms.

"This is my kitchen, my house," Debra told her son.

"I'm not leaving either," Dani said. "Unless Jake wants me to."

Matt's angry face turned sulky until he caught sight of his little brother.

Jake mentally planted his feet. It was harder here, on home turf, where instead of being a Deputy US Marshal, he was his mother's son and Matt and Luke's little brother. Not fair, but life wasn't.

"Don't start, Matt," he warned.

"We're all adults here. Why don't we sit down and talk this over?" Peace-maker Luke set the example by sitting down.

No one followed his lead.

"This is between me, Mom and Phoebe. It's not your business, though I appreciate *your* coming, Dani."

Matt's hands curled into fists. If Jake hadn't been so pissed, he'd have grinned when Dani grabbed hold of Matt's arm and nestled against her husband's side.

"Not my business? You bring a common thief—"

Jake started toward him but found Luke in his way. "That—"

"—is insulting, Deputy," Phoebe said.

It should have been funny, the way his family froze, then turned toward her in varying degrees of discomfort. But it wasn't. He loved her, and his brother was hurting her.

Not that she looked hurt. She leaned against the doorjamb, her arms crossed, her expression . . . hard to read. Her eyelids drooped lazily and her smile was . . . enigmatic. Her clothes were—whoa—definitely in the kick-ass range.

Her brief blue-jean shorts left little leg to the imagination and rode low on her hips. Her equally brief top rode high and snug around her breasts, leaving a lot of midriff bare. An electric-blue ruffle framed her cleavage, then did Daisy Mae off-the-shoulder. Her hair was wet and wild, her lips lush and red.

"I'll have you know," she continued, her voice pure Southern Belle, rich and sultry, "I'm a very *uncommon* thief. The stories I could tell you, if Calvin—that's my lawyer—hadn't advised me to exercise my right to remain silent."

Jake was vaguely aware Luke had dropped back in his chair like a deflated beach ball. Phoebe straightened and sauntered toward the refrigerator, her hip action lighting a wildfire in Jake's gut. Lucky for him his mom wasn't looking at him. No one was.

"You'll just have to take my word for it that the family silver is in no danger." She touched the refrigerator like it was her lover, then looked at Jake's mom. "May I, ma'am? I'm powerful thirsty."

Debra nodded, her eyes wide, but a smile was tugging at the edges of her mouth.

Phoebe opened the door, then bent from the waist, her tightly covered ass almost in Luke's face. When she straightened, Jake realized he'd been holding his breath and expelled it in a rush. Luke looked dazed and, well, awed. Like he'd just had a religious experience.

She popped the top of the Diet Coke she'd snagged and drank, tipping her head back so that they got an unobstructed view of the long, smooth sweep of her soft curves and satiny skin, still glistening with moisture from her recent shower. When she was done, she licked her lips real slow, then, even more slowly, dug into her pocket and produced a dollar bill that she tossed on the table in front of Matt.

"I remember when you could get a Coke for four bits," she said, looking at Matt for a long, pointed moment. When she turned away, Jake thought he saw her wink at Dani, who was having a harder time than his mom not to bust out laughing. "Do I need one of those little electronic anklets to go out into your mama's garden?"

Jake tried to speak, but his throat was too dry, so he shook his head.

"I'll stay well away from the watermelon patch to avoid temptation." She lifted the Coke can in a mock salute, then sauntered out, her hips doing a provocative side-to-side sway again.

No one spoke or moved until the patio door had creaked open, then closed.

Jake rubbed the back of his neck as his powers of speech and thought crept back. Matt looked as if he'd been turned to stone, but Dani gave Jake a delighted smile. "If you let her get away, you deserve to be a bitter, unhappy man, Jake Kirby."

Luke gave himself a shake, like a man waking from an amazing dream, and looked at Matt. "I'm with Louise,"—he gave Dani a quick grin as he used the name she'd given him when they first met—"on this one, bro. That girl is definitely a keeper. You let her get away, I'll kick your ass. Oh, sorry, Mom."

Jake grinned his relief, then turned to Matt, his grin fading abruptly at his brother's grim expression. He didn't intend to let Phoebe get away, even if it cost him his brother, but he hoped it wouldn't. He kinda liked him.

Matt finally looked at him. "This could screw your career, you know."

"Maybe." He hunched his shoulders. "But I'm betting we recruit her. She's not just uncommon, Matt, she's amazing."

Matt stared at him for a long moment, then his face relaxed. "Well, I'll admit she does remind me of someone." He glanced at his wife, who managed to look innocently puzzled and wickedly amused.

It was as close to admitting he could be wrong as Matt would get, which left Mom. What did she think of his lady thief?

Outside, Phoebe found a wooden bench swing that hadn't been visible from her window. Green vines climbed up one side, wound around the beam, then went down the other, leaving a cool, shady place for her to ponder just how much her life sucked.

There was even a cushion to protect her far-too-bare thighs from slivers. She set the swing in motion, then pulled her legs up to her chest, wrapped her arms around them and rested her chin on her knees.

Something wet dropped off her chin and rolled down her leg and across her bare foot. Was it raining? Only if blue sky and bright sun had totally changed their functions.

She touched her face and realized the drop had come from her eyes. Another drop quickly followed, then another. She couldn't be crying. She didn't cry. Maybe she was overflowing? She wasn't sobbing. Her shoulders weren't heaving. Her heart hurt, worse than before, but surely she wasn't crying. Sharp pain spread out from her heart like cracks across glass. It flowed up and out her eyes. It didn't help that she'd always known she couldn't have Jake. Knowing something didn't make it easier to face.

There was a sort of peace in knowing it was better for him. He might be a bit hot for her, but that would pass. People fell out of lust all the time. After the scene in the kitchen, she had her pride, and he had his out. She'd have to find somewhere else to stay, but that would be better anyway. If she spent too much time in the normal zone, who knew what would happen to her?

She heard the patio door creak and quickly wiped her eyes, since teary-eyed didn't match heartless slut. She looked toward the house, expecting to see Jake, not his *mom*.

Debra Kirby walked toward her with a grace that both pleased and intimidated. Phoebe admired her taste. Her linen pants and shirt were coolly elegant. Her slight smile was so like Jake's that the lump tried to crawl up her throat again.

"Do you like gardens?" Debra asked.

This wasn't the scene Phoebe had expected to play. She didn't know her lines. "Yeah, I guess." This seemed pretty lame, so she added, "It's lovely. Real peaceful."

Debra stopped by the swing and looked around, her expression reflective. "It was my husband's domain. He could make anything grow." She sat down next to Phoebe, setting the swing swaying again. "He had some raspberry bushes in that corner that produced the best berries. They made fabulous jam. The boys loved it so much, I could hardly keep it on the shelf."

Phoebe stretched her legs out and hooked her thumbs in

the pockets of her shorts. If Jake's mom was looking to make her feel like she didn't belong, it was working.

"The bushes died the same year John did. Almost as if they knew. Luke dug them out for me and helped me plant tulips there instead. He's very like his father."

"How old—" Phoebe stopped.

"Jake was eight when his father died."

"Old enough to remember." Phoebe stared straight ahead.

"And you?"

"I was three when my father died. I guess that's when Mama started to drink. That's what Kerry Anne said, anyway. I don't remember Mama ever not drinking." Debra might as well know the whole, awful truth about her.

"I thought about getting drunk after John died."

"But you didn't." Phoebe stared into her own past. Her father left them and then her mother might as well have died. As if that wasn't bad enough, Mama turned Montgomery Justice loose in their lives, taking what little was good in their lives and turning it into garbage.

Debra put her hand on Phoebe's, recalling her from the past. "Your mother let you down. Sometimes people do."

"Why didn't you?"

Debra hesitated. "Why didn't you?"

Phoebe blinked. "I don't know."

Debra smiled. "Neither do I. I just didn't. Dani says some people don't know how to go on and some people don't know how to quit." She patted Phoebe's hand. "What happened to you—well, it shouldn't have happened, but it did. At least it brought you to Jake. If you'd had a normal, happy life, you'd probably be married to a Joe Bob or a Billy Ray. I don't know them, but I know my son. Trust me when I say he'll make you a lot happier than either of them."

Phoebe stared at her. "There's no question . . ."

She stood up, her face kind. "But there is, dear. There's a very important question. Will you quit or will you go on?" She rose to leave, then stopped. "Unless you don't love my son?"

Phoebe stared up at her. She tried to make herself say it, but she couldn't.

Debra smiled. "Silly question, wasn't it? How could you not love Jake?"

He'd come outside and was standing on the edge of the deck. She saw him when his mama left her. She couldn't see his expression—the sun was in her eyes—but the sun bathed the rest of him in warm gold light. It loved him, too.

What was she thinking, Jake wondered. Phoebe was in the shadow of the swing, so Jake couldn't see her face. And he'd been too far away to hear what his mother said to her. Or what she'd said to his mother?

Only a few yards separated them, but it might as well be the width of a universe. He didn't know how to get from here to her.

His mom passed him, pausing just long enough to pat his cheek and say, "Faint heart never won fair lady, son." Then she was in the house, and he was alone with Phoebe. He looked over his shoulder. Make that sort of alone. His brothers, his mom and Dani were watching from the window. He waved them away. They waved him on.

Great. An audience. He rubbed the back of his neck. This reminded him of the first time he'd jumped off the high dive. He'd inched his way out on the board until he was over the clear green water. He'd wanted to inch his way back, but his brothers had been standing on the edge of the pool watching him with the same expressions on their faces that they wore now. He'd jumped, because even then he'd had his pride.

The water had rushed toward him, then closed over his head as he went down and down right to the bottom. He'd pushed off for the surface. It took forever before his head broke into the air and his heaving lungs found relief.

Matt had waited until he paddled to the side of the pool, then said, "Yeah, but can you do it again?"

It took three times, he recalled, before he started to enjoy it.

The wooden deck wasn't as high as that board, but the outcome was a lot less certain. He jumped lightly onto the grass and started toward his fair lady.

Chapter Twenty-three

Phoebe watched Jake walk toward her. He looked so . . . *good.* Not just because he was so dang cute, but because he *was* good. His mama was so right. How could she not love him? Be easier to teach her lungs not to breathe, than teach her heart not to love him. Her selfish heart said, grab the boy and don't let go. Her mind said, he deserves better than a messed-up thief.

She sighed. Course someone that good deserved to get what he wanted. And if he really did want her . . .

Her past, her ghosts were all around her as she rose and stepped into the light. It warmed her cold places, while crisp, fresh air filled her lungs, blowing out the stale and the old. Jake stopped as she hesitated and looked back. What had been might have been painful, but it was familiar. Was it her fancy that she saw Kerry Anne sitting there, smiling and urging her on?

Phoebe rubbed her heart. The pain wasn't gone, but it was fading. There'd be scars, but her wounds could finally heal.

She turned and started toward Jake, getting lighter with each step as her ghosts slowly released her. Guess she didn't know how to quit either.

He stopped in front of her and smiled that toe-curling smile of his. She had to smile back. She was in his custody.

"I'm curious again," he said.

The sun must have taken up residence inside her, because she was warming up nicely. "You know what they say about curiosity."

"They're wrong." Jake could feel his family's eyes boring

into his back. It was really cramping his style. He couldn't just jump on the girl. She'd been through hell, could have issues or something. She was so damn young. What if he was taking advantage of her, too? "You want to go for a walk or something?"

Her smile wasn't young. Neither was the look in her eyes. "Definitely *or something.*"

Heat did a fast arc from him to her and back again. "Okay."

Phoebe looked past Jake's shoulder. "Um, your family's watching us out the window."

"I know. Sorry about that." He turned to glare at them. They indicated he should get on with it.

"What do they want?"

As if she didn't know. "A happy ending. Ever since Dani joined the family, we've all become incurable romantics." If he didn't touch her soon, his skin was going to explode.

"Oh."

He had an idea that might partially ease his pain. "We could get them off our backs if we . . . pretended to kiss? You know, a ruse. A trick."

"I am familiar with the concept." Her lashes swept down, then up. "Pretend?"

"If you just stepped a little closer . . ."

She stepped a lot closer. "Like this?"

"Oh, yeah." They still hadn't touched, but only because he couldn't breathe.

"I think I should put my hands around your neck. At least, that's how they do it in the movies."

"Good idea."

She licked her lips as she lifted one hand to his shoulder. Her touch was light, but he trembled. Thought she did, too. He didn't ask, because he couldn't talk, if he could touch her. He just did. His right hand settled on her bare waist, the feel of her skin making his head spin. He felt and heard her small gasp.

"So . . . far . . . so . . . good," he managed to croak.

"Yeah," was her breathy response.

She lifted her second hand up more slowly than the first, dragging it up the side of his arm before sliding it around the back of his head. He had to put his other hand on her waist, too, to steady her. It was the gentlemanly thing to do, especially with his mom watching. The natural consequence of this was to draw her against him.

It was such a relief. He'd come home. Finally.

He leaned his forehead against hers, closed his eyes and confessed, "I love you, Phoebe-Nadine-whoever-you-decide-to-be. To hell with our ruse. Unless you do something to stop me, I'm going to kiss you."

She was close enough, he could feel her mouth smile against his.

"I don't think we fooled them anyway. They're still there."

And if he didn't kiss her soon, she was going to die. She adjusted the angle of her head, to make it easy for him. He did close the distance, but not enough. He kept his tantalizing and yummy mouth just out of reach.

"I got a last name for you, if you'll tell me what I should call you."

She tipped her head back so she could see his true blue eyes. Smoothed his hair back because she could. "Call me . . . in love."

He started to laugh, then swept her off her feet and spun them in a circle that slowed as their mouths finally came together.

Before she lost the ability to think or hear anything, Phoebe thought she heard Kerry Anne laughing.

Epilogue

"Is she nuts?" Dewey asked Phoebe in a low voice as he looked at the guests arriving for a barbecue at Dani and Matt's, an eclectic mix that included her new in-laws, Phoebe's former in-laws already on their way to getting plastered, a gaggle of female friends of Dani's, a mix of law enforcers from various agencies, and, of course, the two, mostly reformed, law breakers.

"She's a romance writer," Phoebe said. Dewey looked happy—contented even—despite the shiny electronic bracelet Bryn had attached to his ankle. A shiny gold band on her left hand kept Phoebe firmly attached to Jake.

"Oh." His gaze found Bryn, lingered for a moment, then turned toward Phoebe. "I've missed you."

Phoebe patted his hand. "She keeps you on a pretty short leash."

"So does yours."

Phoebe smiled. He did indeed. It had been a tumultuous six months. Dewey had given her away, though she'd had to convince Jesse it wasn't the job of the ex-husband. Jake and Jesse would never be close, but they had achieved a sort of truce when the guys realized that Phoebe really was madly in love with her marshal.

For her honeymoon, Jake had arranged a visit to Georgia and a stop by Kerry Anne and Mama's graves. He called it closure; she called it kind. His family had let her in, though she suspected she was still on probation with Matt. That was okay. He was a big brother. Being protective went with the territory. Kept her on her toes to know he was watching. Gave her a goal.

All God's children need a goal. Speaking of. . . .

"Are you ever going to tell her?" Phoebe asked.

Dewey looked at her. "I wondered if you'd figured it out."

"I'm slow, but I get there eventually."

"Does he know?" Dewey nodded in Jake's direction.

"He doesn't ask, I don't tell." It was the one secret she'd kept from Jake. "I wish you could have a happy ending, too."

Dewey grinned. "Maybe I'll consult the romance writer."

"About what?" Bryn had approached unnoticed. In her linen shorts and top, she looked cool and feminine. Was that a slightly softer look in her eyes for Dewey?

Phoebe looked at Dewey. "I think I'm going to go find Jake." She jumped off the fence and headed for her man. Behind her, she heard Dewey say, "Damn, you're cute, girl."

She approached Jake from behind, but he still knew she was there. His hand reached behind him, found hers and pulled her close. His mom smiled a welcome, then her gaze drifted toward the cluster of Dani's female friends, who were laughing, chatting and fending off Mentel boys.

"I wonder . . ." Debra said.

"What?" Phoebe asked.

"Two sons happy. One to go."

Phoebe looked at Luke, who appeared to be talking climbing with Toes. As if he sensed their scrutiny, he turned and gave his mom a "What?" look.

His mom's smile reminded Phoebe of her mamma's red shoes smile.

Just a hint of evil around the edges.